Other books about Discworld

THE DISCWORLD ALMANAK
(with Bernard Pearson)
THE UNSEEN UNIVERSITY CUT-OUT BOOK
(with Alan Batley and Bernard Pearson)
WHERE'S MY COW?
(illustrated by Melvyn Grant)
THE ART OF DISCWORLD
(with Paul Kidby)
THE WIT AND WISDOM OF DISCWORLD
(compiled by Stephen Briggs)
THE FOLKLORE OF DISCWORLD
(with Jacqueline Simpson)

Discworld maps
THE STREETS OF ANKH-MORPORK
(with Stephen Briggs)
THE DISCWORLD MAPP
(with Stephen Briggs)
A TOURIST GUIDE TO LANCRE – A DISCWORLD MAPP
(with Stephen Briggs, illustrated by Paul Kidby)
DEATH'S DOMAIN
(with Paul Kidby)

A complete list of other books based on the Discworld series – illustrated
screenplays, graphic novels, comics and plays, can be found on
www.terrypratchett.co.uk.

Non-Discworld novels
GOOD OMENS
(with Neil Gaiman)
STRATA
THE DARK SIDE OF THE SUN
THE UNADULTERATED CAT
(illustrated by Gray Jolliffe)

Terry Pratchett is one of the most popular authors writing in the UK today. He is the acclaimed creator of the Discworld® series, the first title in which, *The Colour of Magic*, was published in 1983. Worldwide sales of his books are in excess of 55 million, and they have been translated into 36 languages. He has written a number of titles for younger readers, including *The Amazing Maurice and his Educated Rodents*, which won the Carnegie Medal in the UK, and *Nation*, which was a Printz Honor Book in the US.

He was awarded an OBE in 1998, and a Knighthood in 2009 for his services to literature.

Visit **www.terrypratchett**.co.uk
for further news and information.

EXCLUSIVE EDITION FOR WATERSTONE'S

By Terry Pratchett, for young readers
THE CARPET PEOPLE
TRUCKERS
DIGGERS
WINGS
THE BROMELIAD omnibus edition
(includes *Truckers, Diggers, Wings*)

ONLY YOU CAN SAVE MANKIND
JOHNNY AND THE DEAD
JOHNNY AND THE BOMB
THE JOHNNY MAXWELL OMNIBUS EDITION
(includes *Only You Can Save Mankind, Johnny and the Dead, Johnny and the Bomb*)

Discworld novels
THE AMAZING MAURICE AND HIS EDUCATED RODENTS
THE WEE FREE MEN
A HAT FULL OF SKY
WINTERSMITH
THE WEE FREE MEN ILLUSTRATED

25 YEARS OF DISCWORLD®
The Discworld series is a continuous history of a world not
totally unlike our own, except that it is a flat disc carried on the backs of
four elephants astride a giant turtle floating through space, and that it is peopled
by, among others, wizards, dwarves, soldiers, thieves, beggars, vampires and
witches. Within the history of Discworld there are many individual stories,
which can be enjoyed in any order. But reading them in the sequence in which
they were written can increase your enjoyment through the accumulation
of all the fine detail that contributes to the teeming imaginative
complexity of this brilliantly conceived world.

The Discworld series: have you read them all?
1. THE COLOUR OF MAGIC
2. THE LIGHT FANTASTIC
3. EQUAL RITES
4. MORT
5. SOURCERY
6. WYRD SISTERS
7. PYRAMIDS
8. GUARDS! GUARDS!
9. ERIC
(illustrated by Josh Kirby)
10. MOVING PICTURES

TERRY PRATCHETT

NATION

DOUBLEDAY

NATION
A DOUBLEDAY BOOK
EXCLUSIVE EDITION FOR WATERSTONE'S 978 0 385 61712 3

First published in Great Britain by Doubleday,
an imprint of Random House Children's Books
A Random House Group Company

Doubleday hardback published 2008
This exclusive edition published 2009

1 3 5 7 9 10 8 6 4 2

The Random House Group Limited supports the Forest Stewardship Council (FSC),
the leading international forest certification organization. All our titles that are printed
on Greenpeace-approved FSC-certified paper carry the FSC logo. Our paper
procurement policy can be found at www.rbooks.co.uk/environment.

Mixed Sources
Product group from well-managed
forests and other controlled sources
www.fsc.org Cert no. TT-COC-2139
© 1996 Forest Stewardship Council
FSC

RANDOM HOUSE CHILDREN'S BOOKS
61–63 Uxbridge Road, London W5 5SA

www.terrypratchett.co.uk
www.rbooks.co.uk

Addresses for companies within The Random House Group Limited can be found at:
www.randomhouse.co.uk/offices.htm

THE RANDOM HOUSE GROUP Limited Reg. No. 954009

A CIP catalogue record for this book is available from the British Library.

Printed and bound in the UK by CPI Mackays, Chatham ME5 8TD

For Lyn

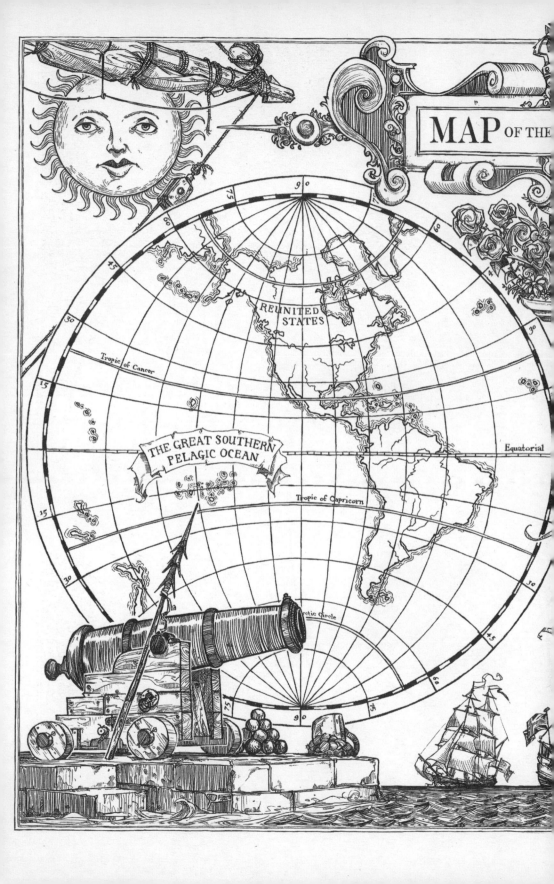

MAP OF THE

REUNITED
STATES

Tropic of Cancer

THE GREAT SOUTHERN
PELAGIC OCEAN

Equatorial

Tropic of Capricorn

Arctic Circle

N

TEE MOUNTAIN

CAVE OF THE
GRANDFATHERS

THE "SWEET JUDY"

HIGH FOREST

BIG PIG
VALLEY

THE WOMEN'S PLACE

TRACK

LOW FOREST

THE VILLAGE

THE BEACH

LITTLE
NATION

THE REEF

The Nation

HOW IMO MADE THE WORLD, IN THE TIME WHEN THINGS WERE OTHERWISE AND THE MOON WAS DIFFERENT

*I*mo set out one day to catch some fish, but there was no sea. There was nothing but Imo. So he spat in his hands and rubbed them together and made a ball of sea. After that he made some fish, but they were stupid and lazy. So he took the souls of some dolphins, who at least had learned to speak, and he mixed them with clay and rubbed them in his hands and changed their shape and they became people. They were clever but they could not swim all day, so Imo dug some more clay and rubbed it in his hands and baked it in the fire of his fishing camp, and that was how the land was made.

Soon the people filled all the lands and were hungry, so Imo took some of the night and rubbed it in his hands and made Locaha, the god of death.

Still Imo was not satisfied, and he said: I have been like

a child playing in the sand. This is a flawed world. I had no plan. Things are wrong. I will rub it in my hands and make a better one.

But Locaha said: The mud is set. People will die.

Imo was angry and said: Who are you to question me?

And Locaha said: I am a part of you, as are all things. So I say to you, Give me the mortal world, and go and make your better one. I will rule here fairly. When a human dies, I will send them to be a dolphin until it is time for them to be born again. But when I find a creature who has striven, who has become more than the mud from which they were made, who has glorified this mean world by being a part of it, then I will open a door for them into your perfect world and they will no longer be creatures of time for they will wear stars.

Imo thought this was a good idea, because it was his own creation, and went off to make his new world in the sky. But before he did this, and so that Locaha would not have things all his own way, he breathed into his hands and made the other gods so that while the people should die, it would be in their right time.

And this is why we are born in water, and do not kill dolphins, and look towards the stars.

CHAPTER 1

THE PLAGUE

*T*he snow came down so thickly that it formed fragile snowballs in the air, which tumbled and melted as soon as they landed on the horses lined up along the dock. It was four in the morning and the place was coming alive and Captain Samson had never seen the dock in such a bustle. The cargo was flying out of the ship, literally; the cranes strained in their efforts to get the bales out as quickly as possible. The ship *stank* of the disinfectant already, stank of the stuff. Every man that came on board was so drenched in it that it dribbled out of his boots. But that wasn't enough; some of them had squelched aboard with big, heavy spray cans, which spat an acid-pink fog over everything.

And there was nothing he could do about it. The agent for the owners was right there on the dockside with his orders in his hands. But Captain Samson was going to try.

'Do you really think we're infectious, Mr Blezzard?' he barked to the man on the dock. 'I can assure you—'

'You are not infectious, Captain, as far as we know, but this is for your own good,' shouted the agent through his enormous megaphone, 'and I must once again warn you and your men not to leave the ship!'

'We have families, Mr Blezzard!'

'Indeed, and they are already being taken care of. Believe me, Captain, they are fortunate, and so will you be, if you follow orders. You *must* return to Port Mercia at dawn. I cannot stress enough how important this is.'

'Impossible! It's the other side of the world! We've only been back a few hours! We are low on food and water!'

'You will set sail at dawn and rendezvous in the Channel with the *Maid of Liverpool*, just returned from San Francisco. Company men are aboard her now. They will give you everything you need. They will strip that ship to the waterline to see that you are properly provisioned and crewed!'

The captain shook his head. 'This is not good enough, Mr Blezzard. What you are asking – it's too much. I— Good God, man, I need more authority than some words shouted through a tin tube!'

'I *think* you will find me all the authority you need, Captain. Do I have your permission to come aboard?'

The captain knew that voice.

It was the voice of God, or the next best thing. But although he recognized the voice, he hardly recognized the speaker standing at the foot of the gangplank. That was because he was wearing a sort of birdcage. At least, that's what it looked like at first sight. Closer, he could see that it was a fine metal framework with a thin gauze around it. The person inside walked in a shimmering cloud of disinfectant.

'Sir Geoffrey?' said the captain, just to be sure, as the man began to walk slowly up the glistening gangplank.

'Indeed, Captain. I'm sorry about this outfit. It's called a salvation suit, for obvious reasons. It is necessary for your protection. The Russian influenza has been worse than you can possibly imagine! We believe the worst is over, but it has taken a terrible toll . . . at every level of society. *Every* level, Captain. Believe me.'

There was something in the way the chairman said 'every' that made the captain hesitate.

'I take it that His Majesty is . . . isn't—' He stopped, unable to force the rest of the question out of his mouth.

'Not only His Majesty, Captain. I said "worse than you can possibly imagine",' said Sir Geoffrey, while red disinfectant dripped off the bottom of the salvation suit and puddled on the deck like blood. 'Listen to me. The only reason the country is not in total chaos at this moment is that most people are too scared to venture out. As Chairman of the Line, I order you – and as an old friend, I beg you – for the sake of the Empire, sail with the devil's speed to Port Mercia and find the Governor. Then you will— Ah, here come your passengers. This way, gentlemen.'

Two more carriages had pulled up in the chaos of the dockside. Five shrouded figures came up the gangplank, carrying larger boxes between them, and lowered them onto the deck.

'Who are you, sir?' the captain demanded of the nearest stranger, who said:

'You don't need to know that, Captain.'

'Oh, don't I, indeed!' Captain Samson turned to Sir Geoffrey with his hands open in appeal. 'Goddammit, Chairman, pardon my French, have I not served the line faithfully for more than thirty-five years? I am the captain of the *Cutty Wren*, sir! A captain must know his ship and all that is on it! I will not be kept in the dark, sir! If I cannot be trusted, I will walk down the gangplank right now!'

'Please don't upset yourself, Captain,' said Sir Geoffrey. He turned to the leader of the newcomers. 'Mr Black? The captain's loyalty is beyond question.'

'Yes, I was hasty. My apologies, Captain,' said Mr Black, 'but we need to requisition your ship for reasons of the utmost urgency, hence the regrettable lack of formality.'

'Are you from the government?' the captain snapped.

Mr Black looked surprised. 'The government? I am afraid not. Just between us, there is little of the government left at the moment, and what there is is mostly hiding in its cellars. No, to be honest with you, the government has always found it convenient not to know much about us, and I would advise you to do the same.'

'Oh, really? I was not born yesterday, you know—'

'No indeed, Captain, you were born forty-five years ago, the second son of Mr and Mrs Bertie Samson, and christened Lionel after your grandfather,' said Mr Black, calmly lowering his package to the deck.

The captain hesitated again. Somehow, that had sounded like the start of a threat; the fact that no actual threat followed made it, for some reason, quite discomfiting.

'Anyway, who do you work for?' he managed. 'I like to know who I'm sailing with.'

Mr Black straightened up. 'As you wish. We are known as the Gentlemen of Last Resort. We serve the Crown. Does that help you?'

'But I thought the king was—' The captain stopped, not wanting to say the dreadful word.

'He is *dead*, Captain Samson. But the Crown itself is not. Let us say that we serve . . . a higher purpose? And to that purpose, Captain, I will tell you that your men will get four times their usual pay for this trip, plus ten guineas a day for every day over the record for the run to Port Mercia, plus a further one hundred guineas on their return. The promotion prospects for every man and officer on board will be much improved. You, Captain, will of course receive enhanced payments as befits your rank and, since we understand your plan is to retire shortly, the Crown will certainly wish to show its gratitude in the traditional way.'

Behind him, Sir Geoffrey spoke and coughed at the same time: 'cough*knighthood*cough.'

'I'm sure Mrs Samson would like that,' said Mr Black.

It was like torture. Captain Samson had a mental picture of what would happen if Mrs Samson ever found out that he had turned down the chance of her becoming *Lady* Samson. It didn't bear thinking about. He stared at the man who called himself Mr Black and said quietly: 'Is something going to happen? Are you trying to prevent something?'

'Yes, Captain. War. The heir to the throne must set foot on English soil within nine months of the monarch's death. It's in Magna Carta, down in the small print or, rather, the tiny writing. The barons didn't want another Richard the Lionheart, you see. And regrettably, since an infected waiter served the soup at the king's birthday party, the next two living heirs to the throne are both somewhere in the Great Southern Pelagic Ocean. I believe you know it well, Captain?'

'Ah, I understand now! That's what's in those boxes,' said the captain, pointing. 'It's a load of English soil! We find him, he sets foot on it and we all shout hurrah!'

Mr Black smiled. 'Well done, Captain! I am impressed! But, alas, that has already been thought of. There is a sub-clause, too. It stipulates that the English soil must be firmly attached to England. We may declare the succession overseas – even crown the man if necessary – but his presence *will* be required on English soil within this time period for full ratification.'

'You know, Mr Black, I thought I knew all of Magna

Carta, but I've never heard of these clauses,' said Sir Geoffrey.

'No, sir,' said the Gentleman of Last Resort patiently, 'that is because they are in the *ratified* version. You don't think barons who could hardly write their name could come up with a complete set of sensible rules for the proper running of a large country for the rest of history, do you? Their clerks put together the full working Magna Carta a month later. It's seventy times bigger, but it is foolproof. Unfortunately, the French have a copy.'

'Why?' asked the captain. Yet another coach had pulled up on the dockside. It looked expensive, and had a crest painted on the door.

'Because if you don't succeed in this enterprise, Captain, it would then be quite likely that a Frenchman would become King of England,' said Mr Black.

'What?' shouted the captain, forgetting all about the new coach. 'No one would stand for that!'

'Wonderful people, the French, wonderful people,' said Sir Geoffrey hurriedly, waving his hands. 'Our allies in the recent unpleasantness in the Crimea and all that, but—'

'Oh, we are the best of chums with the French government on this one, sir,' said Mr Black. 'The last thing they want to see is a Frenchman on any throne, anywhere. It wouldn't do for our Gallic brethren. There are those in France who do, though, and we think it would be a good thing for all concerned if our new monarch could be brought here with a minimum of fuss and a maximum of speed.'

'They killed the last king they had!' said Captain Samson, who wasn't going to waste a good rage. 'My father fought against 'em at Trafalgar! Can't have that, sir, not at any price. I can speak for the men on that, sir! We'll break the record again, sir, coming and going!' He looked around for Sir Geoffrey, but the chairman had hurried down the gangplank and was fussing around two veiled figures who had got out of the coach.

'Are they . . . women?' asked the captain as they swept up onto the *Cutty Wren*'s deck and went past him as if he were of no importance whatsoever.

Mr Black shook some snow off his own veil. 'The smaller one is a maid, and I take it on trust that she is a woman. The tall one, whom your chairman is so eager to please, is a major stockholder in your shipping line and, more importantly, is also the mother of the heir. She is a lady indeed, although my limited experience of her suggests that she is also a mixture of Boadicea without the chariot, Catherine de' Medici without the poisoned rings and Attila the Hun without his wonderful sense of fun. Do not play cards with her, because she cheats like a Mississippi bustout dealer, keep sherry away from her, do everything she says and we might all live.'

'Sharp tongue, eh?'

'Razor blade, Captain. On a lighter note, it is possible that *en route* we might catch up with the heir's daughter, who thankfully was already well on the way to join her father before the plague struck. She is due to leave Cape Town today on the schooner *Sweet Judy*, bound for Port

Mercia via Port Advent. The captain is Nathan Roberts. I believe you know him?'

'What, old "Hallelujah" Roberts? Is he still afloat? Good man, mark you, one of the best, and the *Sweet Judy* is a very trim vessel. The girl is in safe hands, depend upon it.' The captain smiled. 'I hope she likes hymns, though. I wonder if he still makes the crew do all their swearing into a barrel of water in the hold?'

'Keenly religious, is he?' said Mr Black as they headed towards the warmth of the main cabin.

'Just a tad, sir, just a tad.'

'In the case of Roberts, Captain, how big is a "tad"?'

Captain Samson grinned. 'Oh, something about the size of Jerusalem . . .'

At the other end of the world the sea burned, the wind howled, and roaring night covered the face of the deep.

It takes an unusual man to make up a hymn in a hurry, but such a man was Captain Roberts. He knew every hymn in *The Antique and Contemporary Hymn Book*, and sang his way through them loudly and joyously when he was on watch, which had been one of the reasons for the mutiny.

And now, with the End of the World at hand, and the skies darkening at dawn, and the fires of Revelation raining down and setting the rigging ablaze, Captain Roberts tied himself to the ship's wheel as the sea rose below him and felt the *Sweet Judy* lifted into the sky as if by some almighty hand.

There was thunder and lightning up there. Hail rattled off his hat. St Elmo's fire glowed on the tip of every mast and then crackled on the captain's beard as he began to sing, in a rich dark baritone. Every sailor knew the song: '*Eternal Father, strong to save, Whose arm hath bound the restless wave,*' he bellowed into the storm, as the *Judy* balanced on the restless wave like a ballerina. '*Who bidd'st the mighty ocean deep, Its own appointed limits keep . . .*'

How fast were they moving? he wondered as sails ripped and flapped away. The wave was as high as a church, but surely it was running faster than the wind! He could see small islands below, disappearing as the wave roared over them. This was no time to stop praising the Lord!

'*Oh hear us when we cry to Thee, For those in peril on the sea,*' he finished, and stopped and stared ahead.

There was something big and dark out there, coming closer very quickly. It would be impossible to steer around it. It was too big, and in any case the helm didn't answer. He was holding it as an act of faith, to show God that he would not desert Him and hoped that in return God would not desert Captain Roberts. He swung the wheel as he began the next verse, and lightning illuminated a path across the restless wave and there, in the light of the burning sky, was a gap, a valley or cleft in the wall of rock, like the miracle of the Red Sea, thought Captain Roberts, only, of course, the other way round.

The next flash of lightning showed that the gap was full of forest. But the wave would hit it at treetop height. It'd slow down. They might just be saved, even now, in the very jaws of Hell. And here they came . . .

And so it was that the schooner *Sweet Judy* sailed through a rainforest, with Captain Roberts, inspired to instant creativity, making up a new verse explicably missing from the original hymn: '*Oh Thou who built'st the mountains high, To be the pillars of the sky*—' He wasn't totally certain about '*built'st*', but '*bidd'st*' was apparently acceptable – '*Who gave the mighty forests birth*' – branches cracked like gunshots under the keel, thick vines snatched at what remained of the masts – '*And made a Garden of the Earth*' – fruit and leaves rained down on the deck, but a shudder meant that a broken tree had ripped away part of the hull, spilling the ballast – '*We pray to Thee to stretch Thy hand*' – Captain Roberts gripped the useless wheel tighter, and laughed at the roaring dark – '*to those in peril on* the land.'

And three great fig trees, whose buttressed roots had withstood centuries of cyclones, raced out of the future and came as a big surprise. His last thought was: Perhaps *who* raised *the mountains high* would have been a better line in the circums—

Captain Roberts went to Heaven, which wasn't everything that he'd expected, and as the receding water gently marooned the wreck of the *Sweet Judy* on the forest floor, only one soul was left alive. Or possibly two, if you like parrots.

On the day the world ended Mau was on his way home.

It was a journey of more than twenty miles. But he knew the way, oh yes. If you didn't know the way you weren't a man. And he was a man . . . Well, nearly. He'd lived for a month on the island of the boys, hadn't he? Just surviving on that place was enough to make you a man . . .

Well, surviving, and then getting back.

No one ever told you about the Boys' Island, not properly. You picked up stuff as you grew up, but there was one thing you learned very soon: the point about the Boys' Island was that you got *away* from the Boys' Island. You left your boy soul there and got given a man soul when you got back to the Nation.

You had to get back, otherwise something terrible happened: if you didn't get back in thirty days, they came and fetched you, and you'd never be a man, not really. The boys said it would be better to drown than be fetched. Everyone would know you'd failed, and you'd probably never get a wife, and if you did get a wife she'd be a woman none of the real men wanted, with bad teeth and smelly breath.

Mau had lain awake for weeks worrying about this. You were allowed to take only your knife to the island, and he had nightmares about building a canoe in thirty days with just a knife. It couldn't be done. But all the men in the Nation had done it, so there had to be a way, didn't there?

On his second day on the Boys' Island he'd found it.

There was a god anchor in the middle of the island, a stone cube half buried in sand and soil. Heavy vines grew over it and wrapped around a huge tabago tree. Carved deeply into its dry bark in the language for children were the signs: MEN HELP OTHER MEN. Next to it, wedged into the wood, was an *alaki*, a carved black stone on a long handle. Hold it one way, it was an axe. Hold it the other, it was an adze, good for hollowing out a log.

He pulled out the axe, and learned the lesson. So had many other boys; Mau climbed the tree one evening and found the hundreds of marks all the way up the trunk where generations of grateful boys had left the axe, or one like it, for those who came after. Some of them would be Grandfathers now, up in the cave on the mountain, back home.

They would be watching, with eyes that could see for miles, and perhaps they watched him when he found the log, well-seasoned, and not too well-hidden among the pandanuses at the back of the little island. When he got home he'd say he found it, and everyone would say that was lucky, and perhaps the god had put it there. Now he came to think about it, his father and a couple of his uncles had gone off fishing near the island early one morning without inviting him to come with them . . .

It had been a good time. He knew how to make fire, and he'd found the little freshwater spring. He'd made a spear good enough to get fish from the lagoon. And he'd made a good canoe, firm and light, with an outrigger. All you had to build was something that would get you home, but he'd worked on this canoe with knife and skateskin so that it whispered over the water.

He hadn't rushed his last day as a boy. His father had

told him not to. *Clean up the camp*, he'd said. *Soon you will belong to a wife and children. That will be fine. But sometimes you will look back fondly on your last day as a boy. Make it a warm memory, and be back in time for the feast.*

The camp was so clean that you wouldn't know he'd been there. Now he stood in front of the ancient tabago tree for the last time, the axe in his hand and, he was sure, the Grandfathers looking over his shoulder.

It was going to be perfect, he knew. Last night the stars of Air, Fire and Water had been in the sky together. It was a good time for new beginnings.

He found a clear place in the soft bark, and raised the axe. For a moment his eye caught the little blue bead tied to his wrist; it would keep him safe on the journey home. His father had told him how proud he'd be on his way back. But he would need to be careful, and not draw the attention of any gods or spirits to himself. It was not good to be between souls. He'd be like *mihei gawi*, the little blue hermit crab, scuttling from his shell to a new one once a year, easy prey for any passing squid.

It was not a nice thought, but he had a good canoe and a calm sea, and he would scuttle fast, oh yes! He swung the axe, as hard as he could, thinking: Hah! The next boy to pull this out will *deserve* to be called a man.

'Men help other men!' he shouted as the stone hit the bark.

He'd meant it to have an effect. It did, far more than he expected. From every corner of the little island, birds exploded into the air like a cloud of bees. Finches and waders and ducks rose out of the bushes and filled the air with panic and feathers. Some of the larger ones headed out to sea, but most of them just circled, as though terrified to stay but with nowhere else to go.

Mau walked through them as he went down to the beach. Bright wings zipped past his face like hail, and it would have been wondrously pretty if it weren't for the fact that every single bird was taking this opportunity to have a really good crap. If you're in a hurry, there is no point in carrying unnecessary weight.

Something was wrong. He could feel it in the air, in the sudden calm, in the way the world felt suddenly as though something heavy was pressing down on it.

And now it hit Mau, knocking him flat on the sand. His head was trying to explode. It was worse even than that time when he'd played the stone game and had hung on too long. Something was weighing down on the world like a big grey rock.

Then the pain went as fast as it had come, with a zip, leaving him gasping and dazed. And still the birds swarmed overhead.

As Mau staggered to his feet, all he knew was that here was not a good place to be any more, and if it was the only thing he knew, then at least he knew it with every nail and hair of his body.

Thunder rolled in the clear sky, one great hard bolt of it that rattled off the horizons. Mau staggered down to the tiny lagoon while the noise went on, and there was the canoe waiting for him in the white sand of the water's edge. But the usually calm water was . . . dancing, dancing like water danced under heavy rain, although no rain was falling.

He had to get away. The canoe sloped easily into the water, and he paddled frantically for the gap in the reef that led to the open sea. Beneath him and around him, fish were doing the same thing—

The sound went on, like something solid, smashing into the air and breaking it. It filled the whole of the sky. For Mau it was like a giant slap on the ears. He tried to paddle faster, and then the thought rose in his mind: *Animals* flee. His father had told him so. *Boys* flee. A man does *not* flee. He turns to look at his enemy, to watch what he does and find his weakness.

He let the canoe slide out of the lagoon, and easily rode the surf into the ocean, and then he looked around, like a man.

The horizon was one great cloud, boiling and climbing, full of fire and lightning and growling like a nightmare.

A wave crashed in the coral and that was wrong, too. Mau knew the sea, and there was also something wrong with that. The Boys' Island was falling way behind him, because a terrible current was dragging him towards the great bag of storms. It was as if the horizon was drinking the sea.

Men looked at their enemy, yes, but sometimes they turned round and paddled like mad.

It made no difference. The sea was sliding and then, suddenly, was dancing again, like the water in the lagoon.

Mau, trying to think straight, fought to get the canoe under control.

He'd get back. Of course he would. He could see the picture in his head, small and clear. He turned it around, savouring the taste of it.

Everyone would be there. *Everyone.* There could be no exceptions. Old, sick men would prefer to die on mats at the water's edge rather than not be there, women would give birth there if they had to, while watching for the homecoming canoe. It was unthinkable to miss the arrival of a new man. That would bring down terrible bad luck on the whole Nation.

His father would be watching for him at the edge of the reef, and they'd bring the canoe up the beach, and his uncles would come running up, and the new young men would rush to congratulate him, and the boys he'd left behind would be envious, and his mother and the other women would start on the feast, and there would be the . . . thing with the sharp knife, where you didn't scream, and then . . . there would be everything.

And if he could just hold it in his mind, then it would be so. There was a shining silver thread connecting him to that future. It would work like a god anchor, which stopped the gods from wandering away.

Gods, that was it! This was coming from the Gods' Island. It was over the horizon and you couldn't see it even from here, but the old men said it had roared, back in the long ago, and there had been rough water and a lot of smoke and thunder because the Fire god was angry. Maybe he'd got angry again.

The cloud was reaching up to the top of the sky, but there was something new down at sea level. It was a dark grey line, getting bigger. A wave? Well, he knew about waves. You attacked them before they attacked you. He'd learned how to play with them. Don't let them tumble you. Use them. Waves were easy.

But this one was not acting like the normal waves at the mouth of the reef. It seemed as though it was standing still.

He stared at it and realized what he was seeing. It looked as if it was standing still because it was a *big* wave a long way off, and it was moving very fast, dragging black night behind it.

Very fast, and not so far away now. Not a wave, either. It was too big. It was a mountain of water, with lightning dancing along the top, and it was rushing, and it was roaring, and it scooped up the canoe like a fly.

Soaring up into the towering, foaming curve of the wave, Mau thrust the paddle under the vines that held the outrigger and held on as—

– It rained. It was a heavy, muddy rain, full of ash and sadness. Mau awoke from dreams of roast pork and cheering men, and opened his eyes under a grey sky.

Then he was sick.

The canoe rocked gently in the swell while he added, in a small way, to what was already floating there – bits of wood, leaves, fish . . .

Cooked fish?

Mau paddled over to a large *hehe* fish, which he managed to drag aboard. It had been boiled, right enough, and it was a feast.

He needed a feast. He ached everywhere. One side of his head was sticky with, as it turned out, blood. At some point he must have hit it on the side of the canoe, which wasn't surprising. The ride through the wave was an ear-banging, chest-burning memory, the kind of dream you are happy to wake up from. All he'd been able to do was hold on.

There had been a tunnel in the water, like a moving cave of air in the roll of the giant wave, and then there had been a *storm* of surf as the canoe came out of the water like a dolphin. He would swear it had leaped in the air. And there had been singing! He'd heard it for just a few seconds, while the canoe raced down the back of the wave. It must have been a god, or maybe a demon . . . or maybe it was just what you hear in your head as you half fly and half drown, in a world where water and air are changing places every second. But it was over now, and the sea that had tried to kill him was about to give him dinner.

The fish was good. He could feel the warmth entering his bones. There were plenty more, bobbing with all the other stuff. There were a few young coconuts, and he drank the milk gratefully, and began to cheer up. This would be a story to tell! And a wave that big must have washed up at home, so they'd know he wasn't lying.

And home was . . . where? He couldn't see the Boys'

Island. He couldn't see the sky. There were *no islands*. But one horizon was lighter than the other. The sun was setting over *there* somewhere. Last night he'd watched the sun set over the Nation. That had to be the way. He set out steadily, watching that pale horizon.

There were birds everywhere, perching on anything that floated. Mostly they were little finches, chattering madly as the canoe went past. Some of them even fluttered over and perched on the canoe itself, huddling together and staring at him with a sort of desperate, terrified optimism. One even perched on his head.

While he was tying to untangle it from his hair, there was a thump as something much heavier landed on the stern of the canoe, causing the finches to scatter and then flutter back because they were too tired to make it to any-where else. But they kept as far away as possible from the new passenger, because it wasn't particular about who it ate.

It was a big bird, with shiny blue-black feathers and a white chest, and little white feathers covering its legs. Its huge beak, though, was brilliant red and yellow.

It was a grandfather bird, and good luck – to people at least – even if it did slow Mau down and ate one of his fish. Grandfather birds had learned not to be frightened of people; it was bad luck even to shoosh one away. He could feel its beady eyes on the back of his neck as he paddled onwards. He hoped it might *be* lucky. If he had some luck he could be home long before midnight.

There was an 'Erk!' as the grandfather bird took off

again with another of Mau's boiled fish in its beak, making the canoe wallow for a moment. Well, at least I'm a bit lighter, Mau thought. It's not as though I need the fish in any case. I'll be filling up with pork tonight!

The bird landed heavily on a log a little way ahead. Quite a large log, in fact. As he drew nearer Mau saw that it was a whole tree, even with its roots, although a lot of its branches had been torn off.

He saw the axe, tangled, rising out of the water. But part of him already knew he was going to see it. The sight of it raced towards his eyes and became, just for a moment, the centre of the turning world.

The grandfather bird, having juggled the fish so that it could swallow it whole, took off in its gloomy is-this-really-worth-it way and flapped away with its big, slow wings nearly touching the scummy water.

With its weight gone, the tree started to roll back. But Mau was already in the water and caught the axe handle as it was pulled under. Holding his breath, he braced his legs against the tree's trunk and tugged. Oh, he'd been clever, hadn't he, that moment a hundred years ago now, slamming the axe hard into the tree to show the next boy what a big man he was . . .

It should have worked. With his last mighty heave the axe should have come free. That's how it should have been, in a perfect world. But the swollen wood had gripped it firmly.

Mau dived again three more times, and came up every time coughing and spitting sea water. He had a deep, angry feeling that this wasn't right; the gods had sent the axe to him, he was sure of that. They had sent it to him because he was going to need it, he was *certain* of it, and he had failed.

In the end he swam back to the canoe and grabbed the paddle before the grandfather bird was out of sight. They always flew back to land at night, and he was pretty certain that there couldn't be much of the Boys' Island to go back to. The tabago tree was hundreds of years old and it had roots thicker than Mau's waist. It looked as though they had practically held the island together! And there had been a god anchor among them. No wave should have been able to shift a god anchor. It would be like moving the world.

The grandfather bird flapped onward. Ahead of it, the thin line of the horizon grew redder, redder than any Mau had ever seen before. He paddled on as fast as he could, trying not to think about what he was going to find ahead of him; and because he was trying *not* to think them, the thoughts ran around in his head like excited dogs.

He tried to calm them down. Look, the Boys' Island was hardly anything more than a lump of rock surrounded by sandbanks, was it? he thought. It wasn't any good for being anything but a fishing camp or a place for boys to try to be men. The Nation had mountains – well, one good one – had a river, there were caves, there were whole forests, there were men who'd know what to do!

Wouldn't they? And what *could* they do?

But the little picture of his man-soul feast flickered in his head. It wouldn't stay still, and he couldn't find the silver thread that dragged him towards it.

Something dark drifted in front of the sunset, and he almost burst into tears. It was a perfect sunset wave, rolling across the red disc that was just sinking below the horizon. Every man in the Islands of the Sun had that image as his manhood tattoo and in a few hours, he knew it, so would he.

And then, where the wave had been, there was the Nation. He could recognize its outline anywhere. It was five miles away maybe. Well, he could do another five miles. And soon he'd see the light of the fires.

Paddling faster, eyes straining to see the darker shape in the strange twilight, he made out the whiteness of the surf over the reef. And soon, please, soon *he would see the light of the fires*!

Now he could smell them, all the smells of the land except the one he wanted, which was the smell of smoke.

And then, there it was, a sharp little tone in the scents of sea and forest. There was a fire somewhere. He couldn't see it, but where there was smoke there were people. Of course, if the wave had come this way there wouldn't be much dry wood. The wave wouldn't be bad here, not here. He'd seen big waves before, and they would make a mess, and splinter a canoe or two. All right, this one had looked *really* big, but waves did when they went over the top of you! People had gone up the mountain and brought down dry wood. Yes, that's what had happened. That was certainly what had happened. He had worried about nothing. They would be back soon.

That was it. That was how it would be.

But there was no silver thread. He could make the happy pictures in his mind, but they were out there in the dark, and there was no path to them.

It was almost fully dark when he entered the lagoon. He could make out leaves and branches, and hit a big lump of coral that must have been broken off the reef by the wave, but that was what the reef was for. It took the pounding of the storms. Behind the reef, around the lagoon, they were safe.

With a little kiss of crushed sand, the canoe touched the beach.

Mau jumped out, and remembered just in time about the sacrifice. It should be a red fish for a successful journey, and this journey had to be called a success, even if it was a very strange one. He hadn't got a red fish but, well, he was still a boy, and the gods excused boys many things. At least he'd *thought* about it. That must count.

There were no other canoes. There should have been many. Even in this gloom, things looked wrong. There was nobody here; nobody knew he was standing on the shore.

He tried anyway: 'Hello! It's me, Mau! I'm back!'

He started to cry, and that was worse. He'd cried in the canoe, but that was just water escaping from his face and only he knew. But now the tears came in big sobs, dribbling from his eyes and nose and mouth, unstoppably. He cried for his parents, because he was afraid, because he was cold and very tired, and because he was fearful and couldn't pretend. But most of all he cried because only he knew.

In the forest, something heard. And in the hidden fire-light, sharp metal gleamed.

Light died in the west. Night and tears took the Nation. The star of Water drifted among the clouds like a murderer softly leaving the scene of the crime.

CHAPTER 2

THE NEW WORLD

*T*he morning was a lighter shade of night. Mau felt as if he hadn't slept at all, hunched up amongst the broad fallen leaves of a coconut tree, but there must have been times when his body and mind just shut down, in a little rehearsal of death. He awoke or maybe came alive again with the dead grey light, stiff and cold. Waves barely moved on the shore, the sea was almost the same colour as the sky and still it rained tears.

The little river that came down from the mountain was choked with sand and mud and bits of trees, and when he dug down with his hands it didn't flow. It just oozed. In the end Mau had to suck at the rain as it trickled off leaves, and it tasted of ashes.

The lagoon was a mess of broken coral, and the wave had ripped a big hole in the reef. The tide had changed, and water was pouring in. Little Nation, which was barely more than a sandbank on the rim of the lagoon, had been stripped of all its trees but one, which was a ragged stem with, against all hope, a few leaves still on it.

Find food, find water, find shelter . . . these were the things you had to do in a strange place, and this was a strange place and he'd been born here.

He could see that the village had gone. The wave had sliced it off the island. A few stumps marked the place where the long house had stood since . . . for ever. The wave had torn up the reef. A wave like that would not have even noticed the village.

He'd learned to look at coasts when he'd been voyaging with his father and his uncles. And now, looking up, he could see the story of the wave, written in tumbled rocks and broken trees.

The village faced south. It had to. The other three sides were protected by sheer, crumbling cliffs, in which sea caves boomed and foamed. The wave had come from the south of east. Broken trees pointed the trail.

Everyone would have been on the shore, around the big fire. Would they have heard the roar of the wave above the crackle of the flames? Would they have known what it meant? If they had been quick, they would have headed up Big Pig Valley, to the higher ground beyond the fields. But some of the wave would already have been roaring up the eastern slope (all grassy there, nothing much to slow it up) and they would have met it pouring back on them.

And then the rolling cauldron of rocks and sand and

water and people would have broken through the west of the reef and into the deepwater current, where the people would have become dolphins.

But not everyone. The wave had left behind fish and mud and crabs, to the delight of the leg-of-pork birds and the grey ravens and, of course, the grandfather birds. The island was full of birds this morning. Birds Mau had never seen before were squabbling with the familiar, everyday ones.

And there were people, tangled in broken branches, half buried in mud and leaves, just another part of the ruined world.

It took him a few long seconds to realize what he was looking at, to see that what he had thought was a broken branch was an arm.

He looked around slowly and realized why there were so many birds, and why they were fighting . . .

He ran. His legs took him and he ran, screaming out names, up the long slope, past the lower fields, which were covered with debris, past the higher plantations, too high even for the wave, and almost to the edges of the forest. And there he heard his own voice, echoing back from the cliffs.

No one. But there must be someone . . .

But they had all been waiting, for someone who was no longer a boy but had yet to become a man.

He walked up to the Women's Place – totally forbidden for any man, of course – and risked a quick peek through the big hedge that surrounded the gardens, untouched up here by the water, but he saw nothing moving and no voice called out in answer to his cry.

They had been waiting on the beach. He could see them all so clearly in his mind, talking and laughing and dancing in circles around the fire, but there was no silver line, nothing to pull them back.

They had been waiting for the new man. The wave must have hit them like a hammer.

As he went back down to the fields he grabbed a broken branch and flailed ineffectively at the birds. There were bodies everywhere in the area just above the scoured land where the village had been. At first they were hard to see, tangled as they were with debris and as grey as the ashen mud. He'd have to touch them. They had to be moved. The pigs would come down soon. The thought of pigs eating— *No!*

There was some brightness behind the clouds in the east. How could that be? Another night had passed? Had he slept? Where had he been? But tiredness certainly had him now. He dragged some leafy branches up against a big rock for shelter, crawled inside and felt the grey of the mud and the rain and the bruised-looking sky sneak in silently and fill him up and close over him.

And Mau dreamed. It had to be a dream. He felt himself become two people. One of them, a grey body made of mud, began to look for the bodies that the wave hadn't taken. It did it carefully and as gently as it could, while the other Mau stayed deep inside, curled in a ball, doing the dreaming.

And who am I, doing this? thought the grey Mau. Who am I now? I am become like Locaha, measuring the contours of death. Better be him than be Mau, on this day . . . because here is a body. And Mau will not see it, lift it, or look into its eyes, because he will go mad, so I will do it for him. And this one has a face he has seen every day of his life, but I will not let him see.

And so he worked, as the sky brightened and the sun came up behind the plume of steam in the east and the forest burst into song, despite the drizzle. He combed the lower slopes until he found a body, dragged it or carried it – some were small enough to carry – down to the beach and out to the point where you could see the current. There were usually turtles there, but not today.

He, the grey shadow, would find rocks and big coral lumps, and there were plenty of those, and tie them to the body with papervine. And now I must take my knife and cut the spirit hole, thought the grey Mau, so that the spirit will leave quickly, and pull the body out into the waves where the current sinks, and let it go.

The dreaming Mau let his body do the thinking: You lift like *this*, you pull like *this*. You cut the papervine like *that*, and you don't scream, because you are a hand and a body and a knife, and they don't even shed a tear. You are inside a thick grey skin that can feel nothing. And nothing can get through. Nothing at all. And you send the body sinking slowly into the dark current, away from birds and pigs and flies, and it would grow a new skin and become a dolphin.

There were two dogs, too, and that almost broke him. The people, well, the horror was so great that his mind went blank, but the twisted bodies of the dogs twisted his soul. They had been with the people, excited but not knowing why. He wrapped them in papervine and weighed them down and sent them into the current anyway. Dogs would want to stay with the people, because they were people, too, in their way.

He didn't know what to do with the piglet, though. It was all by itself. Maybe the sow had legged it for the high forest, as they did when, in their piggy way, they sensed the water coming. This one hadn't kept up. His stomach said it was food but he said no, not this one, not this sad little betrayed thing. He sent it into the current. The gods would have to sort it out. He was too tired.

It was near sunset when he dragged the last body to the beach and was about to wade out to the current when his body told him: *No, not this one. This is you and you are very tired but you are not dead. You need to eat and drink and sleep. And most of all you must try not to dream.*

He stood for a while until the words sank in, and then trudged back up the beach, found his makeshift shelter and fell into it.

Sleep came, but brought no good thing. Over and over again he found the bodies and carried them to the shore because they were so light. They tried to talk to him, but he could not hear them because the words could not get through his grey skin. There was a strange one, too, a ghost girl, totally white. She tried to talk to him several times but faded back into the dream, like the others. The sun and moon whirled across the sky, and he walked on in a grey world, the only moving thing in veils of silence, for ever.

And then he was spoken to, out of the greyness.

WHAT ARE YOU DOING, MAU?

He looked around. The land looked odd, without colour. The sun was shining, but it was black.

When the voices spoke again, they seemed to come from everywhere at once, on the wind.

THERE IS NO TIME FOR SLEEPING. THERE IS SO MUCH THAT MUST BE DONE.

'Who are you?'

WE ARE THE GRANDFATHERS!

Mau trembled, and trembling was all he could manage. His legs would not move.

'The wave came,' he managed. 'Everyone is dead! I sent some into the dark water!'

YOU MUST SING THE DARK WATER CHANT.

'I didn't know how!'

YOU MUST RESTORE THE GOD ANCHORS.

'How do I do that?'

YOU MUST SING THE MORNING SONG AND THE EVENING SONG.

'I don't know the words! I am not a man!' said Mau desperately.

YOU MUST DEFEND THE NATION! YOU MUST DO THE THINGS THAT HAVE ALWAYS BEEN DONE!

'But there is just me! Everyone is dead!'

EVERYTHING THE NATION WAS, YOU ARE! WHILE YOU ARE, THE NATION IS! WHILE YOU REMEMBER, THE NATION LIVES!

There was a change in the pressure of the air, and the grandfathers . . . went.

Mau blinked, and woke up. The sun was yellow and halfway down the sky and beside him was a flat round metal thing, on top of which was a coconut with the top sliced off, and a mango.

He stared at them.

He was alone. No one else could be here, not now. Not to leave him food and creep away.

He looked down at the sand. There were footprints there, not large, but they had no toes.

He stood up very carefully, and looked around. The creature with no toes was watching him, he was sure. Perhaps . . . perhaps the Grandfathers had sent it?

'Thank you,' he said to the empty air.

The Grandfathers had spoken to him. He thought about this as he gnawed the mango off its huge stone. He'd never heard them before. But the things they wanted . . . how could a boy do them? Boys couldn't even go near their cave. It was a strict rule.

But boys did, though. Mau had been eight when he'd tagged along after some of the older boys. They hadn't seen him as he'd shadowed them all the way up through the high forests to the meadows where you could see to the edge of the world. The grandfather birds nested up there, which was why they were called grandfather birds. The older boys had told him that the birds were spies for the Grandfathers and would swoop on you and peck your eyes out if you came too close, which he knew wasn't true, because he'd watched them and knew that – unless there was beer about – they wouldn't attack anything bigger than a mouse if they thought it might fight back. But some people would tell you anything if they thought you'd be scared.

At the end of the meadows was the Cave of the Grandfathers, high up in the wind and the sunlight, watching over the whole world. They lived behind a round stone door that took ten men to shift, and you might live for a hundred years and only see it moved a few times, because only the best men, the greatest hunters and warriors, became Grandfathers when they died . . .

On the day he had followed the boys, Mau had sat and watched from the thick foliage of a grass tree as they dared one another to go near the stone, to touch it, to give it a little push – and then someone had shouted that he'd heard something, and within seconds they'd vanished into the trees, running for home. Mau had waited a little while, and when nothing happened he had climbed down and gone and listened at the stone. He had heard a faint crackling right on the edge of hearing but then a grandfather bird on the cliff above was throwing up (the ugly-looking things didn't just eat everything, they ate *all* of everything, and carefully threw up anything that didn't fit, taste right, or had woken up and started to protest).

There was nothing very scary at all. No one had ever heard of the Grandfathers coming out. The stone was there for a reason. It was *heavy* for a reason. He forgot about the sound; it had probably been insects in the grass.

That night, back in the boys' hut, the older boys boasted to the younger boys about how they had rolled away the big stone and how the Grandfathers had turned their ancient, dry old faces to look at them, and tried to stand up on their crumbling legs, and how the boys had (very bravely) rolled the big stone back again, just in time.

And Mau had lain in his corner and wondered how many times this story had been told over the last hundreds of years, to make big boys feel brave and little boys have nightmares and wet themselves.

Now, five years later, he sat and turned over in his hands the grey round thing that had acted as a holder for the mango. It looked like metal, but who had so much metal that they could waste it on something to hold food?

There were marks on it. They spelled out *Sweet Judy* in faded white paint – but they spelled out *Sweet Judy* in vain.

Mau was good at reading *important* things. He could read the sea, the weather, the tracks of animals, tattoos and the night sky. There was nothing for him to read in lines of cracked paint. Anyone could read wet sand though. A toeless creature had come out of the low forest, and had gone back the same way.

At some time in the past something had split the rock of the island, leaving a long low valley on the east side that was not very far above sea level and had hardly any soil.

Things had soon taken root even so, because something will always grow *somewhere*.

The low forest was always hot, damp and salty, with the sticky, itchy, steamy atmosphere of a place which never sees much new air. Mau had forced his way into there a few times but there wasn't much of interest, at least not at ground level. Everything happened high above, up in the canopy. There were wild figs up there. Only the birds could get at them, and they fought over the little morsels, which meant there was a steady rain of bird poo and half-eaten figs onto the forest floor, which in turn was a permanent feast for the little red crabs that scuttled around and cleared up anything that dropped in. Sometimes pigs came down to feed on the crabs, so the low forest was worth an occasional look. You had to be careful, though, because you often got a tree-climbing octopus or two in there, after baby birds and anything else they could find, and they were hard to pull off if they landed on your head. Mau knew that you must never let them think you are a coconut. You learned that fast, because they had sharp beaks.*

Now he came round the huge broken rocks that stood at the entrance to the valley, and stopped.

Something much bigger than a bird plop or a pig had hit the forest. It couldn't have been just the wave. Some

---

* The tree-climbing octopus (*octopus arbori*) is found on The Island Where the Sun Is Born, in the Mothering Sunday Islands. They are extremely intelligent, and cunning thieves.

enormous thing had charged through, leaving a line of smashed trees into the distance.

And not just trees; it had left treasure behind. Rocks! Grey round ones, brown ones, black ones . . . Good hard rocks had a lot of uses here, where the mountain rock was too crumbly to make decent weapons.

But Mau resisted the temptation to collect them now, because rocks don't go anywhere and, besides, there was the dead man. He lay by the track, as if the creature had tossed him aside, and he was covered in little red crabs whose big day had come.

Mau had never seen a man like this before, but he'd heard of them – of the pale people in the north who wrapped their legs in cloth so they looked like a grand-father bird. They were called the trousermen, and were as pale as ghosts. This one didn't worry him, not after the memory of yesterday, which screamed all the time behind a door in his head. This was just a dead man. He didn't know him. People died.

Mau didn't know what to do with him either, especially since the crabs did. Under his breath he said: 'Grandfathers, what shall I do with the trouserman?'

There was a sound like the forest drawing its breath, and the Grandfathers said: HE IS NOT IMPORTANT! ONLY THE NATION IS IMPORTANT!

This was not a lot of help, so Mau dragged the man off the broken track and into a deeper part of the forest, with an army of little crabs following in a very determined way. They'd had years of fig seeds and bird plop. They'd put up with this like good little crabs, they seemed to say, but now it was time for their perfect world.

There was another trouserman further along the trail, also dropped by the creature. Mau didn't think about it at all this time, but just dragged him into the tangle of undergrowth, too. It was the best he could do. He had walked too much in the footsteps of Locaha lately. Perhaps the crabs would take the soul of the man back to the trouserman world, but here and now Mau had other things to think about.

Something had come out of the sea on the wave, he thought. Something *big*. Bigger than a sailfin crocodile,* bigger than a war canoe, bigger even than . . . a whale? Yes, that could be it, a big whale. Why not? The wave had hurled big rocks beyond the village, so a whale wouldn't stand a chance. Yes, a whale, that would be it, thrashing around in the forest with its big tail and slowly dying under its own weight. Or one of the really big sea squids, he wondered, or a very big shark.

He had to be sure. He had to find out. He looked around and thought: Yes, but not in the dark. Not in the twilight. In the morning he'd come with weapons. And in the morning it might be dead.

---

* The sailfin crocodile (*crocodylus porosus Maritimus*) is still found in all parts of the Pelagic. It travels immense distances on the surface by means of a large skin and cartilage 'sail' which it can, to some extent, steer.

He selected a couple of useful-looking rocks from the monster's trail, and ran for it.

Night rolled over the jungle. The birds went to bed, the bats woke. A few stars appeared in the desolate sky.

And in the tangle of broken trees at the end of the trail, something sobbed, all night.

Mau awoke early. There was no more fruit on the round metal thing, but a grandfather bird was watching him hopefully, in case he was dead. When it saw him moving, it sighed and waddled off.

Fire, thought Mau. I must make fire. And for that I need punk wood. His punk bag was a muddy mess because of the wave, but there was always punk in the high forest.

He was hungry, but you had to have fire. Without fire and a spear, you could never hope to be a man, wasn't that right?

He spent some time hammering the metal between the two stones he'd taken from the monster's track, and ended up with a long sliver of metal that was pretty bendy but very sharp. That was a good start. Then he chipped one stone against the other until he had enough of a groove to allow him to bind the stone to a stick with papervine. He wound papervine around one end of the new metal knife, to make a kind of handle.

As the sun rose so did Mau, and he raised his new club and his new knife.

Yes! They might be sorry things that a man would have

thrown away, but now he could kill things. And wasn't that part of being a man?

The grandfather bird was still watching him from a safe distance, but when it saw his expression it shuffled off hurriedly and lumbered into the air.

Mau headed up to the high forest, while the sun grew hotter. He wondered when he'd last eaten. There had been the mango, but how long ago? It was hard to remember. The Boys' Island was far away in time and space. It had gone. Everything had gone. The Nation had gone. The people, the huts, the canoes, all wiped away. They were just in his head now, like dreams, hidden behind a grey wall—

He tried to stop the thought, but the grey wall crumbled and all the horror, all the death, all the darkness poured in. It filled up his head and buzzed out into the air like a swarm of insects. All the sights he had hidden from himself, all the sounds, all the smells crept and slithered out of his memory.

And suddenly it all became clear. An island full of people could not die. But a boy could. Yes, that was it! It made sense! *He was dead!* And his spirit had come back home, but he couldn't see out of the spirit world! He was a ghost. His body was on the Boys' Island, yes! And the wave had not been real, it had been Locaha, coming for him. It all made sense. He'd died on land with no one to put him into the dark water, and he was a ghost, a wandering thing, and the people were all around him, in the land of the living.

It seemed to Mau that this was not too bad. The worst had already happened. He would not be able to see his family again, because everyone hung ghost bags around the huts, but he would know that they were alive.

The world breathed in.

WHY HAVE YOU NOT REPLACED THE GOD ANCHORS? WHY HAVE YOU NOT SUNG THE CHANTS? WHY HAVE YOU NOT RESTORED THE NATION?

The little valley of the grandfather birds floated in front of Mau's eyes. Well, at least they would believe him this time.

'I'm dead, Grandfathers.'

DEAD? NONSENSE, YOU ARE NOT *GOOD* ENOUGH TO BE DEAD!

Hot pain struck Mau's left foot. He rolled and yelped, and a grandfather bird who had also decided he was dead and had pecked his foot to make sure, hopped away hurriedly. It didn't go far away, though, in case he died after all. In the grandfather bird's experience, everything died if you watched it for long enough.

All right, not dead, Mau thought, pushing himself upright. But dead tired. A sleep full of dark dreams was no sleep at all, it was like a meal of ashes. He needed fire, and real food. Everyone knew that bad dreams came when you were hungry. He didn't want those dreams again. They were about dark waters, and something chasing him.

Mud and sand covered the fields, but worse than that, the wave had broken down the thorn fences, and the pigs had clearly been rooting all over the fields in the night, when Mau had been in the prison of his dreams. There would probably be something left in the muck if he grubbed about long enough, but a man didn't eat where a pig had eaten.

There was plenty of wild food to eat on the island: upside-down fruit, bad-luck root, malla stems, red star tree, papervine nuts . . . you'd stay alive, but a lot of it you had to chew for a long time and even then it tasted as though someone had eaten it before you. Men ate fish or pork, but the lagoon was still cloudy, and he hadn't seen a pig since he'd been back. They were wily, too. A man by himself might get a lucky shot if a pig came down in the low forest at night to eat crabs, but once they were in the high forest you needed many men to catch one pig.

He found tracks as soon as he entered the forest. Pigs were always making tracks. They were fresh, though, so he poked around a bit to see what they'd been after, and found some mad-root tubers, big and white and juicy; the pigs had probably been so stuffed with the food from the field that they were grubbing around out of pure habit, and didn't have room for one more tuber. Mad-root tubers had to be roasted before they could be eaten, though, or else you went mad. Pigs ate them raw, but pigs probably didn't notice if they were mad or not.

There was no dry punk wood. There were rotten branches all over the place, but they were sodden to the core. Besides, he thought, as he threaded the tubers on a length of papervine, he hadn't found any fire stones yet, or decent dry wood for fire sticks.

Granddad Nawi, who did not go raiding because of his twisted leg, sometimes took the boys tracking and hunting, and he used to talk about the papervine bush. It grew everywhere, its long leaves as tough as anything even when they were crackling dry. 'Take one strip of the vine lengthwise and yes, it needs the strength of two men to pull it apart. But weave five strands of it into a rope and a hundred men can't break it. The more they pull, the more it binds together and the stronger it becomes. That is the Nation.'

They used to laugh at him behind his back because of his wobbling walk, and didn't pay much attention to him, because what could a man with a twisted leg know about anything important? But they made sure that when they laughed they were *well* behind his back, because Nawi always had a faint little smile and an expression that said he already knew far more about you than you could possibly guess.

Mau had tried not to laugh too much because he had liked Nawi. The old man watched how birds flew and always knew the best places to fish. He knew the magic word which would keep sharks away. But he didn't get carefully dried out in the hot sand and taken to the Cave of the Grandfathers when he died, because he'd been *born* with a leg that didn't work properly and that meant he'd been cursed by the gods. He could look at a finch and tell you which island it had been born on; he used to watch spiders make webs, and saw things other people didn't notice. Thinking about it now, Mau wondered why any god would curse someone like that. He'd been born with that leg. What had a baby done to make the gods angry?

One day he'd plucked up the courage to ask him. Nawi was sitting out on the rocks, occasionally looking out to sea in between carving something, but he'd given Mau a look that indicated that company would not be objected to.

The old man had laughed at the question.

'It was a gift, boy, not a curse,' he said. 'When much is taken, something is returned. Since I had a useless leg I had to make myself a clever brain! I cannot chase, so I learn to watch and wait. I tell you boys these secrets and you laugh. When I hunt, I never come back empty-handed, do I? I think the gods looked at me and said to themselves, Well, this one is a sharp one, eh? Let's give him a gimpy leg so he can't be a warrior and will have to stay at home among the women (a fate which has something to recommend it, my boy, believe me), and I thank them.'

Mau had been shocked at this. Every boy wanted to be a warrior, didn't he?

'You didn't *want* to be a warrior?'

'Never. It takes a woman nine months to make a new human. Why waste her effort?'

'But then when you died you could be taken up to the cave and watch over us for ever!'

'Hah! I think I've seen enough of you already! I like the

fresh air, boy. I'll become a dolphin like everyone else. I'll watch the sky turn and I will chase sharks. And since all the great warriors will be shut up in their cave, it occurs to me there will be rather more female dolphins than male ones, which is a pleasing thought.' He leaned forward and stared into Mau's eyes. 'Mau . . .' he said. 'Yes, I remember you. Always at the back. But I could see you thinking. Not many people think, not *really* think. They just think they do. And when they laughed at old Nawi, you didn't want to. But you laughed anyway, to be like them. I'm right, yes?'

How had he spotted that? But you couldn't deny it, not now, not with those pale eyes looking through you.

'Yes. I'm sorry.'

'Good. And now that I have answered your questions, I think you owe me a favour.'

'Do you want me to run an errand? Or I could—'

'I want you to remember something for me. Have you heard that I know a word that drives away sharks?'

'People say so, but they laugh.'

'Oh, yes. But it works. I've tried it three times. The first was when I discovered it, which was when I was about to have my good leg bitten off, and then I tried it out from a raft, just to see if I'd been lucky the first time, and then I swam off the reef one day and frightened away a hammerhead.'

'You mean you went *looking* for a shark?' said Mau.

'Yes. Quite a big one, as I recall.'

'But you might have been eaten!'

'Oh, I'm not bad with a spear, and I had to find out,' said Nawi, grinning. 'Someone had to eat the first oyster, you know. Someone looked at half a shell full of snot and was brave.'

'Why doesn't everybody know?'

Nawi's permanent smile turned down a little. 'I'm a bit strange, yes? And the priests don't like me much. If I told everyone, and someone died, I think things would be very tricky for me. But someone should know, and you are a boy who asks questions. Don't use it until I'm dead, all right? Or until you are about to be eaten by a shark, of course.'

And there on the rocks, as the sunset made a path of red across the sea, Mau learned the shark word.

'It's a trick!' he said, without thinking.

'Not so loud,' snapped Nawi, glancing back at the shore. 'Of course it's a trick. Building a canoe is a trick. Throwing a spear is a trick. Life is a trick, and you get one chance to learn it. And now you know another one. If it saves your life one day, catch a big fish and throw it to the first dolphin you see. With luck, it will be me!'

And now the old man and his leg were only a memory, along with everyone Mau had ever known. Mau wanted to scream with the weight of it. The world had emptied.

He looked down at his hands. And he'd made a club. A weapon for what? Why did it make him feel better? But he had to stay alive. Yes! If he died, then the Nation would never have been. The island would be left to the red crabs and the grandfather birds. There would be no one to say that anyone had been there.

There was a fluttering overhead. A grandfather bird had landed in a shaggy-headed grass tree. Mau knew that, even though he couldn't see up through the tangle of vines; grandfather birds were very clumsy and didn't so much land as crash slowly. It hopped around up there making the *nab-nab* grumbling noises, and then there was the familiar sound of throwing up and a shower of small bones pattered around the forest floor.

The tree shook as the grandfather bird took off again. It flapped out into the open, saw Mau, decided to watch him for signs of being dead, and landed heavily on a branch of a tree that could barely be seen under its weight of strangler vines.

For a moment boy and bird stared at each other.

The branch snapped.

The grandfather bird squawked and leaped away before the rotted wood hit the ground, and disappeared, flapping and squawking with injured pride, into the undergrowth. Mau paid it no attention. He was staring at the cloud of fine yellow dust rising from the fallen branch. It was punk dust, what you got when rot and termites and time hollowed out a dead branch. And this one had been up in the air, out of reach of the damp. The dust was like pollen. It would be the best ever for starting fires.

He took the biggest lump of branch that he could hold, stuffed both ends with leaves and started back down the mountain.

There were pigs rooting in the fields again now, but he had no time to shoo them away. One piece of papervine soon breaks, he thought, and five bound together are strong. That's good to know and it is true. The trouble is, I'm the one piece.

He stopped. He was taking the other, steeper track down to the vill— to the place where the village had been. The wave had surged across the island here, too. Trees were broken and everything stank of seaweed. But on the other side of the shattered trees was a cliff, which overlooked the low forest . . .

Mau carefully tucked the tubers and the punk branch under some grass and pushed his way through the tangle of vines and branches at the edge of the cliff. It was possible to climb all the way up or down the cliff quite easily. He'd done it before. There were so many roots and vines and creepers growing over the stone, and so much soil and old birds' nests had made a home for every drifting seed that it was more like a vertical meadow, with flowers everywhere. There was papervine, too. There was always papervine. He cut enough to make a sling for his club, while whispering belated thank-yous to the Papervine Woman for her ever-reliable hair.

Now he slid to the edge and pushed aside a spray of orchids.

Mists were rising everywhere below him, but he could see the track the monster had left through the forest, a white scar half a mile long. It stopped at the group of fig trees that grew in the highest part of the low forest. They were massive. Mau knew them well. Their trunks had huge buttresses that looked as though they might reach down to the roots of the world. They would stop anything, but the steam and the spread of the tree canopy meant that he couldn't see what it was that had been stopped.

But he heard a voice. It was very faint, but it was coming from somewhere below Mau. It sounded a bit like singing, but not a very big bit. To Mau, it just sounded like 'na, na, na'.

But it was a human voice. Perhaps it was another trouser-man? It was a bit squeaky. Were there trouserwomen? Or it could be a ghost. There would be a lot of ghosts now.

It was past noon. If it was a ghost, then it would be very weak. He was the Nation. He had to do *something*.

He started to climb down the cliff, which was easy enough even with trying to move quietly, although birds flew up all around him. He shivered. He didn't know how to make a ghost bag. That was a woman's task.

The a-bit-like-singing went on. Perhaps it *was* some sort of ghost, then. The birds had made such a racket that any living person would surely have stopped and investigated.

His feet touched the tangle of flaking stone and tree roots that was the floor of the lower forest and he moved silently between the dripping trees.

'Na, na, na' – *clink!* – 'na, na, na' – *clink!*

That sounded like metal. Mau grasped his club in both hands.

– 'give, for, wild, confu-sion, peace' – *clink!* – 'and, hear, us, when, we, cry, to, Thee' – *clink!* – 'for, those in per-ril on the sea!' – *clang!* – 'drat!'

Mau peered round the buttress of a giant fig tree.

There was a lot to see.

Something had been wrecked, but it was not alive. It was some kind of giant canoe, stuck between the trunks of two trees and covered with debris that looked as though it would be worth investigating, but not now. A big hole in the side leaked stones. But all this was background. Much closer to Mau, and staring at him in horror, was a girl – probably. But she could be a ghost; she was very pale.

And a trouserman, too. The trousers were white and frilly, like the feathery legs of a grandfather bird, but she also had some kind of skirt tucked up around her waist. And her hair glowed in the sunlight. She had been crying.

She had also been trying to dig into the forest floor with some odd kind of flat-headed spear, which had the glint of metal about it. That was stupid; it was all roots and rocks, and there was a very small heap of rocks next to her. There was something else, too, large and wrapped up. Perhaps I did walk in the footsteps of Locaha, Mau thought, because I know that there is a dead man in there. And the ghost girl, she was in my nightmares.

I am not alone.

The girl dropped the flat-headed spear and quickly held up something else, something that also shone like metal.

'I kn-know how to use this!' she shouted very loudly. 'One step more and I will pull the trigger, I mean it!' The metal thing waved back and forth in her hands. 'Don't think I'm afraid! I'm not afraid! I could have killed you before! Just because I felt sorry for you doesn't mean you can come down here! My father will be here soon!'

She sounded excited. Mau took the view that she wanted him to have the metal thing, because by the way she was holding it with both hands and waving it about she was obviously very frightened of it.

He reached out for it, she screamed and turned her head away, something went *click*, there was a small fountain of sparks from near one end of the metal thing and, quite slowly, a little round ball rolled out of a hole in the other end and landed in the mud in front of the girl. There were . . . *things* on her feet, he noticed with a sort of horrified fascination; they were like black pods and had *no toes*.

The girl was watching him in round-eyed terror.

Mau gently took the thing away from her, and she flattened herself against the side of the canoe as if *he* were the ghost.

The metal stank of something bitter and foul, but that wasn't the important thing. It had sparked. Mau knew what to do with a spark.

'Thank you for this gift of fire,' he said, and picked up his axe and ran for it before she could do anything dreadful to him.

In the wreckage on the beach Mau crouched over his work. The punk branch was only the start. He had combed the forest for dry twigs and bark. There was always some, even after heavy rain, and he'd carefully made little piles of everything from grass to quite thick twigs. He'd made a small heap of crumbled dried-up papervine bark and punk and now, with great care, picked up the spark-maker.

If you pulled back the piece of metal at the top until it went click, and then pulled the piece of metal at the bottom, and made certain – at least the second time – to keep your fingers out of the way, then a sort of metal claw scraped a dark stone down some metal and sparks would be born.

He tried it again now, holding the spark-maker just above the punk heap, and held his breath as a few sparks dropped onto fine dust, which went black where they fell.

He blew across the heap, which he shielded in his cupped hands, and a tiny wisp of smoke went up. He kept his breath steady, and a little flame crackled into life.

This was the hard part. He fed the flame with great care, teasing it along with grass and bark until it grew fat enough for its first twig. Every move was thoughtful, because fire is so easily scared away. It wasn't until it was crackling and hissing and spitting that he tried the first thin branch, and there was a nasty moment when the flames seemed to choke on it, and then they came up stronger and before long were asking for more. Well, there was no shortage of fuel. Broken trees were everywhere. He dragged them into the flames, and they burst as the heat boiled the water in them. Mau threw more wood on, piling it up so that sparks and steam soared into the dark. Shadows jumped and danced across the beach so that, while the flames burned, there was a sort of life.

After a while he dug out a hole on the edge of the fire, buried the mad-root tubers just under the sand, and scraped glowing embers over them.

Then he lay back. When was the last time he had sat by a fire, here at home? The memory rushed in before he could stop it. It was his last meal as a boy, with all his family there, and in the Nation all his family meant, sooner or later, just about everyone. It was his 'last meal' because the next time he ate on the island it would be as a man, no longer living in the boys' hut but sleeping in the house of the unmarried men. He hadn't eaten much, because he'd been too excited. He'd been too scared, too, because he could just about get the idea that this wasn't only about him; it was also about his family. If he came back ready for a man's tattoos and, obviously, the . . . thing with the knife where you must not scream, then it would be a triumph for them, too. It would mean that he had been brought up in the right way and had learned the right things.

The fire crackled and sent smoke and steam up into the darkness, and he saw them in the firelight, watching him, *smiling* at him. He closed his eyes and tried to force the clamoring memories away, into the dark.

Had he sent any of them into the dark current when he'd walked in the steps of Locaha? Perhaps. But there was no memory there. He'd been curled up in the grey body of the Locaha-Mau, as a part of him trudged back and forth, doing what was needed, taking the dead to become dolphins so that they wouldn't become food for the pigs. He should have sung a burial chant, but he'd never been taught the words, so instead he'd straightened limbs on the bodies as tidily as he could. Perhaps he had seen faces, but then that part of him had died. He tried to remember the face of his mother, but all he could see was dark water. He could hear her voice, though, singing the song about the god of Fire, and how the Papervine Woman got fed up with him chasing her daughters, and bound his hands to his sides with great coils of vine and his younger sister used to laugh at that and chase him with coils of— But a wave passed over his mind, and he was glad it washed the bright memory away.

He could feel the hole inside, blacker and deeper than the dark current. Everything was missing. Nothing was where it should be. He was here on this lonely shore and all he could think of was the silly questions that children ask . . . Why do things end? How do they start? Why do good people die? What do the gods do?

And this was hard, because one of the right things for a man was: Don't ask silly questions.

And now the little blue hermit crab was out of its shell and scuttling across the sand, looking for a new shell, and there wasn't one. Barren sand stretched away on every side, and all it could do was run . . .

He opened his eyes. And now there was just him and the ghost girl. Had she been real? Was he real? Was that a silly question?

The smell of the tubers came up through the sand. His

stomach suggested that *they* might be real, at least, and he burned his fingers digging them up. One would keep until tomorrow. The other one he broke open and stuck his face into the fluffy, crunchy, hot, savoury heart of it, and he went to sleep with his mouth full, while the shadows danced in circles around the fire.

CHAPTER 3

CALENTURE

*I*n the darkness of the wreck of the *Sweet Judy*, a match flared. There were some pings and scraping noises and at last the lamp was alight. It wasn't broken, but she had to be sparing with it because she hadn't found any more oil yet. It was probably underneath everything else. *Everything* was under everything else. It was a mercy she'd wrapped the mattress around her before the *Sweet Judy* tried to sail through trees. She'd remember the snapping and the screams as long as she lived. She'd heard the hull split and the masts crack, and worst of all she had heard the silence.

And she'd climbed out into a steaming morning, full of birdsong, with most of the *Judy* back on the smashed trail behind her, and one word in her head.

The word was 'Calenture'.

It meant a special kind of madness, brought on by the heat. First Mate Cox had told her about it, probably hoping to frighten her because he was that sort of person. Sailors got calenture when they'd been becalmed at sea for too long. They'd look over the side and see, instead of the ocean, cool green fields. They'd leap down into them, and drown. First Mate Cox said he'd seen grown men do it. They'd jumped into a meadow full of daisies and drowned or, as he put it, drown-ded. And he'd probably pushed them in, too.

And there she was, stepping off a boat into the middle of a green jungle. It was like the . . . opposite of madness, in a way. She was quite sane, she was sure of that, but the world itself had gone mad. There were dead men, back on the track. She'd seen dead people before, when her uncle had broken his neck while hunting, and of course there had been that terrible accident with the harvesting machine. Neither of the dead seamen was Cookie, she was shamefully glad to say, and she'd said a quick prayer over them and had run back to the ship to be sick.

Now she rummaged in the mess that had been a neat cabin, and found her writing box. She balanced it on her knees and opened it, taking out one of the gold-edged invitation cards she had got for her birthday, and stared at it for a moment. According to her book of etiquette (another birthday present), there should be a chaperone present if she invited the young man to visit, and the only person she could think of was poor Captain Roberts. He was a real captain, which counted for something, but he was unfortunately dead. On the other hand the book didn't actually say the chaperone had to be alive, only present. Anyway, she had still got the sharp machete stuffed down behind her bunk. It had not been a happy voyage after First Mate Cox had come aboard.

She glanced at the blanket-covered shape in the corner, from which came a continual muttering. She had to keep it covered up or else it'd start to swear again. Some of the words it came out with a respectable young lady should not know the meaning of. The words she *didn't* know the meaning of worried her even more.

She had been unkind to the boy, she knew. You weren't supposed to shoot people, especially if you hadn't even been introduced to them, and it was only a mercy the gunpowder had got wet. It was sheer panic and he'd been working so hard burying those poor people in the sea. At least her father was alive and he would come looking for her, even though there were more than eight hundred places to look in the Mothering Sunday Islands.

She dipped her pen in the ink and crossed out 'Government House, Port Mercia' at the top of the card, and carefully wrote underneath: 'The Wreck of the *Sweet Judy.*'

There were other changes that needed to be made. Whoever had designed the cards had completely overlooked the possibility that you might want to invite someone whose name you didn't know, who lived on a beach, wore hardly any clothing and almost certainly couldn't read. But she did her best, on both sides of the card,* and then signed it 'Ermintrude Fanshaw (the Honourable Miss)' and wished she didn't have to, at least about the 'Ermintrude'.

Then she put on the big oilskin coat that had belonged to poor Captain Roberts, pocketed the last of the mangoes, picked up a cutlass, unhooked the oil lamp, and set out into the night.

Mau awoke with the Grandfathers shouting in his head and the fire a big glowing heap.

REPLACE THE GOD ANCHORS! WHO IS GUARDING THE NATION? WHERE IS OUR BEER?

I don't know, Mau thought, looking up at the sky. The women made beer. I don't know how.

He couldn't go into the Women's Place, could he? He'd already been up there to take a look, although men couldn't go to the Women's Place, and women couldn't go into the valley of the Grandfathers. If these things happened, there would be the end of everything. It was that important.

Mau blinked. How much more of an end could every-thing have? There were no more people, so how could there be rules? Rules couldn't float around by themselves!

He stood up, and saw the golden glitter. A white oblong had been wedged in a piece of broken wood, and there were toeless footprints in the sand. Next to the wood was another mango.

* Where it said 'Dress' she'd written: 'Yes, please.'

She'd been creeping around while he slept!

There were meaningless marks on the white oblong, but on the other side were some pictures. Mau knew about messages, and this one wasn't difficult:

'When the sun is just above the last tree left on Little Nation, you must throw a spear at the big wrecked canoe,' he said aloud. It didn't make any sense, and nor did the ghost girl. But she had given him the spark-maker, although she'd been very frightened. He'd been frightened, too. What were you supposed to do about girls? You had to keep away from them while you were a boy, but he'd heard that when you were a man you got other instructions.

And as for the Grandfathers and the god anchors, he hadn't seen them at all. They were big stones, but the wave hadn't cared. Did the gods know? Had *they* been washed away? It was too complicated to think about. Beer was simpler, but not by much.

Women made the beer, and he knew that there was a big bowl in front of the Cave of the Grandfathers where an offering of beer was poured every day. He knew this and it had just stayed in his head as a thing that he knew, but now questions were rising, like: Why did the dead need beer? Wouldn't it . . . trickle through? If they didn't drink it, who did? And would he get into trouble for even *thinking* these questions?

Who from?

He remembered going into the Women's Place from when he was very small. Around about the time he was seven or eight he started to become unwelcome there. Women shoo'd him away, or stopped what they were doing when he came near and watched him very hard until he went away. The very old women in particular had a way of glaring at you that made you want to be some-where else. One of the older boys told him that they could mutter words that made your wingo fall off. After that, he kept away from the Women's Place and it became like the moon; he knew where it was but didn't even think about going there.

Well, there were no old women now. He wished there were. There was no one to stop him doing anything. He wished there was.

The path to the Women's Place turned off from the track into the forest and then went downhill and south-west and down into a narrow gulley. At the end of it were two big stones, taller than a man, splashed with red paint. That was the only way in, back when there were rules. Now, Mau pulled out the thorn bush that blocked the entrance and pushed through.

And there was the Place, a round bowl of a valley full

of sunlight. Screens of trees kept out the wind, and had thorn and briar bushes woven so thickly among them that nothing except maybe a snake could get through, and today the valley looked as though it was asleep. Mau could hear the sea, but it seemed to be a long way off. There was the tinkle of a little stream, which dribbled out of the rock at one side of the bowl, filled a rocky hollow that was a natural bathing place and lost itself in the gardens.

The Nation grew the big crops in the large field. That was where you found aharo, sugar cane, tabor, boomerang peas and black corn. There men grew the things that made you live.

In the Place, the gardens of the women grew the things that made the living enjoyable, possible and longer: spices and fruits and chewing roots. They had ways of making crops grow bigger or more tasty. They dug up or traded plants and brought them here, and knew the secrets of seeds and pods and things. They raised pink bananas here and rare plantains and yams, including the jumping yam. They also grew medicines here, and babies.

Here and there around the edges of the gardens were huts. Mau approached them carefully, beginning to feel nervous. Someone should be shouting at him, some old woman should be pointing and mumbling, and he should be running away very fast with his hands cupped over his groin, just in case. Anything would be better than this sunny, empty silence.

So there *are* still rules, he thought. I brought them with me. They're in my head . . .

There were baskets in some of the huts, and bunches of roots hung from the ceiling, out of reach of small fingers. They were maniac roots. You learned about them very early on. It made the best beer of all or it killed you as dead as a stone, and the secret ingredient that decided which of these happened was a song that everybody knew.

He found what he was looking for in the hut by the spring. A whole bowl of chopped root was hissing and bubbling gently to itself under a pile of palm leaves. The sharp, prickly smell filled the hut.

How much did some dead men drink? He filled a calabash with the stuff, which should be enough. He was very careful how he poured it, because it was very dangerous at this stage, and hurried away before a ghost could catch him.

He reached the valley of the Grandfathers without spilling much, and tipped the contents of the calabash into the big stone bowl in front of the sealed cave. From the gnarly old trees a couple of grandfather birds watched him carefully.

He spat into the bowl, and the beer seethed for a while. Big yellow bubbles burst on the surface.

Then he sang. It was a simple little song, easy to remember, about the four brothers, all sons of Air, who one day decided to race around the huge belly of their father to see which of them would court the woman who lived in the Moon, and the tricks each one played on the others so that he could be first. Babies learned it. Everyone knew it. And, for some reason, singing that song turned the poison into beer. It really did.

The beer foamed in the bowl. Mau watched the big round stone, just in case, but the Grandfathers probably had a way of drinking beer from the spirit world.

He sang his way through the song, taking care not to miss out any verse, especially the one that was very funny when you did the right gestures. When he finished, the beer had gone clear, with golden bubbles rising to the top. Mau took a sip, to check. His heart didn't stop after one beat, so the beer was probably fine.

He took a few steps back and said, to the wide open sky: 'Here is your beer, Grandfathers!'

Nothing happed. It was a bad thought, but a 'thank you' might have been nice.

Then the world drew a breath and the breath became voices: YOU HAVE FAILED TO DO THE CHANT!

'I have sung the song! It is good beer!'

WE MEAN THE CHANT THAT *CALLS* US TO THE BEER!

A couple more grandfather birds crash-landed in the trees.

'I didn't know there was one!'

YOU ARE A LAZY BOY!

Mau grabbed at this. 'That's right, I'm just a boy! There is no one to teach me! Can you—?'

HAVE YOU RIGHTED THE GOD ANCHORS? NO! And with that the voices snapped into silence, leaving only the sighing of the wind.

Well, it looked like good beer. What was a chant

needed for? Mau's mother had made good beer, and people just turned up.

With a flapping of wings, a grandfather bird landed on the edge of the beer stone and gave him the usual stare which said: *If you are going to die, hurry up. Otherwise, go away.*

Mau shrugged, and walked away. But he hid behind a tree, and he was good at hiding. Maybe the big round stone *would* roll.

It didn't take long for several more grandfather birds to alight on the bowl. They squabbled for a while and then, with the occasional pause for another brief fight, settled down to some serious boozing, rocking backwards and forwards because that is how birds move when they drink, then rocking backwards and forwards and falling over a lot, which is how birds move when they have been drinking fresh beer. One took off and flew backwards into some bushes.

Mau walked back thoughtfully to the beach, stopping on the way to cut himself a spear from the forest. Down on the beach he sharpened it to a point, which he hardened in the fire, occasionally glancing up at the sun.

He did all this slowly, because his mind was filling up with questions. They came out of the black hole inside him so fast that they made it hard to think in a straight line. And soon he would have to see the ghost girl. That was going to be . . . difficult.

He looked at the white oblong again. The shiny metal around the edge was quite soft and useless, and scraped off easily. As for the picture, he thought it might be some kind of magic or charm, like the blue bead. What was the point of throwing a spear at the big canoe? It wasn't something you could kill. But the ghost girl was the only other person on the island, and she had, after all, given him the spark-maker. He didn't need it now, but it was still a wonderful thing.

When the sun was getting close to the Little Nation, he set off along the beach and entered the low forest.

You could *smell* things growing. There was never much light down here, but the big canoe had left a wide trail and daylight was shafting down into places that hadn't seen it for years, and the race was on for a rare place in the sun. New green shoots were fighting for their place in the sky, fronds were unfolding, seeds were cracking open. The forest was coming back with its own green tide; in six months, no one would ever guess what had happened here.

Mau slowed down when the wreck of the big canoe came in sight, but he could see no movement. He would have to be careful about this. It would be so easy to get things wrong.

It was so easy to get things wrong.

She hated the name 'Ermintrude'. It was the 'trude' really. 'Ermin', now, that wasn't bad at all. 'Trudy', too, sounded quite jolly, but her grandmother had said it sounded fast, whatever that meant, and banned her from using it. Even 'Gertrude' would have done. You still had your 'trude', of course, but one of the royal princesses was named Gertrude, and some of the newspapers called her 'Princess Gertie' and that sounded like the name of a girl who might have some fun in life.

But Ermintrude, she thought, was exactly the kind of name that would invite a young man to tea and mess it all up. The coal stove kept smoking, the flour she'd tried to make the scones of had smelled funny, because of the dead lobster in the barrel, and she felt sure some of the flour shouldn't have been moving about either. She'd managed to open the last tin of Dr Poundbury's Patent Ever-Lasting Milk, which said on the tin that it would taste as good after a year as it did on the day it was tinned and, sadly, that was probably true. It smelled like drowned mice.

If only she'd been taught properly! If only someone had thought to spend an afternoon teaching her a few things that would be handy to know if she was shipwrecked on a desert island! It could happen to anyone! Even some hints on making scones would have been a help! But no, her grandmother had said that a lady should never lift any-thing heavier than a parasol and should certainly never set foot in a kitchen unless it was to make Economic Charitable Soup for the Deserving Poor, and her grand-mother didn't think there were very many of *them*.

'Always remember,' she used to say, far too often, 'that it only needs one hundred and thirty-eight people to die and your father will be King! And that means that, one day, you might be Queen!'

Grandmother used to say this with a look in her eye that suggested that she was planning 138 murders, and you didn't have to know the old lady for long to suspect that she'd be quite capable of arranging them. They wouldn't be impolite murders, of course. There wouldn't be any of that desperate business with daggers and pistols. They would be elegant and tactful. A block or stone would fall out of someone's stately home *here*, someone would slip on a patch of ice in the castle battlements *there*, a suspicious blancmange at a palace banquet (arsenic could so easily be confused with sugar) would take care of several at once . . . But she probably wouldn't go that far, not really. Nevertheless, she lived in hope, and prepared her granddaughter for a royal life by seeing to it, wherever possible, that Ermintrude was not taught anything that could possibly be of any practical use whatsoever.

Now here she was, with her wrong name, struggling to make afternoon tea in a wrecked boat in the middle of the jungle! Why hadn't anyone thought this might happen?

And the young man was what her grandmother would have called a savage, too. But he hadn't been savage. She had watched him bury all those people in the sea. He had picked them up gently, even the dogs. He wasn't someone throwing away garbage. He had cared. He had cried tears, but he hadn't seen her, not even when she'd stood in front of him. There had been just one point when his streaming eyes had tried to focus on her, and then he had stepped round her and got on with his work. He'd been so careful and gentle it was hard to believe he was a savage.

She remembered First Mate Cox shooting at monkeys with his pistol when they had moored in that rivermouth in the Sea of Ceramis. He had laughed every time a small brown body dropped into the river, especially if it was still alive when the crocodiles caught it.

She'd shouted at him to stop it, and he'd laughed, and Captain Roberts had come down from the wheelhouse and there had been a terrible row, and after that things had gone very sour on the *Sweet Judy*. But just as she had begun the first part of her journey around the world, there had been a lot in the newspapers about Mr Darwin and his new theory that people had a kind of monkey as their distant ancestor. Ermintrude did not know if this was true, but there when she'd looked into First Mate Cox's eyes she'd seen something much worse than any monkey could be.

At which point a spear crashed through the cracked porthole, hissed across the cabin and left via the porthole on the other side, which had lost all its glass to the wave.

Ermintrude sat very still, firstly out of shock and then because she was remembering her father's advice. In one of his letters to her, he had said that when she joined him in Government House she would be his First Lady, and would be able to meet all kinds of people who might act in ways she found strange at first, and perhaps would even misunderstand. And so she would have to be gracious and make allowances.

Very well. This was about the time the boy would be here. What had she expected him to do when he got here?

Even on a boat that isn't wrecked, it's hard to find a door-bell. Perhaps throwing a spear means: *Look, I've thrown away my spear! I'm not armed!* Yes, that sounds right. It's just like shaking hands, after all, to show you are not hold-ing a sword. Well, I'm glad that's one little mystery solved, she thought.

For the first time since the spear had hissed across the cabin, she breathed out.

Outside, Mau was beginning to wonder if something had gone wrong when there were some wooden noises and the ghost girl's head appeared over the side of the big canoe.

'So kind of you to be punctual,' she said, trying to smile, 'and thank you very much for breaking the window, it was getting very stuffy in here!'

He didn't understand any of this, but she was very nearly smiling and that was a good thing. She wanted him to come into the wreck, too. He did so, very cautiously. The *Sweet Judy* had keeled over a bit when the wave had dropped her at ground level, so everything sloped.

Inside was just a mess, made of many different messes all jumbled up. Everything stank of mud and stale water. But the girl led him into another space, which looked at least as though someone had tried to clean things up a bit, even if they had failed.

'I'm afraid the chairs all got smashed,' said the girl, 'but I'm sure you will find poor Captain Roberts's sea chest an adequate substitute.'

Mau, who had never sat on anything but the ground or

a hut floor when he ate, edged his bottom onto a wooden box.

'I thought it would be nice to get properly acquainted, since we haven't been introduced,' said the ghost girl. 'Obviously the fact that we cannot understand one another will be something of a drawback . . .'

While this gibberish was going on, Mau stared at the fire in its little cave. Steam was coming out of a round black pipe. Next to it was a flat round thing. Pale things on it looked like some kind of bread. This is a Woman's Place, he thought, and I don't know the rules. I must be careful. She might do *anything to me*.

'. . . and the butter had gone runny, but I threw away the flour that had gone really green. Would you like some tea? I expect you don't take milk?'

He watched as a brown liquid was poured into a blue and white bowl. Mau watched it carefully, while the girl went on talking, faster and faster. How do you know what's right and wrong? he wondered. What are the rules when you are all alone with a ghost girl?

He'd not been alone on the Boys' Island. Oh, there hadn't been anyone else there, but he'd felt the Nation around him. He was doing the right thing. But now? What were the right things? The Grandfathers bellowed and complained and ordered him about and didn't listen.

He couldn't find the silver thread either, or the picture of the future. There was no picture now. There was just him and this girl, and no rules to fight the darkness ahead.

Now she had taken the bready things off the fire, and

put them on another of the round metal things which he tried to balance on his knees.

'Most of the crockery got smashed in the wreck,' said the girl sadly. 'It's a miracle I could find two cups. Will you have a scone?' She pointed at the bread things.

Mau took one. It was hot, which was good, but on the other hand it tasted like a piece of slightly rotten wood.

She was watching anxiously as he moved the mouthful around in his mouth, looking for something to do with it.

'I've done it wrong, haven't I?' she said. 'I thought the flour was too damp. Poor Captain Roberts used to keep a lobster in the flour barrel to eat the weevils, and I'm sure that can't be right. I'm sorry, I won't mind if you spit it out.'

And she started to cry.

Mau hadn't understood a word, but some things don't need language. She weeps because the bread is awful. She should not cry. He swallowed, and took another bite. She stared, and sniffed, not certain if it was too early to stop crying.

'Very nice food,' said Mau. He swallowed the thing with a fight and was sure he felt it hit the bottom of his stomach. And then he ate the other one.

The girl dabbed at her eyes with a cloth.

'Very good,' Mau insisted, trying not to taste rotted lobster.

'I'm sorry, I can't understand you,' she said. 'Oh, dear, and I completely forgot to lay out the napkin rings. What must you think of me . . .'

'I don't know the words you say,' said Mau.

There was a long, helpless pause, and Mau felt the two lumps of bad, dreadful bread sitting in his stomach, planning their escape. He was drinking the cup of sour, hot liquid to drown them when he became aware of a faint muttering coming from a corner of the cabin, where a big blanket covered – what? It sounded as though someone under there was muttering angrily to itself.

'It's good to have someone to talk to,' said the girl loudly. 'I see you walking around and it's not so lonely.'

The flour balls in Mau's stomach didn't like the brown drink. He kept very still, fighting to keep them down.

The girl looked at him nervously and said: 'My name is, um . . . Daphne.' She gave a little cough and added, 'Yes, Daphne.' She pointed to herself and held out her hand.

'Daphne,' she said again, even more loudly. Well, she'd always liked the name.

Mau looked obediently at her hand, but there was nothing to see. So . . . she was from Daphne? In the Islands the most important thing about you was the name of your clan. He hadn't heard of the place, but they always said that no one knew all the islands. Some of the poorer ones disappeared completely at high tide and the huts were built to float. They would have gone now . . . so how many were left? Had everyone in the world been washed away?

The ghost girl stood up and walked up the sloping deck to the door. Mau thought this looked promising. With any luck he didn't have to eat any more wood.

She said: 'Could you please help me with poor Captain Roberts?'

She wanted him to go outside, that was clear, and Mau got up quickly. The bad bread wanted to escape, and the smell of the fire was giving him a headache.

He staggered up and out into the fresh afternoon air. The girl was standing on the ground, by the big grey roll Mau had seen yesterday. She looked at him helplessly.

'Poor Captain Roberts,' she said, and prodded it with her foot.

Mau pulled away the heavy cloth and saw the body of an old trouserman with a beard. He was lying on his back, his eyes staring up at nothing. Mau pulled the cloth down further and found that the man's hands were holding a big circle of wood, with things like wooden spikes all round the edge of it.

'He tied himself to the ship's wheel so that he wouldn't get washed away,' said the girl behind him. 'I cut the ropes but his poor hands wouldn't let go, so I found a hammer and knocked the pin out of the wheel, and I tried and tried to bury him but the ground is too hard and I can't move him by myself. I'm sure he wouldn't mind being buried at sea,' she finished, all in one breath.

Mau sighed. She must know I can't understand her but she goes on talking, he thought. She wants this body buried, I can tell. I wonder how long it took her to scrape that pathetic little hole in the rock? But she's lost and far from home, like me.

'I can send him into the dark water,' he said. He made

wave noises and wave shapes with his hand. She looked terrified for a moment, and then laughed and clapped her hands.

'Yes! Yes! That's right! The sea! Whoosh, swoosh! The sea!'

The man and the wooden wheel together were too heavy to lift, but the cloth was very thick and Mau found he could drag the body quite well over the crushed vegetation of the track. The girl helped him over the difficult bits, or at least tried to, and once they reached the shore the grey roll slid well enough over the damp sand, but it was a long tiring drag to the western end of the beach. At last Mau managed to get the captain into the waist-deep water at the very edge of the reef.

He looked into the dead eyes, staring straight ahead, and wondered what they would see down in the dark current. Would they see anything? *Did anyone see anything?*

The shock of the question hit him like a blow. How could he think it?

Once we were dolphins and Imo made us into men! That was true, wasn't it? Why did he even *wonder* if it wasn't? And if that wasn't true, then there was just the dark water and nothing was anything . . .

He stopped those thoughts before they could run away with him. The Daphne girl was watching him and this was no time to be uncertain and hesitant. He twisted papervine together to fasten stones and pieces of broken coral to poor Captain Roberts and his wheel. Papervine got tighter when it was wet and didn't rot for years. Wherever poor Captain Roberts was going, he was going to stay there. Unless he turned into a dolphin, of course. Then, quickly, he made the cut to release his spirit.

On the rocks behind him, the girl sang a song. It wasn't all na-na-na this time. Somehow Mau could hear her voice better, now he'd heard her speak. There were words, probably, although they had no meaning to Mau. But he thought: It's a trouserman chant for the dead. They are like us! But if Imo made them, why are they so different?

The captain was almost underwater now, still holding onto the wheel. Mau held the last stone in one hand and pushed the floating captain forward, feeling all the time with his toes for the edge of the rock. He could sense the cold of the deeps below him, too.

The current was down there. No one knew where it came from, although there were stories of a land to the south where the water fell like feathers. But everyone knew where it went. They could see it. It became the Shining Path, a river of stars that flowed across the night sky. Once in a thousand years, it was said, when Locaha looked among the dead for those who should go to the perfect world, then they would climb that path and send the rest back to be dolphins until it was time for them to be born again.

How does that happen? Mau thought. How does water become stars? How does a dead man become a living dolphin? But that was a child's question, wasn't it? The kind you shouldn't ask? The kind that was silly or wrong, and if you asked 'why' too much you were given chores to do and told 'that's how the world is'.

A wavelet broke over the captain. Mau fastened the last stone to the wheel and, as the captain slid gently under the water, gave him a push out into the current.

A few bubbles came up as the captain sank, very slowly, out of sight.

Mau was just turning away when he saw something rising through the water. It broke the surface and turned over slowly. It was the captain's hat, and now that it had filled with water it began to drift back down again.

There was a splash from behind him and the girl of the Daphne clan floundered past him, her white dress floating around her like a huge jellyfish.

'Don't let it sink again!' she shouted. 'He wants you to have it!' She plunged forward, grabbed the hat, waved it triumphantly – and sank.

Mau waited for her to come back up, but there were just bubbles.

Could it possibly be that there was someone in the world who couldn't—

His body worked without thinking. He ducked under the surface, grabbed the biggest lump of coral he could see, and dived over the edge and into the dark water.

There below him was poor Captain Roberts, drifting gently down towards posterity. Mau went past in a rip of silver.

There were more bubbles below, and a pale shape disappearing at the farthest reach of the sunlight.

Not this one, Mau thought, as loudly as he could. Not now. No one goes alive into the dark. I served you, Locaha. I walked in your steps. You should owe me this one. One life back from the dark!

And a voice came back from the gloom: *I recall no arrangement, Mau, no bargain, covenant, agreement or promise. There is what happens, and what does not happen. There is no 'should'.*

And then he was tangling in the sea anemone of her skirts. He let the stone continue into the dark, found her face, breathed the air from his bursting lungs into hers, saw her eyes open wide, and kicked for the surface, dragging her behind him.

It took for ever. He could feel the long, cold fingers of Locaha grabbing at his feet and squeezing his lungs, and surely the light was fading. The sound of the water in his ears began to sound like whispering: *Would it hurt to stop now? To slide back down into the dark and let the current take him? It would be the end of all grief, a blanking of all bad memories. All he had to do was let her go and—* No! That thought brought back his anger, and the anger brought strength.

A shadow fell across the light and Mau had to swim out of the way as the gently-sinking captain went on past, on the last voyage he'd ever make.

But the light was no nearer, never any nearer. His legs were like stones. Everything stung. And there it was, the silver line, coming back to him again, pulling him forward into a picture of what could be –

– And rock was under his feet. He kicked down, and his head broke through the surf. His feet touched the rock again, and the light was brilliant.

The rest of what happened he watched from inside himself as he dragged the girl onto the rocks, and tipped her upside down and slapped her on her back until she coughed up water. Then it was a run along the beach to lay her down by the fire, where she vomited up more water and groaned. Only then did Mau's mind explain that his body was far too weak to have managed all this, and let it fall backwards into the sand.

He managed to turn over in time to throw up what was left of the dreadful cakes and stared down at the mess. Does not happen, he thought, and the words became a declaration of triumph and defiance. 'Does not happen,' he said, and the words got bigger and dragged him to his feet, and 'Does not happen!' he shouted at the sky. *'Does not happen!'*

A little sound made him look down. The girl was shaking, there on the sand. He knelt down beside her and held her hand, which was still clutching the captain's hat. Her skin was white, and as cold as the touch of Locaha, even in the heat of the fire.

'Cheat! I got her back!' he shouted. 'Does not happen!'

Mau ran further along the beach and onto the track that led into the low forest. Red crabs scuttled out of the way as he bounded along the trail of broken trees. He reached the big canoe and scrambled up the side. There had been— Yes, there was that big blanket in the corner.

He grabbed it and pulled, and something pulled back. He pulled harder, and something landed on the deck with a splintering noise.

A voice said: '*Waark!* Roberts is a dreadful boozer! Show us yer drawers!'

This time the blanket had come away, revealing a broken wooden cage on the floor and a very angry grey bird. It glared at Mau.

'*Waark!* Blessed are the meek, my sainted aunt!'

Mau had no time for birds now, but this one had a worrying glint in its eye. It seemed to demand a reply.

'Does not happen!' he shouted, and ran out of the cabin, the blanket flapping behind him.

He was halfway down the track when there was a flutter of wings overhead and a shriek of 'Does not happen!'

Mau didn't even look up. The world had become too strange. He ran to the fire and wrapped the girl as tight as he could in the blanket. After a while, the shivering stopped, and she seemed to be asleep.

'Does not happen!' screamed the bird from a broken tree. Mau blinked. He'd understood it! And he'd understood it before, and not realized it.

Oh, there were some birds that could speak a few words, like the grey raven and the yellow parakeet, but you could hardly understand them. This bird talked as if it knew what it was saying.

'Where's my grub, you vinegar-faced old piss-pot?' said

the bird, bouncing up and down eagerly. 'Give me my rations, you ol' hypocrite!'

That sounded like trouserman talk, right enough.

The sun was low, but still a hand's span above the sea. A lot had happened in a short space of time which, on the inside, had lasted nearly for ever.

Mau looked down at the sleeping girl. 'Does not happen' was not enough. You couldn't trust Locaha. There were no bargains. Now he had to think about '*Will* not happen'. Death was not going to rule here . . .

He found his spear, and stood guard until morning.

CHAPTER 4

BARGAINS, COVENANTS AND PROMISES

*D*aphne had heard that when you drown, your whole life passes in front of your eyes.

In fact it's when you *don't* drown that this happens, as life races back from the start to get to the last known living moment. Mostly it's a blur, but every life has its important moments which get more and more colourful the longer they are remembered.

In hers, one of them was about the map. Every life should have a map.

The map. Oh yes, the map. She'd found it in the big atlas in the library, one wet winter afternoon. In a week she could have drawn it from memory.

And the name of it was *The Great Southern Pelagic Ocean*. It was half a world of blue sea, but it was stitched together with seams of little dots, tiny dots that her father had called 'island chains'. There were hundreds and thousands of islands and a lot of them were just about big enough for a coconut tree, he'd said. There had to be one coconut tree on every tiny island, by law, so that if someone was shipwrecked then at least he'd have some shade to sit in.* He drew her a picture, of her sitting in the shade of a coconut tree, with her white dress and her parasol, but quickly added, on the pencilled horizon, a ship coming to rescue her.

Much later on, she was able to read the names of the groups of islands: 'The Bank Holiday Monday Islands', 'All Souls Island', 'The Rogation Sunday Islands', 'The Mothering Sunday Islands', 'The Hogmanay Islands' . . . it seemed that the Great Southern Pelagic Ocean had been navigated not with a compass and a sextant but with a calendar.

Her father had said that if you knew where to look you could find Mrs Ethel J. Bundy's Birthday Island, and loaned her a large magnifying glass. She spent long Sunday afternoons lying on her stomach, minutely examining every necklace of dots, and concluded that Mrs Ethel J. Bundy's Birthday Island was a Father Joke, i.e. not

---

* The lonesome palm (*cocos nucifera solitaria*) is common over most of the Pelagic, and is unusual in that an adult tree secretes a poison in its root which is deadly only to other palms. Because of this it is not unusual to find only one such palm on the smaller islands and a thousand cartoons are, therefore, botanically correct.

very funny but sort of loveable in its silliness. But now, thanks to him, she knew the island chains of the Great Southern Pelagic Ocean by heart.

She wanted, there and then, to live on a island that was lost at sea, and so small that you weren't sure if it was an island or just that a fly had done its business on the page.

But that wasn't all. There was a map of the stars at the back of the atlas. Next birthday she'd asked for a telescope. Her mother had been alive then, and had suggested a pony, but her father had laughed and bought her a beautiful telescope, saying: 'Of course she should watch the stars! Any girl who cannot identify the constellation of Orion just isn't paying attention!' And when she started asking him complicated questions, he took her along to lectures at the Royal Society, where it turned out that a nine-year-old girl who had blonde hair *and* knew what the precession of the equinoxes was could ask hugely bearded famous scientists anything she liked. Who'd want a pony when you could have the whole universe? It was far more interesting and you didn't have to muck it out once a week.

'Well, that was a good day,' said her father, when they were coming back from one meeting.

'Yes, Papa, I think Dr Agassiz is certainly providing evidence for the Ice Age theory, and I shall need a bigger telescope if I am to see Jupiter's Great Red Spot.'

'Well, we shall have to see about that,' said her father with hopeless parental diplomacy. 'But please don't let your grandmother know you shook hands with Mr Darwin. She thinks he is the devil.'

'Gosh! Is he?' The prospect had seemed quite interesting.

'As a matter of fact,' said her father, 'I believe he is the greatest scientist who has ever lived.'

'Greater than Newton? I don't think so, Papa. Many of his ideas were first voiced by other people, including his own granddad!'

'Ah-ha. You've been in my library again. Well, Newton said that *he* stood on the shoulders of giants.'

'Yes, but . . . well, he was just being modest!' And they had argued all the way home.

It was a game. He loved it when she assembled her facts and pinned him down with a cast-iron argument. He believed in rational thinking and scientific inquiry, which was why he never won an argument with his mother, who believed in people doing what she told them, and believed it with a rock-hard certainty which dismissed all opposition.

In fact there was always something a little naughty about going to the lectures. Her grandmother objected to them on the grounds that they 'would make the girl restless and give her ideas'. She was right. Ermintrude was already pretty good at ideas, but a few more are always welcome.

At this point the racing line of life speeds up, to get past some dark years she never remembered except in nightmares and whenever she heard a baby crying, and leaps ahead to the day when she first knew she would *see* islands under new stars . . .

Her mother was dead by then, which meant that things at the Hall were now run entirely by her grandmother, and her father, a quiet, hardworking man, didn't have much spirit left to battle with her. The wonderful telescope was locked away, because 'a well-brought-up young lady has no business looking at the moons of Jupiter, whose home life was so different from that of our own dear king!' It didn't matter that Daphne's father very patiently explained that there were at least 36 million miles of difference between Jupiter, the Roman god, and Jupiter, the largest planet in the solar system. She didn't listen. She never listened. And you put up with that or you hit her over the head with a battle axe, and her father didn't do that sort of thing, even though one of his ancestors had once done something really horrible to the Duke of Norfolk with a red-hot poker.

Their Royal Society visits were banned on the grounds that the scientists were nothing but people who asked silly questions, and that was that. Her father came and apologized to her about that, which was horrible.

But there were other ways to explore the universe . . .

One of the things about being a quiet girl in a very big house is that you can, if you try, be invisible in plain view, and it was amazing what you could overhear when you were being a good little girl helping Cook in the kitchen by cutting out pastry shapes. There were always delivery boys or men from the estate after a cup of tea, or Cook's old friends just dropping in for a chat. The secret was to wear ribbons in your hair and skip everywhere. It completely fooled people.

Except her grandmother, unfortunately, who put a stop to the visits below stairs as soon as she took over the running of the household. 'Children should be seen, but not seen listening!' she said. 'Off you go! Quickly, now!'

And that was that. Ermi— Daphne spent most of her time doing embroidery in her room. Sewing, provided you weren't doing it to make something useful, was one of the few things a girl 'who was going to be a lady one day' was allowed to do, at least according to her grandmother.

However, it wasn't all *she* did. To begin with, she found the old dumbwaiter, a sort of elevator just for food, which hadn't been used since the days when her great-great-aunt had lived in Daphne's bedroom on the top floor and all her food had to be hauled up to five floors from the kitchen. Daphne didn't know much about the old woman, but apparently a young man had smiled at her on her twenty-first birthday and she'd gone straight to bed with an attack of the vapours, and stayed there, still gently vaporizing, until she completely vaporized at the age of eighty-six, apparently because her body was fed up with having nothing to do.

The dumbwaiter had never been officially used since then. Daphne, though, had found that with the removal of a few planks and the greasing of some wheels, she could haul it up and down by its pulleys and eavesdrop on several rooms. It became a sort of sound telescope to explore the indoor solar system that revolved around her grandmother.

She gave it a bit of a scrub, and then another because –

yuck – if the maids weren't going to carry a food tray up five floors, then they weren't going to – yuck – carry down anything else, like the guzunder.

It was an interesting education, listening to the big house when it was unaware, but getting it was like tipping out a jigsaw puzzle on the floor and trying to guess at the picture from looking at five pieces.

And it was while listening to two of the maids talking about Albert the stable boy and how naughty he was (a state of affairs they didn't entirely disapprove of, apparently, and which she was starting to suspect very strongly had nothing to do with how he looked after the horses) that she heard the argument in the dining room. Her grandmother's voice cut through the ear like a diamond on glass, but her father was using the calm, flat voice he always used when he was very angry and didn't dare show it. By the time she'd pulled up the dumbwaiter to get a better listen, it had, by the sound of it, been going on for some time:

'. . . and you'll end up in a cannibal's cooking pot!' That was the unmistakable sound of her grandmother.

'Cannibals usually roast their food, Mother, not boil it.' – And that was certainly the quiet voice of her father who, when he was talking to his mother, always sounded as though he was determined not to look up from his newspaper.

'And is that any better, pray?'

'I doubt it, Mother, but at least it is more accurate. In any case, the Rogation Sunday Islanders have never been known to cook anyone *al fresco* in any kind of utensil, as far as we know.'

'I don't see why you have to go to the other end of the world.' – And *that* was her grandmother changing her line of attack.

'Somebody must. We have to keep the flag flying.'

'Why, pray?'

'Oh dear, Mother, I'm surprised at you. It's *our flag*. It has to fly.'

'Do remember that only one hundred and thirty-eight people have to die and you will be King!'

'So you keep telling me, Mother, although Father always said that claim is rather weak when you consider what happened in 1421. In any case, while I'm waiting for that very unlikely death toll, I might as well do my bit in the service of the Empire.'

'Is there any Society there?' Grandmother could say a capital letter so distinctly that you could hear it. 'Society' meant people who were rich or influential or, preferably, both. Although they shouldn't be richer and more influential than her.

'Well, there's the bishop – jolly decent chap, apparently. Goes around the place in a canoe and speaks the lingo like a native. Doesn't wear shoes. Then there's McRather; he runs the dockyard. Teaching the native lads to play cricket. As a matter of fact I'm to take some more bats with me. And of course there will often be a ship in, so as Governor I'll have to entertain the officers.'

'Sun-struck madmen, naked savages—'

'They wear pads, actually.'

'What? What? What *are* you talking about?' Another thing about Grandmother was her belief that a conversation consisted of someone else listening to her talking, so even mild interruptions seemed to her to be some strange, puzzling inversion of the natural order of things, like pigs flying. It baffled her.

'Pads,' said Daphne's father helpfully, 'and protective thingummies. McRather says they've rather confused hitting the wicket with hitting the batsman.'

'Very well then, sun-struck madmen, *semi-naked* savages and the Royal Navy. And you really think I will allow my granddaughter to face these perils?'

'The Royal Navy isn't very perilous.'

'Supposing she marries a sailor!'

'Like Auntie Pathenope did?' Daphne could imagine her father's faint smile, which always made his mother angry, but then, so did practically everything else.

'He was a Rear Admiral!' her grandmother snapped. 'That's not the same thing at all!'

'Mother, there is no need for this fuss. I have told the king that I will go. Ermintrude will follow in a month or two. It will do us good to be away for a while. This house is too cold and too big.'

'Nevertheless, I forbid—'

'It is also too *lonely*. It has too many *memories*! It has too much silenced laughter, too many unheard footsteps, too many soundless echoes since they died!' The words came out like slabs of thunder. 'I have made my decision and it will not be unmade, even by you! I have told the palace to send her out to me as soon as I am settled in. Do you understand? I believe my daughter would!! *And perhaps at the other end of the world there is a place where the screaming can't be heard, and I may find it in my heart to grant God absolution!*'

She heard him walk to the door, while tears met on her chin and soaked her nightgown.

And Grandmother said: 'And the child's schooling, may I ask?'

How did she manage it? How did she come out with something like that, when the silverware and the chandeliers were still jingling with tinny echoes. Didn't she remember the coffins?

Perhaps she did. Perhaps she thought that her son needed to be anchored to the earth. It worked, then, because he stopped with his hand on the doorhandle and said, in a voice that almost didn't shake, 'She will have a tutor in Port Mercia. It will do her good, and broaden her horizons. You see? I have thought about this.'

'It won't bring them back, you know.' That was her grandmother. Daphne put her hand over her mouth in sheer shock. How could the woman be so . . . *stupid*?

She could imagine her father's face. She heard him walk to the dining-room door and open it. She waited for the slam, but that wouldn't be her father. The sharp little click of the door shutting was louder in her head than any slam could be.

* * *

At which point Daphne awoke, glad that she had. The broadened horizon was red but the back of the sky was full of stars; she felt stiff to her very bones, and she felt that she'd never eaten in her life, ever. And this was very convenient, because the smell coming out of the pot was fishy and spicy and was making her dribble.

The boy was standing some way off, holding his spear and looking out to sea. She could just see him in the firelight.

He'd piled on even more logs. They roared and crackled and exploded with steam, sending a thick cloud of smoke and vapour into the sky. And he was guarding the beach. What from? This was a real island, much bigger than many that she had seen on the voyage. Some had been not much more than a sandbank and a reef. Could anyone be left alive within a hundred miles? What was he frightened of?

Mau stared at the sea. It was so flat that all night he had been able to see the stars in it.

Somewhere out there, flying to him from the edge of the world, was tomorrow. He had no idea what shape it would be, but he was wary of it. They had food and fire, but that wasn't enough. You had to find water and food and shelter and a weapon, people said. And they thought that was all you had to have, because they took for granted the most important thing. You had to have a place where you belonged.

He'd never counted the people in the Nation. There

were . . . enough. Enough to feel that you were part of something that had seen many yesterdays and would see many tomorrows, with rules that everyone knew, and which worked because everyone knew them, so much so that they were just part of the way people lived. People would live and die but there would always be a Nation. He'd been on long voyages with his uncles – hundreds of miles – but the Nation had always been there, somewhere over the horizon, waiting for him to come back. He'd been able to *feel* it.

What should he do with the ghost girl? Maybe some other trousermen would come looking for her? And then she'd go, and he'd be alone again. That would be horrible. It wasn't ghosts that frightened him, it was memories. Perhaps they were the same thing? If a woman follows the same path every day to fill a calabash from the waterfall, did the path remember?

When Mau closed his eyes, the island was full of people. Did it remember their footsteps and their faces, and put them in his head? The Grandfathers said he was the Nation, but that couldn't be true. Many could become one, but one could not become many. He would remember them, though, so that if people came here he would tell them about the Nation, and it would come alive again.

He was glad she was here. Without her, he'd walk into the dark water. He'd heard the whispering as he dived down after her in that scream of silver bubbles. It would have been so easy to heed the wily words of Locaha and sink into the blackness, but that would have drowned her, too.

He was not going to be alone here. That was not going to happen. Just him and the voices of the old dead men, who gave orders all the time and never listened? No.

No . . . there would be two of them to stay here, and he would teach her the language, so they would both remember, so that when people came they could say: *Once there were many people living here, and then the wave came.*

He heard her stir, and knew she was watching him. He knew one other thing, too – the soup smelled good, and he probably wouldn't have made it just for himself. It was some whitefish off the reef and a handful of shellfish and some ginger from the Women's Place and some taro chopped up fine to give it all some body.

He used a couple of twigs to drag the pot out of the embers and gave the girl a big half-shell to use as a spoon.

And it was . . . funny, mostly because they both had to blow on the soup to get it cool, and she seemed very surprised that he spat out fish bones into the fire while she very carefully coughed them into a piece of frilly cloth that was very nearly stiff with salt and sand. One of them started giggling, or maybe it was both of them at the same time, and then he was laughing so much he couldn't spit the next bone at all and, instead, coughed it out into his hand with the same little noise that she made, which was 'uh-pur', which made her nearly choke. But she managed to stop laughing long enough to try and spit out a bone, which she couldn't get the hang of at all.

They didn't know why these things were funny. Sometimes you laugh because you've got no more room for crying. Sometimes you laugh because table manners on a beach are funny. And sometimes you laugh because you're alive, when you really shouldn't be.

And then they lay back looking up at the sky, where the star of Air sparkled yellow-white in the east and Imo's Campfire was a sharp red overhead, and sleep hit them like a wave.

Mau opened his eyes.

The world was full of birdsong. It was everywhere, and every kind of song, from the grandfather birds honking up last night's leftovers to – from the direction of the low forest – something that really should not count as bird-song at all, because it went: 'Polly wants a fig, you Bible-thumping ol' fool! *Waark!* Show us yer drawers!'

He sat up.

The girl had gone, but her strange toeless prints led towards the low forest.

Mau looked in the clay pot. There had been hardly any-thing left by the time the shells had scraped it out, but while they had been sleeping something small had licked it clean.

He could try clearing some more of the debris off the fields today. There could be more crops to—

REPLACE THE GOD ANCHORS! SAY THE CHANTS!

Oh, well . . . Up until now it had been a good day, in a horrible kind of way.

The god anchors . . . well, they were things. If you

asked about them you'd be told you were too young to understand. All that Mau knew was that they kept the gods from floating away into the sky. Of course, the gods were in the sky in any case, but asking about that was a silly question. Gods could be anywhere they wanted. But somehow, for reasons that were perfectly clear, or at least perfectly clear to the priests, the gods stayed near the god anchors and brought good luck to the people.

So which god brought the great wave, and how lucky was that?

There had been a great wave before, everyone said. It turned up in stories of the Time When Things Were Otherwise and the Moon Was Different. Old men said it was because people had been bad, but old men always said that kind of thing. Waves happened, people died, and the gods did not care. Why had Imo, who had made everything and *was* everything . . . ? Would He have made *useless* gods? There it was, out of the darkness inside, another thought that he wouldn't even have known how to think a few days ago, and so dangerous he wanted to get it out of his head as soon as possible.

What did he have to do to the god anchors? But the Grandfathers didn't answer questions. There were little mud or wood god stones all over the island. People placed them for all sorts of reasons, from watching over a sick child to making sure a crop didn't spoil. And since it was seriously bad luck to move a god stone, no one did. They were left to fall apart naturally.

He'd seen them so often that he didn't look at them any

more. The wave must have moved hundreds of them, and washed them away. How could he put them back?

He looked along the beach. Most of the branches and broken trees had gone now, and for the first time he saw what wasn't there.

There had been three *special* god stones in the village – the god *anchors*. It was hard, now, to remember where they had been, and they certainly weren't there now. Those anchors were big cubes of white stone, almost too heavy for a man to lift, but the wave had even snapped the house posts and thrown lumps of coral the size of a man across the lagoon. It wouldn't have worried about some stone blocks, no matter what they anchored . . .

He walked along the beach, hoping to see signs leading him to one almost buried in the sand. He didn't. But he could see a god stone on the floor of the lagoon, now that the water had cleared a bit. He dived in to fetch it, but it was so heavy that bringing it out needed several goes. The lagoon had been scoured by the wave and shelved quite deeply at the west end. He had to carry it along the bed, sometimes leaving it behind and coming up to fill his lungs with air, until he found a place shallow enough to bring it out. And of course it weighed more out of the water for some magical reason no one understood; he was out of breath by the time he'd rolled it end over end up the beach.

He remembered this one. It had been next to the chief's house. It was the one with the strange creature carved on it. It had four legs, like a hog but much longer, and a head like an *elas-gi-nin*. People called it the Wind, and gave it fish and beer for the god of Air before they went on a long journey. Birds and pigs and dogs took the fish and the beer soaked into the sand, but that didn't matter. It was the spirit of the fish and the spirit of the beer that mattered. That's what they said.

He dived in again. The lagoon was a mess. The wave had scattered house-sized bits of the reef everywhere, as well as tearing a new entrance for the sea. But he had seen something white over there.

As he got near he saw how big the new gap was. A ten-man canoe could have got through it sideways.

Another god stone was right under Mau's feet. He dived, and a school of small silver fish fled from him.

Ah, the Hand, the anchor for the Fire god. This one was smaller, but it was deeper, and further from the beach. It took him more than an hour to steal it back from the seas, in short slow underwater bounds across the white sand.

There was another one he'd glimpsed right in the new gap, where the surf swirled dangerously. But that would be Water, and right now he felt that Water had taken too many sacrifices lately. Water could wait.

GATHER THE STONES AND GIVE HUMBLE THANKS OR YOU WILL BRING BAD LUCK ON THE NATION! said the Grandfathers in his head.

How did they get into his mind? How did they know things? And why didn't they understand?

The Nation had been strong. There were bigger islands,

but they were a long way off and weren't as favoured. They were too dry, or the winds were bad or they didn't have enough soil, or were at places where the currents were wrong and the fishing was poor or they were too close to the Raiders, who never came this far into the islands these days.

But the Nation had a mountain, and fresh water all the time. It could grow lots of vegetables, ones that most of the islands couldn't grow. It had plenty of wild pigs and jungle fowl. It grew maniac roots and had the secret of the beer. It could *trade*. That was where the jade bead had come from, and the two steel knives, and the three-legged cook pot, and cloth from far away. The Nation was rich and strong and some said it was because it had the white stone anchors. There was no stone like that anywhere else in the islands. The Nation was blessed, people said.

And now a little boy wandered around on it, doing the best he could, always getting things wrong.

He tumbled the block called the Hand onto the sand near the fire. You left something on the anchor of the Hand if you wanted success in hunting or war. If you were lucky, it was probably a good idea to give it something else when you got back, too.

Right now he gave it his bum. I fished you out of the sea, he thought. The fishes wouldn't have left you offerings! So excuse me if I offer you my tiredness. He heard the rage of the Grandfathers, but tried to ignore it.

Give thanks to the gods or you will bring bad luck, he thought. What, right now, would be bad luck? What could the gods do to him that was worse than what they had done already? A wave of anger rose in him like bile, and he felt the darkness in him open up. Had the people called on the gods when the wave broke? Had his family clung to these stones? Did the gods watch them as they tried to reach higher ground? Did the gods laugh?

His teeth chattered. He felt cold under the hot sun. But fire filled his head, burning up his thoughts.

'Did you hear their screams?' he yelled to the empty sky. 'Did you watch them? You gave them to Locaha! I will not thank you for my life! You could have saved theirs!'

He sat down on the Hand, trembling with anger and apprehension.

There was no reply.

He looked up into the sky. There were no storm clouds, and it didn't look as if it was about to rain snakes. He glanced at the blue bead on his wrist. It was only supposed to work for a day. Could a demon have crept in while he'd slept? Surely only a demon could have thought those thoughts!

But they were *right*.

Or maybe I have no soul at all, maybe the darkness inside is my dead soul . . . He sat with his arms around himself, waiting for the trembling to stop. He had to fill his mind with everyday things, that was it. That would keep him safe.

He sat and looked along the naked beach, and thought: I'd better plant some coconuts, there's plenty being washed up. And pandanuses, I'll plant some of those, too, for shade. That didn't sound demonic. He could see the picture of what it would be in his mind's eye, overlaid on the horrible mess that the beach had become, and in the middle of the image was a white dot. He blinked, and there was the ghost girl, coming towards him. She was covered in white, and carried some kind of round white thing above her head, to keep the sun off, perhaps, or to stop the gods seeing her.

She had a determined expression on her face and he saw, under the arm that wasn't holding the sunshade, what looked like a slab of wood.

'Good morning, Mau,' she said.

'Daphne,' said Mau, the only word he was certain of.

She looked down meaningfully at the block he was sitting on, and gave a little cough. Then her face went bright pink. 'I'm *so sorry*,' she said. 'I am the one who's being bad-mannered, aren't I! Look, we need to be able to talk, and I had this idea because you're always looking at the birds . . .'

The wooden slab . . . wasn't. It split open when Daphne pulled at it. Inside, it looked like sheets of papervine, rolled flat instead of being twisted up. There were marks on it. Mau couldn't read them but Daphne ran her finger over them and said loudly:

'Birds of the Great Southern Pelagic Ocean,
by Colonel H. J. Hookwarm, M.R.H, F.R.A.
With sixteen hand-coloured illustrations by the Author.'

Then she turned over the sheet . . .

Mau gasped. Her words were gibberish to his ears, but he knew how to speak pictures . . . It was a grandfather bird! There, right on the paper! It looked real! In wonderful colours! No one on the island had been able to make colours like that, and they never turned up in trade. It looked as though someone had pulled a grandfather bird out of the air!

'How is this done?' he said.

Daphne girl tapped it with a finger. 'Pantaloon bird!' she said. She looked expectantly at Mau, then pointed to her mouth and made a sort of snapping motion with her thumb and forefinger.

What does that mean? Mau wondered. 'I'm going to eat a crocodile'?

'Pant-aa-loooon birddd,' she said, very slowly.

She thinks I'm a baby, thought Mau. That's how you talk to babies when you want them to un-der-stand. She wants me to *say* it!

'Pant-aaa-looooon birrrrdd,' he said.

She smiled, as if he'd just done a good trick, and pointed to the thickly feathered legs of the bird. 'Pantaloons,' she said, and this time she pointed to her frilly trousers, peeking from under her torn skirt. 'Pantaloons!'

All right, it looks as though 'pantaloon bird' means 'trouser bird', Mau told himself. Those frilly legs did look just like the bird's strange feathered legs. But she's got the name wrong!

He pointed to the picture again and said, in a talking-to-babies voice: '*Graaaand-faaather* birrrrd!'

'Grandfather?'

Mau nodded.

'Grandfather?' The girl still looked bewildered.

Oh. She needed to be shown one. Well, he wasn't going to roll away the big stone for *anyone* but . . .

It was quite a performance. Mau stroked an invisible long beard, staggered around leaning on a non-existent walking stick, muttered angrily while waving a finger in the air, and – he was proud of this bit – tried to chew a tough piece of pork with invisible non-existent teeth. He'd watched the old men eating, and made his mouth look like two rats trying to escape from a bag.

'Old man?' shouted Daphne. 'Oh yes! Very droll! The Old Man Bird! Yes, I see what you mean! They always look so annoyed!—'

After that, things happened quite fast, with the aid of the sand, a stick and some pebbles and a lot of acting. Some things were easy, like canoe, sun and water. Numbers were not too bad, after a false start (one pebble is, in addition to being a pebble, one). They worked hard. Bird, big bird, small bird, bird flying . . . Nest! Egg!

Fire, cook, eat, good, bad (good was a mime of eating followed by a big smile, bad was Daphne's unladylike but realistic pantomime of throwing up). They got the hang of here and there, and probably something that did the job of 'this is' or 'here is'. Mau wasn't too sure of a lot of it, but at least they had the start of . . . something.

Back to the sand. Mau drew a stick figure and said 'Man'.

'Man,' said Daphne, and took the stick from him. She drew another figure, but the legs were thicker.

Mau thought about it. 'Pantaloon man?' he tried.

'Trouser man,' said Daphne firmly.

What does that mean? Mau wondered. Only trouser-men are proper men? I don't wear them. Why should I? Imagine trying to swim in them!

He took the stick and carefully drew a stick woman, which was like a stick man with a woven papervine skirt and two added circles and two dots. Above the skirt.

The stick was snatched out of his hand and, at speed, Daphne hastily drew a new figure. It was a woman, probably, but as well as the skirt there was another skirt thing covering the top of her body, with only the arms and head sticking out. Then she stuck the stick in the sand and crossed her arms defiantly, her face red.

Ah, right. This was like the time before his older sister

went off to live in the unmarried girls' hut. Suddenly, everything he said and did had been wrong, and he never knew why. His father had just laughed when he told him, and said he'd understand one day, and it was best to keep away.

Well, he couldn't keep away here, so he grabbed the stick and tried, as best he could, to draw a second skirt on the top half of the stick woman in front of him. It wasn't very good, but Daphne's look told him he'd done the right thing, whatever it was.

But it put a cloud in the sky. It had been fun, playing with the words and pictures, a sort of game which filled his world and kept the visions of dark water away. And now he'd hit a rule he didn't understand, and the world was back to what it was before.

He squatted down on the sand and stared out to sea. Then he looked down at the little blue bead on his wrist. Oh, yes . . . and he had no soul. His boy soul had vanished with the island, and he'd never get a man soul now. He was the blue hermit crab, hurrying from one shell to another, and the big shell he had thought he could see had been taken away. A squid could snap it up in a second, only it wouldn't be a squid for *him*, it would be some demon or ghost. It would enter his head and take him over.

He started to draw in the sand again, little figures this time, men and – yes – women, women that he remembered, not covered-up trousermen women, and smaller figures, people of all sizes, filling the sand with life. He drew dogs and canoes and huts and –

– he drew the wave. The stick seemed to do it all by itself. It was a wonderful curve, if you didn't know what it had done.

He shifted along a little and drew one stick figure, with a spear, looking out at the flat horizon.

'I think all that means sadness,' said the girl behind him. Gently, she took the stick out of his hand and drew another figure beside the first one. It was holding a portable roof, and wore pantaloons. Now two figures looked out at the endless ocean.

'Sadness,' said Mau. 'Saad ness.' He turned the word over on his tongue. 'Saaad nesssss.' It was the sound of a wave breaking. It meant you could hear the dark waters in your mind. Then—

'Canoe!' said Daphne. Mau looked along the beach, his head still full of sadness. What about canoe? They'd already done canoe, hours ago, hadn't they? Canoe was sorted out!

And then he saw the canoe, a four-man canoe, coming through the reef. Someone was trying to steer it, and not doing a bad job, but the water tumbled and swirled in the new gap and a canoe like that needed at least two people to guide it.

Mau dived into the lagoon. As he surfaced he could see that the lone paddler was already losing control; the gap in the reef was indeed big enough for a four-man canoe to come through it sideways, but any four-man canoe that actually tried anything as stupid as that while the tide was running would soon be overturned. He fought his way through the churning surf, expecting every second to see the thing break up.

He surfaced again after a big wave passed over him, and now the paddler was trying to fend the canoe off the ragged edges of the gap. He was an old man. But he wasn't alone. Mau heard a baby crying, somewhere in the bottom of the canoe.

Another big surge made the canoe spin, and Mau grabbed at it. It rammed his back against the coral before turning away once more, but he was ready for it when it swung round for a second try at crushing him and he swung himself up and into the canoe a moment before it crunched into the reef again.

There was someone else lying under a blanket in the rocking canoe. He paid them no attention but grabbed a paddle and dug it into the water. The old man had some sense, at least, and kept the canoe off the rocks while Mau tried to move it towards the beach. Panic wouldn't help here; you just had to pull it out of the churning mass of water a few inches at a time, with long, patient strokes, which got easier as you drove it free, until suddenly it was in calmer water and moving quickly. He relaxed a little then, but not too much, because he wasn't sure he'd have the strength left to move it again if it stopped.

He leaped out as the canoe was about to hit the beach, and managed to pull it a little further up onto the sand.

The man almost tumbled out – and tried to lift the other person out from under the blanket. A woman. The old man was a bag of bones, and with far more bones than bag. Mau helped him carry the woman and the baby close to the fire, and laid them on the blanket. At first he thought the woman was dead, but there was a flicker of life around her lips.

'She needs water,' croaked the old man, 'and the child needs milk! Where are your women? They will know!'

Daphne came running up, parasol bobbing. 'Oh, the poor things!' she said.

Mau took the baby from the woman, who made a weak

and pitiful attempt to hang onto it, and handed it to the girl.

He heard 'Oh, isn't he *lovely – ur, yuck*!' behind him as he hurried to the river and came back with a couple of brimming coconut shells of water that still had the taste of ashes.

'Where are the other women?' asked the old man as Daphne held the dripping baby at arm's length and looked around desperately for somewhere to put it.

'There's just this one,' said Mau.

'But she's a trouserman woman! They are not proper human beings!' said the old man.

This was news to Mau. 'There's only the two of us here,' he said.

The old man looked crestfallen. 'But this is the Nation!' he wailed. 'An island of stone, beloved of the gods! I trained as a priest here. All the time I paddled I was thinking, the Nation will have survived! And there's just a boy and a cursed girl from the unbaked people?'

'Unbaked?'

'Have you been taught nothing? Imo made them first, when He was learning, but He did not leave them long enough in the sun. And you will learn that they are so proud they cover themselves in the sun. They really are very stupid, too.'

They have more colours than we do, Mau thought, but he didn't say so.

'My name is Mau,' he said, because at least that wouldn't start an argument.

'And I must speak to your chief. Run, boy. Tell him my name. He may have heard of Ataba the priest.' There was a sad but hopeful sound to that last sentence, as if the old man thought this was not very likely.

'There is no chief, not since the wave. It brought the trouserman girl here, and everyone else it . . . took away. I did tell you, sir.'

'But this is such a big island!'

'I don't think the wave cared.'

The baby started to cry. Daphne tried to cuddle it without getting too close, and made embarrassed shushing noises.

'Then an older man—' Ataba began.

'There isn't anyone,' said Mau patiently. 'There's just me, and the trouserman girl.' He wondered how many times he would have to say this before the old man managed to find the right-shaped space for it in his bald head.

'Only you?' said Ataba, looking bewildered.

'Believe me, sir, sometimes I don't believe it either,' Mau said. 'I think I'll wake up and it will all be a dream.'

'You had the wonderful white god anchors,' said the old man. 'I was brought here to see them when I was a small boy, and that was when I decided I wanted to be a—'

'I think I'd better give this little boy back to his mummy,' said Daphne quickly. Mau didn't understand the words, but the tone of determination translated itself very well. The baby was screaming.

'His mother cannot feed him,' said Ataba to Mau. 'I

found her on a big raft with the child, only yesterday. There was food on it, but she wouldn't eat and the child takes no nourishment from her. It will die soon.'

Mau looked at the little bawling face, and thought: No. Does not happen.

He caught the ghost girl's eye, pointed to the baby and made eating motions with his mouth.

'You *eat* babies?' said Daphne, stepping back. Mau picked up the tone of horror, and it took a lot of creative miming to get her to understand that the one who was going to be fed was the baby.

'What?' said Daphne. 'Feed it? What with?'

Oh, well, Mau thought, the baby is screaming and I'm in trouble whatever happens. But . . . does not happen. He waved vaguely at her flat chest, under its slightly grubby white frills.

Daphne went bright pink. 'What? No! How dare you! You have to . . .' She hesitated. She wasn't really sure about this, since everything she knew on the subject of the lumps at the front was based on an overheard, giggly conversation between the housemaids, which she had found unbelievable, and a strange lecture from one of her aunts, in which the phrase 'when you're old enough' had turned up a lot and the rest of it sounded unlikely.

'You have to be married,' she said firmly. It didn't matter that he didn't understand, she felt better for saying it.

'Does she know anything? Has she borne children?' said Ataba.

'I don't think so!'

'Then there will be no milk. Please fetch another woman, one who has not long had— Oh.' The old man sagged as he remembered.

'We have food,' said Mau.

'It must be milk,' said the old man flatly. 'The baby is too young for anything else.'

'Well, at least there can be a hut for the mother, up at the Women's Place. It's not too far. I can light a fire there,' said Mau.

'You dare to go into a Women's Place?' The priest looked shocked, and then smiled. 'Ah, I see. You are only a boy.'

'No, I left my boy soul behind me. I think the wave washed it away.'

'It washed away too many things,' said Ataba. 'But you have no tattoos, not even the Sunset Wave. Have you learned the chants? No? No manhood feast? You were not given a man's soul?'

'None of those.'

'And the thing with the knife where you—?'

'Not that, either,' said Mau quickly. 'All I have is this.' He held out his wrist.

'The blue jade stone? They're only protection for a day or so!'

'I know.'

'Then it could be that behind your eyes is a demon or a vengeful spirit.'

Mau thought about this. He agreed with it. 'I don't know what's behind my eyes,' he said. 'All I know is that it is very angry.'

'On the other hand, you did save us,' said the old man, smiling at him a little nervously. 'That doesn't sound like any demon I've ever heard of. And I hope you gave thanks to the gods for your salvation?'

'Gave . . . *thanks?*' said Mau.

'They may have plans for you,' said the priest cheerfully.

'Plans,' said Mau, his voice as cold as the dark current. 'Plans? Yes, I see. Someone must be alive to bury the rest, was that it?' He took a step forward, his fists clenched.

'We cannot know the reasons for all that happ—' Ataba began, backing away.

'*I saw their faces!* I sent some of them into the dark water! I tied small stones to little bodies. The wave took everyone I love, and everything I am wants to know why!'

'Why did the wave spare you? Why did it spare me? Why did it spare that baby which will die soon enough? Why does it rain? How many stars are in the sky? We cannot know these things! Just be thankful that the gods spared your life!' shouted the old man.

'I will not! To thank them for my life means I thank them for the deaths. I want to find reasons. I want to understand the reasons! But I can't because there are no reasons. Things happen or do not happen, and that is all there is!'

The roar of the Grandfathers' anger in Mau's head was so loud that he wondered why Ataba hadn't heard it.

YOU SCREAM OUT AGAINST THE GODS, BOY. YOU KNOW NOTHING. YOU WILL BRING DOWN THE WORLD. YOU WILL DESTROY

THE NATION. ASK FORGIVENESS OF IMO.

'I will not! He gave this world to Locaha!' roared Mau. 'Let him ask forgiveness of the dead. Let him ask forgiveness of me. But don't tell me that I am supposed to thank the gods that I'm alive to remember that everyone else died!'

Someone was shaking Mau, but it seemed to be happening to someone else, a long way off.

'Stop this! You're making the baby cry!' Mau stared at Daphne's furious face. 'Baby, food,' she said insistently. Her meaning was very clear, even if he didn't understand the actual words.

Did she think he was a magician? Women fed babies, everyone knew that! There was no milk on the island. Didn't she understand? There was no— He stopped, because a bit of his raging brain had just opened up and was showing him pictures. He stared at them, and thought: Could that work? Yes, there it was, the silver thread to a small part of the future. It might work. It *had* to work.

'Baby, food!' Daphne repeated, insistently, trying to pull him up.

He gently pushed her arms out of the way. This needed thinking about, and careful planning. The old man was looking at him as if he were on fire, and stepped back quickly when Mau picked up his fish spear and strode into the lagoon. At least, he tried to make it look like a good manly stride, but inside his mind was full of rage.

Were the Grandfathers mad? Was Ataba mad? Did

they *really* think he should thank the gods for his life? If it hadn't been for the ghost girl, he'd have taken himself to the dark water!

Babies and milk was a smaller problem, but it was noisier, and closer to hand. He could see the answer. He could see a little picture of how it would have to work. It depended on many things. But there was a path. If he followed the steps, there should be milk. And it had to be easier to get milk for a baby than to understand the nature of the gods.

He stared down into the water, not actually seeing anything other than his thoughts. He'd need more tubers, and maybe some beer, but not too much. First, though, he'd have to catch a fish—

And there one was, only a little way away from his feet, white against the white sand so that only its pale shadow gave it away. It floated there like a gift from the gods— No! It was there because he had been so still, as a hunter should be. It was completely unaware of him.

He speared the fish, cleaned it and took it to the priest, who was sitting between the two big god anchors.

'You know how to cook fish, sir?'

'Are you here to blaspheme against the gods, demon boy?' said Ataba.

'No. It would only be blasphemy to say they didn't exist if they were real,' said Mau, keeping his voice level. 'Now, can you cook fish?'

By the look of it, Ataba was not going to argue religion when there was fresh food around.

'Since before you were born,' said the old man, eyeing the fish greedily.

'Then let the ghost girl have some, and please make a gruel for the woman.'

'She won't eat it,' said Ababa flatly. 'There was food on her raft. There is something wrong in her head.'

Mau looked at the Unknown Woman, who was still by the fire. The ghost girl had brought along more blankets from the *Sweet Judy*, and at least the woman was sitting up now. Daphne was sitting beside her, holding her hand and talking to her. They are making a Women's Place, he thought. The language doesn't matter.

'There will be others,' said Ataba, behind him. 'Lots of people will end up here.'

'How do you know?'

'The smoke, boy! I saw it from miles away! They will come. We weren't the only ones. And maybe the Raiders will come, too, from their great land. You will call upon the gods then, oh yes! You will grovel before Imo when the Raiders come.'

'After all this? What's left for them? What have we still got that they would want?'

'Skulls. Flesh. Their pleasure in our death. The usual things. Pray to the gods, if you dare, that those cannibals do not come this far.'

'Will that help?' said Mau.

Ataba shrugged. 'What else do we have?'

'Then pray to the gods to send milk for the child,' said Mau. 'Surely they can do something so simple?'

'And what will you do, demon boy?'

'Something else!' Mau paused then, and thought: He's an old man. He came many miles, and he did stop for the woman and her baby. That is important. He let his anger subside again. 'I don't mean to insult you, Ataba,' he said.

'Oh, I understand,' said the old man. 'We all rage against the gods sometimes.'

'Even you?'

'Yes. First thing every morning, when my knees go click and my back aches. I curse them then, you can be certain of it. But quietly, you understand. And I say, "Why did you make me old?"'

'And what do they reply?'

'It doesn't work like that. But as the day wears on and there is maybe some beer, I think I find their answer arising in my mind. I think they tell me: "It is because you will prefer it to the alternative."' He looked at Mau's puzzled expression. 'Not dead, you see?'

'I don't believe that,' said Mau. 'I mean, I think you're just hearing your own thoughts.'

'Do you wonder where your thoughts come from?'

'I don't think they come from a demon!'

Ataba smiled. 'We shall see.'

Mau stared at the old man. He had to be proud about this. This was Mau's island. He had to act like a chief.

'There is something I am going to try,' he said stiffly. 'This is for my nation. If I don't come back, you can stay here. If you stay, there are the huts at the Women's Place. If I come back, I will fetch you beer, old man.'

'There is beer that happens and beer that does not happen,' said the priest. 'I like the beer that happens.'

Mau smiled. 'First there must be the milk that happens,' he said.

'Fetch it, demon boy,' said Ataba, 'and I'll believe anything!'

CHAPTER 5

THE MILK THAT HAPPENS

*M*au hurried up to the Women's Place and entered more boldly than he had done before. There was no time to waste. The sun was dropping down the sky, and the ghost of the moon was rising.

This had to work. And he'd have to concentrate, and time it right and he probably wouldn't get another go.

First, get some beer. That wasn't hard. The women made mother-of-beer every day, and he found some fizzing gently to itself on a shelf. It was full of dead flies, but they would be no problem. He did the beer ceremony and sang the Song of the Four Brothers as the beer required, and took down a big bunch of plantains and some whistling yams. They were old and wrinkled, just right for pigs.

The Nation had been rich enough to have four

three-legged cauldrons, and two of them were up here in the Place. He got a fire going under one and dumped the plantains and the yams into one of them. He added a bit of beer, let it all boil until the roots were soft and floury, and then it was just a matter of pounding it all together into one big beery mess with the butt of his spear.

Even so, the shadows were getting longer by the time he continued on towards the forest, with the oozing, beery mash dripping in a woven punk-wood bag and a small calabash under his other arm. It was the best one he could find: someone had been very careful to scrape out as much of the orange flesh as possible and dry the rind with care so that it was light and strong, without any cracks.

He left his spear propped up outside the Women's Place. For a lone man, a spear was no good against an angry hog – a furious boar would bite one in half, or spit itself on the shaft and keep on going, a ball of biting, slashing rage that didn't know when it was dead. And the sows were worse when they had piglets at heel, so he was probably going to die, if the beer didn't work.

At least there was a little piece of luck. There was a fat old sow on the track, piglets all around her, and Mau saw her before she saw him, but only just. He stopped dead. She gave a snort and shifted her big wobbling body, uncertain at the moment whether to charge but ready to do so if he made a wrong move.

He took the big ball of mash out of the bag and tossed it towards her. He was running away before it hit the forest floor, crashing away like a frightened creature. He stopped after a minute, and listened. From some way behind him came some very satisfied grunting.

And now for the dirty bit. He moved a lot quieter now, making a big circle to bring himself back onto the path some way behind her. She'd come from the big mucky wallow the pigs had made where a stream crossed the track. They loved it, and it was filthy. It stank of pig, and Mau rolled in it until he did, too.

Globs of the slimy stuff slithered off him as he crept back along the track. Well, he certainly didn't smell human any more. He probably never would again.

The old sow had trampled herself a nest in the undergrowth and was making happy, beery snoring noises, with her family crawling and fighting all over her.

Mau dropped to the ground and began to crawl forward. The sow's eyes were shut. Surely she wouldn't smell him through all the muck? Well, that was a risk he had to take. Would the piglets, already shoving one another aside to get at the teats, work out what he was? They squealed all the time in any case, but did they have a special squeal that would set the sow on him? He'd find out. Would he even be able to get the milk out? He'd never heard of anyone milking a pig before. Something else to find out. He'd have to learn a lot in a short time. But he'd fight Locaha everywhere he spread his dark wings.

'Does *not* happen,' he whispered, and slid forward into the brawling, squalling mass of pork.

Daphne tugged another log onto the fire, straightened up

and glared at the old man. He might do a bit of work, she thought. Some clothes could only help, too. But all he did was sit by the fire and nod at her occasionally. He'd eaten more than his fair share of the baked fish (she'd measured it with a stick) and she had been the one to mash up some of the fish with her own hands and feed it to the Unknown Woman, who looked a bit better now and had at least eaten a few mouthfuls. She was still clutching her baby, but it wasn't crying any more, and that was more worrying than the crying had been . . .

Something screamed up in the hills, and went on screaming, and then went on screaming *louder*.

The old man creaked to his feet and picked up Mau's axe, which he could barely lift. When he tried to raise it over his shoulder he went over backwards.

The scream arrived, followed by the screamer, something that looked human but was dripping green mud and smelled like a swamp on a very hot day. It thrust a warm, heavy gourd towards Daphne, who took it before she could stop herself. Then it shouted 'MILK!' and ran on into the dark. There was a splash as it dived into the lagoon.

The smell hung in the air for quite a long time. When a faint breeze blew it over the fire, the flames burned blue for a moment.

Mau spent the night much further along the beach, and went for another swim as soon as it was light. The smell had this about it: he could sit on the bottom of the lagoon and scrub himself with sand and weeds and then swim underwater in any direction and yet, as soon as he surfaced, there the smell was, waiting for him.

He caught some fish and left them where people could see them. At the moment, they were fast asleep; the mother and her baby were curled up in their blanket, sleeping so peacefully that Mau envied them, and the old man was sleeping with his mouth open and looked as if he was dead, although by the sound of it he wasn't. The girl had gone back to the *Sweet Judy*, for some strange trouser-man reason.

He tried to keep away from the others during the day, but the ghost girl seemed to be looking out for him all the time, and he was running out of nonchalant ways to avoid her. In the end she found him in the evening, while he was repairing the field fences with fresh thorns, to keep the pigs out. She didn't say anything, but just sat and watched him. That can be quite annoying when people do it for long enough. A big cloud of silence builds up like a thunderstorm. But Mau was good at silence, and the girl wasn't. Sooner or later, she had to talk or burst. It didn't matter that he couldn't understand nearly everything she said. She just had to talk, to fill up the world with words.

'My family owns more land than there is on this whole island,' she said. 'We have farms, and once a shepherd gave me an orphan lamb to look after. That's a baby sheep, by the way. I haven't seen any here, so you probably don't know what they are. They go *maaaa*. People say they go *baaa*, but they don't. Sheep can't pronounce their "b"s, but people still go on saying it because they don't listen properly. My mother made me a little shepherdess outfit, and I looked so sweet it would make you *sick*, and the wretched creature used to take every opportunity to butt me in the— to butt me. Of course, all this won't mean very much to you.'

Mau concentrated on weaving the long thorns between the stakes. He'd have to go and get some more from the big thickets on the north slope, he thought. Perhaps I ought to go and get some right now. If I run, perhaps she won't try to follow me.

'Anyway, the thing is that the shepherd showed me how to get a lamb to suck milk off your fingers,' the girl went on relentlessly. 'You have to sort of dribble the milk slowly over your hand. Isn't that funny? I can speak three languages and play the flute and the piano, but it turns out that the most useful thing I've ever learned is how to make something small and hungry suck milk off my fingers!'

That sounds as though she's said what she thinks is an important bit, Mau told himself, and so he nodded and smiled.

'We also own lots of pigs. I've seen them with the little piglets and everything,' she continued. 'I'M TALKING ABOUT PIGS. Oink oink, grunt grunt.'

Ah, though Mau, this is about pigs, and milk. Oh, good. Just what I wasn't hoping for.

'Oink?' he said.

'Yes, and, you see, I want to get something sorted out. I *know* you can't milk a pig like you can a sheep or a cow because they don't have' – she touched her chest for a moment, and then rapidly put her hands behind her back – 'they don't have uddery parts. There's just the little . . . the little . . . tubes.' She coughed. 'THEY CAN'T BE MILKED, UNDERSTAND?' And now she moved her hands up and down, as if she was pulling ropes, while at the same time making squish-squish noises for some reason. She cleared her throat. 'Er . . . so I think the only way you could have got the baby's milk, excuse me, is to sneak up on some sow with a litter of little ones, which would be very dangerous indeed, and crawl up when she was feeding them – they make such a noise, don't they? – and, er . . .' She screwed up her lips and made a sucking sound.

Mau groaned. She'd worked it out!

'And, er, well, I mean, YUCK!' she said. 'And then I thought, Well, all right, yuck, but the baby is happy and has stopped crying, thank goodness, and even his mother is looking better . . . so, well, I thought, I bet even great heroes of history, you know, with helmets and swords and plumes and everything, I bet they wouldn't get down in the dirt because a baby was dying of hunger and crawl up to a pig and . . . I mean, when you think about it, it's still YUCK, but . . . in a good way. It's still yucky, but the reason you did it . . . it makes it sort of . . . holy . . .' At last her voice trailed away.

Mau had understood 'baby'. He was also pretty sure about 'Yuck', because her tone of voice practically drew a picture. But that was all. She just sends words up into the sky, he thought. Why is she going on at me? Is she angry? Is she saying I did a bad thing? Well, round about the middle of the night I'm going to have to do it again, because *babies need feeding all the time.*

And it'll be worse. I'll have to find another sow! Ha, ghost girl, you weren't there when she realized something was going on! I'd swear her eyes had shone red! And run? Who'd have thought that something that big could go that fast that quickly! I only outran her because the piglets couldn't keep up! And soon I'll have to do it all again, and go on doing it until the woman can feed the baby herself. I must, even though I may have no soul, even though I may be a demon who thinks he's a boy. Even though I may be an empty thing and in a world of shadows. Because . . .

His thoughts stopped, just there, as if they had run into sand. Mau's eyes opened wide.

Because what? Because 'Does not happen'? Because . . . I must act like a man, or they will think less of me?

Yes, and yes, but more than that. I need there to be the old man and the baby and the sick woman and the ghost girl, because without them I would go into the dark water right now. I asked for reasons, and here they are, yelling and smelling and demanding, the last people in the world, and I need them. Without them I would be just a figure on the grey beach, a lost boy, not knowing who I am. But they all know me. I matter to them, and that is who I am.

Daphne's face glistened in the firelight. She'd been crying. All we can do is talk baby talk, Mau thought. So why does she talk all the time?

'I set some of the milk to keep cool in the river,' said Daphne, idly drawing on the sand with a finger. 'But we will need some more tonight. MORE MILK. Oink!'

'Yes,' said Mau.

They fell into another of those awkward silences, which the ghost girl ended with: 'My father will come, you know. He will come.'

Mau recognized this. He looked down at what she had absent-mindedly been drawing in the dirt. It was a picture, of a stick girl and a stick man, standing side by side on a big canoe, which he knew was called a boat. And when he watched her he thought: She does it, too. She sees the silver line into the future, and tries to pull herself towards it.

The fire crackled in the distance, sending sparks up towards the red evening sky. There wasn't much wind today, and the smoke went up to the clouds.

'He *will* come, whatever you think. The Rogation Sunday Islands are much too far away. The wave could never reach them. And if it did, Government House is built of stone and very strong. He is the Governor! He could send out a dozen ships to look for me if he wanted! He already has! One will be here in a week!'

She was crying again. Mau hadn't understood the words, but he understood the tears. You're not sure of the future either. You thought you were, it was so close you could see it in your head, and now you think it's washed away, so you're trying to talk it into coming back.

He felt her hand touch his. He didn't know what to do

about that, but squeezed her fingers gently a couple of times, and pointed up at the column of smoke. There couldn't be many fires burning in the islands now. It was a sign that must show up for miles.

'He will come,' he said.

Just for a moment, she looked astonished. 'You think he will come?' she said.

Mau rummaged around in his small collection of phrases. Repetition should do it. 'He will come.'

'See, I *told* you he would come,' she said, beaming. 'He'll see the smoke, and steer right here! A pillar of fire by night and a pillar of smoke by day, just like Moses.' She jumped up. 'But while I'm still here, I'd better go and see to the little boy!'

She ran off, happier than he'd ever seen her. And all it had taken was three words.

Would her father come to find her in his big boat? Well, he might. The smoke of the fire streamed across the sky.

Someone would come.

The Raiders, he thought . . .

They were a story. But every boy had seen the big wooden club in the chief's hut. It was studded with shark teeth, and Mau hadn't even been able to lift it the first time. That was the last time they came as far east as the Nation. After that, they knew better!

Every boy tried to lift the trophy axe, every boy listened wide-eyed to the descriptions of the big dark canoes, their prows hung with bloody skulls, their oars rowed by captives who were near-skeletons themselves, and how the prisoners were lucky, because when they were too weak to row any more they were just beheaded for their skulls. The prisoners who were taken back to the Land of Fires weren't treated quite so well, even *before* they got turned into dinner. You got told this in detail.

At this point, when you were sitting there with your mouth open or perhaps your fingers over your ears, you were just trying not to wet yourself.

But then you were told about Aganu, the chief who fought the leader of the Raiders in single combat, as was their custom, and took the shark-tooth club from his dead hand, and the Raiders ran back to their war canoes. They worshipped Locaha himself, and if He was not going to give them a victory there was no point in staying, was there?

After that, you were given another chance to lift the club, and Mau had never heard of a boy failing to lift it this second time. And only now did he wonder: Was it really because the story made boys stronger, or did the old men have some way of making it heavier?

YOU INSULT THE MEMORY OF YOUR ANCESTORS!

Aargh. They had been quiet all day. They hadn't even said anything about him milking the pig.

'It's not insulting,' he said aloud. 'I'd use a trick, if it was me. A trick to give them hope. The strong boys wouldn't need it and the boys that are not so strong would feel stronger. Every one of us dreamed of being the one who'd beat their champion. Unless you believe that you might, you can't! Weren't you ever boys?'

There was no grumbling roar in his head.

I don't think they *think*, he thought. Perhaps they used to really think, but the thoughts have worn out from being thought so often?

'I will keep the baby alive if I have to milk every pig on this island,' he said, but it was horrible to think that he might have to.

No reply.

'I thought you might like to know that,' he said, 'since he will be taught about you. Probably. He'll be a new generation. He'll call this place home. Like I do.'

The reply came slowly, and sounded grinding and cracked: YOU SHAME THE NATION! HE IS NOT OF OUR BLOOD . . .

'Do you have any?' snapped Mau, out loud.

'Do you have any?' a voice echoed.

He looked up into the ragged crown of a coconut tree. The grey parrot looked down on him with its mouth open. 'Show us yer drawers! Do you have any? Do you have any?' it squawked.

That's what they are, he thought. They're just parrots.

Then he stood up, grasped his spear, turned to face the sea, and guarded the Nation from the darkness.

He didn't sleep, of course, but at some point he blinked and when he opened his eyes again the stars were bright and it was only a couple of hours to dawn. That was not too much of a problem. A snoring old sow would be easy enough to find. She wouldn't ask any questions if she found a nice big beery mash in front of her, and when the time came to run he might even be able to see where he was going.

He told himself this to cheer himself up, but you couldn't get away from it: milking a pig would be much harder the second time, because you'd have to forget how horrible it had been the first time.

In the dark the surf shone where it broke over the reef, and it was time to go through it all again. He'd rather have been going into battle.

The Grandfathers certainly thought he should. They'd had time to pull some pig thoughts together. IS THIS THE WAY OF THE WARRIOR? they growled. DOES THE WARRIOR ROLL IN THE MUCK WITH HOGS? YOU SHAME US!

Mau thought, as loudly as he could: This warrior is fighting Death.

The baby was already grizzling. The young woman gave him a sad little smile when he took the empty calabash and washed it out. She never said anything even now.

Once again, he didn't bother to take the spear. It'd only slow him down.

The old man was sitting on the slopes above the beach, staring up at the fading night. He nodded at Mau. 'Going milking again, demon boy?' he said and grinned. He had two teeth.

'Want to try it, sir? You've got the mouth for it!'

'Ha! But not the legs! I did my bit, though. Last night I begged the gods to let you succeed!'

'Well, have a rest tonight,' said Mau, 'and I'll go and lie in the muck without a prayer. And tomorrow I'll get some sleep and you can pray to the gods to make it rain milk. I think you will find lying in the muck is more reliable.'

'Are you trying to be smart, boy?'

'Trying not to be dumb, sir.'

'Games with words, boy, games with words. The gods are in everything we do. Who knows? Perhaps they see a use for your sorrowful blasphemy. You mentioned beer yesterday . . .' he added hopefully.

Mau smiled. 'Do you know how to *make* beer?' he said.

'No,' said Ataba. 'I have always seen it as my duty to do the drinking part. Making beer is women's business. The trouserman girl does not know how to make beer, no matter how much I shout at her.'

'I'll need all that is left,' said Mau firmly.

'Oh, dear, are you sure?' said Ataba, his face falling.

'I'm not going to try to suck milk out of a sober pig, sir.'

'Ah yes,' said Ataba sadly. 'Well, I shall pray . . . and for the milk, also.'

It was time to go. Mau realized that he had just been putting things off. He should have been listening to himself; if you didn't believe in prayer, then you had to believe in hard work. There was just enough time to make a dash and find a sow before they woke up. But the old man was still staring at the sky.

'What are you looking for?' said Mau.

'Omens, portents, messages from the gods, demon boy.'

Mau looked up. Only the star of Fire was visible this close to dawn. 'Have you seen any?' he said.

'No, but it would be terrible to miss one, wouldn't it?' said Ataba.

'Was there one before the wave? Was there a message in the sky?'

'Quite possibly, but we were not good enough to know what it meant.'

'We would have, if they had shouted a warning. We'd have understood that! Why didn't they just *shout*?'

'HELLO!' It was so loud it seemed to echo off the mountain.

Mau felt the shock down his body, and then his brain cut in with: It came from the sea! There's a light on the water! And it's not Raiders, because they wouldn't shout 'Hello!'

But the old man was on his feet, mouth open in a horrible grin. 'Ah-ha, you believed!' he crowed, waving a skinny finger at Mau. 'Oh yes you did, just for a second! And you were fearful, and rightly so!'

'There's a canoe with a lobster-claw sail!' said Mau, trying to ignore him. 'They're coming round the point! Look, they even have a torch burning!'

But Ataba hadn't finished gloating. 'For just one moment you—'

'I don't care! Come on! There's more *people*!'

* * *

The canoe was coming through the new gap in the reef. Mau made out two figures, still shadowy against the rising light, lowering the sail. The tide was right and the people knew what they were doing, because the craft slid easily into the lagoon, as if it were steering itself.

It nudged the beach gently, and a young man jumped down and ran towards Mau.

'Are there women here?' he said. 'Please, my brother's wife is going to have a baby!'

'We have one woman, but she is sick.'

'Can she sing the calling song?'

Mau glanced at the Unknown Woman. He'd never heard a word from her, and he wasn't at all sure she was right in the head.

'I doubt it,' he said.

The man sagged. He was young, only a few years older than Mau. 'We were taking Cahle to the Women's Place on the Overshoal Islands when the wave hit,' he said. 'They're gone. So many places have . . . gone. And we saw your smoke. Please, where is your chief?'

'I'm here,' said Mau firmly. 'Take her up to the Women's Place. Ataba here will show you the way.' The old priest sniffed and scowled but didn't argue.

The young man stared at Mau. '*You* are the chief? But you are just a boy!'

'Not just. Not even. Not only. Who knows?' said Mau. 'The wave came. These are new days. Who knows what we are? We survived, that's all.' He paused, and thought: *And we become what we have to be . . .* 'There is a girl who can help you. I will send her up to the Women's Place,' he said.

'Thank you. It is going to be very soon! My name is Pilu. My brother is Milo.'

'You mean the ghost girl?' hissed Ataba in his ear as the boy ran back down the beach. 'That's not right! She doesn't know the birthing customs!'

'Do *you*?' said Mau. 'Can *you* help her?'

Ataba backed away as if he'd been burned. 'Me? No!'

'Then stay out of the way. Look, she *will* know what to do. Women always do,' said Mau, trying to sound certain. Besides, it was true, wasn't it? Boys had to live on the Island and build a canoe before they were officially a man, but with girls it just happened somehow. Then they magically knew things, like how to hold babies the right way up and how to go 'Ooozeewididwidwden?' without the baby screaming until its little face went blue. 'Besides, she's not a man, she can talk and she's alive,' he finished.

'Well, I suppose, in the circumstances . . .' Ataba conceded.

Mau turned to look at the two brothers, who were helping a very pregnant woman onto the beach. 'Show them the way. I'll be quick!' he said, and ran off.

Are trousermen women the same as real women? he wondered as he ran. She got very angry when I drew that picture! Do they ever take their clothes off? Oh, please, please don't let her say no!

And his next thought, as he ran into the low forest,

which was alive with birdsong, was: Who did I just say 'please' to?

Daphne lay in the dark with a towel around her head. It was stuffy in the wreck, and damp and smelly. But you had to maintain standards. Her grandmother had been very keen on Maintaining Standards. She positively looked for standards to maintain, and if she didn't find any she made some up, and Maintained them.

Sleeping in the captain's hammock probably wasn't maintaining standards, but her mattress was damp and sticky with salt. *Everything* was damp. Nothing dried properly down here, and of course she couldn't hang her washing out up above the beach, in case men saw her underthings, which would definitely not maintain any standards at all.

The hammock swung gently back and forth. It was very uncomfortable, but it had the big advantage that the little red crabs couldn't get onto it. She *knew* they would be scuttling around on the floor again, getting into everything, but at least with the towel around her head she couldn't hear the little *scrittle scrittle* noise they made as they ran about.

Unfortunately, it didn't cut out what, back home, would have been called the dawn chorus, but that just wasn't the right word for the explosion of noise that was happening outside. It was like a war with whistles; everything with a feather on it went crazy. And the wretched pantaloon birds' supper also came up as the sun rose (she could hear it pattering on the deck above her) and, by the sound of it, Captain Roberts's parrot still hadn't run out of swear words. Some of them were foreign, which made it worse. But she could still tell it was swearing. She just could.

Sleep came and went in patches, but in every fuzzy half-awake dream the boy moved.

When she had been younger, she'd been given a book full of patriotic pictures about the Empire, and one had stuck in her mind because it was called 'the Nobbly Savage'. She hadn't understood why the boy with the spear and the skin as golden-brown as freshly poured bronze was called nobbly, since he looked as smooth as cream, and it wasn't until years later that she realized how you were supposed to pronounce the word that was spelled 'noble'.

Mau looked like him, but the boy in the picture had been smiling, and Mau didn't smile, and he walked like something trapped in a cage. She was sorry now that she had shot at him.

Her memory swirled in the ripples of her sleepy brain. She remembered him on that first dreadful day. He'd moved around as though he were some kind of engine, and hadn't heard her, hadn't even *seen* her. He was carrying the bodies of dead people and his eyes were looking into another world. Sometimes, she thought they still were. He seemed angry all the time, in the way that Grandmother got angry when she found out that Standards were not being Upheld.

She groaned as there was a pattering overhead. Another pantaloon bird had thrown up the remains of last night's dinner, vomiting little bones all over the deck. Time to get up.

She unwrapped the towel from her head, and sat up.

Mau was standing by the bed, watching her. How'd he got in? How had he walked across the deck without treading on a crab? She would have heard! Why was he staring like that? Why, oh why hadn't she worn her one clean nightshirt?

'How dare you walk in like—?' she began.

'Woman baby,' said Mau urgently. He had only just arrived, and had been wondering how to wake her up.

'*What?*'

'Baby come!'

'What's wrong with it now? Did you get the milk?'

Mau tried to think. What was that word she used to mean one thing after another thing. Oh yes . . .

'Woman *and* baby!' he said.

'What about them?'

He could see that it hadn't worked, either. Then an idea struck him. He held his arms out in front of him, as if there was a huge pumpkin in front of him. 'Woman, baby.' Then he folded his arms and rocked them.

The ghost girl stared at him. If Imo made the world, Mau thought, why can't we understand one another?

This is impossible, Daphne thought. Is it about that poor woman? But she can't possibly be having another baby! Or maybe he means . . . ?

'People come island?'

'Yes!' shouted Mau, relieved.

'A woman?'

Mau did the pumpkin act again. 'Yes!'

'And she's . . . *enceinte*?' It meant pregnant, but her grandmother said a lady would never use that word in polite company. Mau, who was certainly not what her grandmother would have thought of as polite company, looked blank.

Blushing furiously, Daphne did her own version of the pumpkin act. 'Uh, like this?'

'Yes!'

'Well, that's nice,' said Daphne, as steel terror rose up inside her. 'I hope she's very happy. Now I've really got to do some washing—'

'Women's Place, you come,' said Mau.

Daphne shook her head. 'No! It's nothing to do with me, is it? I don't know anything about . . . babies being born!' Which wasn't true, but she wished, oh how she wished it was true. If she closed her eyes she could still hear . . . no! 'I'm not coming! You can't make me,' she said, pulling back.

He gripped her arm, softly but firmly. 'Baby. You come,' he said, his voice as firm as the grip.

'You didn't see the little coffin next to the big one!' she screamed. 'You don't know what that was like!'

And it came to her like a blow. *He does.* I watched him bury all those people in the sea. He knows. How can I refuse?

She let herself relax. She wasn't nine years old any more, sitting at the top of the stairs cowering and listening and getting out of the way quickly when the doctor came thundering up the stairs with his big black bag. And the worst of it all, if you could find the highest wave in a sea of worsts, was that *she hadn't been able to do anything*.

'Poor Captain Roberts had a medical book in his sea chest,' she said, 'and a box of drugs and things. I'll go and fetch them, shall I?'

The brothers were waiting at the narrow entrance to the Women's Place when Mau arrived with Daphne, and that was when the world changed yet again. It changed when the older brother said: 'This is a trouserman girl!'

'Yes, the wave brought her,' said Mau.

And then the younger brother said something in what sounded like trouserman, and Daphne almost dropped the box she was carrying, and spoke quickly to him in the same language.

'What did you say to her?' said Mau quickly. 'What did she say to you?'

'I said: "Hello, lovely lady"—' the young man began.

'Who cares what anyone said to anybody? She's a woman! Now get me in there!'

That was Cahle, the mother-to-be, hanging heavily between her husband and her brother-in-law, and very big and very angry.

The brothers looked up at the rocky entrance. 'Er . . .' the husband began.

Ah, fear of the safety of the wingo, thought Mau. 'I'll help her in,' he said quickly. 'I'm not a man. I *can* go in.'

'Do you really have no soul?' said the younger brother. 'Only, the priest said you had no soul . . .'

Mau looked around for Ataba, but the old man suddenly had business elsewhere.

'I don't know. What does one look like?' he said. He put his arm around the woman and, with a worried Daphne supporting her on the other side, they headed into the Place.

'Sing to the baby a good song to welcome it, pretty lady,' shouted Pilu after them. Then he said to his brother: 'Do you trust him?'

'He is young and he has no tattoos,' said Milo.

'But he seems . . . older. And maybe he has no soul!'

'Well, I've never seen mine. Have you seen yours? And the trouserman girl in white . . . you remember the praying ladies in white we saw that time, when we helped carry Bos'n Higgs to that big house for makin' people better and how they sewed up the gash in his leg so neat? She is like them, you bet. She knows all about medicine, for sure.'

CHAPTER 6

A STAR IS BORN

*D*aphne flipped despairingly though the medical book, which had been published in 1770, before people had learned to spell properly. It was stained and falling apart like a very crumbly pack of cards. It had crude woodcut diagrams like 'How to Saw a Leg Off' – aargh aargh aargh – 'How to Set Bones' – yuck – and cut-away diagrams of— Oh, no – aargh aargh aargh!

The book's title was *The Mariners' Medical Companion*, and it was for people whose medicine cabinet was a bottle of castor oil, whose operating table was a bench sliding up and down a heaving deck, and whose tools were a saw, a hammer and a bucket of hot tar and a piece of string. There wasn't much in there about childbirth, and what there was – she turned the page – aargh! An illustration that she really did not want to see; it was for those times when things were so bad that not even a surgeon could make them worse.

The mother-to-be was lying on a woven bed in one of the huts, groaning, and Daphne wasn't sure if this was good or bad. But she was absolutely certain that Mau shouldn't be watching her, boy or not. This was called the Women's Place, and it didn't get more womanly than it was about to be.

She pointed at the door. Mau looked astonished.

'Shoo, out! I mean it! I don't care if you're human or a ghost or a demon or whatever you are, but you aren't a female one! There's got to be *some* rules! That's it, right out! And no listening at the keyh— piece of string,' she added, pulling the grass curtains that did, very badly, the job of a door.

She felt better for all that. A good shouting at somebody always makes you feel better and in control, especially if you aren't. Then she sat down by the mat again.

The woman grabbed her arm and rattled out a question.

'Er . . . I'm sorry, I don't understand,' Daphne said, and the woman spoke again, gripping her arm so tightly that the skin went white.

'. . . I don't know what to do . . . Oh, no, don't let it go wrong . . .'

The little coffin, so small on top of the big one. She'd never forget it. She'd wanted to look inside, but they wouldn't let her, and they wouldn't listen, wouldn't let her explain. Men came round to sit with her father, so the house was full of people all night, and there wasn't a new baby brother or sister, and that wasn't all that had gone from her world. So she'd sat there on the top landing all night, next to the coffins, wanting to do something and not daring to do it, and feeling so sorry for the poor little dead boy crying, all alone.

The women arched her body and yelled something. Hold on, there had to be a song, yes? That's what they said. A song to welcome the baby. What song? How would she know?

Maybe it wouldn't matter what song it was, so long as it was a welcoming song, a good song for the child's spirit to hear, so that it would hurry up to be born. Yes, that sounded like a good idea, but why did she have, just for the moment, the *certainty* that it was supposed to be a good one? And here *came* a song, so old in her mind that she could not remember not knowing it, a song her mother sang to her, in the days when she still had a mother.

She leaned down, cleared her throat carefully, and sang: '*Twinkle, twinkle, little star, how I wonder what you are—*'

The woman stared at her, seemed puzzled for a moment, and then relaxed.

'*Up above the world so high, Like a diamond in the sky—*' sang Daphne's lips, while her brain thought: She's got a lot of milk, she could easily feed two babies, so I should get them to bring the other woman and her child up here. And this thought was followed by: Did I just think that? But I don't even know how babies are born! I hope there's no blood, I hate the sight of blood—'

'When the blazing sun is gone,
When the nothing shines upon,
Then you show your little light,
Twinkle, twinkle all the night.
Then the traveller in the dark,
Thanks you for your tiny spark . . .'

And now something was happening. She carefully pulled aside the woman's skirt. Oh, so *that's how.* My goodness. *I don't know what to do!* And here came another thought, as if it had been lying in wait: *This* is what you do . . .

The men were waiting outside the gateway to the Place, feeling unnecessary and surplus to requirements, which is exactly the appropriate feeling in the circumstances.

At least Mau had time to learn their names. Milota-dan (big, the oldest, who was head and shoulders taller than anyone Mau had ever seen) and Pilu-si (small, always rushing and hardly ever not smiling).

You found out that Pilu did all the talking: 'We went on a trouserman boat for six months once, all the way to a big place called Port Mercia. Good fun! We saw huge house made of stone, and they had meat called beef and we learned trousermen talk and when they dropped us off back home they gave us big steel knives and needles and a three-legged pot—'

'Hush,' said Milo, raising a hand. 'She's singing! In trouserman! Come on, Pilu, you're the best at this!'

Mau leaned forward. 'What's it about?'

'Look, our job was to pull on ropes and carry things,' Pilu complained. 'Not work out songs!'

'But you said you could speak trouserman!' Mau insisted.

'To get by, yes! But this is very complicated! Um . . .'

'This is *important*, brother!' said Milo. 'This is the first thing my son will hear!'

'Quiet! I think it's about . . . stars,' said Pilu, bent in concentration.

'Stars is good,' said Milo, looking around approvingly.

'She's saying the baby—'

'He,' said Milo firmly. 'He will be a boy.'

'Er, yes, certainly. He will be, yes, like a star, guiding people in the dark. He will twinkle, but I don't know what that means . . .'

They looked up at the dawn sky. The last of the stars looked back, but twinkled in the wrong language.

'He will guide people?' said Pilu. 'How does she know about this? This is a powerful song!'

'I think she's making it up!' Ataba snapped.

'Oh?' said Milo, turning on him. 'Where did you come from? Do you think my son *won't* be a great leader?'

'Well, no, but I—'

'Hold on, hold on,' said Pilu. 'I think . . . he will seek to know what the stars mean, I'm pretty sure of that. And – look, I'm having to work hard on this, you know – *because* of this wondering, people won't . . . be in the dark,' he finished quickly, and then added, 'That was really hard to do, you know! My head aches! This is priest stuff!'

'Quiet,' said Mau. 'I just heard something . . .'

They fell silent, and the baby cried.

'My son!' said Milo as the others cheered. 'And he will be a great warrior!'

'Er, I'm not sure it meant—' Pilu began.

'A great man, anyway,' said Milo, waving a hand. 'They say the birth song can be a prophecy, for sure. That type of language at this time . . . it's telling us what will be, right enough.'

'Do the trousermen have gods?' asked Mau.

'Sometimes. When they remember— Hey, here she comes!'

The outline of the ghost girl appeared in the stone entrance to the place.

'Mr Pilu, tell your brother he is the father of a little boy and his wife is well and sleeping.'

That news was passed on with a whoop, which is easy to translate.

'And he be called Twinkle?' Milo suggested, in broken English.

'*No!* I mean, no, don't. Not Twinkle,' said the ghost girl quickly. 'That would be wrong. Very, very wrong. Forget about Twinkle. Twinkle, NO!'

'Guiding Star?' said Mau, and that met with general approval.

'That would be very auspicious,' said Ataba. He added, 'Is there going to be beer by any chance?'

The choice was also translated for the ghost girl, who

indicated that any name that wasn't Twinkle was bound to be good. Then she asked – no, *commanded* – that the other young woman and her baby be brought up and all sorts of things carried to the Place from the wreck of the *Sweet Judy*. The men jumped to it. There was a purpose.

… And now it was two weeks later, and a lot had happened. The most important thing was that time had passed, pouring thousands of soothing seconds across the island. People need time to deal with the now before it runs away and becomes the then. And what they need most of all is nothing much happening.

And this is me, looking at all that horizon, Daphne thought, looking at the wash of blue that stretched all the way to the end of the world. My goodness, Father was right. If my horizon was any broader it would have to be folded in half.

It's a funny saying, 'broaden your horizons'. I mean, there's just *the* horizon, which moves away from you, so you never actually catch up with it. You only get to where it's been. She'd watched the sea all around the world, and it had always looked pretty much the same.

Or maybe it was the other way round; maybe *you* moved, *you* changed.

She couldn't believe that back in ancient history, she'd given the poor boy scones that tasted like rotting wood and slightly like dead lobster! She'd fussed about napkins! And she'd tried to shoot him in the chest with poor Captain Roberts's ancient pistol, and in any book of etiquette that was a wrong move.

But then, was that her back there? Or was *this* her, right here, in the sheltered garden that was the Women's Place, watching the Unknown Woman sitting by the pool but holding her little son tightly, like a little girl holds a favourite dolly, and wondering if she shouldn't take the child again, just to give it some time to breathe.

It seemed to Daphne that the men thought all women spoke the same language. That had seemed silly and a bit annoying, but she had to admit that in the Place, right now, the language was Baby. It was the common language. Probably everyone makes the same sort of cooing noises to babies, everywhere in the world, she thought. We kind of understand it's the right thing to do. Probably no one thinks that the thing to do is to lean over it and hit a tin tray with a hammer.

And suddenly, that was very interesting. Daphne found herself watching the two babies closely, in between the chores. When they didn't want feeding they turned their heads away, but if they were hungry their little heads bobbed forward. It's like shaking your head for no and nodding it for yes. Is this where it comes from? Is it the same everywhere? How can I find out? She made a note to write this down.

But she was really worried about the mother of the baby that, in the privacy of her head, Daphne called the Pig Boy. She was sitting up now, and sometimes walked around, and smiled when you gave her food, but there was something missing. She didn't play with her baby as much as Cahle, either. She let Cahle feed it, because there must have been some lamp still burning in her brain that knew it was the only way, but afterwards she'd grab it and scuttle off to the corner of a hut, like a cat with a kitten.

Cahle was already bustling round the place, always with her baby under her arm, or handed to Daphne if she needed to use both hands. She was a bit puzzled about Daphne, as if she wasn't quite sure what the girl was but was going to be respectful anyway, just in case. They tended to smile at one another in a slightly wary 'we're getting on fine, I hope' kind of way when their eyes met, but sometimes, when Cahle caught Daphne's attention, she made a little motion towards the other woman and tapped her own head sadly. That didn't need a translation.

Every day one of the men brought some fish up, and Cahle showed Daphne some of the plants in the Place. They were mostly roots, but there were also some spicy plants, including a pepper that made Daphne go and lie with her mouth in the stream for three minutes, although she felt very good afterwards. Some of the plants were medicines, as far as she could tell. Cahle was good at pantomime. Daphne still wasn't sure whether the little brown nuts on the tree with the red leaves made you sick or stopped you being sick, but she tried to remember everything anyway. She was always superstitious about remembering useful things she had been told, at least outside lessons. You would be bound to need it one day. It was a test the world did to make sure you were paying attention.

She tried to pay attention when Cahle showed her cookery stuff; the woman seemed to think it was very important, and Daphne tried hard to hide the fact that she'd never cooked anything in her life. She'd learned how to make some kind of drink, too, which the woman was . . . emphatic about.

It smelled like the Demon Drink, which was the cause of Ruin. Daphne knew this because of what happened when Biggleswick the butler broke into her father's study one night and got Rascally Drunk on whisky and woke up the whole house with his singing. Grandmother had sacked him on the spot, and refused to relent even when Daphne's father said that Biggleswick's mother had died that day. The footmen pulled him out of the house and carried him out to the stables and left him crying in the straw with the horses trying to lick the tears off his face, for the salt.

What upset Daphne, who had quite liked Biggleswick, especially the way he walked with his feet turned out so that he looked as if he might split in two at any moment, was that he lost his job because of *her*. Grandmother had stood at the top of the stairs like some ancient stone goddess, pointed at Daphne (who had been watching with interest from the upper landing) and screamed at her father: 'Will you stand there doing nothing when your only child is exposed to such Lewdness?'

And that had been it for the butler. Daphne had been sorry to see him go, because he was quite kind and she'd very nearly mastered his waddle. Later she'd heard via the dumbwaiter that he'd met a Bad End. And all because of the Demon Drink.

On the other hand, she'd always wondered what the Demon Drink was like, having heard her grandmother talk about it so much. This particular Demon Drink was made very methodically out of a red root that grew in one corner of the Place; Cahle peeled it very carefully with a knife, and then washed her hands just as carefully in the pool, at the place where it overflowed into the little stream again. The root was mashed with a stone and a handful of small leaves was added. Cahle stared at the bowl for a moment and then cautiously added another leaf. Water was poured in from a gourd, taking care not to splash, and the bowl was left on a shelf for a day.

By next morning the bowl was full of a churning, hissing, evil-looking yellow foam.

Daphne went to climb up to see if it smelled as bad as it looked, and Cahle gently but firmly pulled her back, shaking her head vigorously.

'Don't drink?' Daphne had asked.

'No drink!'

Cahle took the bowl down and set it down in the middle of the hut. Then she spat in the bowl. A plume of what looked like steam went up to the thatched roof of the hut, and the churning mixture in the bowl hissed even more.

This, thought Daphne, watching in a kind of fascinated shock, is not at all like Grandmother's sherry afternoons.

At this point, Cahle began to sing. It was a jolly little song, with the kind of tune that sticks in your mind even when you don't know the words. It bounced along and you just *knew* you wouldn't be able to get it out of your head. Even with a chisel.

She was singing to the beer. And the beer was listening. It was calming down, like an excited dog being reassured by its master's voice. The hissing began to grow less, the bubbles settled down and what had looked like a foul mess was actually becoming transparent.

Still Cahle sang, beating time with both hands. But they weren't *just* beating time; they made shapes in the air, following the music. The beer-calling song had lots of little verses with the same chorus between each one, so Daphne started to sing along and wave her hands in time. She got the feeling that the woman was pleased about this because she leaned over, still singing, and moved Daphne's fingers into the right positions.

Strange, oily ripples passed across the stuff in the bowl, which got a bit clearer each time. Cahle watched it closely, still counting . . . and then stopped.

The bowl was full of liquid diamond. The beer sparkled like the sea. A small wave rolled across it.

Cahle dipped a shell into it and offered it to Daphne with an encouraging nod.

Well, refusing would certainly be what Grandmother called a *Faux Pas*. There was such a thing as good manners, after all. It might cause offence, and that would never do.

She tried it. It was like drinking silver, and made her eyes water.

'For man! Husbun!' said Cahle, grinning. 'For when too much husbun!' She lay on her back and made very loud snoring noises. Even the Unknown Woman smiled.

Daphne thought: I'm learning things. I hope I find out soon what they are.

Next day she worked it out. In a language made up of a few words and a lot of smiles, nods and gestures – some very embarrassing gestures, which Daphne knew she should be shocked about, except that here on this sunny island there was just no point – she, Cahle, was teaching her the things she needed to know so that she would be able to get a husband.

She knew she shouldn't laugh, and tried not to, but there was no way to explain to the woman that her way to get a husband was to have a very rich father who was Governor of a lot of islands. Besides, she was not at all certain that she even wanted a husband, since they seemed a lot of work, and as for children, after seeing the birth of Guiding Star she was certain that if *she* ever wanted children she'd buy some ready-made.

But this wasn't something she could tell two new mothers, even if she knew how, so she tried to understand what Cahle was trying to tell her, and even let the name-less woman do her hair, which gave the poor woman some comfort and, Daphne thought, looked pretty good but far too grown-up for thirteen. Her grandmother would *not approve*, in italics, although the other side of the world was probably too much even for her beady eyes.

At any moment her father's ship would come into view,

of course. That was a certainty. It was taking some time because there were so many islands to search.

And supposing he didn't come?

She pushed that thought out of her mind.

It pushed back. She could see thoughts that were waiting on the other side of it, waiting to drag her down if she dared to think them.

More people had arrived on the day after Guiding Star had been born, a small boy called Oto-I and a tiny wizened old lady, both of them parched and hungry.

The old lady was about the same size as the boy and had taken over a corner of one of the huts, where she ate everything that was given to her and watched Daphne with small bright eyes. Cahle and the other women treated her with great respect and called her by a long name that Daphne couldn't pronounce. She called her Mrs Gurgle because she had the noisiest stomach Daphne had ever heard, and it was a good idea to keep upwind of her at all times.

Oto-I, on the other hand, had recovered in the speedy way that children do, and she had sent him off to help Ataba, and from here she could see the old man and the boy working on the pig fence, just below her, and if she walked to the edge of the fields, she could see a steadily growing pile of planks, spars and sailcloth on the beach. Since there was going to be a future, it would need a roof over its head.

The *Judy* was dying. It was sad, but they were only finishing what the wave had begun. It would take a long time, because a boat is quite hard to take to bits, even when you've found the carpenter's toolbox. But what a treasure it was, on an island that, before the wave, owned two knives and four small three-legged cauldrons. Together, Mau and the brothers pecked away at the boat like grandfather birds at a carcass, dragging everything to the shore and then all the way along the beach. It was hot work.

Pilu swanked a bit about knowing the names of the tools in the box, but it seemed to Mau that when you got right down to it, a hammer was a hammer whether it was made of metal or stone. It was the same with chisels. And skateskin was as good as this sandpaper, wasn't it?

'All right, but what about pliers?' said Pilu, holding up a pair. 'We've never had pliers.'

'We could have done,' said Mau, 'if we'd wanted to. If we'd needed them.'

'Yes, but that's the interesting thing. You don't know you need them until you haven't got them.'

'We've never had them to want to need!' said Mau.

'You don't have to get angry.'

'I'm not angry!' snapped Mau. 'I just think we manage all right!'

Well, they did. The island always had. But the little galley of the *Sweet Judy* was annoying him in ways he didn't quite understand, which was making him feel even worse. How did the trousermen get to have all this stuff? They'd piled it up where the low forest met the beach, and it was *heavy*. Pots, pans, knives, spoons, forks . . . There was a big fork which, with the simple addition of a shaft, would make the finest fishing spear *ever*, and there were lots like it, and knives as big as swords.

It was all so . . . arrogant. The wonderful tools had been treated by the crew as if they were worth hardly anything, thrown in together to rattle around and get scratched. On the island, a fork like that would have been hung on a hut wall and cleaned every day.

There was probably more metal on this one boat than there was in all the islands. And according to Milo there had been lots of boats in Port Mercia and some of them had been much bigger than the *Judy*.

Mau knew how make a spear, from picking a shaft to chipping a good sharp point. And when he'd finished it was truly his, every part of it. The metal spear would be a lot better, but it would just be a . . . a thing. If it broke, he wouldn't know how to make another one.

It was the same with the pans. How were they made? Not even Pilu knew.

So we're not much-better than the red crabs, Mau thought, as they dragged the heavy box down to the beach. The figs fall out of the trees, and that's all they know. Can't we be better than them?

'I want to learn trouserman,' he said as they sat down to rest before going back inside the stifling, smelly heat of the wreck, yet again. 'Can you teach me?'

'What do you want to say?' said Pilu, and then he grinned. 'You want to be able to talk to the ghost girl, right?'

'Yes, since you ask. We talk like babies. We have to draw pictures!'

'Well, if you want to talk to her about loading and unloading and pulling ropes, I might I might be able to help,' said Pilu. 'Look, we were on a boat with a lot of other men. Mostly they grumbled about the food. I don't think you want to say "This meat tastes like you cut it off a dog's arse", do you? I know that one.'

'No, but it would be nice to be able to talk to her without asking you for words all the time.'

'Cahle is saying the ghost girl is learning to speak our language very well,' Milo rumbled. 'And she makes better beer than anyone.'

'I know! But I want to talk to her like a trouserman!'

Pilu grinned. 'You and her all by yourself, eh?'

'*What?*'

'Well, she's a girl and you are a—'

'Look, I'm not interested in the ghost girl! I mean I—'

'Leave it to me, I know just what you need.' Pilu rummaged in the heap of things they had already taken from the wreck and held up what looked to Mau to be just another plank but, after Pilu had banged at them and hammered at them for a while, turned out to be—

'Trousers,' said Pilu, holding them up and winking at his brother.

'Well?' said Mau.

'The trousermen ladies like to see a man in trousers,' said Pilu. 'When we were in Port Mercia we weren't allowed to go ashore unless we wore some, otherwise the trousermen women would give us funny looks and scream.'

'I'm not going to wear them here!'

'The ghost girl might think you're a trouserman and let you—' Milo began.

'I'm *not interested* in the ghost girl!'

'Oh, yeah, you said.' Pilu pulled at the trousers for a moment and then stood them on the beach. They were so encrusted with mud and salt that they stood up by themselves. They looked fearsome.

'They're powerful magic, they are,' Milo said. 'They're the future. Sure enough.'

Mau tried to avoid crunching the red crabs when they went back along the track to the wreck. They probably didn't know if they were alive or dead, he thought. I'm certain they don't believe in little sideways crab gods, and here they are, after the wave, as many as ever. And the birds knew it was coming, too. We didn't. But we are smart! We make spears and trap fish and tell stories! When Imo made us out of clay, why didn't he add the bit that tells us that the wave would come?

Back in the *Sweet Judy*, Pilu whistled cheerfully as he levered up planks with a long metal bar from the toolbox. It was a cheerful and jaunty tune and unlike anything Mau had heard before. They used to whistle the dogs when they were hunting, but this sounded . . . complicated.

'What is that?' he said.

'It's called "I've Got a Lovely Bunch of Coconuts",' said Pilu. 'One of the men on the *John Dee* taught it to me. It's a trouserman song.'

'What does it mean?'

'It means I've got a lot of coconuts and I want you to throw things at them,' said Pilu as a piece of the deck began to come free.

'But you don't have to throw things at them if you've already got them out of the tree,' Mau pointed out, leaning on the toolbox.

'I know. The trousermen take coconuts back to their own country and stand them on sticks and throw things at them.'

'Why?'

'For fun, I think. It's called a coconut shy.' The plank came up with a long-drawn-out scream of nails. It was a horrible noise. Mau felt that he was killing something. All canoes had a soul.

'Shy? What does that mean?' he said. It was better to talk about nonsense than about the death of the *Judy*.

'It is meaning coconuts want to hide from people,' Milo volunteered, but he looked a bit uncertain at this.

'Hide? But they are in the trees! We can *see* them.'

'Why do you ask so many questions, Mau?'

'Because I want so many answers! What does "shy" really mean?'

Pilu looked serious, as he always did when he had to think; generally he preferred talking.

'Shy? Well, the crew said to me, "You're not shy like your brother." That was because Milo never said anything much to them. He just wanted to earn a three-legged cauldron and some knives, so he could get married.'

'Are you telling me the trousermen throw things at coconuts because coconuts don't talk?'

'Could be. They do crazy things,' said Pilu. 'The thing about the trousermen is, they are very brave and they sail their boats from the other end of the world, and they have the secret of iron, but there is one thing that they are frightened of. Guess what it is?'

'I don't know. Sea monsters?' Mau wondered.

'No!'

'Getting lost? Pirates?'

'No.'

'Then I give in. What are they afraid of?'

'Legs. They're scared of *legs*,' said Pilu triumphantly.

'They are scared of legs? Whose legs? Their own legs? Do they try to run away from them? How? What with?'

'Not their own legs! But trousermen women get very upset if they see a man's leg, and one of the boys on the *John Dee* said a young trouserman fainted when he saw a woman's ankle. The boy said the trousermen women even put trousers on table legs in case young men see them and think of ladies' legs!'

'What's a table? Why does it have legs?'

'That is,' said Pilu, pointing towards the other end of the big cabin. 'It's for making the ground higher.'

Mau had noticed it before, but had paid it no attention. It was nothing more than a few short planks held off the deck by some bits of wood. It sloped, because the wreck of the *Sweet Judy* lay on her side and the table was nailed to it. There were twelve pieces of dull metal nailed to the wood. These turned out to be called plates ('What are they for?'), which were nailed down so that they didn't slip off in stormy weather and could be washed up by someone sloshing a bucket of water ('What's a bucket?') over it. The deep marks in the plates were because mostly the food was two-year-old salt-pickled beef or pork, which was very hard to cut even with a steel knife, but Pilu had loved it because you could chew it all day. The *Sweet Judy* had big barrels of pork and beef. They were feeding the whole island. Mau liked the beef best; according to Pilu, it came from an animal called a cattle.

Mau rapped on the table top. 'This table doesn't wear trousers,' he said.

'I asked about that,' said Pilu, 'and they said there was nothing in the world that would stop a sailor thinking about ladies' legs, so it would be a waste of trousers.'

'A strange people,' said Mau.

'But there's something about the trousermen,' Pilu went on. 'Just when you think they are mad, you see something like Port Mercia! Great big huts made of stone, higher than a tree! Some of them are like a forest inside! More boats than you can count! And the horses! Oh, everyone should see the horses!'

'What are horses?'

'Well, they're . . . well, you know hogs?' said Pilu, ramming the bar under another plank.

'Better than you can imagine.'

'Oh, yes. Sorry. We heard about that. It was very brave of you. Well, they are not like hogs. But if you took a hog and made it bigger and longer, with a longer nose and a tail, that's a horse. Oh, and much more handsome. And much longer legs.'

'So a horse is not really like a pig at all?'

'Well, yes, I suppose so. But it's got the same number of legs.'

'Do *they* wear trousers?' said Mau, thoroughly confused.

'No. Just people and tables. You should try them!'

They made her do it. That was probably a good thing, Daphne admitted. She'd wanted to do it, but didn't dare do it, but they'd made her do it, although really they'd made her make herself do it, and now she'd done it she was glad. Glad, glad, *glad*. Her grandmother would not have approved but that was all right because: a) she wouldn't find out; b) what she'd done was entirely sensible in the circumstances; and c) her grandmother really wouldn't find out.

She had removed her dress and all but one of her petticoats. She was only three garments away from being totally naked! Well, four if you included the grass skirt.

The Unknown Woman had made it for her, much to Cahle's approval; she'd used lots of the strange vine that grew everywhere here. It seemed to be a sort of grass, but instead of growing upwards it just unrolled itself, like an endless green tongue. It tangled up with other plants, blew up into the trees and generally just got everywhere. According to quite a good pantomime from Cahle, you could make a so-so soup of it, or wash your hair in its juice, but mostly you used it as string or made clothes and bags out of it. Like this skirt the Unknown Woman had made. Daphne knew she had to wear it, because it was quite something for the poor woman to let go of her baby for any reason other than to let Cahle feed it, and that was a good thing and ought to be encouraged.

The skirt rustled when she walked, in a most disconcerting way. She thought she sounded like a restless haystack. The wonderful breeze got in, though.

This must be what Grandmother called 'Going Native'. She thought that being foreign was a crime, or at least some sort of illness that you could catch by being out in the sun too much, or eating olives. 'Going Native' was giving in and becoming one of them. The way to *not* go native was to act exactly as if you were at home, which included dressing for dinner in heavy clothes and eating boiled meat and brown soup. Vegetables were 'unwholesome', and you should also avoid fruit because 'you don't know where it's been'. That had always puzzled Daphne because, after all, how many places could a pineapple go?

Besides, wasn't there a saying, *When in Rome, do as the Romans do?* But her grandmother would probably say that meant bathing in blood, throwing people to the lions and eating peacocks' eyeballs for tea.

And I don't care, she thought. This is rebellion! But obviously she wasn't going to take off her bodice or her pantaloons or her stockings. This was no time to go totally mad. You had to maintain standards.

And then she realized she had thought that last thought in her grandmother's voice.

'You know, on you they look good!' said Pilu, down in the low forest. 'The ghost girl will say, "Aha, it's a trouserman." And then you can kiss her.'

'I told you, this is not about kissing the ghost girl!' snapped Mau. 'I . . . just want to see if they have any effect on me, that's all.'

He took a few steps. The trousers had been swirled around in the river and bashed on a rock a few times to get the stiffness out of them, but they still made creaking noises as he walked.

This was foolish, he knew, but if you couldn't put your trust in gods, then trousers might do. After all, in the Song of the Four Brothers, didn't the North Wind have a cloak that carried him through the air? And if you couldn't believe in a song that turned poison into beer, what could you believe in?

'Do you feel anything?' said Pilu.

'Yes, they really chafe the sresser!'

'Ah, that would be because you're not wearing Long-Johns,' Pilu pointed out.

'Long John's what?'

'It's what they call soft trousers that you wear underneath the outside trousers. I think they are named after a pirate.'

'So even the *trousers* wear trousers?'

'That's right. They think you can't have too much trouser.'

'Hold on, what are these things called?' said Mau, fumbling around in them.

'I don't know,' said Pilu cautiously. 'What do they do?'

'They're like little bags inside the trousers. Now, that's clever!'

'Pockets,' said Pilu.

But trousers alone weren't something that changed the world. Mau could see that. Trousers would be useful if you were hunting in thorny scrub, and the bags for carrying things were a wonderful idea, but it wasn't the trousers that gave the trousermen their metal and their big ships.

No, it was the toolbox. He'd been cool about it in front of Pilu, because he did not like to admit that the Nation was behind the trousermen in any way, but the toolbox had impressed him. Oh, everyone could invent a hammer, but there were things in that box – beautiful, gleaming wooden and metal things – that not even Pilu knew the use of. And they spoke to Mau somehow.

We never thought of pliers because we didn't need them. Before you make something that is truly new, you first have to have a new thought. That's the important thing. We didn't need new things so we didn't think new thoughts.

We need new thoughts now!

'Let's get back to the others,' he said. 'But we'll take the tools this time.' He stepped forward, and fell over. 'Aargh, there's a huge stone here!'

Pilu pulled aside the ever-growing papervine as Mau tried to rub some life back into his foot.

'Ah, it's one of the *Judy*'s cannon,' he announced.

'What's a cannon?' said Mau, peering at the long black cylinder.

Pilu told him.

The next question was: 'What's gunpowder?'

Pilu told him that, too. And Mau saw the little silver picture of the future again. It wasn't clear, but cannon fitted into it. It was hard to believe in gods, but the *Judy* was a gift from the wave. It held what they needed – food, tools, timber, stone – so perhaps they needed what it held, even if they didn't know it yet, even if they didn't want it yet. But now they should be getting back.

They each took a handle of the toolbox, which even by itself was almost too much to carry. They had to stop every few minutes to get their breath back, while Milo trudged on with the planks. In fact, Mau got his breath back while Pilu chatted. He talked all the time, about anything.

Mau had learned this about the brothers: it wasn't a case of big stupid Milo and little clever Pilu. Milo didn't talk as much, that was all. When he did talk, he was worth listening to. But Pilu swam through words like a fish through water, he painted pictures in the air with them, and he talked all the time.

Eventually Mau said, 'Don't you wonder about your people, Pilu? About what happened to them?'

And, for once, Pilu slowed down. 'We went back. All the huts were gone. So were the canoes. We hope they made it to one of the stone islands. When we have rested and the baby is fine and strong, we'll go looking for them. I hope the gods took care of them.'

'Do you think they did?' said Mau.

'The best of the fish were always taken to the shrine,' said Pilu, in a flat voice.

'Here they are – I mean they *were* – left on the god anchors,' said Mau. 'The pigs ate them.'

'Well, yes, but only what's left.'

'No, the whole fish,' said Mau bluntly.

'But the spirit goes to the gods,' said Pilu, his voice seeming to come from a distance, as if he were trying to draw back from the conversation without actually backing away.

'Have you ever seen it happen?'

'Look, I know you think there are no gods—'

'Perhaps they do exist. I want to know why they act as if they don't – I want them to explain!'

'Look, it's happened, all right?' said Pilu wretchedly. 'I'm just grateful I'm alive.'

'Grateful? Who to?'

'Glad, then! Glad that we are all alive, and sad that others died. *You* are angry, and what good is that going to do?' said Pilu, and now his voice had a strange kind of growl to it, like some small harmless animal that has been trapped in a corner and is ready to fight back in a fury.

To Mau's astonishment Pilu was crying. Without knowing why, but also knowing, absolutely *knowing*, down to his bones, that it was the right thing to do, he put his arms around him as enormous shuddering sobs escaped from Pilu, mixed with broken words and tangled in snot and tears. Mau held him until he stopped shaking and the forest was given back to birdsong.

'They went to be dolphins,' Pilu murmured. 'I am sure of it.'

Why can't I do this? Mau thought. Where are my tears when I need them? Maybe the wave took them. Maybe Locaha drank them, or I left them in the dark water. But I can't feel them. Perhaps you need a soul to cry.

After a while the sobbing stopped and became coughs and sniffs. Then Pilu very gently pushed Mau's arms away and said: 'Well, this isn't getting things done, is it? Come on, let's get going! You know, I'm sure you gave me the heavy end to carry!'

And there was the smile, as if it had never gone away.

You didn't have to know Pilu for long to see that he floated through life like a coconut on the ocean. He always bobbed up. There was some sort of natural spring of cheerfulness that bubbled to the surface. Sadness was like a cloud across the sun, soon past. Sorrow was tucked away somewhere in his head, locked up in a cage with a blanket over it, like the captain's parrot. He dealt with troubling thoughts by simply not thinking them; it was as if someone had put a dog's brain in a boy's body and, right now, Mau would have given anything to be him.

'Just before the wave came, all the birds flew up into the air,' he said as they walked out from under the canopy and into the full light of the afternoon. 'It was as if they knew something, something that I didn't!'

'Well, birds fly up when hunters go into the forest,' said Pilu. 'It's what they do.'

'Yes, but this was nearly a minute before the wave came. The birds knew! How did they know?'

'Who knows?' And that was the other thing about Pilu: no thought stayed in his head for very long, because it got lonely.

'The ghost girl has got a – a thing called a book, you know? Made out of something like papervine. And it's full of birds!' He wasn't sure what he was trying to do now. Perhaps he just wanted to see the light of interest in Pilu's eyes.

'Squashed?'

'No, like . . . tattoos, but the proper colours! And the trouserman name for grandfather bird is "pantaloon bird"!'

'What's a pantaloon?'

'Trouserman trousers for trouserwomen,' Mau explained.

'Silly to have a different name,' said Pilu.

And that was it. Pilu had a soul to fill him, so he lived happily enough. But Mau looked into himself and found questions, and the only answers seemed to be 'because', and 'because' was no answer at all. Because . . . the gods, the stars, the world, the wave, life, death. There are no reasons, there is no sense, only 'because' . . . 'because' was a curse, a struck blow, it was putting your hand in the cold hand of Locaha—

WHAT WILL YOU DO, HERMIT CRAB? WILL YOU PULL DOWN THE STARS? WILL YOU SMASH THE MOUNTAINS LIKE SHY COCONUTS TO FIND THEIR SECRETS?

THINGS ARE AS THEY ARE! EXISTENCE IS ITS OWN 'BECAUSE'! ALL THINGS IN THEIR RIGHT PLACE. WHO ARE YOU TO DEMAND REASONS? WHO ARE YOU?

The Grandfathers had never been as loud as this before. Their thundering made his teeth ache and he collapsed to his knees, the box of tools crashing into the sand.

'Are you all right?' said Pilu.

'Ugh,' said Mau, and spat bile onto the sand. It wasn't just that the old men got into his head, although that was bad enough, but they left everything in a mess when they went away again. He stared at the sand until the bits of his thoughts came back together again.

'The Grandfathers spoke to me,' he mumbled.

'I didn't hear anything.'

'Then you're lucky! Ugh!' Mau clutched at his head. It had been really bad this time, the worst ever. And there was something extra, too. It had sounded as though there had been more voices, very weak or a long way off, and they had been shouting something different, but it had got lost in the clamour. More of them, he thought gloomily. A thousand years of Grandfathers, all shouting at me, and never shouting anything new.

'They want me to bring up the last of the god anchors,' he said.

'Do you know where it is?'

'Yes, it's in the lagoon, and it can stay there!'

'All right, but what actual harm would it do to bring it up?'

'Harm?' said Mau, trying to understand this. 'You want to thank the god of Water?'

'You don't have to mean it, and people will feel better,' said Pilu.

Something whispered in Mau's ear, but whatever it was trying to say was far too faint to be understood. It's probably some ancient Grandfather who was a bit slow, he thought sourly. And even though I am the chief, my job is to make people feel better, is it? Either the gods are powerful but didn't save my people, or they don't exist and all we're believing in is lights in the sky and pictures in our heads. Isn't that the truth? Isn't that important?

The voice in his head answered, or tried to. It was like watching someone shouting at the other end of the beach. You could see them jumping up and down and waving their arms and maybe even make out their lips moving, but the wind is blowing through the palms and rustling the pandanuses and the surf is pounding and the grandfather birds are throwing up unusually loudly, so you can't hear but you do know that what you can't hear is definitely shouting. In his head it was exactly like that, but without the beach, the jumping, the waving, the lips, the palms, the pandanuses, the surf and the birds, but with the same feeling that you are missing something that someone really, really wants you to hear. Well, he wasn't going to listen to their rules.

'I'm the little blue hermit crab,' said Mau under his breath. 'And I am running. But I will not be trapped in a shell again, because . . . yes, there has to be a because . . . because . . . any shell will be too small. I want to know why. Why *everything*. I don't know the answers, but a few days ago I didn't know there were questions.'

Pilu was watching him carefully, as if uncertain whether he should run or not.

'Let's go and see if your brother can cook, shall we?' said Mau, keeping his voice level and friendly.

'He can't, usually,' said Pilu. He broke into his grin again, but there was something nervous about it.

He's frightened of me, Mau thought. I haven't hit him or even raised my hand. I've just tried to make him think differently, and now he's scared. Of thinking. It's magic.

It can't be magic, Daphne thought. Magic is just a way of saying 'I don't know'.

There were quite a few shells of beer fizzing on the shelves in the shed. They all had little bubbles growing and bursting from the seals at the top. It was beer that hadn't been sung to yet. Mother-of-beer, they called it at that stage. She could tell quite easily, because there were dead flies all round it. They didn't drown in it; they died and became little fly statues as soon as they drank it. If you were looking for the *real* Demon Drink, this was it.

You spit in it, you sing it a song, you wave your hands over it in time to the said song, the demon is magically sent back to, er, wherever, and there's just the good drink left. How does that happen?

Well, she had a theory; she'd spent half the night thinking it up. The ladies were at the other end of the Place, picking blossoms. They probably wouldn't hear her if she sang quietly. The spitting . . . well, that was for luck, obviously. Besides, you had to be scientific about these things, and test one bit at a time. The secret was in the hand movements, she was sure of it. Well, slightly sure.

She poured a little of the deadly pre-beer into a bowl and stared at it. Or perhaps it was in the song, but not in the words? Perhaps the frequency of the human voice did something to the tiny atomic substances, such as happened when the famous operatic soprano Dame Ariadne Stretch broke a glass by singing at it? That sounded very promising, especially when you knew that only women were supposed to make beer and they, of course, had higher voices!

The Demon Drink stared back at her, rather smugly in her view. *Go on*, it seem to say, *impress me*.

'I'm not sure I know all the words to this one,' she said, and realized that she had just apologized to a drink. That was the trouble with being brought up in a polite household. She cleared her throat. 'Once my father took me to the music hall,' she said. 'You might enjoy this one.' She cleared her throat again, and began:

> 'Let's all go down the Strand,
> ('ave a banana!)
> Oh! What a happy land,
> I'll be leader, you can march behind . . .'

No, that sounded a bit complicated for a beverage, and

the banana only confused matters. What about . . . ? She hesitated, and thought about songs. Could it be *that* simple? She started to sing again, counting on her fingers as she sang.

'*Baa, baa, black sheep, have you any wool? Yes, sir, yes, sir, three bags full—*'

She sang sixteen of the verses, counting all the time, singing to the beer as it bubbled, and noted whether it was suddenly as clear and sparkly as a diamond. Then she tested her conclusion, like a proper scientist would, on a third bowl of mother-of-beer, feeling rather certain and more than a little pleased with herself. Now she had a working hypothesis.

'*Baa, baa, black—*'

She stopped, aware of people trying to be quiet. Cahle and the Unknown Woman were standing in the doorway, listening with interest.

'Men!' said Cahle cheerfully. She had a flower tucked in her hair.

'Er . . . what?' said Daphne, flustered.

'I want to go and see my husbun!'

Daphne understood that, and there was no rule against it. Men weren't allowed into the Place, but women could come and go as they pleased.

'Er . . . good,' she said. She felt something touch her hair, went to brush it away, and realized that the Unknown Woman was undoing her plaits. She went to stop her, and caught Cahle's warning look. In her head the Unknown Woman was coming back from somewhere bad, and every sign of her being a normal person again was to be encouraged.

She felt the plaits being gently teased apart.

Then she smelled a whiff of perfume, and realized the woman had stuck a flower behind her ear. They grew everywhere in the Place, huge floppy pink and purple blooms that knocked you down with their scent. Cahle generally wound one into her hair in the evenings.

'Er, thank you,' she said.

Cahle took her gently by the arm, and Daphne felt the panic rise. *She* was going to the beach as well? But she was practically naked! She had nothing under the grass skirt but one petticoat, her pantaloons and a pair of Unmentionables! And her feet were bare right up to the ankles!

Then it went strange, and for ever afterwards she never quite understood how it was done.

She should go down to the beach. The decision floated there in her head, clear and definite. She had decided it was time to go down to the beach. It was just that she couldn't *remember* deciding. It was a strange sensation, like feeling full even though you can't recall having lunch. And there was something else, fading away fast like an echo without a voice: *Everyone has toes!*

Milo was a pretty good cook, Mau had to admit. He really knew how to bake fish. The smell hung over the camp when they got back, and the air practically dribbled.

There was still plenty of the *Sweet Judy* left. It would

take months, maybe years to break her right down. They had the tools now, yes, but not enough people; it would need a dozen strong men to shift some of the bigger timbers. But there was a hut, even if its canvas sides rattled in the wind, and there was fire, and now there was a hearth. And what a hearth! The entire galley had been dragged here, every precious metal bit of it, except for the big black oven itself. That could wait, because there was already a fortune in pots and pan and knives.

And we didn't make them, Mau thought as the tools were passed around. We can build good canoes, but we could never build the *Sweet Judy*—

'What are you doing?' he said to Milo. The man had taken up a hammer and a metal chisel and was bashing away at a smaller chest among the pile of salvage.

'It is locked,' said Milo, and showed him what a lock was.

'There's something important inside, then?' he said. 'More metal?'

'Maybe gold!' said Pilu. That had to be explained, and Mau remembered the shiny yellow metal around the strange invitation the ghost girl had given him. Trousermen loved it almost as much as trousers, said Pilu, even though it was too soft to be useful. One small piece of gold was worth more than a really good machete, which showed how crazy they were.

But when the hasp broke and the lid was thrown back, the chest was found to contain the smell of stale water and—

'Books?' said Mau.

'Charts,' said Pilu. 'That's like a map but, well, looks like this.' He held up a handful of the charts, which squelched.

'What good are they?' said Ataba, laughing.

A soggy chart was laid out on the sand. They inspected it, but Mau shook his head. You probably had to be a trouserman to begin to understand.

What did it all mean? It was just lines and shapes. What good *were* they?

'They are . . . pictures of what the ocean would look like if you were a bird, high in the sky,' said Pilu.

'Can trousermen fly, then?'

'They have tools to help them,' said Pilu uncertainly. Then he brightened and added: 'Like this.' Mau watched as Pilu pulled a heavy round item from his pile of spoils. 'It's called a compass. With a compass and a chart, they are never lost!'

'Don't they taste the water? Don't they watch the currents? Don't they smell the wind? Don't they *know* the ocean?'

'Oh, they are good seamen,' said Pilu, 'but they travel to unknown seas. The compass tells them where home is.'

Mau turned it around in his hand, watching the needle swing.

'And where it isn't,' he said. 'It has a point at both ends. It shows them where unknown places are, too. Where are we on their chart?' He pointed to a large area of what was, apparently, land.

'No, that's Nearer Australia,' said Pilu. 'That's a *big* place. We are' – he rummaged through the damp charts and pointed to some marks – 'here. Probably.'

'So where are we, then,' said Mau, straining to see. 'It's just a lot of lines and squiggles!'

'Er, those squiggles are called numbers,' said Pilu nervously. 'They tell the captains how deep the sea is. And these are called letters. They say "Mothering Sundays". That's what they call us.'

'We got told that on the *John Dee*,' said Milo helpfully.

'*And* I'm reading it here on the chart,' said his brother, giving him a sharp look.

'Why are we called that?' Mau asked. 'We are the Sunrise Islands!'

'Not in their language. Trousermen often get names wrong.'

'And the island? How big is the Nation?' said Mau, still staring at the chart. 'I can't see it.'

Pilu looked away, and mumbled something.

'What did you say?' said Mau.

'It's not actually drawn here, there. It's too small . . .'

'*Small?* What do you mean, *small*?'

'He's right, Mau,' said Milo solemnly. 'We didn't want to tell you. It's small. It's a small island.'

Mau's mouth was open in astonished disbelief. 'That can't be right,' he protested. 'It's much bigger than any of the Windcatcher Islands.'

'Islands which are even smaller,' said Pilu, 'and there's lots of them.'

'Thousands,' said Milo. 'It's just that . . . well, as big islands go—'

'– this is one of the smaller ones,' Pilu finished.

'But the best one,' said Mau quickly, 'and no one else has got the tree-climbing octopus!'

'Absolutely,' said Pilu.

'Just so long as we remember that. This is our home,' said Mau, standing up. He pulled at the trousers. 'Aargh. These really itch! All I can say is, trousermen don't walk about much!'

A sound made him look up, and there was the ghost girl – at least, it looked like the ghost girl. Behind her stood Cahle with a big grin, and the Unknown Woman, smiling her faint, faraway smile.

Mau looked down at his trousers, and then up at her long hair with the flower in it, while she looked down at her toes and then up at his trousers, which were so much longer than his legs that he appeared to be standing in a pair of concertinas, and the captain's hat floated on his curls like a ship at sea. She turned to look at Cahle, who stared up at the sky. He looked at Pilu, who looked down at his feet, although his shoulders were shaking.

Then Mau and the ghost girl looked directly into one another's eyes and there was only one thing they could do, which was to laugh themselves silly.

The others joined in. Even the parrot squawked, 'Show us yer drawers!' and did its doo-dahs on Ataba's head.

But Milo, who took things sensibly, and who happened to be facing the sea, stood up and pointed and said: 'Sails.'

CHAPTER 7

DIVING FOR GODS

*I*t rained gently, filling the night with a rustling.

Three more canoes, Mau thought, staring into the dark. Three all at once, sailing on the gentle wind.

Now there were two babies and another coming soon, one little girl, one boy, eleven women including the ghost girl, and eight men not including Mau, who had no soul – and three dogs.

He'd missed dogs. Dogs added something that even people didn't, and one of the dogs was sitting by his feet, here in the darkness and the gentle rain. It wasn't bothered much about the rain or what might be out there on the unseen sea, but Mau was a warm body moving about in a sleeping world and might at any moment do something that called for running around and barking. Occasionally it looked up at him adoringly and made a slobbery gulping noise which possibly meant 'Anything you say, boss!'

More than twenty people, Mau thought as the rain dripped off his chin like tears. It wasn't enough, if the Raiders came. Not enough to fight, but too many to hide. And certainly enough for a few good dinners for the people-eaters . . .

No one had *seen* the Raiders. They were coming from island to island, people said, but it was always a rumour. On the other hand, if you had seen the Raiders, then they had seen you . . .

There was a slight greyness to the air now, not really light but the ghost of it. It would get stronger, and the sun would come up and maybe the horizon would be black with canoes, and maybe it wouldn't.

Inside Mau's head there was one bright memory. There was the ghost girl, looking silly in the grass skirt, and there was him, looking even sillier in the trousers, and everyone was laughing, even the Unknown Woman, and everything had been . . . right.

And then there had been all these new people, milling around and worried and ill and hungry. Some of them were not even sure where they'd ended up, and all of them were scared.

They were a rabble, according to the Grandfathers. They were the people the wave had not swallowed. Why? Not even they knew. Maybe they had held onto a tree while others had been swept away, or on higher ground, or had been at sea, like Mau.

Those afloat had gone back to people and villages that weren't there, and had scavenged what they could and set out to find other people. They'd followed the current, and had met up, and had become a kind of floating village – but one of children without parents, parents without children, wives without husbands, people without all those things around them that told them what they were. The wave had shaken up the world, and left broken pieces. There might be hundreds more out there.

And then, and then . . . from where had they come, the rumours of the Raiders? A shout from other refugees, fleeing too urgently to stop? An old woman's dream? A corpse floating by? Did it matter when terrified people had set out again in anything that would still float, with little to eat and brackish water?

And so the second wave came, drowning people in their own fear.

And at last they had seen the smoke. Nearly all of them knew the Nation. It was rock! It couldn't be washed away! It had the finest god anchors in the world!

And what they had found was rag-tag – not much better off than themselves, with one old priest, a strange ghost girl and a chief who was not a boy and not a man and didn't have a soul and might be a demon.

Thank you, Ataba, Mau thought. When people are not sure what you are, they don't know what you might do. The newcomers seemed awkward about a chief who wasn't a man, but a touch of demon got respect.

He'd dreamed about the island being full of people

again, but in his dream it was the people who used to be there. *These* people didn't belong. They didn't know the chants of the island, they didn't have the island in their bones. They were lost, and they wanted their gods.

They had been talking about it yesterday. Someone asked Mau if he was sure that the Water anchor had been in its right place before the wave. He'd had to think hard about that, keeping his expression blank. He must have seen the god anchors nearly every day of his life. Were all three there when he went to the Boys' Island? Surely he'd have noticed if one was missing? The empty space would have cried out to him!

Yes, he'd said, they were all there. And then a grey-faced woman had said: 'But a man could lift one, yes?' And he saw how it was going. If someone had moved the stone and rolled it into the water, couldn't that have caused the wave? That would explain it, wouldn't it? That would be the reason, wouldn't it?

He'd looked at all the haggard faces, all of them willing him to say yes. Say yes, Mau, and betray your father and your uncles and your nation, just so that people would have a reason.

The Grandfathers had thundered their anger in his head until he thought his ears would bleed. Who were these beggars from little sandy islands to come here and insult them? They urged his blood to sing war chants in his veins and Mau had to lean on his spear to stop himself from raising it.

But his eye had stayed on the grey woman. He couldn't

remember her name. She'd lost her children and her husband, he knew. She was walking in the steps of Locaha. He saw it in her eyes, and kept his temper.

'The gods let you down. When you needed them they weren't there. That is it, and all of it. To worship them now would be to kneel before bullies and murderers.'

Those were the words he'd wanted to say, but with her looking at him he'd rather bite his tongue off than say them. They would be true, he knew it, yet here and now that didn't mean anything. He'd looked around at the anxious faces, still waiting for his answer, and remembered how shocked and hurt Pilu had been. A thought could be like a spear. You do not throw a spear at the widow, the orphan, the grieving . . .

'Tomorrow,' he'd told them, 'I will bring up the anchor of Water.'

And people sat back and looked at one another in satisfaction. It wasn't smugness, it wasn't a look of triumph, but the world had wobbled a bit and was now back where it should be.

And now it was tomorrow, somewhere beyond the hissing rain.

I'll bring the three stones together, he thought. And what will happen next? Nothing! The world has changed! But they'll catch fish to put on the stones, and cower!

Light was leaking slowly through the rain, and something made him turn.

There was a figure standing a handful of paces away. It had a large head which looked, as he concentrated, as if it was more like some enormous beak. And the rain made a slightly different noise as it landed, more a click than a patter.

There were stories about demons. They came in all shapes; they could come disguised as a human, or an animal or anything in between, but—

– there were no demons. There couldn't be. If there were no gods, then there were no demons, so what was standing there in the rain was *not* a creature with a beak bigger than a man's head that looked quite capable of slicing Mau in two. It couldn't exist, and he had to prove it. Somehow, though, rushing up and shouting at it didn't seem the sensible next thing to do . . .

I've got a brain, haven't I? he thought. I will *prove* it's not a monster.

There was a small gust of wind and the creature flapped a wing.

Ugh . . . but remember the toolbox. There was nothing special about the trousermen. They'd just been lucky. Pilu said they came from a place where, sometimes, the weather could get so cold the sky shed freezing feathers, like the hail you sometimes got in storms, but more fluffy, and so they had to invent trousers to stop their wingos getting frozen and big boats to find places where the water never got hard. They had to learn new ways of thinking: a new toolbox.

This isn't a demon. Let's find out what it is.

He stared. The feet looked human. And what he thought was that the flapping didn't really look like a wing; when you watched carefully, it was more like cloth blowing in the breeze. The only demon was in his fear.

The thing made a cooing noise. This was so undemonic that Mau splashed over to it, and saw someone who'd draped themselves in a tarpaulin from the *Sweet Judy*, which was so stiff that it had formed a sort of hood.

It was the Unknown Woman, cuddling her baby in the dry while the rain trickled around them. She gave him her haunted little smile.

How long had she been there? Before the light began to rise, he was certain. What was she doing there? Well, why was he there, if it came to that? It just felt right. Someone had to watch over the Nation. Perhaps she thought the same thing.

The rain was slackening off now and he could see the surf. Any minute now, the—

'Show us yer knickers! Roberts is on the gin again!'

– parrot would be waking up.

Pilu said that cry meant 'Show me your small trousers'. Perhaps it was the way trousermen recognized one another.

He had small trousers now. He'd cut the legs off at the knee and used the material to make more of what made trousers really worthwhile, which were pockets. You could keep so many things in them.

The Unknown Woman had walked back up the beach, and there were the sounds of people waking up.

Do it now. Give them their gods . . .

He slipped out of the half-trousers with their so-useful pockets, ran forward and dived into the lagoon.

The tide was just about to turn, but the water around the break was calm. The wave had really pounded through here; he could see deep blue water beyond the gap.

The anchor of Water gleamed below him, right in the gap. It was deeper than the others had been, and further from the shore. It would take ages to bring it back. Better start now, then.

He dived, got his arms around the stone cube, and heaved. It didn't budge.

Mau brushed aside some weeds. The white block was trapped by a piece of coral. Mau tried to move that, too.

About five seconds later his head broke water and he swam back, slowly and thoughtfully, to the shore. He found Ataba using a metal hammer from the toolbox on a slab of salt-pickled beef. The stuff went down well with nearly everyone except the priest, who didn't have enough teeth and couldn't often find anyone prepared to do the chewing for him. He sat down and watched the old man in silence.

'You've come to laugh at me in my infirmity, demon boy?' said Ataba, looking up at him.

'No.'

'Then you might at least have the decency to take over the hammering.'

Mau did so. It was hard work. The blows just bounced off it. You could make a shield out of the stuff.

'Something on your mind, demon boy?' said the priest

after a while. 'You haven't insulted the gods for at least ten minutes.'

'I need some advice, elderly one,' said Mau. 'It's about the gods, actually.'

'Yes? But you do believe in them today? I watched you yesterday night; you learned that belief is a complicated matter, yes?'

'There are three gods, yes?'

'Correct.'

'Not four, ever?'

'Some say Imo is the fourth god, but he is the All in which they and us, and even you, exist.'

'Imo has no god anchors?'

'Imo Is, and since He Is, He Is everywhere. Since He Is everywhere, He is not anywhere. The whole universe is His anchor.'

'What about the star Atindi, which is always close to the sun?'

'That is the son of the moon. Surely you know this?'

'He has no god anchors?'

'No,' said Ataba. 'It is nothing more than the clay that Imo had left over after he made the world.'

'And the red star called Imo's Campfire?'

Ataba gave Mau a suspicious look. 'Boy, you *know* that is where Imo baked the mud to make the world!'

'And the gods live in the sky, but also are close to their anchors?'

'Don't be smart with me. You know this one. The gods are everywhere, but can have a greater presence in certain places. What is this about? Are you trying to trap me in some way?'

'No. I just want to understand. No other island has white stone god anchors, right?'

'Yes!' snapped Ataba. 'And you are trying to make me say something wrong!' He looked around suspiciously, in case of lurking heresy.

'Have I succeeded?'

'No, demon boy! What I have told you is right and true!'

Mau stopped hammering, but held onto the hammer. 'I've found another god anchor. It's not the one for Water. So that means I've found you a new god, old man . . . and I think he's a trouserman.'

In the end they worked from one of the big canoes.

Milo, Mau and Pilu took turns to dive with the hammer and steel chisel from the *Sweet Judy*'s toolbox, and pound at the coral which held the white cube in its grip.

Mau was hanging onto the canoe to get his breath when Pilu surfaced on the other side.

'I don't know if this is a good thing or a bad thing,' he said, glancing up nervously at Ataba's hunched figure in the stern, 'but there is another one down there, behind the first one.'

'Are you sure?'

'Come and see. It's your turn anyway. Careful, though, the tide's really tugging now.'

It was. Mau had to fight against the pull of the water as

he swam down. As he did so, Milo dropped the hammer
and chisel and swam up past him. It seemed as though
they had been doing this for hours. It was hard to hammer
under the water; the hammer just didn't seem to work so
well.

There was the stone Mau had first dived for. It looked
free of coral now, but where it had been broken away there
was the corner of *another* cube, in the unmistakable white
stone. What did all this mean? Not more gods, he
thought; we've had enough trouble with the ones we've
got.

He ran his fingers over the shape cut in the first of the
new stones. It looked like a tool from the trouserman toolbox, one that he'd held in his hand and wondered about,
until Pilu had told him what it was for. But there had been
no trousermen around even when his grandfather was a
boy, he knew that. And coral was *ancient*. One of these
cubes had been right inside the rock, even so, like a pearl
in an oyster. He would never have found it if the wave
hadn't smashed up the reef.

He heard the splash above, and a hand reached past
him and snatched the hammer. He looked up into the
furious features of Ataba, just as the old man brought
the hammer down on the stone. Bubbles rose as the priest
man shouted something. Mau tried to grab the hammer
and got a surprisingly powerful kick in the chest. There
was nothing for it but to kick out for the surface with what
breath he had left.

'What happened?' said Pilu.

Mau hung onto the side of the canoe, wheezing. The old fool! Why did he do that?

'Are you all right? What is he doing? Helping at last?' said Pilu, with the cheeriness of someone who doesn't know what's happening yet.

Mau shook his head and dived again.

The old man was still hammering madly at the stones, and it occurred to Mau that he didn't have to risk getting another kick. All he had to do was wait. Ataba needed air, just like everyone else, and how much of it could that skinny chest hold?

More than he expected.

Ataba was hammering wildly as if he intended to be down there all day . . . And then there was an explosion of bubbles as the last of his air ran out. That was chilling, and also quite insane. What was so dangerous about a rock that the old fool would waste his last breath trying to smash it?

Mau fought his way down through the running tide, grabbed the man's body and dragged it back up to the surface, almost flinging Ataba into the arms of the brothers. The canoe rocked.

'Drain the water out of him!' he yelled. 'I don't want him to die! I can't scream at him if he's dead!'

Milo had already turned Ataba upside down and was slapping him on the back. A lot of water came out, chased by a cough. More coughs followed, and he lowered the old man to the deck.

'He was trying to smash the new stones,' said Mau.

'But they look like god anchors,' said Milo.

'Yes,' said Mau. Well, they did. Whatever you thought about the gods and their stones, these looked like god anchors.

Milo pointed to the groaning Ataba. 'An' he's a priest,' he said. Milo believed in laying out the facts of the matter. 'An' he was trying to smash the stones?'

'Yes,' said Mau. There was no doubt about it. A priest, trying to smash god stones.

Milo looked at him. 'I'm puzzled,' he said.

'One of those down there has got chart dividers carved on it,' said Pilu cheerfully. 'The trousermen use chart dividers to measure distance on their charts.'

'That means nothing,' Milo intoned. 'Gods are older than the trousermen an' they can make what they like on the stones— Hey!'

Ataba had jumped over the side again. Mau saw his feet disappear under the water.

'That was the caliper stone he was trying to smash!' he growled, and dived.

The water was pouring through the gap now. It grabbed Mau as he swam after the skinny figure, tried to play with him, tried to throw him against the jagged coral.

It had got the priest already. He was struggling down towards the blocks but the racing tide snatched at him, banged him against the coral and tumbled him away, struggling, with a thin trail of blood blooming in the water behind him.

Never fight the tide! It was always stronger! Didn't the old fool know that?

Mau swam after him, curving his body like a fish, using all his energy to keep away from the edges of the gap. Ahead of him, Ataba struggled to the surface, tried to grab a handhold and was spun away into the foam.

Mau rose to take a breath and swam on—

Blood in the water, Mau, said Locaha, swimming alongside him. *And there will be sharks outside the reef. What now, little hermit crab?*

Does not happen! thought Mau, and tried to swim faster.

Demon boy, he calls you. He smiles in your face but tells people you are mad. What is he to you?

Mau tried to keep his mind blank. Out of the corner of his eye he could see the grey shadow, easily keeping up with him.

There's no shell for you here, little hermit crab. You are heading for the open sea.

Things happen or do not happen, thought Mau, and he felt the deep water open up under him. The sunlight shone blue through the waves above, but below Mau it was green, shading to black. And there was Ataba, hanging in the light, not moving. Blood uncoiled in the water around him like smoke from a slow fire.

A shadow passed over the sun, and a grey shape slid overhead.

It was the canoe. As Mau grabbed the priest there was a splash, and Pilu swam out of a cloud of bubbles. He pointed frantically.

Mau turned to see a shark already circling. It was a small grey, although when there is blood in the water then no shark is small, and this one seemed to fill the whole of Mau's world.

He thrust the old man towards Pilu, but kept his attention on the shark, looking into its mad, rolling eye as it swam past. He thrashed around a little to keep its attention on him and didn't relax until, behind him, he could feel the boat rocking as Ataba was hauled up for the second time.

The shark was going to rush him on the next pass, Mau could tell. And—

– suddenly it didn't matter. This was the world, all of it, just this silent blue ball of soft light, and the shark and Mau, without a knife. A little ball of space, with no time.

He swam gently towards the fish, and this seemed to worry it.

His thoughts came slowly and calmly, without fear. Pilu and Ataba would be out of the water now, and that was what mattered.

When a shark is coming at you, you are already dead, old Nawi had said, and since you were already dead, then anything was worth trying . . .

He rose gently, and gulped a lungful of air. When he sank back down again, the shark had turned and was slicing through the water towards him.

Wait . . . Mau trod water gently as the shark came onward, as grey as Locaha. There would be one chance.

More sharks would be here at any second, but a second passed slowly in the arena of light.

Here it came . . .

Wait. Then . . . *Does not happen*, said Mau to himself, and let all his breath out in a shout.

The shark turned as if it had hit a rock, but Mau did not wait for it to come back. He spun in the water and raced for the canoe as fast as he dared, trying to make the maximum of speed with the minimum of splash. As the brothers hauled him aboard, the shark passed underneath them.

'You drove it away!' said Pilu, heaving him up. 'You shouted and it turned and ran!'

Because old Nawi was right, Mau thought. Sharks don't like noise, which sounds louder underwater; it doesn't *matter* what you shout, so long as you shout it loud!

It probably wouldn't have been a good idea if the shark had been really hungry, but it had *worked*. If you were alive, what else mattered?

Should he tell them? Even Milo was looking at him with respect. Without quite being able to put words to it, he felt that being mysterious and a little dangerous was not a bad thing right now. And they would never know that he'd pissed himself on the way back to the canoe, which as far as sharks were concerned was nearly as bad as blood in the water, but the shark was unlikely to tell anyone. He looked around, half expecting to see a dolphin waiting for him to throw it a fish – and it would feel . . . *right* . . . to do so. But there was no dolphin.

'It was scared of me,' he said. 'Perhaps it was scared by the demon.'

'Wow!' said Pilu.

'Remind me when we get back that I owe a fish to Nawi.' Then he looked along the little deck to Ataba, who was lying in a heap. 'How is he?'

'He's been banged about on the coral, but he'll live,' said Milo. He gave Mau a questioning look, as if to say 'If that's all right with you?' He went on, 'Er . . . who's Nawi? A new god?'

'No. Better than a god. A good man.'

Mau felt cold now. It had seemed so warm in the blue bubble. He wanted to shiver but he daren't let them see. He wanted to lie down, but there was no time for that. He needed to get back, he needed to find ou—

'Grandfathers?' he said under his breath. 'Tell me what to do! I do not know the chants, I do not know the songs, but just once, help me! I need a chart for the world, I need a map!'

There was no reply. Perhaps they were just tired, but they couldn't be more tired than him. How tiring was it, being dead? At least you can lie down.

'Mau?' Milo rumbled, behind him. 'What is happening here? Why did the priest try to smash the holy stones?'

This was not the time to say 'I don't know'. The brothers had begging, hungry looks, like dogs waiting to be fed. They wanted an answer. It would be nice if it was the right answer, but if it couldn't be then any answer would do, because then we will stop being worried . . . and then his mind caught alight.

That's what the gods are! An answer that will do! Because there's food to be caught and babies to be born and life to be lived and so there is no time for big, complicated and worrying answers! Please give us a simple answer, so that we don't have to think, because if we think we might find answers that don't fit the way we want the world to be.

So what can I say now?

'I think he thinks they aren't really holy,' Mau managed.

'It's because of the chart dividers carving, yes?' said Pilu. 'That's what he was trying to smash! He thinks you're right. They were made by the trousermen!'

'They were inside coral,' said Milo. 'Reefs are old. Trousermen are new.'

Mau saw Ataba stir. He went and sat down next to him as the brothers manoeuvred the canoe round and fought it back through the gap. People had gathered on the beach, trying to see what was happening.

When the brothers were busy, Mau leaned down. 'Who made the god anchors, Ataba?' he whispered. 'I know you can hear me.'

The priest opened one eye. 'It's not your place to question me, demon boy!'

'I saved your life.'

'It's a ragged old life and not worth saving,' said Ataba, sitting up. 'I don't thank you!'

'It's very ragged indeed and smells of beer, but you must

pay me back, otherwise it belongs to me. You can buy it back but I set the price!'

Ataba looked furious. He struggled as if he were being boiled in anger and resentment, but he knew the rule as well as anyone.

'All right!' he snapped. 'What do you want, demon boy?'

'The truth,' said Mau.

The priest pointed a finger at him. 'No you don't! You want a special truth. *You* want the truth to be a truth that *you* like. You want it to be a pretty little truth that fits what you already believe! But I will tell you a truth you will not like. People want their gods, demon boy. They want to make holy places whatever you say.'

Mau wondered if the priest had been reading his mind. He would have needed good eyesight because rosy clouds of exhaustion floated across Mau's mind, as if he were dreaming. Sleep always wanted paying; if you put off sleeping for days on end, then Sleep would sooner or later turn up with its hand out.

'Did the gods carve the white stone?' His tongue slurred the words.

'Yes!'

'That was a lie,' Mau managed. 'The stones have trouser-man tool marks on them. Surely gods don't need tools.'

'*Men* are their tools, boy. They put the idea of carving into the minds of our ancestors!'

'And the other stones?'

'Not only gods can get into a mind, boy, as you should know!'

'You think they are *demons*?' said Mau. '*Demon* stones?'

'Where you find gods, you find demons.'

'That might be true,' said Mau. Behind him, he heard Milo snort.

'It is my position to know the truth of things!' Ataba shouted.

'Stop that, old man,' said Mau, as gently as he could. 'I'll ask you one more time, and if I think you are lying then I will let the gods blow your soul over the edge of the world.'

'Ha! But you don't believe in the gods, demon boy! Or do you? Don't you listen to yourself, boy? I do. You shout and stamp and yell that there are no gods, and then you shake your fist at the sky and revile them for not existing! You need them to exist so that the flames of your denial will warm you in your self-righteousness! That's not thinking, that's just a hurt child screaming in pain!'

Mau's expression did not change, but he felt the words clang back and forth in his head. What *do* I believe? he thought. What do I really believe? The world exists, so perhaps Imo exists. But He is far away and does not care Locaha exists, that is certain. The wind blows, fire burns and water flows for good and bad, right and wrong. Why do they want gods? We need people. That is what I believe. Without other people, we are nothing. And I believe I am more tired than I can remember . . .

'Tell me who you think carved the stones, Ataba,' he said, keeping his voice calm. 'Who brought them here and carved them, so long ago they lie under the rocks?

Tell me this, because I think you are screaming, too.'

All sorts of thoughts twisted their way across the priest's face, but there was no escape. 'You will be sorry,' he moaned. 'You will wish you didn't know. You will be sorry that you did this to me.'

Mau raised his finger as a warning. It was all he could manage. The pink hogs of tiredness trampled through his thoughts. In a minute he would fall over. When Ataba spoke next, in a whispered hiss, it echoed as if Mau were hearing it inside a cave. The darkness was made of too many thoughts, too much hunger, too much pain.

'Who brings rocks here and leaves them, boy? Think on that. How many people will you hurt even more with your wonderful truth?'

But Mau was already sleeping.

Mr Black hammered on the door of the *Cutty Wren*'s wheelhouse for the second time.

'Let me in, Captain! In the name of the Crown!'

A hatch in the door slid back. 'Where is she?' said a voice, full of suspicion.

'She's below!' the Gentleman shouted above the roar of the wind.

'Are you certain? She has a habit of jumping out!'

'She's below, I assure you! Open the door! It's freezing!'

'Are you positive?'

'For the last time, man, let us in!'

'Who's "us", exactly?' said the voice, not to be fooled easily.

'For heaven's sake! Mr Red is with me!'

'Is he alone?'

'Open in the name of the Crown, Captain!'

The door opened. A hand dragged both men inside. Behind them, bolts snapped into place with a noise like gunshots.

At least it was warmer in there, and the wind was held at bay. Mr Black felt as though some giant had stopped punching him.

'Is it always like this?' he said, shaking the water off his oilskins.

'This? This fine day in the Roaring Forties, Mr Black! I was about to go and have a sunbathe! You've come about the signal, I dare say.'

'There was something about a tidal wave?'

'A big one. Got this from a navy ship out of Port Mercia an hour ago. Flooding throughout the Western Pelagic. Great loss of life and damage to shipping. Port Mercia safe, it says here. Source of the wave estimated as seventy miles south of the Mothering Sundays.'

'That's still well to the north of us.'

'And this happened weeks ago!' said Mr Red, who had been scrutinizing the pencilled message.

'That is true, gentlemen. But I've been working things out, and I'm wondering where the *Sweet Judy* might have been about that time. Old Roberts likes to island-hop and the *Judy* isn't the fastest ship. The Heir's daughter is on board the *Judy*.'

'So the Heir might have been caught up in this?'

'Could be, sir,' said the captain gravely. He coughed. 'I could set a course to pass through there, but it would slow us down.'

'I need to think about this,' snapped Mr Black.

'And I need a decision soon, sir. It's a matter of wind and water, see? They are not yours to command, nor mine.'

'Who do the Mothering Sundays belong to?' said Mr Black to Mr Red, who shrugged.

'We lay claim to them, sir, to keep the Dutch and French out. But they're all tiny and there's no one there. No one to speak of, anyway.'

'The *Wren* could cover a lot of ocean, sir,' the captain offered. 'And it sounds like the king is safe and, of course, you get some rum types fetching up in out-of-the-way places like that . . .'

Mr Black stared ahead. The *Cutty Wren* was flying like a cloud. The sails boomed, the rigging sang. It sneered at the miles.

After some time he said, 'For all kinds of good reasons, beginning with the fact that we cannot be certain of the *Sweet Judy*'s course, and there are many of these islands, too much time has passed, His Majesty would certainly have sent out searchers—'

Mr Red said, 'He doesn't know he is king, sir. He may well have led the search himself.'

'There's cannibals and pirates to the north-west,' said the captain.

'And the Crown requires that we find the king as soon

as possible!' said Mr Black. '*Would either of you gentlemen like to make this decision for me?*'

There was a dreadful silence, broken only by the roar of their speed.

'Very well,' said Mr Black, rather more calmly. 'Then we follow our original orders, Captain. I will sign the log to this effect.'

'That must have been a hard decision to make, sir,' said Mr Red sympathetically.

'Yes. It was.'

CHAPTER 8

IT TAKES A LIFETIME TO LEARN HOW TO DIE

*D*aphne was eating for Mrs Gurgle, who had no teeth. She did this by chewing her food for her, to get it good and soft. It was, she thought as she chomped dutifully on a lump of salt-pickled beef, very unlike life at home.

But life at home seemed unreal now, in any case. What home was – really was – was a mat in a hut, where she slept every night a sleep so deep that it was black, and the Place, where she made herself useful. And she *could* be useful here. She was getting better at the language every day, too.

But she couldn't understand Mrs Gurgle at all. Even Cahle had difficulty there and had told Daphne, 'Very old speaking. From the long ago.' She was known all over the islands, but none of the survivors remembered her as anything but ancient. The boy Oto-I could only remember that she had plucked him off a floating tree and only drank sea water so that he could have the fresh water in her water bag.

The old woman tapped her on the arm. Daphne absent-mindedly spat out the lump of meat and handed it over. It wasn't, she had to admit, the most pleasant way of passing the time; there was a certain amount of *aarghaarghaargh* about it if you let your mind dwell on it, but at least the old *woman* wasn't chewing food for *her*.

'Ermintrude.'

The word hung in the air for a moment.

She looked around, shocked. *No one* on the island knew that name! In front of her, in the garden, a few women were tending the plants, but most people were working in the fields. Beside her, the old woman sucked enthusiastically at the newly softened meat with the sound of a blocked drain.

It had been her own voice. She must have been day-dreaming, to take her mind off the chewing.

'Bring the boy here. Bring the boy here now.'

There it was again. *Had* she said it? Her lips hadn't moved – she would have felt them do so. This wasn't what people really meant when they said 'you're talking to yourself'. This was herself talking to *her*. She couldn't ask 'Who are you?' – not to her own voice.

Pilu had said Mau heard dead grandfathers in his head, and she'd thought, well, something like that would be bound to happen after all the boy had been through.

Could she be hearing his ancestors?

'Yes,' said her own voice.

'Why?' she asked.

'Because this is a sacred place.'

Daphne hesitated. Whoever was doing this knew her name, and *no one* here knew her real name, no one. It wasn't a secret you'd like to put about. And she wasn't mad, because surely a mad person wouldn't have spent the last half an hour chewing food for Mrs Gurgle . . . er, perhaps that wasn't the best example, because her grandmother and people like her would say that for a girl who would be queen if one hundred and thirty-nine people died to be chewing up the food of someone who looked, sounded and smelled like Mrs Gurgle was just about as mad as you could get without actually dribbling.

Maybe it was God, but that didn't feel right. She'd listened hard for God in church, especially after that horrible night, but of course He was a busy person. Apparently there were lesser gods here, though. Perhaps this was one of them.

She looked around her. There were no pews, and certainly no polished brass, but there was a quiet busyness about it, a silence with a texture of breezes. The wind never seemed to blow hard in here, and loud noises got lost among the trees.

It *was* a sacred place, and not because of some god or other. It was just . . . sacred, because it existed, because pain and blood and joy and death had echoed in time and made it so.

The voice came again. 'Quickly, now!'

Daphne looked around the Place. A couple of women were gardening, and didn't even look up. But there had been something about that 'Quickly, now!' that went straight to her feet.

I must have been talking to myself, she thought as she hurried out of the Place. People often do that. It's perfectly normal when you are a shipwrecked sailor, I'm sure.

She ran down the hill. There was a small crowd there. At first she thought some more survivors had turned up, and then she saw the figure slumped against the corner of the new hut.

'What have you done to him?' she shouted as she ran. Pilu turned, while the rest of the group drew back hurriedly in the face of her anger.

'Us? I've tried to make him lie down, but he fights me! I'd swear he's asleep, but I've never seen anyone sleep like *that!*'

Daphne hadn't, either. Mau's eyes were open wide, but she got the uneasy feeling that if they were looking at a beach, it certainly wasn't this one. His arms and legs were twitching as if they wanted to move but couldn't.

She knelt down beside Mau and put her ear to his chest. She hardly needed to get that close. His heart was trying to break free.

Pilu stepped closer to her and whispered, 'There's been trouble!' He managed to suggest that the trouble had not been made by him, very definitely not by him, and that he was against trouble of any kind, particularly any trouble up close. Ever since the Twinkle song, he had always been a little nervous of Daphne. She was a woman of power.

'What kind of trouble?' she said, looking around. But she didn't need an answer, because Ataba was standing with a ferocious expression. By the look of it there had been, as Cook back home would have put it, '*words*'.

He turned to look at her, his face like a smacked bottom (Cook again), and then snorted and turned to face the lagoon.

At that moment the water mounded and Milo walked up the sloping, white floor, water pouring off him. He had a god stone on his shoulder.

'I want to know what's been going on!' said Daphne. She was ignored. Everyone was watching the approaching Milo.

'I told you! I forbid you to bring that ashore!' Ataba yelled. 'I am a priest of Water!'

Milo gave him a long, slow look, and then kept on coming, his muscles moving like oiled coconuts under his skin. Daphne could hear the sand being crushed under his feet as he plodded over to the god anchors and set his burden down with a grunt. It sank a little into the beach.

There were already four lying the sand. That isn't right, is it? she wondered. Weren't there supposed to be three but one got lost? Where did the other ones come from?

She saw the big man stretch himself out with a cracking of joints before turning to the little crowd and saying, in the slow and solemn voice of a man who tests the truth of every word before letting it go: 'If anyone touches the stones they answer to me.'

'That one was made by a demon!' shouted Ataba. He looked at the crowd for some support here, but didn't find any. The people weren't on anyone's side, as far as Daphne could tell. They just didn't like shouting. Things were bad enough as they were.

'Demon,' rumbled Milo. 'You like that word? Demon boy, you call him. But he saved you from the shark, right? And *you* said we made the god anchors. You did! I heard you!'

'Only *some*,' said Ataba, backing away. 'Only some!'

'You never said "some"!' said Milo quickly. 'He never said "some",' he announced to the crowd. 'He was speaking for his life an' he never said "some"! I have good ears and he never said "some"!'

'Who cares what he said?' said Daphne. She turned to the nearest woman. 'Get Mau some blankets! He's as cold as ice!'

'Mau did rescue Ataba from a shark,' said Pilu.

'That is a lie! I was in no danger—' the priest began, and stopped, because Milo had started to growl.

'You should have seen it!' said Pilu quickly, turning to the crowd with his eyes wide open and his arms outspread. 'It was the biggest one I have ever seen! It was as long as a house! It had teeth like, like, like huge teeth! As it came towards us, its speed made waves that almost sank the canoe!'

Daphne blinked, and looked sideways at the people. Their eyes were as wide as Pilu's. Every mouth hung open.

'And Mau just waited, treading the water,' the boy went

on. 'He did not turn and flee! He did not try to get away! He looked it in the eye, there in its own world! He waved at the shark, the shark with the teeth like machetes, the shark with teeth like needles, to call it to him! He called it to him! Yes, he did! I was in the water and I saw! He was waiting for it! And the shark came faster! It came like a spear! Faster and faster it came!'

In the audience, someone started to whimper.

'And then I saw an amazing thing!' Pilu went on, his eyes wide and gleaming. 'It was the most amazing thing I have ever seen! I will never see anything like it if I live to be a hundred! As the shark charged through the water, as the shark with the huge teeth sped towards him, as the shark as long as a house came through the water like a knife, Mau – he pissed himself!'

The little waves of the lagoon lapped at the sand of the lagoon with little *sup-sup* noises, suddenly loud in the bottomless moment of silence.

The woman bringing a grubby blanket from the hut almost walked into Daphne because she couldn't bear to take her eyes off Pilu.

Oh, thank you, Pilu, she thought bitterly as the magic drained away. You were doing so well, you had their hearts in the palm of your hand, and then you had to go and spoil it by—

'And that was when I saw,' whispered Pilu, lowering his voice and staring around the circle of faces, catching every eye. 'That is when I knew. That is when I understood. He was no demon! He was no god, no hero. No. He was nothing but a man! A man who was frightened! A man like you and me! But would we wait there, full of fear, as the shark with huge teeth came to eat us? *He* did! I saw him! And as the shark was upon him he shouted at it in scorn! He shouted these words: *Da! Na! Ha! Pa!* '

'Da! Na! Ha! Pa!' several people mumbled, as if they were in a dream.

'And the shark turned and fled from him. The shark could not face him. The shark turned about and we were saved. I was there. I saw this.'

Daphne realized that her hands were sweating. She had felt the shark brush past her. She had seen its terrible eye. She could draw a picture of its teeth. *She* had been there. *She* had seen it. Pilu's voice had *shown* it to her.

She remembered when Mr Griffith from the Nonconformist chapel had been invited to speak in the parish church. The sermon was rather damp, because he spat a fine spray when he shouted, but the man was so full of God that it overflowed everywhere.

He preached as if he had a flaming sword in his hand. Bats fell out of the rafters. The organ started up by itself. The water sloshed in the font. All in all, it was very unlike the sermons of the Reverend Fleblow-Poundup, who on a fine day could get through a mumbled service in half an hour, with his butterfly net and collecting jar leaning against the pulpit.

When they had got home her grandmother had stood in the hall, taken a deep breath and said, 'Well!' And that was that. Normally people tended to be very quiet in the parish church. Perhaps they were afraid of waking God up in case He asked pointed questions or gave them a test.

But Pilu had unfolded the story of the shark like Mr Griffith had preached. He had unfolded a picture in the air and then made it move. Was it true? Had it really happened like that? But how could it not be true, now? They had been there. They had *seen* it. They had *shared* it.

She looked down at Mau. His eyes were still open and his body was still twitching. And then she looked up, and into the face of Cahle, who said: 'Locaha has taken him.'

'You mean he's dying?'

'Yes. The cold hand of Locaha is on him. You know him. He does not sleep. He eats not enough. He carries all weights, runs every distance. In his head, too much thinking. Has anyone here seen him not working, guarding, digging, carrying? He tries to carry the world on his back! And when such people weaken, Locaha springs.'

Daphne leaned down to Mau. His lips were blue. 'You're not dying,' she whispered. 'You can't be dying.'

She shook him gently, and there was a rush of air from his lips, faint as a spider's sneeze: '*Does . . .*'

'Does not happen!' she said triumphantly. 'See? Locaha hasn't got him yet! Look at his legs! He is *not* dying! In his head he is *running*!'

Cahle looked carefully at Mau's twitching legs, and put her hand on his forehead. Her eyes widened. 'I have heard of this,' she said. 'It's shadow stuff. It will kill him, even so. The Sky Woman will know what to do.'

'Where is she, then?'

'You chew her food for her,' said Cahle, smiling. The Unknown Woman appeared behind her, staring at Mau in horror.

'*Mrs Gurgle?*' said Daphne.

'She is very old. A woman of great power.'

'Then we'd better hurry!'

Daphne put her hands under Mau's shoulders and pulled him up. To her astonishment the Unknown Woman handed her baby to Cahle and took Mau's feet. She looked at Daphne expectantly.

Together, they ran up the hill, leaving everyone else behind after they had gone a little way. By the time they arrived in the hut, Mrs Gurgle was waiting for them with her little black eyes gleaming.

As soon as Mau was laid on a mat, she changed.

Up until now Mrs Gurgle had been rather a strange, half-sized person to Daphne. She had lost most of the hair on her head, moved on all fours like a chimpanzee, and looked as if she'd been made out of old leather bags. Also, she was, frankly, grabby when it came to food, and tended to fart in an unladylike way, although that was mostly the fault of the salt-pickled beef.

Now she crawled around Mau carefully, touching him gently here and there. She listened intently at his ears and lifted each of his legs in turn, watching the twitching as intently as if she were watching a new species of wild animal.

'He can't die!' Daphne blurted out, unable to bear the suspense. 'He just doesn't sleep! He spends all night on guard! But you can't die of not sleeping! Can you?'

The ancient woman gave her a wide grin and picked up one of Mau's feet. Slowly she ran a stubby black fingernail along his twitching sole, and seemed disappointed in whatever it was she learned by it.

'He isn't dying, is he? He can't die!' Daphne insisted as Cahle came in. Other people crowded around the door.

Mrs Gurgle ignored them, and gave Daphne a look which said, unmistakably, 'Oh? And who are you, who knows everything?' and did some more leg-lifting and prodding just to make the point that she was in charge. Then she looked up at Cahle and spoke at high speed. At one point Cahle laughed, and shook her head.

'She says he is in the—' Cahle stopped, and her lips moved as she tried to find a word she thought Daphne might understand. 'The place between,' she said. 'Shadow place. Not alive. Not dead.'

'Where is it?' said Daphne

This was another difficult one. 'A place with no place – you cannot walk there. Cannot swim there. On sea, no. On land, no. Like shadow. Yes! Shadow place!'

'How can I get there?' This one was relayed to Mrs Gurgle, and the reply was abrupt.

'*You?* Cannot!'

'Look, he saved me from drowning! He saved my life, do you understand? Besides, it's your custom. If someone saves your life, it's like a debt. You must pay it back. And I want to!'

Mrs Gurgle seemed to approve of this when it was translated. She said something.

Cahle nodded. 'She says that to get to the shadow world you have to die,' she translated. 'She is asking if you know how to?'

'You mean it's something you have to *practise*?'

'Yes. Many times,' said Cahle calmly.

'I thought you only got one go!' Daphne said.

Mrs Gurgle was suddenly in front of the girl. She stared at her fiercely, moving her head this way and that as if she were trying to find something in her face. Then, before Daphne could move, the old woman suddenly grabbed her hand, dragged it onto her own heart and held it there.

'Boom-boom?' she said.

'Heartbeat? Er . . . yes,' said Daphne, trying very hard and very unsuccessfully not to feel embarrassed. 'It's quite faint – I mean, you've got a very . . . a lot of—'

The heartbeat stopped.

Daphne tried to pull her hand away, but it was held tight. Mrs Gurgle's expression was blank and slightly preoccupied, as if she were trying to do a mildly complicated sum in her head, and the room seemed to darken.

Daphne couldn't help herself. She started to count under her breath.

'. . . fifteen . . . sixteen . . .'

And then . . . *boom* . . . so faint you could easily have missed it . . . *boom* . . . a little louder this time . . . *boom-boom* . . . and it was back. The old woman smiled.

'Er . . . I could try it—' Daphne began. 'Just show me what to do!'

'There is no time to teach you, she says,' said Cahle. 'She says it takes a lifetime to learn how to die.'

'I can learn very fast!'

Cahle shook her head. 'Your father looks for you. He is a trouserman chief, yes? If you are dead, what do we say? When your mother weeps for you, what do we say?'

Daphne felt the tears coming, and tried to shut them out. 'My mother . . . cannot weep,' she managed.

Once more Mrs Gurgle's dark little eyes looked into Daphne's face as if it were clear water – and there Daphne was, on the stairs in her nightdress with the little blue flowers on it, hugging her knees and staring in horror at the little coffin on top of the big one, and sobbing because the little boy would be buried all alone in a box instead of with his mother, and would be so frightened.

She could hear the lowered voices of the men, talking to her father, and the clink of the brandy decanter, and smell the ancient carpet.

There was the sound of a busy stomach, and there was Mrs Gurgle, too, sitting on the carpet chewing salt-pickled beef, and watching her with interest.

The old woman stood up and reached for the little coffin, laying it gently on the carpet. She reached up again and lifted the lid of the big coffin, and looked at Daphne expectantly.

There were footsteps below in the hall as a maid

crossed the tiled floor and disappeared through the green baize door to the kitchens, sobbing.

She knew what to do. She'd done it in her imagination a thousand times. She lifted the small cold body from his lonely coffin, kissed his little face and tucked him in beside their mother. The crying stopped—

– she blinked at Mrs Gurgle's bright eyes, there in front of her again. The sound of the sea filled her ears.

The old woman turned to Cahle, and she rattled and spluttered out what sounded like a long speech, or perhaps it was some kind of command. Cahle started to reply, but the old woman raised a finger, very sharply. Something had changed.

'She says it is you who must fetch him back,' said Cahle, a bit annoyed. 'She says there is a pain taken away, there at the other end of the world.'

Daphne wondered how far those dark eyes could see. *There at the other end of the world.* Maybe. *How did she do that?* It hadn't felt like a dream; it felt like a memory! But a pain was fading . . .

'She says you are a woman of power, like her,' Cahle went on reluctantly. 'She has walked often in the shadow world. I know this to be true. She is famous.'

Mrs Gurgle gave Daphne another little smile.

'She says she will send you into the shadows,' Cahle went on. 'She says that you have very good teeth and have been kind to an old lady.'

'Er . . . it was no trouble,' said Daphne, and thought furiously: *How did she know? How did she do it?*

'She says there is no time to teach you, but she knows another way, and when you come back from the shadows you will be able to chew much meat for her with your wonderful white teeth.'

The little old woman gave her a smile so wide that her ears nearly fell into it.

'I certainly will!'

'So now she will poison you to death,' Cahle went on.

Daphne looked at Mrs Gurgle, who nodded encouragingly.

'She will? Er . . . really? Er, thank you,' said Daphne. 'Thank you very much.'

Mau ran. He didn't know why; his legs were doing it all by themselves. And the air was . . . not air. It was thick, as thick as water, and black, but somehow he could see through it a long way, and move through it fast, too. Huge pillars rose out of the ground around him, and seemed to go up for ever, to a roof of surf.

Something silvery and very fast shot past him and disappeared behind a pillar, and was followed by another one, and another.

Fish, then, or something like fish. So he was underwater. Underwater, looking up at the waves . . .

He was in the Dark Current.

'Locaha!' he shouted.

Hello, Mau, said the voice of Locaha.

'I'm not dead! This is not fair!'

Fair? I'm not sure I know that word, Mau. Besides, you are nearly dead. Certainly more dead than alive, and dying a little more every moment.

Mau tried to go faster, but he was already running faster than he had ever run before.

'I'm not tired! I can keep going for ever! This is some kind of a trick, right? There must be rules, even to a trick!'

I agree, said Locaha. *And this* is *a trick.*

'This is safe, isn't it?' said Daphne. She was lying down on a mat by Mau, who still seemed as limp as a doll apart from the twitching legs. 'And it *will* work, won't it?' She tried to keep the wobble out of her voice, but it was one thing to be brave, and two things to be brave *and* determined when it was really only an idea at the moment – and definitely another matter entirely when you could see Mrs Gurgle out of the corner of your eye, busy at work.

'Yes,' said Cahle.

'You are sure, are you?' said Daphne. Oh, it sounded so *weedy*. She was ashamed of herself.

Cahle gave her a little smile and went over to Mrs Gurgle, who was squatting by the fire. Baskets of dried . . . *things* had been brought down from their hanging place in one of the huts, and Daphne knew the rule: the nastier and more dangerous, the higher. These had practically been on the roof.

When Cahle spoke to her, acting like a pupil talking to a respected teacher, the old woman stopped sniffing at a handful of what looked like dusty bean pods and looked across at Daphne. There was no smile or wave. This was

Mrs Gurgle at work. She said something out of the corner of her mouth and threw all the pods into the little three-legged cauldron in front of her.

Cahle came back. 'She says safe is not sure. Sure not safe. There is just do, or do not do.'

I was drowning, and he saved me, thought Daphne. Why did I ask that stupid question?

'Make it sure,' she said. 'Really sure.' On the other side of the room, Mrs Gurgle grinned. 'Can I ask another question? When I'm . . . you know, *there*, what should I do? Is there anything I should say?'

The reply came back: 'Do what is best. Say what is right.' And that was it. Mrs Gurgle did not go in for long explanations.

When the old woman hobbled across with half an oyster shell, Cahle said: 'You must lick up what is on the shell and lie back. When the drop of water hits your face you . . . will wake up.'

Mrs Gurgle gently put the shell in Daphne's hand and made a very short speech.

'She says you will come back because you have very good teeth,' Cahle volunteered.

Daphne looked at the half-shell. It was a dull white, and empty except for two little greeny-yellow blobs. It didn't seem much for all that effort. She held it close to her mouth and looked up at Cahle. The woman had put her hand in a gourd of water, and now she held it high over Daphne's mat. She looked down. With a drop of water glistening on the end of her finger.

'Now,' she said.

Daphne licked the shell (it tasted of nothing) and let herself fall back.

And then there was the moment of horror. Even as her head hit the mat, the drop of water was falling towards it.

She tried to shout, 'That's not enough ti—'

And then there was darkness, and the boom of the waves, overhead.

Mau ran onward, but the voice of Locaha still sounded very close.

Are you tiring, Mau? Do your legs ache for rest?

'No!' said Mau. 'But . . . these rules. What are they?'

Oh, Mau . . . I only agreed there must be rules. That doesn't mean I have to tell you what they are.

'But you must catch me, yes?'

You are correct in your surmise, said Locaha.

'What does that mean?'

You guessed right. Are you sure *you are not tiring?*

'Yes!'

In fact strength flowed into Mau's legs. He had never felt so alive. The pillars were going past faster now. He was overtaking the fish, which panicked away, leaving silvery trails. And there was light on the dark horizon. It looked like buildings, like white buildings as big as the ones Pilu had told him about in Port Mercia. What were buildings doing down here?

Something white flashed past under his feet. He glanced down, and almost stumbled. He was running over white blocks. They were blurred by his speed, and he didn't dare to slow down, but they looked exactly the right size to be god anchors.

This is wonderful, wonderful, said Locaha. *Mau, did you bother to wonder if you are running the wrong way?*

Two voices had said those words and now arms grabbed him.

'*This way!*' screamed Daphne, right in his ear as she tugged him back the way he had come. 'Why didn't you hear me?'

'But—' Mau began, straining to look back at the white buildings. There was something like a twist of smoke coming out of them . . . or perhaps it was a clump of weeds, flapping in the current . . . or a ray, skimming towards them.

'I said *this* way! Do you want to die for ever? Run! Run!'

But now, where was the speed in his legs? It *was* like running through water now, real water. He looked at Daphne, who was half towing him.

'How did you get here?'

'Apparently I'm dead – will you *try* to keep up! And whatever you do now, don't look back!'

'Why not?'

'Because I just did! Run faster!'

'Are you really dead?'

'Yes, but I'm due to get well soon. Come on, Mrs Gurgle! The drop was falling!'

Silence fell like a hammer made of feathers. It left holes in the shape of the sound of the sea.

They stopped running, not because they intended to, but because they had to. Mau's feet hung uselessly above the ground. The air turned grey.

'We are in the steps of Locaha,' he said. 'He has spread his wings over us.'

Words seized Daphne's tongue. It was only a few weeks since she'd heard them before, at the funeral of cabin-boy Scatterling, who had been killed in the mutiny. He'd had red hair and spots and she hadn't liked him much, but she'd cried when the sailcloth-wrapped body had disappeared under the waves. Captain Roberts was a member of the Conducive Brethren, who accepted a version of the Gospel of St Mary Magdalene as, well, gospel.[*] She'd never heard this piece read down at Holy Trinity, but she had tucked it into her memory and now it came out, screamed like a battle cry:

'And those that perish in the sea, the sea shall not hold them!
Tho' they be broken and scattered, they will be made whole!
They will rise again on that morning, clad in new raiment!
In ships of the firmament they will climb among stars!

'Mrs Gur—!'

---

[*] She was quite sure that there had been a female disciple because, as she explained to a surprised Captain Roberts, 'Our Lord is always shown wearing white, and someone must have seen to it that he always had a clean robe.

CHAPTER 9

ROLLING THE STONE

Water splashed on Daphne's face. She opened her eyes, and her mouth said: '—gle!'

Cahle and the old woman looked down on her, smiling. As she blinked in the light, she felt Mrs Gurgle gently pulling something out of her hair. But something else was happening. Memory was flowing out of her mind in a tide. The face of death . . . the great pillars of the world . . . the white slabs . . . they sped into the past like silver fish, fading as they went.

She turned to the mat beside her. Mau lay still, and snored.

No reason to get excited, she thought, feeling a little light-headed. He had been so cold, and she'd brought him up here to keep him warm. There had been . . . something that happened. The shape of it was still in her head, but she couldn't fill it in. Except . . . 'There was a silver fish?' she wondered aloud.

Mrs Gurgle looked very surprised, and said something to Cahle, who smiled and nodded.

'She says you are indeed a woman of power,' Cahle said. 'You pulled him out of a dark dream.'

'I did? I can't remember. But there was a fish in it.'

The hole in her memory was still there when Cahle had gone, and there was still a fish in it. Something big and important had happened and she had been there, and all she could remember was that there was a fish in it?

Mrs Gurgle had curled up in her corner, and it looked as if she was asleep. Daphne was certain that she wasn't. She'd be peeking through eyelids that were *almost* closed and listening so hard that her ears would try to flap. All the women took far too much interest in her and Mau. It was like the maids back home gossiping. It was silly and quite unnecessary, it really was!

Mau looked quite small on the mat. The twitching had stopped, but he had curled up in a ball. It was a shock, now, to see him so still.

'Ermintrude,' said her voice in the air.

'Yes,' she said, and added, 'You *are* me, aren't you?'

'When he is asleep, he still dreams of dark waters. Touch him. Hold him. Warm him. Let him know he is not alone.'

It sounded like her own voice, and it made her blush. She could feel the hot pinkness rising up her neck. 'That wouldn't be seemly,' she hissed, before she could stop herself. Then she wanted to shout: 'That wasn't me! That was some old woman's stupid granddaughter!'

'So who are you?' said the voice in the air. 'Some creature who knows how to feel but not how to touch? Here? In *this* place? Mau is alone. He thinks he has no soul, so he is building himself one. Help him. Save him. Tell him the stupid old men are wrong.'

'The stupid old—' Daphne began, and felt a memory uncoil. 'The Grandfathers?'

'Yes! Help him roll away the stone! He is a woman's child and he is crying!'

'Who are you?' she asked the air.

The voice came back like an echo: 'Who are *you?*' Then the voice went, leaving not even a shape in the silence.

I've got to think about this, Daphne thought. Or perhaps not. Not now, in this place, because maybe there's such a thing as too much thinking. Because however much of a Daphne you yearn to be, there is always your Ermintrude looking over your shoulder. Anyway, her thoughts added, Mrs Gurgle is here, so she counts as a chaperone, and a better one than poor Captain Roberts, since she's nothing like as dead.

She knelt down by Mau's mat. The voice had been right: there was a trickle of tears down his face, even though he seemed fast asleep. She kissed the tears because this felt like the right thing to do, and then tried to get an arm under him, which was really hard to manage and in any case her arm went to sleep and then got pins-and-needles, and she had to pull it out. So much for romance, she decided. She dragged her own mat over to his and lay down on it, which meant that an arm could go over him without too much difficulty but also that she had to rest rather awkwardly with her head on her other arm. But after a while his hand came up and grasped hers, gently, at which point, and despite the extreme discomfort, she fell asleep.

Mrs Gurgle waited until she was sure that Daphne was sleeping, and then uncurled her hand and looked at the little silver fish she had picked out of the girl's hair. It coiled backwards and forwards in her palm.

She swallowed it. It was only a dream fish, but such things are good for the soul.

Daphne woke up just as the first light of dawn was painting the sky pink. She was stiff in muscles she'd never known she possessed. How did married couples manage? It was a mystery.

Mau was snoring gently, and didn't stir at all.

How could you help a boy like that? He wanted to be everywhere and do everything. And so he'd probably try to do more than he should and end up in trouble again and she would have to sort it out again. She sighed a sigh that was older than she was. Her father had been the same, of course. He'd spend all night working on dispatch boxes for the Foreign Office, with a footman on duty at all times to bring him coffee and roast duck sandwiches. It was quite usual for the maids to find him still at his desk in the morning, fast asleep with his head on a map of Lower Sidonia.

Her grandmother used to make sniffy remarks like: 'I suppose His Majesty doesn't have *any* other ministers?' But now Daphne understood. He'd been like Mau, trying to fill the hole inside with work so that it didn't overflow with memories.

Right now she was glad she was alone. Apart from the snoring from Mau and Mrs Gurgle there was no sound but the wind and the boom of the waves on the reef. On the island, that was what counted as silence.

'Show us yer drawers!' floated in through the doorway.

Oh, yes, and the wretched parrot. It really was very annoying. You often didn't see it for days, because it had picked up a deep, cheerful hatred of the pantaloon birds and took a huge delight in annoying them at every opportunity. And then, just when you had a moment that was quiet and a bit, well, spiritual, it was suddenly all over the place shouting, 'Show us your . . . underthings!'

She sighed. Sometimes the world ought to be better organized. Then she listened for a while, and heard it fly off up the mountain.

Right, she thought, first things first. So, first, she went out to the fireplace, and set some salt-pickled beef to simmering in a pot. She added some roots that Cahle had said were OK, and one half of a very small red pepper. It had to be just one half because they were so hot a whole one burned her mouth, although Mrs Gurgle ate them raw.

Anyway, she owed the old woman a lot of chewed beef.

And now for the big test. Things shouldn't be allowed to just happen. If she was going to be a woman of power, she had to take charge. She couldn't always be the ghost girl, pushed around by events.

Right. Should she kneel? People didn't seem to kneel here, but she didn't want to be impolite, even if she was talking to herself.

Hands together. Eyes closed? It was so easy to get things wrong—

The message came right away.

'You did not put a spear into Twinkle's hand,' said her own voice in her own head, even before she'd had time to think how to begin. She thought: Oh dear, whoever it is, they know that I still think of him as Twinkle.

'Are you a heathen god of some sort?' she said. 'I've been thinking about this and, well, gods do talk to people, and I understand there are quite a lot of gods here. I just want to know if there is going to be any thunder and lightning, because I really don't like that. Or I've gone mad and I'm hearing voices. However, I have dismissed this hypothesis because I don't believe that people who have really gone mad think they have gone mad, so wondering if you *have* gone mad means that you haven't. I just want to know who I'm talking to, if you don't mind.'

She waited.

'Er, I apologize for calling you heathen,' she added.

There was still no reply. She didn't know whether to be relieved or not and decided instead to be a bit hurt.

She coughed. 'All right. Very well,' she said, standing up. 'At least I tried. I'm sorry to have trespassed on your time.' She turned to leave the hut.

'We would take the newborn child and make his little hand grasp a spear, so that he will grow up to be a great warrior and kill the children of other women,' said the voice. '*We* did it. The clan said so, the priests said so, the gods said so. And now you come, and what do you know of the custom?' the voice went on. 'And so the first thing the baby touches is the warmth of his mother, and you sing him a song about stars!'

Was she in trouble? 'Look, I'm really sorry about the twinkle song—' she began.

'It was a good song for a child,' said the voice. 'It began with a question.'

This was getting very strange. 'Have I done something wrong or not?'

'How is it that you hear us? We are blown about by the wind, and our voices are weak, but you, a trouserman, heard our struggling silence! How?'

Had she been listening? Daphne wondered. Perhaps she'd never stopped after all those days in the church after her mother died, saying every prayer she knew, waiting for even a whisper in reply. She hadn't been looking for an apology. She wasn't asking for time to run backwards. She just wanted an explanation that was better than 'It's the will of God', which was grown-up speak for 'because'.

It had seemed to her, thinking about it in her chilly bedroom, that what had happened was very much like a miracle. After all, it had been a terrible storm, and if the doctor had managed to get there *without* his horse being struck by lightning, that would have been a miracle, wouldn't it? That's what people would have said. Well, in that big, dark, rainy, roaring night, the lightning had managed to hit quite a small horse among all those big thrashing trees. Didn't that look like a miracle, too? It was almost exactly the same shape, wasn't it? In any case, besides, didn't they call something like this an 'act of God'?

She'd been very polite when she put the question to the archbishop, and in her opinion it had been really unreasonable for her grandmother to scream like a baboon and drag her out of the cathedral by her ear.

But she had kept looking out for a voice, a whisper, a word that would let it all make sense. She just wanted it all . . . sorted out.

She looked up into the gloomy roof of the hut.

'I heard you because I was listening,' she said.

'Then listen to us, girl who can hear those who have no voices.'

'And you are—?'

'We are the Grandmothers.'

'I've never heard of the Grandmothers!'

'Where do you think little grandfathers come from? Every man has a mother, and so does every mother. We gave birth to little grandfathers, and filled them with milk, and wiped their bottoms and kissed their tears away. We taught them to eat, and showed them what food was safe, so that they grew up straight. We taught them the songs of children, which have lessons in them. And then we gave them to the grandfathers, who taught them how to kill other women's sons. The ones who were best at this were dried in the sand and taken to the cave. We went back to the dark water, but part of us remains, here in this place where we were born and gave birth and, often, died.'

'The Grandfathers shout at Mau all the time!'

'They are echoes in a cave. They remember the battle cries of their youth, over and over again, like the talking bird. They are not bad men. We loved them, as sons and husbands and fathers, but old men get confused and dead men don't notice the turning of the world. The world must turn. Tell Mau he must roll away the stone.'

And they left. She felt them slide out of her mind.

That, thought Daphne, was impossible. Then she thought: Up until now, anyway. They were *real*, and they're still here. They're what I felt when Twinkle was being born, as if the Place was alive and on my side. Perhaps some voices are so old *everyone* understands them.

The light came back slowly, grey at first like the dawn. Daphne heard a faint noise close at hand, looked round and saw a young girl standing in the hut doorway, staring at her in horror. She couldn't remember the girl's name, because she had only been here a few days, and was about to tell her off when she did remember that although the girl had arrived with some other survivors, none of them had been her relatives. And she'd been about to shout at her.

Moving very carefully, she crouched down and held out her arms. The child looked as though she was one heartbeat away from fleeing.

'What is your name?'

The girl looked down at her feet and whispered something that sounded like 'Blibi'.

'That's a *nice* name,' said Daphne, and gently drew the child to her. As the sobs began to shake the little body she made a note to tell Cahle. People were turning up every day now, and people who needed looking after were looking after others. That wasn't such a bad thing, but while everyone got food to eat and a place to sleep, there were other things that were just as important that tended to get overlooked when everyone was busy.

'Do you know about cooking, Blibi?' she asked. There was a kind of muffled nod. 'Good! And do you see that man lying on the mat?' Another nod. 'Good. Good. I want you to watch over him. He has been ill. The meat in the pot will be ready when the sun has moved a hand-width above the trees. I'm going to look at a stone. Tell him he must eat. Oh, and you must eat, too.'

Where will I end up? she wondered as she hurried out of the Place. I've slept in the same room as a young man without an official chaperone (would Mrs Gurgle count?), made beer, have been going around practically *naked*, and let gods talk with my mouth, like the Pelvic Oracle in Greece in ancient times, although the voices of the Grandmothers probably didn't count as gods and, come to think of it, it was the Delphic Oracle, anyway. And technically I was nursing him, so that was probably permissible . . .

She stopped, and looked around. Who cared? Who, on

this island, cared a fig? So who was she apologizing to? Why was she making excuses?

'Roll away the stone?' Why did everyone want him to *do* things? She'd heard about the stone. It was in a little valley in the side of the mountain, where women weren't supposed to go.

There was no reason to go now, but she was angry at everyone and she just wanted to get out in the fresh air and do something people didn't want her to. There were skeletons, probably, behind the stone, but so what? A lot of *her* ancestors were in the crypt of the church at home, and they never tried to get out and they never spoke to people. Her grandmother would have had something to say about it if they did! Besides, it was broad daylight, and obviously they'd only come out at night – except, of course, it would be pure superstition to believe that they came out at all.

She set out. There was a clear track leading uphill. The forest wasn't very big, she'd heard, and the track ran right through it. There were no man-eating tigers, no giant gorillas, no ferocious lizards from ancient times . . . in fact it wasn't very interesting at all. But the thing about a forest that's only a few square miles in area is that when it's scrunched up into little criss-crossing valleys and every growing thing is fighting every other living thing for every ragged patch of sunlight, and you cannot see more than a few feet in any direction, and you can't judge where you are by the sound of the sea because the sound of the sea is very faint and in any case all around you, then the forest seems not only very big but also appears to be growing all the time. That's when you began to believe it hated you as much as you hated it.

Following the track was no use, because it soon became a hundred tracks, splitting and rejoining all the time. Things rustled in the undergrowth, and sometimes creatures that sounded a lot bigger than pigs galloped away on paths she could not see. Insects went *zing* and *zip* all around her, but they weren't as bad as the huge spiders that had woven their webs right across the paths and then hung in them, bigger than a hand and almost spitting with rage. Daphne had read in one of her books about the Great Southern Pelagic Ocean islands that 'with a few regrettable examples, the larger and more fearsome the spider is, the less likely it is to be venomous'. She didn't believe it. She could see Regrettable Examples everywhere, and she was sure that some of them were drooling.

– and suddenly there was clear daylight ahead. She would have run towards it, but there was – good fortune not apparent at the time – a Regrettable Example using its web as a trampoline and she had to ease her way past it with caution. This was just as well, because while the end of the path offered vast amounts of fresh air, there was a total insufficiency of anything to stand on. There was a little clearing, big enough for a couple of people to sit and watch the world, and then a drop all the way to the sea. It wasn't a totally sheer drop; you'd bounce off rocks several times before you ever hit the water.

She took the opportunity to take a few breaths that

didn't have flies in them. It would have been nice to see a sail on the horizon. In fact it would be narratively satisfying, she considered. But at least she could see that the day was getting on. She wasn't scared of other people's ghosts, much, but she did not fancy an evening walk through this forest.

And getting back shouldn't be too hard, should it? All she had to do was take a downward path every time she found one. Admittedly taking the upward path at every opportunity, or at least every up path not blocked by a particularly evil-looking Regrettable Example, had completely failed to work, but logic had to triumph in the end.

In a way, it did. After a change of path she stepped out into a small valley, held in the arms of the mountain, and there, ahead of her, was the stone. It couldn't be anything else.

There were trees here and there in the valley, but they were sorry-looking things, and half dead. The ground beneath them was covered with bird doo-dahs.

A little way in front of the stone a large bowl, also of some kind of stone, sat on a tripod made of three big rocks. She peered into it, with a kind of shameful curiosity because, to make no bones about it, it was, in this place, just the kind of big stone bowl that you'd expect to have a few skulls in it. There was something in the brain that said: Sinister-looking valley + half-dead trees + ominous doorway = skulls in a bowl, or possibly on a stick. But even by listening to it, she felt she was being unfair to Mau and Cahle and the rest of them. Human skulls never came up in day-to-day conversation. More importantly, they never came up at lunch.

The sickly smell of sour, sticky Demon Drink rose from the bowl. It was stale, but couldn't have been very good to start with. It was a terrible thing to admit, but she was getting really good at making beer. Everyone said so. It was just some kind of a knack, Cahle had said, or at least had partly said and partly gestured, and that being able to make beer so well meant she would be able to get a very fine husband. Her getting married still seemed to be the big topic of discussion in the Place. It was like being in a Jane Austen novel, but one with far less clothing.

It was windy up here, and colder than it was down below. It wasn't a place where you'd want to be at night.

Oh, well, time to say what she had to say.

She marched up to the stone, stuck her fists on her hips, and said: 'Now listen to me, you! I know about ancestors! I've got lots of ancestors! One of them was a king, and that's about as ancestral as you can be! I'm here about Mau! He tries to do everything, and you just bully him all the time! He's doing wonderful things, and he's nearly killed himself and you never even thank him! Is that any way to behave?'

Well, it's how *your* ancestors behave, said her conscience. What about the way their pictures all stare at you in the Long Gallery? What about the way your father keeps spending all that money on the Hall just because his great-great-great-great-grandfather built it? *Yes, what about your father?*

'I know what happens to people who get bullied,' she shouted, even louder this time. 'They end up thinking they really are no good! It doesn't matter that they work so hard they fall asleep at their desks, it's still never enough! They get timid and jumpy and make wrong decisions, and that means more bullying because, you see, the bully is never going to stop, whatever they do, and my— the person being bullied will do anything make it stop, but it never will! I'm not going to put up with that, do you understand? If you don't mend your ways in very short order, there will be trouble, understand?'

I'm shouting at a rock, she thought as her voice echoed off the mountain. What am I expecting it to do? Reply?

'Is there anyone *listening*?' she yelled, and thought: What do I do if someone says 'yes'? For that matter, what do I do if they say 'no'?

Nothing happened, in quite an offensive way, considering she'd taken a lot of trouble to get up here.

I've just been snubbed by a cave full of dead old men.

Someone was standing behind her. Someone she hadn't heard coming. But she was angry at all sorts of things and right now was mostly angry at herself for shouting at a rock, and whatever it was behind her, it was going to get the sharp end of her tongue.

'One of my ancestors fought in the Wars of the Roses,' she announced haughtily, without looking round, 'and in those wars you were supposed to wear a red rose or a white rose to show whose side you were on, but he was very attached to a pink rose called Lady Lavinia, which we still grow at the Hall, actually, so he ended up fighting both sides at once. He lived, too, because everyone thought it was bad luck to kill a madman. That's what you need to know about my family: we might be pig-headed and stupid, but we *do* fight.' She spun round. 'Don't you dare creep up on— Oh.'

Something went *pnap*. It was a pantaloon bird staring up at her with an affronted expression on its beak. That wasn't the most noticeable thing about it, however, which was that it was not alone. There were at least fifty of the birds, with more flying in. Now there was sound, because the big birds had the aerodynamics of a brick in any case, and in aiming to land near Daphne they were now put off their concentration and mostly crashed on other pantaloon birds, in clouds of feathers and angry beak-snapping: *Pnap! Pnap!*

It was a bit like being in a snowfall. It's all fun and games at the start, a winter wonderland, and you think because it's soft it's harmless. And then you realize you can't see the path any more and it's getting dark and the snow is blotting out the sky—

A big bird, out of sheer luck, landed on her head, scrabbling for a foothold in her hair with claws like old men's hands. She screamed at it, and managed to force it off. But they were still piling up around her, pushing and *pnapping* at one another. She could hardly think, in the storm of noise and stink and feathers, but it seemed they weren't actually attacking her. They just wanted to be where she was, wherever that was.

Oh yes, the stink. Nothing stank like a lot of pantaloon birds up close. On top of the ordinary dry, bony bird smell, they had the worst breath of any living creature. She could feel it hitting her skin like scrubbing brushes. And all the time they *pnapped*, each trying to out-*pnap* all the others, so that she nearly didn't hear the cry of rescue.

'Show us yer drawers! Once I was an awful drinker, now I am a dreadful stinker!'

The birds panicked. They hated the parrot as much as it hated them. And when a pantaloon bird wants to get away fast, it makes sure it leaves behind anything not wanted on the journey.

Daphne crouched down and put her hands over her head as a rain of bones and lumps of fish pattered down. Perhaps the noise was the worst part, but when you got down to it, it was *all* worst.

A golden-brown shape leaped past her, with a coconut in each hand. It kicked and staggered its way through the panicking birds until it reached the big stone bowl, which was full of pantaloon birds like flowers in a vase. It raised shells high in the air over the bowl, and in one sharp movement smashed them together.

Beer poured out, filling the air with its scent. Instantly the birds' beaks swung towards the bowl, seeking the beer like a compass needle seeks north. Daphne was immediately forgotten.

'I wish I was dead,' she said to the world in general, pulling bones out of her hair. 'No, I wish I was in a nice warm bath, with proper soap and towels. And after that I wish I was in *another* bath, because, believe me, this is a two-bath head. And then I wish I was dead. I think this is the worst thing' – she paused, because, yes, there had been something worse, and always would be, and went on – 'the second worst thing that has ever happened to me.'

Mau crouched down beside her. 'Men's Place,' he said, grinning.

'Yes, it looks like one,' snapped Daphne. She stared at Mau. 'How are you?'

Mau's brow wrinkled, and she knew that one wasn't going to work. They had got a language working pretty well now, thanks to Pilu and Cahle, but it was for simple everyday things and 'How are you?' was too complicated because it didn't really ask the question you thought it asked. She could see Mau working it out.

'Er, I am because one day my mother and my father—' he began, but she had been halfway ready for this.

'I mean *here!*' she said loudly. There were several soft thumps while he thought about this. The pantaloon birds were falling over, like an elderly lady who has had too much sherry on Christmas Day. Daphne wondered if they were poisoned by the beer, because none of them had sung a song, but she didn't think so. She had seen one eat a whole dead crab that had been lying in the sun for days. Besides, as they lay there, their beaks trembled and they made happy little *pnap-pnap* noises. As they fell over, thirsty ones took their place.

'The little girl told me you had said something about a stone,' said Mau. 'And then I had to have a bowl of beef.

She insisted. And then I came as fast as I could, but she can't run very fast.' He pointed. Blibi was walking up the valley, treading carefully in order to avoid snoring birds. 'She said you told her she has to watch over me.'

They sat and waited, avoiding each other's gaze. Then Mau said: 'Er, the way it works is that the birds drink the beer, but the *spirit* of the beer flies to the Grandfathers. That's what the priests used to say.'

Daphne nodded. 'We have bread and wine at home,' she said, and thought, Oops, I won't try to explain that one. They have *cannibals* down here. It could get . . . confusing.

'I don't think it's true though,' said Mau.

Daphne nodded, and then thought a bit more. 'Perhaps things can be true in special ways?' she suggested.

'No. People say that when they want to believe lies,' Mau said flatly. 'And they usually do.'

There was another pause, which was filled by the parrot. With its mortal enemies paralysed by the Demon Drink it had swooped down and was industriously pulling their pants off them, which meant very neatly and carefully plucking out every white feather on their legs while making happy but fortunately muffled parrot noises.

'They look very . . . pink,' said Daphne, glad of something innocent, more or less, to talk about.

'Do you remember . . . running?' said Mau, after a while.

'Yes. Sort of. I remember the fish.'

'Silver fish? Long and thin?'

'Like eels, yes!' said Daphne. Feathers were drifting across the valley in clumps.

'So it did happen, did it?'

'I suppose so.'

'I mean, was it a dream or was it real?'

'Mrs Gurgle says yes,' said Daphne.

'Who is Mrs . . . Gurgle, please?'

'The very old woman,' Daphne explained.

'You mean Mar-isgala-egisaga-gol?'

'Probably.'

'And she says yes to what?'

'Your question. I think she means it wasn't the right one. Look, does Locaha talk to you?'

'Yes!'

'Really?'

'Yes!

'In your head? Like your dreams?'

'Yes, but I know the difference!' said Mau.

'That's good, because the Grandmothers have been talking to me.'

'Who are the Grandmothers?'

Blibi, if that was really her name, had caught up with them long before Daphne had finished talking and Mau had finished understanding. She sat at their feet, playing with pantaloon bird feathers.

Mau picked up a feather and twiddled it in his fingers. 'They don't like warriors, then.'

'They don't like people being killed. Nor do you.'

'Have you heard of the Raiders?' asked Mau, brushing a feather off his face.

'Of course. Everyone's talking about them. They have great war galleys, and they hang the skulls of their enemies along the sides of them. Oh, and enemy means everyone else.'

'We have perhaps thirty people here, now. Some more arrived this morning, but most of them can hardly stand. They survived the wave, but they weren't going to wait for the Raiders to come.'

'Well, you've got enough canoes. Can't we just head east?' She said that without thinking, and then sighed. 'We can't, can we?'

'No. If we had more able-bodied people, and time to get provisions together, then we could try it. But it's eight hundred miles of open ocean.'

'The weaker people would die. They came here to be safe!'

'They call this island "the place where the sun is born" because it's in the east. They look to us.'

'Then we could hide until the Raiders go away. Roll away the stone, the Grandmothers said.'

Mau stared at her. 'And hide among the dead men? Do *you* think we should?'

'No! We should fight!' She was amazed at how fast the words came out. They had been pushed out by her ancestors, all those calm stone knights down in the crypt. They'd never ever *thought* about hiding, even when it was the sensible thing to do.

'Then I will think of a way,' said Mau.

'What do the Grandfathers say?'

'I don't hear them any more. I just hear . . . clicks, and insect noises.'

'Perhaps the Grandmothers have told them off,' said Daphne, giggling. 'My grandmother was always telling my grandfather off. He knew everything there is to know about the fifteenth century but he was always coming down to breakfast without his teeth in.'

'They fell out in the night?' said Mau, puzzled.

'No. He used to take them out to clean them. They were new teeth made out of animal bone.'

'You trousermen can give an old man new teeth? What will you tell me next? That you can give him new eyes?'

'Um . . . yes, actually something very much like that.'

'Why are you so much *smarter* than us?'

'I don't think we are, really. I think it's just that you have to learn to make things when it's cold for half the year. I think we got our Empire because of the weather. Anything was better than staying at home in the rain. I'm pretty certain people looked out of the window and rushed off to discover India and Africa.'

'Are they big places?'

'Huge,' said Daphne.

Mau sighed, and said, 'With the people who leave stones.'

'Who?'

'The god anchors,' said Mau. 'I understand Ataba now. I don't think he believes in his gods, but he believes in belief. And he also thinks trousermen came here a long time ago,' he added, shaking his head. 'Maybe they brought the stones as ballast. It must have happened like that. Look at all the stone Judy the Sweet brought. Worthless rock to you, all kinds of tools to us. And maybe they gave us metal and tools, like giving toys to children, and we carved the stones because we wanted them to come back. Isn't that how it would go? We are a little island. Tiny.'

The Phoenicians, thought Daphne glumly. They went on long, long voyages. So did the Chinese. What about the Aztecs? Even the Egyptians? Some people say they visited Further Australia. And who knows who might have been around thousands of years ago? He's probably right. But he looks so sad.

'Well, you might be a small island,' she said, 'but you are an old one. The Grandmothers must have some reason for telling you to roll away the big stone.'

They looked at the stone which glowed a golden yellow in the afternoon light.

'You know, I can't remember a longer day than this,' said Daphne.

'I can,' said Mau.

'Yes. That was a long day, too.'

'It takes ten strong men to move that stone,' said Mau after a while. 'We don't have that many.'

'I've been thinking about that,' said Daphne. 'How many would it take if one of them was Milo, and he had a crowbar made of steel?'

* * *

It took time. There was a groove in the rock that had to be scraped out, and tree trunks to be dragged into position to stop the door falling outwards as it moved. The sun was starting to fall down the sky by the time Milo stepped up to the stone with a six-foot bar of steel in his hand.

Mau looked at it glumly. It was useful and he was glad to have it, but it was a trouserman thing, another present from the *Sweet Judy*. They were still stripping her like termites.

Even canoes had a soul, of a kind. Everyone knew that; sometimes it wasn't a good soul, and the craft was hard to handle, even though it seemed to be well built. If you were lucky you got a good soul, like the one he'd built on the Boys' Island, which always seemed to know what he wanted. The *Sweet Judy* had a good soul, he could tell. It was a shame to break her up, and another kind of shame to know that, once again, they had to rely on the trousermen to get things done. He was almost ashamed of carrying one of the smaller crowbars himself, but they were so *useful*. Who but the trousermen had so much metal that they could afford to make sticks out of it. But the bars were wonderful. They opened anything.

'There may be a curse on the door,' said Ataba, behind Mau.

'Can you tell if there is?'

'No! But this is wrong.'

'These are my ancestors. I seek their guidance. Why should they curse me? Why should I fear their old bones? Why are you afraid?'

'What is in the dark should be left alone.' The priest sighed. 'But no one listens to me now. The coral is full of white stones, people say, so which ones are holy?'

'Well, which?'

'The three old ones, of course.'

'You could test them,' said Daphne, without thinking. 'People could leave a fish on a new stone and see how their fortune changes. Hmm, I'd need to work out a scientific way—' She stopped, aware that everyone was watching her. 'Well, it would be interesting,' she finished lamely.

'I did not understand any of that,' said Ataba, looking coldly at her.

'I did.'

Mau craned to see who had spoken and saw the tall skinny figure of Tom-ali, a canoe builder who had arrived with two children who were not his, one boy and one girl.

'Speak, Mr Tom-ali,' he said.

'I would like to ask the gods why my wife and son died and I did not.' There was some murmuring from the crowd.

Mau already knew him. He knew all the newcomers. They walked the same way, slowly. Some just sat and watched the sea. And there was a greyness about them all. Why am I here? their faces said. Why me? Was I a bad person?

Tom-ali was repairing the canoes now, with the boy helping him, while the girl helped out in the Place. Some of the children were coping better than the adults; after the wave, you just found a place that fitted. But Tom-ali had said what a lot of people didn't want to hear said, and the best thing to do was to give them something else to think about, right now.

'We all want answers today,' Mau said. 'Please, all of you, help me move the stone. No one else has to set foot inside. I will go in by myself. Perhaps I'll find the truth.'

'No,' said Ataba firmly, 'let *us* go in there *together* and find the truth.'

'Fine,' said Mau. 'That way we can find twice as much.'

Ataba stood next to Mau as the men took up their positions. 'You say you are not frightened. Well, *I* am frightened, young man, to my very toes.'

'The truth will be the dead men in there, that's all,' said Mau. 'Dried up. Dust. If you want to be frightened, think about the Raiders.'

'Do not dismiss the past so lightly, demon boy. It may still teach you something.'

Milo forced the bar between the rock and the stone, and heaved. The stone creaked, and moved an inch.

They did it carefully and slowly, because it would certainly crush anybody it fell on. But cleaning out the groove had been a good idea. It ran smoothly, until half of the cave entrance could be seen.

Mau looked inside. There was nothing there. He'd imagined all kinds of things, but not *nothing*. The floor was quite smooth. There was a bit of dust on the floor, and a few beetles scuttled off into the dark, and that was all the cave held. Except depth.

Why had he expected bones to fall out when the door

was opened? Why should it be full up? He picked up a piece of rock and threw it into the darkness as hard as he could. It seemed to bounce and rattle for a long time.

'All right,' he said, and the cave threw his voice back at him. 'We're going to need those lamps, Daphne.'

She stood up, with one of the *Sweet Judy*'s lamps in each hand. 'One red one and one green one,' she said. 'The spare port and starboard lights. Sorry about that but we haven't got very many cabin lamps left, and we're short of oil.'

'What about that white lamp next to you?' said Mau.

'Yes, that's the one I'm going to bring,' said the ghost girl, 'and to save time, shall we pretend we've had the argument and I won?'

More trouserman things, Mau thought as he picked up his lamp. I wonder what we used to use? The low ceiling told him when he touched it. His fingers came away covered in soot.

Torches, then. You could make decent ones out of hog fat. If there was enough of the stuff to spare, they were good for night fishing, because the fish would rise to the light. We've been living off fish and the *Sweet Judy*'s salt-pickled beef, because that's easy, he thought, so now we'll have to find our dead by trouserman lamplight.

CHAPTER 10

BELIEVING IS SEEING

*T*he cave was waiting. It might contain anything, Mau thought. And that was the point, wasn't it? You had to find out. You had to *know*. And Daphne didn't seem concerned. Mau told her that there would probably be bones, and she said that was fine, because bones didn't try to kill you, and that since she had got the message from the Grandmothers she was going to see it through, thank you so very much.

They found the Grandfathers right at the point where you could just see the waning daylight, and Mau began to understand. They weren't scary, they were just . . . sad. Some of them still sat as they had been put, with their knees up under their chin, staring towards the distant light with flat dead eyes. They were just husks and crumbled bones. If you looked carefully, you could see that they had been held together with papervine. It really did have many uses, even after death.

They stopped when the daylight was a little dot at the end of the tunnel.

'How many more can there be?' Ataba wondered.

'I'm counting,' said Mau. 'There's more than a hundred of them so far.'

'One hundred and two,' said Daphne. There seemed to be no end to them, sitting one behind the other like the world's oldest rowing crew, sculling into eternity. Some of them still had their spear or club, tied to their arms.

They went on, and the light vanished. The dead passed in their hundreds and she lost count. She kept reminding herself how scared she wasn't. After all, hadn't she quite enjoyed that lecture on anatomy she had attended? Even though she had kept her eyes shut throughout?

However, if you were going to look at hundreds and thousands of dead men, it didn't help to see the light from Ataba's lamp flicker over them. It seemed to make them move. And they had been men of the islands; she could see, on ancient, leathery skin, blurred tattoos, like the ones every man – well, every man except Mau – wore even now. A wave, curling across the face of the setting sun . . .

'How long have you been putting people in here?' she asked.

'For ever,' said Mau, running on ahead. 'And they came from the other islands, too!'

'Are you tired, sir?' said Daphne to Ataba, when they were left alone.

'Not at all, girl.'

'Your breathing does not sound good.'

'That is my affair. It is not yours.'

'I was just . . . concerned, that's all.'

'I would be obliged if you would stop being concerned,' Ataba snapped. 'I know what is happening. It starts with knives and cooking pots, and suddenly we belong to the trousermen, yes, and you send priests and our souls do not belong to us.'

'I'm not doing anything like that!'

'And when your father comes in his big boat? What will happen to us then?'

'I . . . don't know,' said Daphne, which was better than telling the truth. We do tend to stick flags in places, she had to admit it herself. We do it almost absent-mindedly, as though it's a sort of chore.

'Hah, you fall silent,' said the priest. 'You are a good child, the women say, and you do good things, but the difference between the trousermen and the Raiders is that sooner or later the cannibals go away!'

'That's a terrible thing to say!' said Daphne hotly. 'We don't eat people!'

'There are different ways to eat people, girl, and you are clever, oh yes, clever enough to know it. And sometimes the people don't realize it's happened until they hear the belch!'

'Come quickly!' That was Mau, whose lamp was a faint green glow in the distance.

Daphne ran, to stop Ataba seeing her face. Her father, well, he was a decent man but, well, this century was a game of empires, apparently, and no little island was allowed to belong to itself. What would Mau do if someone stuck a flag on his beach?

There he was now, looking green, and pointing to the line of Grandfathers.

As she got closer she saw the white stone on the edge of the passage. There was a Grandfather sitting on it like a chieftain, but with his hands clasped around his knees like the rest. And he was facing down the corridor, away from the cave mouth, towards the unknown.

In front of him the line of dead warriors continued, all now turned to face . . . what? The light of day was behind them now.

Mau was waiting, a glint in his eye, when Ataba hobbled up. 'Do you know why they are facing the wrong way, Ataba?' he asked.

'They look as though they are protecting us from something,' said the priest.

'Down here? From what? There's nothing down here but darkness.'

'And something best forgotten, perhaps? Do you think the wave never happened before? And the last time it never went away. It was a wave that never ebbed. It ended the world.'

'That's just a story. I remember my mother telling it to me,' said Mau. 'Everyone knows it: "In the Time When Things Were Otherwise and the Moon Was Different . . . Men were becoming troublesome and so He swept them away with a great wave." '

'Was there an ark? I mean, er, some sort of big boat?' said Daphne. 'I mean, how did anyone survive?'

'There were people on the sea and high ground,' said Mau. 'That's the story, isn't it, Ataba?'

'What had they done that was so bad?' Daphne asked.

Ataba cleared his throat. 'It is said they tried to make themselves into gods,' he said.

'That's right,' Mau went on. 'I wonder if you can tell me what we did wrong this time?'

Ataba hesitated.

Mau did not, and he spoke sharp and fast, like a spring unwinding: 'I am talking about my father, my mother, my whole family, my whole *nation*! They all *died*! I had a sister who was seven years old. Just give me the reason. There must have been a reason! Why did the gods let them die? I found a little baby stuck in a tree. How had it offended the gods?'

'We are small. We cannot understand the nature of the gods,' said Ataba.

'No! You don't believe that, I can hear it in your voice! I don't understand the nature of a bird, but I can watch it and listen to it and learn about it. Don't you do this with the gods? Where are the rules? What did we do wrong? Tell me!'

'*I don't know!* Don't you think I haven't asked them?' Tears started to roll down Ataba's cheeks. 'You think I am a man alone? I haven't seen my daughter or her children since the wave. Do you hear what I say? It is not all about you! I envy your rage, demon boy. It fills you up! It feeds you, gives you strength. But the rest of us listen for the certainty, and there is nothing. Yet in our heads we know there must be . . . something, some reason, some pattern, some order, so we call upon the silent gods, because they are better than the darkness. That is it, boy. I have no answers for you.'

'Then I'll look for them in the darkness,' said Mau, holding up the lantern. 'Come further with us,' he said, in a quieter voice.

The light glistened off the tears streaming down the priest's face. 'No,' he said hoarsely.

'We'll have to leave you here,' said Mau. 'Among the dead men, which I think is no place for you. Or you can come with us. At least you'll have a demon and a ghost on your side. We may need your wisdom, too.'

To Daphne's surprise, the old man smiled. 'You think I have some left?'

'Certainly. Shall we continue? What can you find that is worse than me?'

'I'd like to ask a question,' said Daphne quickly. 'How often is a new grandfather put in here, please?'

'Once or twice in fifty years,' said Ataba.

'There are *thousands* here. Are you sure?'

'This place has been here since the world was made, and so have we,' said Mau.

'On that, at least, we are in full agreement,' said Ataba stoutly.

'But that's a very long time ago!'

'And that is why there are so many Grandfathers!' said Mau. 'It's very simple.'

'Yes,' said Daphne, 'when you put it like that, I suppose it is.' They set off, and then she said: 'What was that noise?'

They stopped, and this time they all heard the faint crackling and rustling from behind them.

'Are the dead rising?' said Ataba.

'You know, I really hoped nobody was going to suggest that,' said Daphne.

Mau walked a few steps back along the cave, which was full of tiny crackling sounds. The dead don't walk, he thought. That's one of the ways you know they are dead. So what I'm doing is standing here, a long way from the sky, and I have to work out what they *are* doing. So what is the reason? And where have I heard this noise before?

He walked a little way further up the tunnel, where there was no noise at all, and waited. After a while, the crackling started again, and he thought of sunshine on hot days. It was crackling where he had left the others, too. 'Let's keep going,' he said, 'and it will stop, provided we keep moving.'

'They won't wake up?' said Ataba.

'It's the papervine bindings on the Grandfathers,' Mau said. 'Even when it's bone dry it crackles and pops when it's warmed up. The heat of the lamps and our bodies sets it off if we stay in one place too long. That's all it is.'

'Well, it was frightening *me*,' said Daphne. 'Well done. Deductive reasoning based on observation and experiment.'

Mau ignored that, because he didn't have the faintest

idea what it meant. But he felt pleased. The Grandfathers didn't wake up. The noise he had heard as a boy was just papervine getting hotter or colder. That was true, and he could prove it. It wasn't hard to work out, so why is it all I can do not to wet myself? Because papervine moving doesn't sound interesting and walking skeletons do, that's why. Somehow, they make us feel more important. Even our fears make us feel important, because we fear that we might not be.

He watched Ataba move close to a Grandfather, and step back hurriedly when it began to creak.

My body is a coward but *I* am not fearful. I will fear nothing, ever, he thought. Not now.

There was a glow ahead. It appeared suddenly as they walked round a long curve – red, yellow and green, flickering as they got closer. Ataba groaned and stopped walking, and because he did that, Mau knew *he* couldn't. He looked down the slope ahead.

'Stay and look after the old man,' he said to the ghost girl. 'I don't want him to run away.'

I will not fear my bladder that wants to explode, he told himself as he sped down past the silent sentries, or my feet that want to turn and flee, and I will not fear the pictures that are running, screaming, through my head. He ran on, the light racing ahead of him, repeating the vow until, like Captain Roberts, he found it necessary to change the words in a hurry. I will not fear the shadow that is walking out of the pretty light, because I have found my fear down here in the dark, and I shall reach out and touch him as he reaches out to touch me . . .

His fingers met his reflection and touched smooth golden metal, in a slab about the size of a man.

Mau put his ear to it, but there was no sound. When he pushed it, it didn't move.

'I want you to stay up where you are,' he told the others when they caught him up. 'Both of you. We've come down a long way. There may be water on the other side of this.'

He prodded at the metal with his crowbar. It was very soft, and also very thick, but the stone around it was the ordinary island stone, and that seemed a better bet. It soon started to flake away under some blows from the pointed end of the bar, and after some work there was a hiss and the smell of wet salt. So the sea *was* somewhere near, but at least they were above it.

He called the others down, and hacked at the stone again, amazed at how easily he could crack it with the metal bar, opening up a gap into blackness. It was damp; he could hear a soft lapping of water in the dark. By the light of the lamp he could just make out some white steps, leading down.

So that was it? All this way for some sea cave? There were a lot of them at the bottom of the cliffs on the western side of the island. Kids had explored them since time began, and had never found anything to get excited about.

But the lamplight glinted on something in the dark.

'I'm going to come in with you,' said Daphne behind him.

'No. Stay here. It might be dangerous.'

'Yes, and that's why I ought to go in with you.'

'It's been shut up since for ever! What's going to hurt me?'

'What? *You* were the one who said it might be dangerous!' Daphne said.

'I will enter first,' said Ataba, behind her. 'If Locaha is in there, I will take his hand.'

'I'm not going to wait out here with all these dead men crackling at me!' Daphne protested. 'Yes, I know it's just the vines but *it really doesn't help*.'

The three of them looked at one another in the lamplight and then, as one, tried to get through the narrow gap into a space full of bad air. It tasted rotten, if air could rot.

The steps beyond were god stones, every one. They had carvings on them, just like the ones on the beach, but many of the carvings went across several stones. Here and there, stones were cracked or missing.

Lumps of stone, thought Mau. Why did we think they were worthy things to worship? He held the lamp higher and saw the reason.

Ahead of him, knee-deep in the water, gigantic and gleaming white and sparkling all over, were the gods – the huge-stomached Air with his four sons on his shoulders, the brilliant Water, the ferocious Fire, with his hands bound to his side just as the story said. Air and Water each held a big stone globe in their hands, but Fire's globe was balanced on his head and had a red glitter to it. There was a fourth statue, pale and smashed, with no head and one arm fallen down into the water. For a moment Mau thought: That's Imo. Broken. Would I dare to find His face?

Ataba screamed (and outside in the tunnel a dead man moved slightly). 'Do you see them? Do you *see* them?' the priest managed, in between great gasps of sour air. 'Behold the gods, demon boy!' He bent double with a fit of coughing. It definitely was *not* good air; you sucked it down, but there was no life in it.

'Yes, I see them,' said Mau. 'Gods of stone, Ataba.'

'Why should they be of flesh? And what stone shines like that? I am right, demon boy, in my faith I am right! You can't deny it!'

'I can't deny what I see, but I can question what it is,' said Mau as the old man wheezed again.

Mau looked across the darkness, to the glow of light that was Daphne's lantern.

'Let's get back right now!' he shouted. 'Come on! Even the flames are choking!'

'Those are just statues!' Daphne called back. 'But this . . . this is *amazing*!'

There was the grinding noise of stone moving from somewhere near her.

Ataba was wheezing horribly. It sounded as though every breath was being sawn out of a tree.

Mau looked at the flickering flame of his lantern, and yelled, 'We must get back!'

'And there's a skeleton here!' Daphne called out. 'And he's got— I don't believe this. Oh, you must see this! You must see what he's got in his mouth!'

'Do you want to run back up the tunnel in the dark?' he shouted back as loudly as he could (and outside in the corridor, a Grandfather shifted).

That seemed to do it. He saw her lamp begin to move towards the door. She was panting when she reached him, and the light was a dark orange.

'You know, I thought all this could be Greek,' she said, 'or Egyptian! That we trousermen ... well, togamen, I suppose—'

'So we even begged our gods from your people, too?' snapped Mau, putting an arm around the priest's shoulders.

'What? No! It's more—'

Mau pulled her after him though the narrow gap. 'No more talking!' he said. 'Now, come *on*!'

The 'on!' echoed up and down the corridor. The ancient and oldest Grandfather beside Mau fell over backwards with a little click, and then crumbled into powder and strips of dry papervine, but not before it had tipped over the one behind it . . .

They watched in horror as the line of toppling, crumbling Grandfathers overtook the lamplight, filling the air with cloying, acrid dust.

They looked at one another, and made an immediate and group decision.

'Run!'

Dragging the stumbling old man between them, they dashed up the gentle slope. The dust stung their eyes and clawed at their throats, but around the fortieth collapsing

skeleton they overtook the cascading bones. They didn't
bother to stop; the dust behind them was almost a solid,
billowing mass, as keen to escape as they were. And they
ran on, into better air, until the noise died away.

Daphne was surprised when Mau slowed down, but he
pointed to the white stone that stuck out of the wall, with
the hunched Grandfather on it.

'We can rest for a moment,' he said. 'That one's too
high to be pushed over.'

He propped up Ataba, whose breathing almost rattled.
But he was smiling, even so.

'I *saw* the gods,' he panted, 'and you did, too, Mau.'

'Thank you,' said Mau.

The priest looked puzzled. 'For what?'

'Not calling me demon boy.'

'Ah, I can be generous in victory.'

'They were made of stone,' said Mau.

'Magic stone! The milk of the world! Have you ever
seen so much of it? What human hand could carve it?
What mind could imagine them? They are a sign. In the
heart of darkness, I have found illumination! I was
right!'

'They were stone,' said Mau patiently. 'Did you not see
the slabs on the floor? There are your god stones! They
were made to tread on! They fell into the sea and you
think they are holy!'

'A man in darkness may be misled, it's true. But in the
stones we saw a hint of the truth. The gods made you their
tool, boy. You scorned them and spurned them, but the

faster you ran from them, the closer you came to them. You—'

'We ought to move,' said Daphne to a distant background of crashing bones. 'Even if they can't get closer, that dust can. *Move*, I said!'

They obeyed, as wise men do when a woman puts her foot down, and went on along the tunnel at the best speed that Ataba could hobble.

But Daphne hesitated. The crashing tide of Grandfathers was nearly at the stone and, yes, it should be able to stop them, but Mau had sounded too confident, which to her mind meant that even he was not all that certain. He didn't need to stop, but Ataba was suffering. He actually cares about the old man, she thought. A demon wouldn't—

Crash . . . The tumbling bones hit the stone and stopped.

At least, all but one did.

It was probably a rib, she thought later. It sprang out of the mess and into the air like a salmon, and hit the skull of the Grandfather who was perched on the stone; he rocked backwards and fell onto the skeleton on the other side of the stone, which fell over.

And that was it, like a trick with dominoes. *Crash, crash, crash* . . . The floor was more level here, and the bones rolled faster. Why hadn't she been expecting something like this? The Grandfathers had been stuck in this mouldy cave for ever. They wanted to get out!

She ran after the men, before the dust rose. She'd heard

that when you took a breath, you breathed in a tiny, tiny amount of everyone who had ever lived, but, she decided, there was no need to do it all at once.

'*Run again!*' she yelled.

They were already turning to look. Daphne grabbed the old man's other arm and used him to tow Mau until they had got all six legs sorted out.

The entrance was a little white dot again, a long way off, and after only a few steps Ataba was groaning.

'Leave the lamps here,' panted Mau. 'We don't need them now. I'm going to carry him!'

He scooped up the priest and slung him over his back.

They ran. The dot didn't seem to get bigger. No one looked back. There was no point. All you could do was face the speck of day and run until your legs screamed.

They only looked at the god statues, thought Daphne, trying to keep her mind off what was crashing down behind them. They should have looked at the walls! But of course they wouldn't have known what they were looking at! It's lucky I'm here . . . in a way.

Something crunched under her foot. She risked a quick glance down and saw little bit of bone bouncing along, overtaking her.

'They're right behind us!'

'I know,' said Mau. 'Run faster!'

'I can't. The dust is going to get me!'

'Does not happen! Give me your hand!' Mau shifted the dead weight of the old priest on his back, and grabbed her hand, almost jerking her off her feet. Mau's legs were pounding across the rock as if driven by steam. All she could do was kick at the ground whenever it came near, to stop herself being dragged along it.

Now the circle of daylight was getting closer, and having been so tiny for so long, it was opening fast. The ancient dust, which stung the skin and choked the throat, ran ahead of them across the ceiling, cutting out the daylight.

– they burst into evening sunlight, suddenly and intensely bright after the gloom of the tunnel. It dazzled the eyes and Daphne felt herself begin to stumble into the sea of white that had taken the place of the world. Mau must have been blinded, too, because he let go of her. There was nothing for it but to put her arms over her head and hope for a soft place to fall.

She staggered and folded up, while the dust of the Grandfathers, free after thousands of years, escaped at last on the wind, streaming away across the mountain.

It would have been nice if she'd heard thousands of little voices fading away as the cloud of dust was scattered to the wind, but to her regret she didn't. Reality so often fails when it comes to small, satisfying details, she thought,

She could hear people now, and her sight was coming back. She could make out the ground in front of her as she carefully pushed herself up.

The dry, dusty grass crackled softly and someone walked into her view.

There were boots! Big sturdy boots with tight laces, caked with sand and salt! And above the boots, there were trousers! Real, heavy trouserman trousers! She said he would come and he had! Just in time, too!

She stood up, and the shock hit her like a shovel.

'Well, well, your ladyship, here's a stroke of luck,' said the man, grinning at her. 'So the ol' *Judy* fetched up here, eh? Who'd have thought the ol' bugger could manage it. Didn't do him any good, I see, bein' as it's his hat I do see on that darkie's head. What happened to the old fool? Ate him, did they? And never said no Grace aforehand, too, I have no doubt. I bet that made him wild!'

Foxlip! Not the worst of the mutineers, but that didn't mean much because he had two pistols in his belt, and they don't care who pulls the trigger.

Most of the islanders were in the clearing. They must have led the men up here. Why shouldn't they? She'd been saying for weeks that her father would find her. Most of them had probably never even seen a trouserman before.

'Where's your friend, Mr Foxlip? Is Mr Polegrave with you?' she said, managing a smile.

'Right here, miss,' said a hoarse voice.

She shuddered. Polegrave! And where she could not see him, which was even worse. He'd sidled up behind her, which was his way, the sneaky little worm.

'And will we be joined by Mr Cox?' she asked, trying to hold onto the smile.

Foxlip looked around the little valley. He was counting people; she could see his lips moving.

'Him? I shot 'im,' said Foxlip.

Liar, she thought. You wouldn't dare. You're not that

brave. You're not even that stupid. If you missed he'd have cut your heart out. Good heavens, a couple of months ago I wouldn't have been able to even think a sentence like that. How broad can horizons get?

'Well done, you,' she said.

Her thoughts tumbled through her head. Two men with pistols. And they'd fire them, too. If she said the wrong thing, someone would get killed. She had to get them away from here – get them away and remind them that she was valuable to them.

'My father will pay you a great deal if you get me to Port Mercia, Mr Foxlip,' she said.

'Oh, I dare say there will be a lot of payin' one way or another, yes, I dare say,' said Foxlip, looking around again. 'There's ways and ways, oh yes. So you're the queen of the savages, are you? One white girl, all by yourself. Terrible shame. I bet you could do with a bit o' civilized company, such as might be provided by a pair of gentlemen such as us – well, I *say* us, but o' course Mr Polegrave here does indulge in the questionable habit o' wiping his bogeys on his sleeve, but bishops have been known to do worse.'

And, later on, she thought, it could still have worked if it hadn't been for Ataba.

He'd seen the gods, in the darkness underground. And now he was spinning with the holy memory. He was out of breath and confused, but he had seen the gods, and all uncertainty had been blown away with the dust of history. They were made of stone, indeed, but they had gleamed in their hidden home, and he was sure they had spoken to him, told him that everything he believed was true, and that in this new world he would be their prophet, delivered out of the darkness on the burning wings of certainty.

And there were . . . *trousermen*! The bringers of all that was bad! They were a disease which weakened the soul! They brought steel and beef and infernal devices, which made people lazy and stupid! But now the holy fire had filled him, just in time.

They all heard him scream ancient curses and march across the clearing with his knees clicking loudly. Daphne barely understood any of it. The words tumbled out on top of one another, fighting to be heard. Who knew what his blazing eyes were really seeing as he snatched a spear from a young man and waved it menacingly at Foxlip—

– who shot him dead.

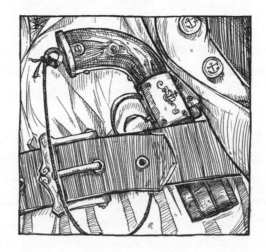

CHAPTER 11

CRIMES AND PUNISHMENTS

*T*he *crack* of the pistol echoed around the mountain. It was even louder in Daphne's head. Ataba fell over backwards, like a falling tree.

Only Milo and Pilu know what's just happened, she thought. No one else here has even *seen* a gun before. There was a loud noise and the old man fell over. I might just be able to stop everyone being killed. Mau was crouched over the body of Ataba, halfway towards getting up. She waved at him frantically to stay down.

Then Foxlip committed suicide. He didn't know it at the time, but that's how it started.

He pulled out his other pistol and growled, 'Tell 'em not to move. First one who does, he's a dead darkie. You tell 'em that right now!'

She stepped forward with her hands up. 'I know these

men! They're Foxlip and Polegrave! They were crew on the *Sweet Judy*. They kill people! They shot Mister Wainsly and Mister Plummer! They laughed about it! They – Pilu, tell them what a gun is!'

'They are bad men!' said Milo.

'Yes! They are! And they've got more pistols. Look! Stuck in their belts!'

'You mean the spark-makers?' said Mau, still crouched. She could see his muscles, wound up to spring.

Oh dear, thought Daphne, what a time to have a good memory . . .

'There's no time to explain. They can point them at you and kill you better than any spear. And they *will* kill you, do you understand? And they probably won't kill me. I'd be worth too much. Keep away. This is between . . . trouserpeople!'

'But you pointed one at me—'

'*There's no time to explain!*' hissed Daphne.

'You're talking a good deal too much, missie,' said Foxlip. And just behind Daphne, Polegrave sniggered. She felt the barrel of a pistol pressed into the small of her back.

'Saw a feller shot inna spine once, miss,' the man whispered. 'It stuck there, indeed it did. Funny thing was, he started dancin', right there, legs goin' like mad and him screaming. Didn't fall over for ten minutes. Amazin' thing, nature.'

'Stow that!' said Foxlip, watching the clearing nervously. The islanders had mostly slid away into the bushes but those that remained did *not* look too happy. 'What did that silly ol' devil want to get hisself shot for? Now they're all worked up!'

'Pretty raggedly lot, though,' said Polegrave. 'We could hang on 'til the others come—'

'I told you to shut up!'

They don't know what to do now, Daphne thought. They are stupid and scared. The trouble is, they are stupid and scared *with guns*. And there's others coming. Imo made us smart, Mau said. Am I smarter than a stupid man with a gun? Yes, I think I am.

'Gentlemen,' she said, 'why don't we deal with this like civilized people?'

'Are you having a little laugh, your majesty?' said Foxlip.

'Get me to Port Mercia and my father will give you gold and a pardon. Who's going to give you a better offer this day? Look at this from a mathematical point of view. You've got guns, yes, but how long can you stay awake? There's a lot more' – she forced the word out – 'darkies than you. Even if one man stays awake, he's only got two shots before his throat is cut. Of course, they might not start with the throat since they are, as you point out, savages and not as civilized as you. You must have a boat here. You don't dare stay.'

'But you're our hostage,' said Polegrave.

'You might be mine. I just have to scream. You shouldn't have shot the priest.'

'That old man was a priest?' said Polegrave, looking panicky. 'It's bad luck to kill a priest!'

'Not heathen ones,' said Foxlip, 'and the bad luck was all his, eh?'

'But they got these spells, they can shrink your head—!'

'When did they shrink yours?' said Foxlip. 'Don't be such a damn fool! As for you, princess, you're coming with us.'

Princess, she thought. That was just like the mutineers. They called her baby names all the time. She hated it. It made her flesh crawl. It was probably meant to. 'No, Mr Foxlip, I'm not a princess,' she said carefully, 'but you're coming with me all the same. Keep close.'

'And have you lead us into a trap?'

'It's near sunset. Do you want to be up here in the dark?' She held out a hand, and added, 'And the rain, too.' A squall had blown in, and the first drops began to fall. 'The people here can see in the dark,' she went on. 'And they can move as silently as the wind. Their knives are so sharp that they can cut a man's—'

'Why's it happening like this?' Polegrave demanded of Foxlip. 'I thought you were smart! You said we'd get the best pickings. You told me—'

'And now I'm telling you to shut up.' Foxlip turned to Daphne. 'All right, my lady, I'm not falling for that malarkey. We'll take you off this rock at first light. Might even get you as far as dear old dad. But there'd better be gold at the end of it, or else. No tricks, right?'

'Yeah, we got four loaded pistols, missie,' said Polegrave, waving one at her, 'and they'll stop anything, you hear?'

'They won't stop the fifth man, Mr Polegrave.'

She rejoiced in the change in his expression as she turned to Foxlip. 'Tricks? From me? No. I want to get home. I don't know any tricks.'

'Swear on your mother's life,' said Foxlip.

'What?'

'You always were a stuck-up kid on the *Judy*. Swear it, like I said. Then I might even believe yer.'

Does he know about my mother? Daphne wondered, calm thoughts floating in a sea of fury. I think poor Captain Roberts did, and I told Cookie, but not even Cookie would gossip about that sort of thing to the likes of Foxlip. But *no one is entitled* to ask for an oath like that!

Foxlip growled. Daphne had been silent for too long for his liking.

'Cat got your tongue?' he said.

'No. But it is an important swear. I had to think about it. I promise I won't try to run away, I won't tell you any lies, and I won't try to deceive you. Is that what you want?'

'And you swear that on your mother's life?' Foxlip insisted.

'*Yes, I do.*'

'That's very handsome of you,' said Foxlip. 'Don't you think so, Mr Polegrave?'

But Polegrave was watching the dripping forest on either side of the path. 'There's *things* in there,' he moaned. 'There's stuff creepin' about!'

'Lions and tigers and elephants, I shouldn't wonder,' said Foxlip cheerfully. He raised his voice. 'But there's a hair trigger on this pistol, so if I even *think* I hear a sound out of place, missie will be put to considerable embarrassment. One footfall and she's ready for the bone yard!'

As soon as Daphne and the two trousermen had rounded a bend in the track and were out of sight, Mau stepped forward.

'We could rush them. The rain's on our side,' Pilu whispered.

'You heard the big one. I can't risk her being killed. She saved my life. Twice.'

'I thought you saved *her* life.'

'Yes, but the first time I saved her life I saved mine, too. Do you understand? If she hadn't been here I'd have held the biggest rock I could find and gone into the dark current. One person is nothing. Two people are a nation.'

Pilu's forehead wrinkled in puzzlement. 'What are three people?'

'A bigger nation. Let's catch them up . . . carefully.'

And she saved me from Locaha a second time, he thought as they set off again, silent as ghosts in the rain. He'd woken up, his mind full of silver fishes, and the old woman had told him. He'd been running to the white city under the sea, and then Daphne had been there, pulling him up faster than Locaha could swim. Even the old woman had been impressed.

The ghost girl had a plan, and she couldn't tell him what it was. All they could do, with their sticks and spears, was follow her—

No, they didn't have to follow her. He knew where she was going. He stared at her, pale in the dusk, as she led the men down the sloping path to the Place.

Who would be in here now? Daphne wondered. She'd seen Mrs Gurgle up at the cave, because everyone who could walk had been up there. There were some sick people in the far huts, though. She would have to be careful . . .

She lit some dry grass from the fire outside the hut, and cautiously transferred the flame to one of the *Judy*'s lamps. She did it very carefully, thinking about each movement, because she did not want to think about what she would be doing next. She had to keep herself in two parts. Even so, her hand shook, but a girl had a right to tremble a bit when two men were pointing guns at her.

'Do sit down,' she said. 'The mats are not as bad as the ground, at least.'

'Much obliged,' said Polegrave, looking around the hut.

It almost broke her heart. Once upon a time some woman had taught the man his manners, but to thank her he'd grown up to be a weasel, thief and murderer. And now, when he was worried and ill at ease, an actual bit of politeness drifted up from the depths, like a pure clear bubble from a swamp. It wasn't going to make things any easier.

Foxlip just grunted, and sat down with his back to the inner wall, which was solid rock.

'This is a trap, right?' he said.

'No. You asked me to swear on my mother's life,' said Daphne coldly, and thought: And that was a sin. Even if you have no god at all, that was a sin. Some things are a sin all by themselves. And I'm going to murder you, and that is a mortal sin, too. But it won't look like murder . . .

She said: 'Would you like some beer?'

'Beer?' said Foxlip. 'You mean real *beer*?'

'Well, it's like beer. It's the Demon Drink, anyway. I've always got some freshly made.'

'You make it? But you're a nob!' said Polegrave.

'Perhaps I make "nobby" beer,' said Daphne. 'Sometimes you have to do what needs doing. Do you *want* some?'

'She'll poison us!' said Polegrave. 'It's all a trick!'

'We'll have some beer, princess,' said Foxlip, 'but we'll watch you drink it first. 'Cos we were not born yesterday.' He gave her an unpleasant wink, full of guile and mischief and with no humour in it all.

'Yeah, you look after us, missie, an' we'll look after you when Cox's cannibal chums come for a picnic!' said Polegrave.

She heard Foxlip hissing at him for this as she stepped outside, but she'd never for one minute believed that they intended to 'rescue' her. And Cox had found the Raiders, had he? Who should she feel sorry for?

She went next door to the beer hut, and took three bubbling shells of beer off the shelf. Taking care to brush all the dead flies off.

What I am about to do *won't* be murder, she told herself. Murder is a sin. It *won't* be murder.

Foxlip would make sure she drank some beer first, to prove it wasn't poisoned, and up until now she had never drunk much, just a tiny amount when she had been experimenting with a new recipe.

Just one drop of beer would turn you into a madman, her grandmother had said. It made you defile yourself and neglect your children and break up families, amongst quite a lot of other things. But this was *her* beer, after all. It hadn't been made in a factory somewhere, with who knew what in it. It was just made of good, honest . . . poison.

She came back balancing three wide, shallow clay bowls, which she put down on the floor between the mats.

'Well now, you've got a lovely bunch of coconuts,' said Foxlip in his disgustingly *unfriendly* friendly way, 'but I'll tell you what, missie, you'll mix the beer up so's we all get the same, right?'

Daphne shrugged, and did as he said, with both men watching closely.

'Looks like horse piss,' said Polegrave.

'Well, horse piss ain't too bad,' said Foxlip. He picked up the bowl in front of him, looked at the one in front of Daphne, hesitated for a moment and then grinned his unpleasant grin.

'I reckon you're too smart to put poison in your bowl and expect me to be daft enough to swap them over,' he said. 'Drink up, princess!'

'Yeah, down the little red lane!' said Polegrave. There it was again, another tiny arrow into her heart. Her own mother had said that to her when she wouldn't eat her broccoli. The memory stung.

'The same beer is in every bowl. You made me swear,' she said.

'I said, *drink up!*'

Daphne spat into her bowl and began to sing the beer song – the island version, not her own. 'Baa, Baa, Black Sheep' just wouldn't work now.

So she sang the Song of the Four Brothers, and because most of her mind was taken up with that, a smaller part took the opportunity to remind her: Air is the planet Jupiter, which we believe to be made of gases. Isn't that a coincidence! And she faltered a moment before recovering herself, because some tiny part of her mind was worrying her with what she was about to do.

There was a stunned silence when she finished, and then Foxlip said, 'What the hell was that all about? You *gobbed* in your drink!'

Daphne tipped up the bowl and took a good swig. It was a little more nutty than usual. She paused to feel it bubbling down, and saw them still staring.

'You have to spit in the bowl and then sing the beer song.' She burped and put a hand over her mouth. 'Pardon *me*. I can teach it to you. Or you can just hum along. Please? It is an ancient custom . . .'

'I'm not singing no pagan mumbo-jumbo!' said Foxlip, and he snatched up his bowl and took a long swig, while Daphne tried not to scream.

Polegrave hadn't touched his beer. He was still

suspicious! His beady little eyes flicked from his fellow mutineer to Daphne, and back again.

Foxlip put down his bowl, and belched. 'Well, it's a long time since—'

Silence exploded. Polegrave reached for his pistols, but Daphne was already moving. Her bowl hit him on the nose, with a crunch. The man screamed and went over backwards, and Daphne snatched his pistols from the floor.

She tried to think and not think at the same time.

Don't think about the man you just killed. [It was an execution!]

Think about the man you may have to kill. [But I can't prove *he*'s a murderer! He didn't kill Ataba!]

She fumbled with a pistol as Polegrave, spitting blood, tried to get up, and cursed. The gun was heavier than it looked and she choked back a curse, courtesy of the *Sweet Judy*'s Great Barrel of Swearing, as clumsy fingers disobeyed her.

Finally she pulled the hammer back, just as Captain Roberts had taught her. It clicked twice, what Cookie called the two-pound noise. When she had asked him why, he'd said, 'Because when a man hears that in the dark, he loses two pounds of . . . weight, quickly!'

It certainly made Polegrave go very quiet.

'I *will* fire,' she lied. 'Don't move. Good. Now, listen to me. I want you to go away. You didn't kill anyone here. Go away. Right away. If I see you again I will – well, you will regret it. I'm letting you go because you had a mother.

Someone actually loved you once, and tried to teach you manners. You won't understand that at all. Now get up, and get out. Get out! Get out and run far away! Quickly now!'

Trying to run and crouch at the same time, holding his hand over his ruined nose, dribbling strings of snot and blood, and certainly not looking back, Polegrave scuttled into the sunset like a crab running for the safety of the surf.

Daphne sat down, still holding the pistol in front of her, and waited until the hut stopped spinning.

She looked at the silent Foxlip, who hadn't moved at all.

'Why did you have to be so – so stupid?' she said, prodding him with the pistol. 'Why did you kill an old man who was shaking a stick at you? You shoot at people without a thought and you call *them* savages! Why are you so stupid as to think *I* was stupid? Why didn't you *listen* to me? I *told* you we sing the beer song. Would it have hurt to hum along? But no, you knew better, because they are savages! And now you are dead, with a stupid little smile on your stupid face! You needn't have died, but you didn't listen. Well, you've got just enough time to listen now, Mr Stupid! The thing is, the beer is made from a very poisonous plant. It paralyses you, all at once. But there's some chemical in human spit, you see, and if you spit into the beer and then sing the beer song, it turns the poison into something harmless with a lovely nutty flavour which, incidentally, I have improved very considerably, everyone says. It takes a little less than five minutes to make the beer safe, which is just long enough to sing the official beer song, but "Baa, Baa, Black Sheep" sung about sixteen times also works, you see, because it's not the song that matters, you see, it's *the waiting*. I worked that out using scientific thinkink' – she burped – 'sorry, I mean thinking.'

She stopped to throw up the beer and then, by the feel of it, to throw up everything she'd eaten in the last year. 'And it could have been such a lovely evening,' she said. 'Do you know what this island is? Have you *any idea* what this island is? Of course you don't, because you're so stupid! And dead! And I'm a murderer!'

She burst into tears, which were large and sticky, and began to argue with herself.

'Look, they were mutineers! If they were in a court of law, they'd be hung!'

[Hanged, not hung. But that's the point of having courts. It's to stop people murdering other people just because they think they deserve it. There's a judge and jury, and if they were found guilty they would be hanged by the hangman, neatly and properly. He'd have his breakfast first, very calmly, and perhaps say a prayer. He would hang them calmly and without anger, because at that moment he would be The Law. That's how it works.]

'But everyone *saw* him shoot Ataba!'

[Correct. So *everyone* should have decided what to do.]

'How could they? They didn't know what I know! And you know what they're like! They had four pistols between them! If I hadn't got them out of the way, they'd have shot other people! They were talking about taking over the island!'

[Yes. What you did was murder, even so.]

'What about the hangman? Doesn't he do murder, then?'

[No, because enough people say it isn't. That's what a courtroom is for. It's where the law happens.]

'And that makes it right? Didn't God say "thou shalt not kill"?'

[Yes. But after that it got complicated.]

There was movement in the doorway, and her hand raised the pistol. Then her brain lowered it again.

'Good,' said Mau. 'I do not want to be shot a second time. Remember?'

The tears started again. 'I'm sorry about that. I thought you were . . . I thought you were a savage,' Daphne managed.

'What's a savage?'

She pointed the pistol towards Foxlip. 'Someone like him.'

'He's dead.'

'I'm sorry. He insisted on drinking his beer.'

'We saw the other one run off towards the low forest. He was bleeding and snorting like a sick pig.'

'He wouldn't drink his beer!' Daphne sobbed. 'I'm sorry, I brought Locaha here.'

Mau's eyes gleamed. 'No, they brought him, and you sent him away full,' he said.

'More are going to come! They talked about it,' Daphne

managed. Mau said nothing, but put an arm around her. 'Tomorrow, I want a trial,' she said.

'What's a trial?' said Mau. He waited for a while, but the only reply was a snore. He sat with her, watching the eastern sky darken. Then he carefully settled her down on her mat, hoisted the rigid body of Foxlip over his shoulder and went down to the beach. The Unknown Woman watched him load the body into a canoe and paddle out into the ocean, where Foxlip went over the side with a lump of coral tied to his foot, to be eaten by whatever was hungry enough to eat carrion.

She watched him return and go back up the mountain, where Milo and Cahle had been watching over the body of Ataba, so that he would not become a ghost.

In the morning, they followed him down to the beach, where the Unknown Woman and a few others joined them. The sun was rising now, and Mau was not surprised to see the grey shadow drifting beside him. At one point, Milo walked through it without noticing.

Two more deaths, Hermit Crab, said Locaha.

'Do they make you happy?' growled Mau. 'Then send this priest to Perfect World.'

How can you ask that, little hermit crab who does not believe?

'Because *he* did. And he cared, which is more than his gods did.'

No bargains, Mau, even for another.

'At least I'm trying!' Mau yelled. Everyone stared at him. The shadow faded.

On the edge of the reef, above the dark current, Mau tied broken coral to the old man and watched him sink beyond the reach of sharks.

'He was a good man!' he shouted to the sky. 'He deserved better gods!'

Down in the steams of the low forest, someone shivered.

It had not been a good night for Arthur Septimus Polegrave, who would have been known to his friends, if he had any friends, as 'Septic'. He knew he was dying, he just knew it. He must be. There couldn't be a single thing in this jungle that hadn't tried to bite, peck or sting him during the last dark soupy hour. There were spiders – giant, horrible things, waiting at nose-height on every path – there were the insects, every one armed, by the feel of it with red-hot needles. Things had bitten his ears and climbed up his trousers. Things had trodden on him. In the middle of the night something horrible had flopped down from the trees and onto his head, which it had tried to unscrew. As soon as he could see clearly, he would take his chances and make a run for the boat and a getaway. All in all, he thought as he pulled something with far too many legs out of his ear, things were about as bad as they could get.

There was a rustling in the tree above him, and he looked up just as a well-fed grandfather bird threw up in time for breakfast, and found that he was wrong.

Later that morning Daphne marched up to Pilu with the log of the *Sweet Judy* in her hand and said: 'I want a fair trial.'

'That's good,' said Pilu. 'We're going to look at the new cave. Are you going to come?' Most of the population were gathered around him; news of the gods had got around fast.

'You don't know what a trial is, do you?'

'Er, no,' said Pilu.

'It's where you decide if someone has done something wrong and if they should be punished.'

'Well, you punished that trouserman,' said Pilu cheerfully. 'He killed Ataba. He was a pirate!'

'Er, yes . . . but the question is, should I have done it? I had no authority to kill him.'

Milo loomed behind his brother, bent down and whispered to him.

'Ah, yes,' said Pilu, 'my brother reminds me of the time we were in Port Mercia and a Navy man had been found thieving, and they tied him to the mast and beat him with some leather thing. Is this what we're talking about? I think we've got some leather.'

Daphne shuddered. 'Er . . . no, thank you. But, er, don't you ever have crime on the islands?'

It took some while to get the idea settled in Pilu's head, and then he said, 'Ah, I've got it. You want us to tell you that you didn't do a bad thing, yes?'

'The ghost girl is saying that there must be rules and there must be reasons,' said Mau, right behind Daphne. She hadn't even known he was there.

'Yes, but you're not to say I did a good thing just because you like me,' she added.

'Well, we didn't like *him*,' said Pilu. 'He killed Ataba!'

'I think I see what she means,' said Mau. 'Let's try it. It sounds . . . interesting.'

And so the Nation had its first court. There was no question of judge and jury; everyone sat around in a circle, children too. And there was Mau, sitting in the circle. No one was more important than anyone else . . . and there was Mau, sitting in the circle just like everybody else.

Everyone should make up their own mind . . . and there was Mau, sitting in the circle. Not big, not even tattooed, not shouting orders – but somehow *being* slightly more there than anyone else. And he had the cap. He was the captain.

Daphne had heard some of the newcomers talking about him. They used a kind of code, about 'the poor boy', and how hard it must be, and somewhere in it all there was, unspoken yet still present, the suggestion that he wasn't old enough to be a chief – and around that point, either Milo or Cahle turned up like an eclipse of the sun and the conversation turned to fishing or babies. And every day Mau was a little older, and still chief.

Pilu was in charge of the court. It was the sort of thing he was born for. But he did need some help . . .

'We must have a prosecutor,' Daphne explained. 'That's someone who thinks what I did was wrong, and a defender, who says what I did was right.'

'Then I'll be the defender,' said Pilu cheerfully.

'And the prosecutor?' said Daphne.

'That would be you.'

'Me? I have to be someone else!'

'But everyone knows that man killed Ataba. We saw him!' said Pilu.

'Look, hasn't there ever been a killing in these islands?'

'Sometimes too much beer, a fight over women, such things as these. Very sad. There is a story, a very old story, about two brothers who fought. One killed the other, but in the battle it could have been otherwise, and the other one dead. The killer fled, knowing the punishment and taking it upon himself.'

'Was it awful?'

'He would be sent far away from the islands, far from his people, from his family, never to walk in the steps of his ancestors, never to sing a death chant for his father, never to hear the songs of his childhood, never again to smell the sweet water of home. He built a canoe and sailed in new seas far away, where men are baked into different colours and for half of every year trees die. He lived for many lifetimes and saw many things but one day he found a place that was best of all, because it was the island of his childhood, and he stepped onto the shore and died, happily, because he was home again. Then Imo made the brothers into stars, and put them in the sky so that we shall remember the brother who sailed so far away that he came back again.'

Oh my word, thought Daphne as the picture of the dying brother faded in her mind, that is so sad. And it's a story about something else, about sailing so far that you come back again . . . Oh, I *must* go back into that cave!

'But the ghost girl is already banished,' Mau pointed out. 'The wave banished her to us.' And so there had to be even more discussion.

Half an hour later matters were not much improved. The whole population of the island sat in a circle around Daphne, trying to be helpful. Trying to understand as the trial went on.

'You say they were bad trousermen,' said Mau.

'Yes. The worst kind,' said Daphne. 'Murderers and bullies. You say you walk in the shadow of Locaha, but they walked in his loincloth when he has not bathed for many months.' That got a laugh. She'd probably said it wrong.

'And how did they walk in Locaha's loincloth?' said Pilu, and got a slightly smaller laugh, to his obvious disappointment.

'That's the wrong question,' said Mau. The laughter stopped. He went on: 'You say you told them about the beer song, and they didn't listen? It is not your fault the man was a fool, is it?'

'Yes, but you see, it was a trick,' Daphne said. 'I knew they wouldn't take any notice!'

'Why would they not listen?'

'Because . . .' She hesitated, but there was no way of avoiding it. 'I'd better tell you everything,' she said. 'I want to tell you everything. You should know what happened on the *Sweet Judy*. You should know about the dolphins and the butterfly and the man in the canoe!'

And while the circle listened with open mouths, she told them what she had seen, what Cookie had told her, and what poor Captain Roberts had written in the ship's log. She told them about First Mate Cox, and the mutiny and the man in the canoe . . .

. . . who had been brown and, like Mrs Gurgle, looked as if he'd been made out of old leather. The *Sweet Judy* had caught up with him out among the islands, where he had been paddling a small canoe very industriously towards the horizon.

According to First Mate Cox, the man made a rude gesture. Foxlip and Polegrave backed him up on that, but in his log the captain, who had spoken to them all separately, made a point of noting that they weren't clear about what the gesture was.

Cox had shot at the man, and had hit him. Foxlip fired, too. Daphne remembered him laughing. Polegrave was the last to fire, and that was just like him. He was the kind of weasel who would kick a corpse, because it was unlikely to fight back. Polegrave giggled all the time, and never took his eyes off Daphne when she was on deck. But he was probably smarter than Foxlip, although once you got past the swaggering and the bullying, there were probably lobsters who were smarter than Foxlip.

The two of them tended to hang around with Cox in a way that was hard to understand until you found out that there are fish that swim alongside a shark, or even in its mouth, where they are safe from other fish and never get eaten. Nobody knows what's in it for the shark; maybe it doesn't notice, or is saving them up for a secret midnight snack.

Of course, Cox was not like a shark. He was worse. Sharks are just eating machines. They don't have a choice. First Mate Cox had a choice, every day, and had chosen to be First Mate Cox. And that was a strange choice, because if evil was a disease, then First Mate Cox would have been in an isolation ward on a bleak island somewhere. And even then, bunnies nibbling at the seaweed would start to fight one another. Cox was, in fact, contagious. Where his shadow fell, old friendships snapped and little wars broke out, milk soured, weevils fled from every stale ship's biscuit and rats queued up to jump into the sea. At least, that was how Cookie had put it, although he was given to mild exaggeration.

And Cox grinned. It wasn't the nasty, itchy little grin of Polegrave, that made you want to wash your hands after seeing it. It was the grin of a man who is happy in his work.

He'd come on board at Port Advent, after five of the crew didn't come back from shore leave. That often happened, the cook told Daphne. A captain who strictly forbade card games, whistling, alcohol and swearing found any crew hard to keep at any price. It was a terrible thing, said Cookie, to see religion get such a hold on a decent soul. But *because* he was a decent soul, and a good captain, a lot of the crew stayed with him voyage after voyage, even though stopping sailors from swearing was a terrible thing to do (they got around it by sticking an old barrel of water right down in the scuppers and swearing into it when it all got too much; try as she might, Daphne couldn't make out all the words, but at the end of a difficult day the water in the barrel was hot enough to wash with).

Everyone knew about Cox. You didn't hire First Mate Cox. He turned up. If you didn't need a first mate because you already had one, then the one you had was suddenly very keen indeed on being a second mate once again, yes indeed, much obliged . . .

And if you were an innocent man, you accepted all the glowing references of the other captains without wondering why they would be so happy to see Cox on someone else's ship. But Cookie said that in his opinion Roberts knew all about Cox and had been filled with missionary zeal at the chance to save such a big ripe sinner from the Pit of Damnation.

And maybe Cox, when he found himself working for a captain who held compulsory prayer meetings three times a day, was filled with a different kind of zeal, which would have been black with flames around the edges. Evil likes company, Cookie said.

Amazingly, he went to the services willingly and joined in *and paid attention.* Those who knew about him walked carefully. Cox ate and drank mischief, and if you couldn't work out what he was up to, then it was the really dark stuff.

When he had nothing else to do, Cox shot at things. Birds, flying fish, monkeys, anything. One day a large blue butterfly, blown from one of the islands, landed on the deck. Cox shot it so neatly that there were just two wings left, and then gave Daphne a wink, as if he'd done something clever. She'd had a cousin like that – Botney was his name – who never left a frog unsquashed, a kitten unkicked or a spider unflattened. In the end, she'd accidentally broken two of his fingers under the nursery rocking horse, told him she'd put a wasps down his trousers next time if he didn't mend his ways and then burst into tears when people came running. You didn't come from a family of ancient fighters like hers without at least a pinch of ruthlessness.

Sadly, there had been no one there to set Cox's feet on the right path and his fingers in plaster. But, some of the crew whispered, it seemed that he'd changed. He still shot at things, but he was always in the front row for the services, watching old Roberts like a botanist watching a rare beetle. It was as if Cox was *fascinated* by the captain.

As for Captain Roberts – he might have wanted to save Cox's soul from the Fires of Perdition, but he hated the man himself and didn't mind showing it. This did not sit well with Cox, but shooting captains always caused a bit too much of a stir so, Cookie said, he must have decided to beat the captain on the man's own ground, or water, destroying him from the inside.

Cox shot things because they were alive, but to him that was just killing time. He had greater ambitions for the captain. He wanted to shoot him in the faith.

It began with Cox sitting up straight during the prayer meetings and shouting 'Halleluja' or 'Amen' every time the captain finished a sentence, and clapping loudly. Or he'd ask puzzled questions like 'What did they feed the lions and tigers with in the Ark, sir?' and 'Where did all the water go?' Then there was the day when he asked Cookie to try to make a meal for the whole crew out of five loaves and two fishes. Then when the captain said the story was not meant to be taken literally, Cox gave him a smart salute and said: 'Then what is, Cap'n?'

It started to get bad. The captain got humpty. Crew who'd served with him for a long time said he was a decent man and a good captain, and they'd never seen him get humpty before. Everyone suffered under a humpty captain, who'd find fault with everyone and turn every day into a chore. Daphne spent a lot of time in her cabin.

And then there was the parrot. No one was ever sure who taught the bird its first swear word, although the wobbling finger of suspicion pointed at Cox, but by then the whole crew was ill at ease. Cox had his supporters, and the captain had staunch allies of his own. Fights broke out, and things, small things, were getting stolen. That was terrible, according to Cookie; nothing broke up a crew like the thought that a man had to watch his possessions all the time. Dooms and reckonings would be upon them all, he forecast. Probably more dooms than reckonings, he added.

And the next day, Cox shot the old man in the canoe. Daphne would like to report that every sailor in the crew was angry because the old man had been shot, and in a way it was true, but many of the men were less concerned about the sanctity of souls than they were about the possibility that the old man had relatives nearby with fast canoes, sharp spears and an unwillingness to listen to explanations. And there were even a few who held that one old man more or less didn't matter, but Cox and his cronies had been shooting at dolphins, too, and that was cruel and unlucky.

In the end there was a war, and so much bad blood had been bubbling that there seemed to Daphne to be more than two sides. She sat it out in her cabin, seated on a small barrel of gunpowder with a loaded pistol in her hand. The captain had told her that if Cox's men won she should fire the pistol into the barrel 'to save her honour', but she was uncertain how much a saved honour would be worth when it was falling out of the sky in tiny pieces, along with the rest of the cabin. Fortunately she did not have to find out, because Captain Roberts ended the mutiny by detaching one of the *Sweet Judy*'s swivel guns and aiming it at the mutineers. The gun was intended for firing lots of small lead balls at any pirates who might try to board the ship. It was not intended to be a hand cannon, and if he had fired the thing, the recoil would probably have thrown him into the air, but everyone in front of it would have died of terminal perforations. There was a fury about him that even Cox took note of, Cookie had told her. The captain had the look in his eye of the Almighty confronting a particularly wicked city, and maybe Cox was just sane enough to recognize that here was some-one who might be even madder than him, at least for the time it took to turn Cox and those around him into much smaller lumps. Or, Cookie said, the captain had been about to commit wild murder right up until he realized that this was what Cox wanted, and the devil of a man would drag the captain's soul to hell along with his own.

But the captain didn't fire the gun, said Cookie. He laid it on the deck, straightened up with his arms folded and a grim little smile on his face, and Cox just stood there, looking puzzled, and then every single loyal crewman pointed a pistol at his head. The steam got knocked out of the mutiny. Cox and his chums were herded into the ship's boat with food, water and a compass. And then of course there was the matter of the guns. The mutineers still had friends among the crew, who said that leaving them in uncertain waters without weapons was a death sentence. In the end the guns were left for them on a little island a mile away, despite Captain Roberts declaring that in his opinion, any pirate or slaver who ran into Cox and his men would have a new captain in very short order indeed. He ordered the swivel guns primed and ready day and night, and said that the boat would be fired on instantly if it was ever seen again.

The boat was set adrift and sailed, her crew silent and worried except for Polegrave and Foxlip, who jeered and spat. That was because they were too dumb to realize, said Cookie, that they were heading off into bad waters with a murderous madman in command.

The *Judy* never really recovered, but she kept on course. People didn't talk much, and kept to themselves when they were off watch. She wasn't a happy ship at all. Five men had previously jumped ship at Port Henry and so, without the mutineers, there weren't enough men to crew the ship properly when the wave came.

And that was the story Daphne told. She tried to be honest, and where she'd relied on Cookie's rather excitable stories she said so. She wished she had Pilu's talent; he could make tripping over a stone sound like a desperate adventure.

There was silence when she finished. Most people turned to look at Pilu. She'd done her best in a foreign language, but she'd seen the puzzled looks.

What Pilu gave them was the story all over again, but with acting, too. She could make out the character of Captain Roberts, heavy and pompous, and surely the one who sidled around was Polegrave, and the one who stamped and roared was Cox. They shouted at one another all the time, while Pilu's fingers popped like pistols and somehow, in the middle of the air, the story unfolded.

A certain extra touch of slightly mad realism was added by the parrot, who danced madly in the top of a coconut palm and shouted things like, 'What about Darwin, then? Waark!'

Pilu's translation lagged behind Daphne's account, but when he was about to deal with the old man's shooting, he stopped for guidance.

'He killed a man in a canoe because he was not a trouserman?'

She was ready for this. 'No. The man I kill— the dead man would have done that, but I think Cox just killed the old man because he couldn't see anything else to shoot at.'

'Er . . . my English is no so good—' Pilu began.

'I am sorry to say you heard me correctly.'

'He kills for Locaha and adds glory, like the Raiders?'

'No. Just because he wants to.'

Pilu looked at her as if this was going to be a hard one to get across. It was. From the sound of it, no one thought he was making sense.

He went on doggedly for a few more sentences and turned to Daphne. 'Not dolphins,' he said. 'No sailor would kill a dolphin. You must be wrong.'

'No. He really did.'

'But that is killing a soul,' said Pilu. 'When we die we become dolphins until it is time to be born again. Who would kill a dolphin?' Tears of puzzlement and anger raced down his face.

'I'm sorry. Cox would. And Foxlip shot at it, too.'

'Why?'

'To be like Cox, I think. To seem like a big man.'

'Big man?'

'Like the remora fish. Er, you call them suckfish. They swim with the sharks. Perhaps they like to think they are sharks.'

'Not even the Raiders would do this, and they worship Locaha! It is beyond belief!'

'I saw them. And poor Captain Roberts wrote it down in the ship's log. I can show you.' Too late, she remembered that Pilu didn't so much read as recognize writing when it was pointed out to him. His look now was a plea for help, so she stood close to him and found the right place: '*Once again Cox and his cronies have been discharging their pistols at the dolphins, against all decency and the common laws of the sea. May God forgive him, because no righteous sailor will. Indeed, I suspect that in this case even the Almighty will find his mercy overly strained!!!*'

She read it aloud. In the circle, people were getting restless. There was a lot of loud whispering that she couldn't understand, and it looked as if some sort of agreement was being arrived at. The nods and whispers ran around the circle of people in opposite directions until they met at Mau, who cracked a thin smile.

'These were men who would shoot a brown man for no reason,' he said. 'And they would shoot dolphins, which even trousermen respect. You could see inside their heads, ghost girl. Isn't that right? You could see how they thought?'

Daphne couldn't look at his face. 'Yes,' she said.

'Savages, we are to them. Some sort of animal. *Darkies.*'

'Yes.' She still did not dare to look up, in case she met his gaze. She'd pulled the trigger, she remembered, on that first day. And he had *thanked* her for the gift of fire.

'When the ghost girl first met me—' Mau began.

Oh, no, he's not going to *tell* them, is he? she thought. Surely he won't. But that little smile of his, that's the smile he smiles when he's really angry!

'— she gave me food,' Mau went on, 'and later she gave me a gun to help me light a fire, even though she was far from home and frightened. She was thoughtful enough, too, to take out the little ball that flies and kills, so that I would come to no harm. And she invited me into the *Sweet Judy* and gave me wonderful lobster-flavoured cakes. You all know the ghost girl.'

She looked up. Everyone was staring at her. Now Mau stood up and walked into the centre of the circle.

'These men were different,' he said, 'and the ghost girl knew how their minds worked. They would not sing the beer song because they thought we were a sort of animal, and they were too proud and great to sing an animal's song. She knew this.' He looked around the circle. 'The ghost girl thinks she killed a man. Did she? You must decide.'

Daphne tried to make out what was said next, but people all started talking at once, and because everyone was talking at once, everyone started talking louder. But something was happening. Little conversations got bigger, and then were picked up and rolled from tongue to tongue around the circle. Whatever the result was going to be, she thought, it probably was not going to be one simple word. Then Pilu wandered around the circle, hunkering down here and there, joining in for a little while, and then strolling on to another point and doing the same thing again.

No one stuck up their hands and there was no voting, but she thought, I wonder if it was like this in ancient Athens? This is pure democracy. People don't just get a vote, they have a say . . .

And now it was settling down. Pilu got up from his last conversation and walked back to the centre of the ring. He nodded to Mau and started to speak: 'A man that will kill a priest, or kill a man for the pleasure of seeing him die, or kill a dolphin' – this one got a big groan from the circle – 'could not be a man at all. It must have been an evil demon haunting the shell of a man, they say. The ghost girl could not have killed him, because he was already dead.'

Mau cupped his hands over his mouth. 'Is this what you think?' There was a roar of agreement.

'Good.' He clapped his hands together and raised his voice. 'We've still got to finish the pig fence, everyone, and we still need timber from the *Judy*, and the fish trap is not going to build itself!'

The circle rose and became a criss-crossing of hurrying people. No one had banged a table with a wooden hammer, or worn a wig. They had just done a thing that needed doing, without much fuss, and now, well, there was the pig fence to repair.

'Is this what you wanted?' asked Mau, suddenly beside her.

'Sorry? What?' She hadn't even seen him approaching. 'Oh, yes. Er, yes. Thank you. That was a very good, er, judgement,' she said. 'And you?'

'I think they have decided and I think it is settled,' said Mau briskly. 'The man brought Locaha here and his pistols serve him. But Locaha is no one's servant.'

CHAPTER 12

CANNON AND POLITICS

Mau sat down on a god stone.

'Where is Cox now, do you think?'

'I hope to goodness the wave drowned him!' said Daphne. 'I know I shouldn't, but I do.'

'And you fear that it did not,' said Mau. It wasn't a question.

'That's true. I think it would take more than a wave. Hah, Foxlip said he killed Cox. That was just because he wanted to look big, I'm sure. But Polegrave said something about Cox having cannibal chums. Could that happen?'

'I don't know. The Raiders kill for glory and skulls. You say he kills for no reason. He kills things because they are alive. He sounds like a bad dream, a monster. They will not know what to make of him.'

'Soup?' Daphne suggested.

'I doubt it,' said Mau. 'A cannibal has to be careful who he eats. Milo would make them strong, Pilu would give them a magic voice and I would give them . . . indigestion. Who would want to eat a madman?'

Daphne shuddered. 'Just so long as they don't eat me!'

'No, they would never eat a woman,' said Mau.

'That's very gentlemanly of them!'

'No, they would feed you to their wives, so that they become beautiful.'

There was one of those pauses that are icy-cold and red-hot at the same time. It was stuffed with soundless words, words that should not be said, or said another time, or in a different way, or could be said or needed to be said but couldn't be said, and they would go on tumbling through the pause for ever, or until one of them fell out—

'Ahem,' said Daphne, and all the other words escaped, for ever. Much later, and many times, she wondered about what might have happened if she hadn't chosen a word that clearly belonged to her grandmother. And that was that. For some people, there is only one right moment for the right word. This is sad, but there seems to be nothing that can be done about it. 'Well, I don't see him being eaten by anybody, or even left on the side of the plate,' she went on quickly, to drown out the last echoes of 'Ahem' in her head. 'I'm sure the captain was right when he said Cox will take over any vessel that finds him, like a disease. It's amazing what you can do if you don't care who you kill. And he *will* kill. Those two were sent as scouts, I'm sure of it. And that means he's found a *bigger* boat.'

'The boat they came in is still here, but a canoe was stolen last night,' said Mau. 'I think we are not good at understanding this sort of thing.'

'I don't think it will make any difference.'

'That's true. The Raiders are following – hunting the survivors. They will get here sooner or later. But I want to—'

'Er . . .'

It was a small boy. Daphne could not remember his name but he was hopping up and down like someone who does not want to intrude but needs to, well, intrude.

'Yes, Hoti?' said Mau.

'Er . . . please, they say they are running out of thorns to fence the big field,' said the child nervously.

'Run and tell them there is a big stand to the west of the Grandfathers' cave.' As the boy ran off Mau shouted after him, 'Tell them I said to cut the lengths much longer! It's a waste to cut them short!'

'And you must defend your island,' said Daphne.

He reacted as if he'd been struck. 'Do you think I won't, ghost girl? Do you think that?'

'It's not just your people! You must defend your gods!'

'What? How can you say this to me?'

'Not the metaphysical . . . the ones with the god stones and the sacrifices and all the rest of it! I mean the statues and all the other things in the cave!'

'Those? Just more stones. Worthless . . . stuff.'

'No! No, they aren't worthless. They tell you who you are!' She sagged a little. Things had been quite busy lately, and 'ghost girl' said so sharply had hurt. It did. Of course, they all called her ghost girl, even Mau sometimes, and it had never worried her. But this time it told her to go away, trouserman girl, you are not one of us.

She pulled herself together. 'You didn't look. You didn't see what I saw in the cave! You remember Air, Fire and Water all with their globes? And the headless statue?'

'I'm sorry,' said Mau, putting his head in his hands.

'Pardon?'

'I've upset you. I know when you're upset. Your face goes shiny, and then you try to act as if nothing has happened. I'm sorry I shouted. It's all been . . . well, you know.'

'Yes. I know.'

They sat in the silence you get when thoughts are too tangled to become words. Then Daphne coughed.

'Anyway, you saw the broken one? And that arm sticking out of the water?'

'Yes. I saw everything,' said Mau, but he was watching a woman hurrying towards them.

'No! You didn't! The air was getting too foul! The broken statue had been holding something. I found it while you were arguing with Ataba. It was the world. The world turned upside down. Come and see.' She took his hand in hers and pulled him towards the path up the mountain. 'Everyone must see! It's very—'

'Yes, Cara?' said Mau to the woman, who was now hovering where she was sure to be noticed.

'I'm to tell you the river's gone all cloudy,' the woman said, with a nervous look at Daphne.

'A pig's got into the east meadows and is wallowing in the spring,' said Mau, standing up. 'I will go and—'

'You are going to come with me!' shouted Daphne. The woman backed away quickly as Daphne turned and went on, 'Get a stick and walk up to the valley until you find a pig in the water and prod the pig! It's not hard! Mau, you are the chief. What I want to show you is not about pigs! It's important . . .'

'Pigs are impor—'

'This is more important than pigs! I want you to come and see!'

By the end of the day everyone saw, if only for a few minutes. People moving up and down the long cave were shifting the air around, and it was nothing like as foul as it had been, but the lamps were used a lot. Every single lamp from the *Judy* had been pressed into service.

'The world,' said Mau, staring. 'It's a ball? But we don't fall off?'

The ghost girl seemed to be on fire with words. 'Yes, yes, and you know this! You know the story about the brother who sailed so far he came back home?'

'Of course. Every child knows this.'

'I think people from this island sailed around the world, a long, long time ago. You remembered, but over the years it became a story for little children.'

Even down in the dark, Mau thought. He ran a hand over what Daphne called 'the globe', the biggest one, which had rolled onto the floor when the statue had broken. Imo's globe. The World. He let his fingertips just brush the stone. It came up to his chin.

So this is the world, he thought, letting his fingers follow a line of gleaming gold across the stone. There were a lot of these lines, and they all led to the same place – or, rather, away from it, as though some giant had thrown spears around the world. And he was my ancestor, he told himself as he lightly touched the familiar symbol that told him this was no place built by trousermen. His people carved the stone. His people *carved* the gods.

In his memory he could hear the spirit of Ataba, roaring, 'That doesn't mean a thing, demon boy! The gods themselves guided their tools.' And Mau thought, Well, it means something to me. Yes, it means a lot.

'Your land was a big place, as big as Crete, I think,' said the ghost girl behind him. 'I'll show you Crete on the map later. Your people went everywhere! Mostly Africa and China and the middle Americas, and you know what? I think James Croll's theory about the ice sheets is right! I went to his lecture at the Royal Society. That's why so much of Europe and North America is just not there – er, not because he gave his lecture, I mean, but because it was covered in ice! Do you know what ice is? Oh. Well, it's when water goes very cold until it becomes like crystal. Anyway, the other end of the world was a snowball, but down here it was still warm and you did *amazing* things!'

'Ice,' murmured Mau. He felt as if he was on an unfamiliar sea. With no map and no familiar smells, while her voice washed over him. The globe was a kind of map, like the *Judy*'s charts. Where his island was now, where all the islands in the chain had been, it showed a mighty land, made of gold. People from here had sailed everywhere. And then . . . something had happened. The gods got angry, as Ataba had said, or as the ghost girl said, the crystal world of the trousermen melted. It meant the same thing. The sea rose.

If he closed his eyes he could see the white buildings under the sea. Had it come in a rush, that great wave? Did the land shake and the mountains catch fire? It must have been sudden, because the water rose and the land became a pattern of islands, and the world changed.

'When the world was otherwise,' he whispered.

He sat down on the edge of what everyone was calling the god pool. His mind was too full of thoughts; he needed a bigger head. The . . . ancestors had brought the milk stone here and used it to make steps and wall carvings and gods, perhaps all out of the same piece of stone. And there was the broken statue of Imo. His head was probably in the depths of the pool. Imo had fallen, and so had the world.

Something had been returned. The Nation had been old, older than the reef, she was saying. The people of the Nation had sailed beyond the seas they knew, under unfamiliar stars.

He looked up, and saw unfamiliar stars. The light moved as groups of people moved around the hall. The roof glittered, just like statues. They were made of glass, she'd said. They looked like stars in the night sky, but they were not his stars. They were crystal stars, stars of a different sky.

'I want the right people to see this,' said Daphne behind him.

'The right people *are* seeing it,' said Mau.

After a few moments' silence he heard the girl say, 'I'm sorry. I meant that there are learned men in the Royal Society who could tell us what it means.'

'Are they priests?' asked Mau suspiciously.

'No. Very much no! In fact some of them don't get on with priests *at all*. But they search for answers.'

'Good. Send them here. But I know what this place means. My ancestors wanted to tell us that they were here, that's what it means,' said Mau. He could feel the tears welling up, but what was propelling them was a fierce, burning pride. 'Send your wise trousermen,' he said, trying not to let his voice shake, 'and we will welcome the brothers who travelled to the other end of the world, and came back at last to the place they had left behind. I am not stupid, ghost girl. If we sailed to those places long ago, wouldn't we have settled there, yes? And when your learned men come here, we will say to them: The world is a globe – the further you sail, the closer to home you are.'

He could barely see Daphne in the gloom, but when she spoke he could tell that her voice was shaking. 'I will tell you something even more amazing,' she said. 'All around the world people have carved stones into gods. All around the world. And all around the world people have said that the planets are gods, as well. But your ancestors knew things that nobody else knew. Mau, the god of Air has four little figures sitting on his shoulders. They are his sons, yes? They raced around their father to see which of them would court the Woman who lives in the Moon? It's in the beer song.'

'And what do you want to tell me about them?'

'We call the Air planet Jupiter. Jupiter has four moons that race around it. I've seen them in my telescope at home! And then there is Saturn, which you call Fire. The Papervine Woman tied his hands to his belt to stop the god stealing her daughters, yes?'

'It's just another god story for babies. I don't believe it.'

'It's true. Oh, well. In a way – I don't know about the Papervine Woman, but the planet Saturn has rings around it, and I suppose they do look like that when you see them at the right angle.'

'It's just a story.'

'No! It's been *turned* into a story. The moons are real! So are the rings! Your ancestors saw them, and I wish I knew how. Then they made up these songs and mothers sing them to their children! That's how the knowledge gets passed down, except that you didn't know it was knowledge! See how the gods shine? There are little plates of glass all over them. Your ancestors made *glass*. I've got an idea about that, too. Mau, when my father comes and I get back home, this place will be the most famous cave in—'

It was horrible to watch her face change. It went from

a kind of desperate excitement to dark despair, in gentle slow motion. It was as though a shadow had drifted across a landscape.

He caught her before she fell, and felt her tears on his skin. 'He will come,' he said quickly. 'There is so much ocean.'

'But he would know the course of the *Judy*, and this is a big island! He should have got here by now!'

'The ocean is much bigger. And there was the wave! He could be looking south, thinking the *Judy* capsized. He could be looking north, in case you were swept along. Oh, he will come. We must be ready.' Mau patted her on the back, and looked down. The children, who had soon got fed up with looking at big dark things they didn't understand, had gathered round and were watching them with interest. He tried to shoo them away.

The sobbing stopped. 'What was that little boy holding?' said Daphne hoarsely.

Mau beckoned the child over, and borrowed the new toy from him. Daphne stared at it and started to laugh. It was more like a panting noise, in fact, the noise made by someone too astonished to draw breath. She managed to say: 'Where did he get these, please?'

'He says Uncle Pilu gave them to him. He has been diving in the god pool.'

Uncle Pilu, Daphne noted. There were lots of uncles and aunts on the island now, and not many mothers and fathers.

'Tell the little boy I will give him an arm's length of

sugar cane for them,' she said, 'and he can stretch as much as he likes. Is that a trade?'

'Well, he's grinning,' said Mau. 'I think just hearing the words "sugar cane" was enough!'

'A mountain of sugar would not have been enough.' Daphne held up her purchase. 'Shall I tell you what these are? They were made by someone who did not just watch the skies and sail to new lands. He thought about small things that make life better for people. I've never heard of them being made of gold before, but these are definitely false teeth!'

When she was a lot older and had to deal with meetings all the time, Daphne remembered the council of war. It was probably the only one ever to have children running around in it. It was certainly the only one to have Mrs Gurgle scuttling around in it with her new teeth. She had snatched them out of Daphne's hand when she was demonstrating them to Cahle, and it was impossible to get anything off Mrs Gurgle if she didn't want you to take it. They were too big for her and almost certainly she couldn't eat with them, but if she opened her mouth in daylight it was like looking at the sun.

Pilu did most of the talking, but always with one eye on Mau. He talked so fast and hard that the words formed pictures in front of her eyes, and what she saw was the Agincourt speech from *Henry the Fifth*, or at least what it might have been like if Shakespeare had been small and dark and wore a little loincloth instead of trousers, or tights in Shakespeare's case. But there was lot more in there, and Pilu had one wonderful talent for a speaker: he began with the truth and then he hammered it out until it was very thin but gleamed like Mrs Gurgle's new teeth at noon.

They were the oldest people! He told them their ancestors had invented canoes and sailed them under new skies, to land so far away they ended up back home! And they had seen further than any other people! They had seen the four sons of Air race across the sky! They had seen the Papervine Woman lash her vines around the Fire god! They had built wondrous devices, back in the long ago, when the world was otherwise!

But now bad men were coming! They were very bad men indeed! So Imo himself had sent them the *Sweet Judy*, the first ship ever built, which had come back on the great wave, carrying everything they would need in this dark time, including the wonderful salt-pickled beef and the ghost girl, who knows the secrets of the sky and makes wonderful beer—

Daphne blushed at this, and tried to catch Mau's eye, but he looked away.

And Pilu was shouting, 'And with the help of the *Sweet Judy* we shall blow the Raiders across the seas!'

Oh no, she thought, he knows about the cannon! He's found the *Judy*'s cannon.

There was cheering as Pilu finished. People surrounded Mau.

There had always been wars, even among the local

islands. From what she could work out, they were mostly not much worse than a fight among the stable boys and a good way of getting impressive scars and a story to exaggerate for your grandchildren. And there were often raids from one island to another to steal brides, but since the women arranged it all beforehand, they hardly counted.

But . . . cannon! She'd seen gun drill on the *Judy*, and even Cox handled them with care. There was one right way of firing a cannon, and lots of wonderfully explosive ways of getting it wrong.

When the crowd was gathering around Pilu for some patriotic singing, Daphne strode up to Mau and glared at him.

'How many cannon?' she demanded.

'Milo has found five,' said Mau. 'We are going to put them on the hill above the beach. Yes, I know what you're going to say, but the brothers know how to use them.'

'Really? They might have watched! Pilu thinks he knows how to read, but mostly he just guesses!'

'The cannon give us hope. We know who we are now. We are not beggars outside the trouserman world. We are not children. Once *we* were the bold sailors, all the way to the other end of the world. Perhaps *we* wore the trousers.'

'Er, I think Pilu might have been going too far with that—'

'No, he is clever. Should he tell them the truth? Should he tell them that all I've got is a few things I know and a handful of guesses and a big hope, and that we are so weak, and that if I am wrong, those of us not dead by sunset on the day the Raiders attack will wish they were? That will only make them fear. If a lie will make us strong, a lie will be my weapon.' He sighed. 'People want lies to live by. They cry out for them. Have you looked at the *Judy* lately? I must show you something.'

The path through the low forest was well worn. So much had been dragged out to the beach in the past months that even high-speed vines and voracious grasses had not been able to keep up everywhere. In places the forest floor was just shards of crumbling stone.

'We go to the *Sweet Judy* for everything,' said Mau as he led the way. 'It gives us wood and food and light. Without the *Judy* and her cargo, where would we be? What could we want that the *Judy* could not give us? That's what people say. And now, since our gods have failed us . . .'

He stood back.

Someone had nailed a red fish to the planking of the ship. By the smell, it had been there for several days. And below it were a stick man and a stick woman, drawn very crudely in red, white and black. Daphne stared at them.

'That's supposed to be me, isn't it,' she said, 'and that's you with poor Captain Roberts's cap on.'

'Yes,' sighed Mau.

'It's a good one of the cap,' said Daphne diplomatically. 'Where did they get the white?'

'There's a stick of it in the carpenter's toolbox,' said Mau gloomily.

'Ah, that would be called chalk,' said Daphne. 'I suppose all these round things they have drawn here are barrels?'

'Yes. This is a god place now. I've heard them talking, sometimes. Some of them think the gods sent the *Judy* here to help them! Can you believe that? Then who sent the wave? They'll believe in anything! This morning I heard one of the new ones talking about "The Cave the Gods Made"! *We* made it! Men made the gods, too. Gods of cold stone, which we made so that we could hide from thc dark in a shell of comfortable lies. But when the Raiders come, there will be five cannon on the beach, made by men! And when they speak, they will not tell lies!'

'You will blow yourself up! Those cannon have been thrown about and dragged over rocks and they were old and rusty to start with! Cookie said they'd turn into a tin banana if you fire them with more than half a load. They'll blow up!'

'We will not run. We cannot run. So we must fight. And if we fight, we must win. But at least we know *how* they will fight.'

'How can you possibly know that?'

'Because when the Raiders come they will pour onto the beach and challenge our chief to single combat.'

'You? But you can't—'

'I have more than one plan. Please trust me.'

'You will fire the cannon?'

'Perhaps. They worship Locaha. They think he protects them. They collect skulls for him. They eat the flesh of men in his honour. They believe the more men they kill, the more slaves they will have in his country when he takes them. They don't care if they die. But Locaha makes no bargains with *anyone*.'

They were back on the beach now. In the distance, a couple of men were, very slowly, carrying a cannon up the track.

'I don't think we have much time,' said Mau. 'The man with the big bleeding nose will tell Cox that we are an island of invalids and children and no trousermen. Except you.'

'He won't care who gets killed. He shot a butterfly in half, remember?' said Daphne.

Mau shook his head. 'How can he rise up every morning and decide to be him?'

'I think that if you could understand him, you'd be him. That's what he does. He turns people into creatures like himself. That's what happened to Foxlip. And he'll make sure that the only way to kill him is to be worse than him. It nearly worked on poor Captain Roberts. Make sure it doesn't happen to you, Mau!'

Mau sighed. 'Let's get back before they start worshipping us, shall we?'

They followed the cannon and Daphne trailed behind a little. Even wearing the trousers, which were far too big for him, Mau still walked like a dancer. Daphne had been taken to the ballet several times by her grandmother, who wanted to make sure she grew up to be a proper lady and not marry a godless scientist. She'd been bored silly, and the dancers were nothing like as graceful as she had expected. But Mau walked as if every part of his body knew where it was and where it was going to and exactly how fast it had to go to get there. People would have paid good money just to see the muscles on his back move like they were doing now. She understood the maids back home a lot more when the sun gleamed on his shoulders. Ahem.

In the morning, they fired a cannon, an enterprise which consisted of lighting a really long fuse and then everyone running very fast in the opposite direction. The bang was impressive and most people got back on their feet in time to see the splash when the ball hit the water on the other side of the lagoon.

But Daphne didn't join in the celebrations. Of course, according to Cookie, everything on the *Judy* was far too old and ready for the scrap heap, but she'd looked into the barrels of the cannon, and they *were* a mess. Four of them had cracks in, and the last one, inside, looked as knobbly as the moon. They did not look like the kind of cannon you wanted to fire if you had been raised in the belief that, when it came to cannon, the ball should come out of the *front*. But Mau wouldn't listen to her when she tried to talk to him about it, and a look came over his face that she'd seen before. It said: 'I know what I'm doing. Don't bother me. Everything will be all right.' And in the meantime Milo and Pilu banged mysteriously at empty tins from the *Judy*'s galley, down by the fire, hammering them flat for no reason they were prepared to give. Some of the men and older boys were trained in firing the cannon, but since there wasn't any gunpowder to spare for actually firing any more of the things, they made do with pushing wooden cartridges into the barrel and proudly shouting, 'Bang!' They got quite good at that, and were proud at the speed with which 'Bang!' could be shouted. Daphne said she hoped the enemy would be trained to say, 'Aargh!'

Nothing happened and went on happening. They finished the pig fence, which meant that the last of the planting could be done. They started a new hut, but this was a lot higher up the slope. Trees were planted. One of the men got his leg ripped open on the first boar hunt since the wave and Daphne sewed it up again, washing the wound in mother-of-beer to keep it clean. Mau stood guard on the beach every night, often with the Unknown Woman nearby, but now at least she trusted people enough to leave her little boy with them. And that was just as well, because she had taken a sudden interest in paper-vine, cutting the longest leaves of it from all over the island and then endlessly plaiting them into string after green string. So now, because it's how people's minds work, the Unknown Woman was known as the Papervine Woman.

Once she solemnly handed her baby to Daphne, and Cahle made a remark that Daphne didn't quite catch but which made all the women laugh, so it was almost certainly something like, 'It's about time you made one!'

People relaxed.

And the Raiders came, just at dawn.

They came with drums, and torchlight.

Mau ran up the beach to the huts, shouting, 'The Raiders are coming! The Raiders are coming!'

People woke up and ran, mostly into one another, while outside the clanging and drumming went on. The dogs barked and got under people's feet. In ones and twos men hurried up to the cannons on the hill, but by then it was too late.

'You're all dead,' said Mau.

Out on the lagoon the mists faded. Milo and Pilu stopped their drumming and banging and paddled their canoe back to the beach. People looked around feeling stupid and annoyed. Nevertheless, up on the hill a man shouted 'Bang!' at the top of his voice and looked very pleased with himself.

Later, though, Mau asked Daphne what the casualties were.

'Well, one man dropped his spear on his own foot,' she said. 'A woman sprained her ankle because she tripped over her dog, and the man up on the cannon got his hand stuck up in the barrel.'

'How can you possibly get your hand stuck up the barrel of a cannon?' said Mau.

'Apparently he was pushing the ball in and it rolled back onto his fingers,' said Daphne. 'Perhaps you should write a letter to the cannibals, telling them not to come. I know you don't know how to write, but they probably don't know how to read.'

'I must organize people better,' sighed Mau.

'No!' said Daphne. 'Tell them to organize *themselves*! There should be lookouts. There should always be a man up on the guns. Tell the women to make sure they know where to go. Oh, and tell them that the fastest gun crew will get extra beer. Make them *think*. Tell them what's got to be done, and let them work out how. And now, thank you, I've got some beer half made!'

Back in her hut, with the reassuringly homely smells of the cauldron, the beer and Mrs Gurgle, she wondered about Cookie: whether *he* had survived the wave, because if anyone should have done, it was Cookie.

Daphne had spent a lot of time in the *Sweet Judy*'s galley, because it was only another type of kitchen, and she was at home in kitchens. It was also a safe place. Even at the height of the mutiny, everyone was friends with Cookie, and he had no enemies. Every seaman, even a madman like Cox, knew that there was no point in upsetting the cook, who had all kinds of little opportunities to get his own back, as you might find out one night when it was *you* hanging over the rail, trying to throw up your own stomach.

And on top of this Cookie was good company and seemed to have sailed to everywhere on just about any kind of ship, and he was constantly rebuilding his own coffin, which he'd brought aboard. It was now part of the furniture of the galley, and for most of the time the saucepans were piled up on top of it. He seemed surprised that Daphne thought all this was a touch on the odd side.

Perhaps this was because the most important thing about this coffin was that Cookie did not intend to die in it. He intended to live in it instead, because he had designed it to float. He had even built a keel on it. He took great pleasure in showing her how well appointed it was inside. There was a shroud, in case he actually did die, but which could easily be used as a sail until that unlucky day; there was a small folding mast for this very purpose. Inside the coffin, which was padded, there were rows of pockets which held ship's biscuits, dried fruit, fish hooks (and fishing line), a compass, charts and a wonderful device for distilling drinking water from the sea. It was a tiny floating world.

'I got the idea off of a harpooner I met when I was working on the whalers,' he told her one day as he was adding yet another pocket to the insides of the coffin. 'He was a rum 'un and no mistake. Had more tattoos than the Edinburgh festival and all his teeth filed as sharp as daggers, but he lugged this coffin onto every ship he sailed with so's if he died he'd have a proper Christian funeral and not be chucked over the side sewn up in a bit o' canvas with a cannon ball for company. I thought about it myself – it's a good basic idea, but it needs a little bit of changing. Anyway, I didn't stay long on that ship on account of coming down with bowel weevils just before we rounded the Cape and I had to put ashore at Valparaiso. It was probably a blessing in disguise, 'cos I reckon that ship was heading for a bad end. I've seen a few mad captains in my time, but that one was as crazy as a spoon. And you may depend upon it, when the captain is crazy, so is the ship. I often wonder what happened to 'em all.'

Daphne finished making the mother-of-beer and walked down the slope until she could see the little crumbling cliff that overlooked the beach. Mau was there, and so were all the gunners, including the Papervine Lady, for some reason.

The cannon are useless, she thought. He must know that. So what does he think he's doing?

There was a distant shout of 'Bang!' and she sighed . . .

Two of the Gentlemen of Last Resort ran up onto the deck and joined the captain at the ship's rail.

'What is the emergency?' said Mr Black. 'Surely we're nowhere near the Mothering Sundays yet?'

'The lookout said he saw a maroon fired,' said the captain, his telescope to his eye. 'Some poor soul's been shipwrecked, I dare say. There's an island there. It's not on the charts. Technically, Mr Black, I need your permission to change course.'

'Of course you must, aha, change course, Captain,' said Mr Black. 'Indeed, I note that you already have.'

'That is correct, sir,' said the captain carefully. 'The sea has its own laws.'

'Well done, Captain. I should listen to your advice.'

There was a moment's silence, caused by *nobody mentioning the king's daughter*.

'I'm sure Roberts got her through, sir,' said the captain, looking carefully at the distant island again.

'It's kind of you to say so.'

'In the meantime,' the captain went on, cheerfully, 'I do believe I am looking at a very lucky shipwrecked mariner. Someone else may have discovered an island over there before us. I can see a fire, and a man fishing from a—' He stopped, and adjusted the telescope. 'Well, I have to say he seems to be sitting in a coffin . . .'

There was no alarm on the next day, but there was one the day after, which Mau said went well. Every morning, people became better and better at shouting 'Bang!' And every day Daphne wondered what Mau was really planning.

CHAPTER 13

TRUCE

*T*he Raiders came, just before dawn.

They came with drums, and torchlight making red suns in the mists.

Mau's ears heard them. In his eyes the flames were reflected. Then he awoke from what was not exactly a sleep, and felt the future happening.

How did that work? he wondered. On the very first day he'd stood guard on the Nation, he'd had the memory of this. It had been flying towards him from the future. He'd always had that trick with the silver thread that pulled him towards the future he pictured in his head. But this time it was the future that had been tugging at him, pulling him to this place, at this time.

'They are here,' someone whispered beside him. He looked at the Unknown Woman. He'd never seen much of an expression on her face before, but now it terrified the life out of him. It was sheer poisonous hatred.

'Ring the bell!' he snapped, and she hurried up the beach. Mau walked backwards, watching the mist. He hadn't expected that. He hadn't *seen* it!

The sound of the *Sweet Judy*'s bell sang out across the lagoon. Mau ran up the track, and was relieved to see faint shapes hurrying through the damp billows. Where was the sun? It must be time for dawn!

Over towards the low forest, the first grandfather bird threw up, and was immediately attacked by its arch enemy.

'*Waark!* Yer lying ol' hypocrite!'

And with that the dawn chorus exploded, with every bird, frog, toad and insect screaming its head off. Golden light rolled in from the east, melting ragged holes in the mist. It was a beautiful picture, apart from the black and red war canoes. Most of them were too big to enter the lagoon. They had grounded on the spit of land by Little Nation, and figures were pouring onto the sand.

No voices in my head, Mau thought. No dead people. It's just me in here. I've got to get this right . . .

Pilu hurried up with a heavy package wrapped in papervine cloth. 'It's been kept dry. It will be fine.'

Mau looked along the high ground. Someone was standing by each cannon with a long fuse in his hand, or in the case of one, *her* hand. They were watching him anxiously. *Everyone* was watching him.

He looked down at the beach again, and saw Cox, towering over the Raiders.

He'd been expecting someone like Foxlip, skinny and unhealthy-looking, but this man was a good foot taller and nearly the same size as Milo. He had feathers sticking up around his trouserman hat. They were red, the feathers of a chief. So he'd done what the ghost girl had said he'd do: he'd taken over. That was their law. The strongest man led. That made sense. At least, it made sense to strong men.

The Raiders were holding back, though. They were staying near their boats; only one was coming up the beach, with his spear held over his head.

In a way, and it was a strange kind of way, it was a big relief. He didn't like having two plans.

'He looks very young,' said the ghost girl behind him. He spun round and there she was, dwarfed beside Milo, who was carrying a club the size of a medium-sized tree; in fact it *was* a medium-sized tree, without the branches.

'You should have gone into the forest with the others!' he said.

'Really? Well, now I'm coming with you.'

Mau glanced at Milo, but he'd get no help there. Since Guiding Star had been born, the ghost girl could do no wrong as far as his father was concerned.

'Besides,' she said, 'it's going to end up the same way for all of us, if this goes wrong. Why aren't they charging towards us?'

'Because they want to talk.' Mau pointed to the approaching man. He was young, and trying not to be afraid.

'Why?'

The young man stuck his spear into the sand, and then turned and ran.

'Maybe it's because they have seen the cannon. I was hoping for this. Look at them. They're not happy.'

'Can we trust them?'

'With a truce? Yes.'

'Really?'

'Yes. There are rules. Pilu and Milo will talk to them. I'm just a boy, with no tattoos. They won't speak to me.'

'But you are the chief!'

Mau smiled. 'Yes, but don't tell them.'

Was it like this at the Battle of Waterloo? Daphne wondered as they walked down to the beach and the waiting group. This is . . . strange. It's so . . . civilized, as if a battle is something that starts when somebody blows a whistle. There are rules, even here. And here comes Cox. Oh Lord, even the air he breathes needs a wash afterwards.

First Mate Cox came towards them, smiling like someone greeting a long-lost friend who owed him money. You never saw Cox frown. Like crocodiles and sharks, Cox always had a grin for people, especially when he had them at his mercy, or at least where his mercy would be if he had any.

'Well now, here's a thing,' he said. 'Fancy seeing you here, young lady. The *Judy* got this far, then? And where's old Roberts and his upstanding crew? At prayer?'

'They are here and armed, Mr Cox,' Daphne said.

'Are they indeed?' said Cox cheerfully. 'Then I'm the

Queen of Sheba.' He pointed to the upper slope, where the cannon were clearly visible. 'Those guns are from the *Judy*, right?'

'I'm not telling you anything, Mr Cox.'

'Then they are. A load of scrap iron, as I recall. That skinflint Roberts was too mean to get new ones. I know I'm right. First time you use them they'll split like a sausage! Seems to have put the wind up my jolly loyal subjects though. Oh, yeah, I'm their chief, as a matter of fact. See my new hat? It's quite the style, ain't it? Me, King o' the Cannibals.' He leaned forward. 'You got to be nice to me now I'm a king,' he said. 'You should call me Your Majesty, eh?'

'And how did you become a king, Mr Cox?' said Daphne. 'I'm *sure* it involved killing people.' She had to make an effort not to back away, but backing away from the man never worked.

'Only one, so don't be so hoity-toity. We'd just got a nice new boat courtesy of a bunch of Dutchmen of a charitable disposition, and then just after we'd chucked them over the side, a load of our brown chums comes up on us all in rush, and we had a bit of an argument. I shot this big devil, all war paint and feathers, just as he's about to flatten me with his big hammer – lovely gun, the cheese-eater captain had, far too good for a Dutchman, which is why I grabbed it off him before we threw him to the sharks – but anyway, I let a bit of air into Johnny Savage, lovely action that gun's got, smooth as a kiss – and next thing you know, abracadabra, I'm king of 'em.

And then it's all off to a nice island for a big coronation feast. An' don't you look at me like that – I had the fish.'

He looked around. 'Oh dear me, where are my manners? May I introduce to you the lads from what they call the Land of Many Fires. I dare say you've heard of them? As black-hearted a bunch of villains as you might find in a dozen chapels!' He waved a hand theatrically at a group of men, lesser chiefs perhaps, who had gathered around Pilu and Milo, and went on: 'They are a bit whiffy on the nose, my word, yes, but that's 'cos of their diet. Not enough roughage, see? Leave the clothes *on*, I tell 'em, the buttons'll do you good! But they don't listen. Nearly as bad as me, and I don't spread praise like that around in a hurry. These lads here are the gentry, believe it or not.'

She took a look at some of the said gentry and, to her shock, recognized them. She knew them. She'd lived among them for most of her life. Well, not actual cannibals, obviously (although there had been all those rumours about the 10th Earl of Crowcester, but dinner-party opinion picked up via the trusty dumbwaiter was that he had just been very hungry and extremely short-sighted).

These old men had bones in their noses and shells in their ears, but there was something familiar there, too. They had the well-fed, important, careful look of people who took care not to be at the top. A lot of government people like them had dined at the Hall. They had learned over the years that the top was not a happy or safe place to be. One rung down, that was the place for a sensible man.

You advised the king, you had a lot of power, in a quiet kind of way, and you didn't get murdered anything like as often. And, if the ruler started to get funny ideas and became a bit of an embarrassment, you just . . . took care of things.

The nearest one gave her a nervous smile, although later she realized that he might have just been hungry. In any case, if you took away the long hair, which was curled up into a headdress with a feather stuck in it, and then added a pair of silver spectacles, he would look *exactly* like the Prime Minister back home, or at least like the Prime Minister would look after a year in the sun. She could see his wrinkles under his paint.

Cannibal Chief, she thought. It's such a nasty name. But she could see the polished skull on his belt, and his necklace was made of little white shells and finger bones, and as far as she knew, the Prime Minister didn't have a big black club studded with sharks' teeth.

'Amazin' resemblance, ain't it?' said Cox, as if he'd been reading her thoughts. 'And there's one back there who could pass for the Archbishop of Canterbury in a poor light. Just goes to show what a haircut and a Savile Row suit will do, eh?'

He winked his horrible wink, and Daphne, who had vowed not to rise to this sort of thing, heard herself say: 'The Archbishop of Canterbury, Mr Cox, is not a cannibal!'

'He doesn't think so, miss. Wine and wafers, m'lady, wine and wafers!'

TRUCE

Daphne shuddered. The man had an uncanny ability to look inside your head, and leave it feeling grubby. Even on the beach she wanted to apologize to the sand for letting him tread on it, but the looks on the faces of the wrinkled old men with him made her heart leap. They were glaring! They hated him! He'd brought them here, and now they were under the barrels of cannon! They might get killed, and they had spent a lifetime not getting killed. All right, he'd killed the last king, but that was just because he had the magic gun stick. He smelled of madness. Tradition was fine, but sometimes you had to be practical . . .

'Tell me, Mr Cox, can you speak the language of your new subjects?' she asked sweetly.

Cox looked astonished. 'What, me? Catch me speaking their heathen lingo! Ugga wugga this, lugga mugga that! That's not for me! I'm learnin' 'em English, since you ask. I'll civilize 'em if I have to shoot every mother's son of 'em, trust me on that. Talking of ugga wugga, what's all this chin-wagging about?'

Daphne listened out of the corner of her ear. War negotiations were going rather oddly. The enemy warriors listened to Pilu, but looked up at Milo when they replied, as Pilu himself was not important.

Mau was taking no part in things at all. He stood behind the brothers, leaning on his spear and listening. Daphne went to push her way through them and found she didn't need to; cannibal chiefs shuffled out of her way as fast as they could.

'What's *happening*?' she whispered. 'Are they worried about the cannon?'

'Yes. They believe in single combat, one chief against another. If our chief beats their chief, they will go away.'

'Can you trust them?'

'Yes. This is about belief. If their god doesn't smile on them, they won't fight. But Cox wants them all to fight, and they know they should obey him. He wants a massacre. He's telling them that the cannon won't work.'

'You think they will, though,' said Daphne.

'I think one will,' said Mau quietly.

'One? *One!*'

'Don't *shout*. Yes, one. Just one. But that isn't going to matter, because we don't have enough gunpowder for more than one shot.'

Daphne was speechless. She finally managed to say, 'But there were three kegs!'

'That's true. The little one from your cabin was half empty. The others are full of gunpowder soup. The water got in. It's just stinking muck.'

'But you fired a cannon weeks ago!'

'The little keg had enough for two firings. The first one we tried with what looked like the least rotten gun. It worked. You saw it. But there's a crack all along it now, and it was the best one. But don't worry, we repaired it.'

Daphne's brow furrowed. 'How can you repair a cannon? You can't repair a cannon, not here!'

'A trouserman might not be able to, but I can,' said Mau proudly. 'Remember, you didn't know how to milk a pig!'

'All right then, *how* do you repair a broken cannon?' said Daphne.

'Our way,' said Mau, beaming. 'With string!'

'With str—?'

'*Waark!* Cox is the prawn of the devil!'

Even Daphne, mouth open to object, turned to look—

But Cox was quicker than all of them. His hand moved fast as the parrot glided over the beach. He cocked, aimed and fired in one movement, three shots, one after another, The parrot squawked and tumbled into the papervine thickets above the beach, leaving a few bits of feather floating in the air.

Cox looked at the watchers, and bowed and waved, like a musician who had just played a very difficult piano concerto. But the Raiders glanced at him as if he were a little boy who was proud of having wet himself.

Daphne was still trying to deal with string, but on top of that floated: Three shots in a row! The Dutch captain's gun was a revolver!

'I think this is the time,' Mau said. 'Pilu should have got them confused enough by now. Turn my words into Trouserman, will you?'

And he strode off down the beach before she could argue. He pushed his way into the circle before anyone knew he was there, and faced the Raiders.

'Who says our guns do not fire?' he bellowed. 'Enough arguing! *Fire!*'

Up on the cliff, the unknown Papervine Woman, who had been crouched obediently over her green cannon, touched the slow match to the fuse and, as instructed, ran away very fast and stood behind a tree until the thunder had died away, and then ran back even faster. She ignored the cannon, which was under a cloud of steam, and looked at the lagoon.

The ball had splashed in the middle, capsizing three boats. Figures were in the water. She smiled, and went back to the cannon. Wordless though she was, she'd *begged* to be allowed to fire it. Hadn't she gathered all the paper-vine? Hadn't she woven it into ropes from dawn to dusk, tangling into it the inexhaustible hatred in her heart? Hadn't Mau seen her helping Pilu shaping metal plates over the cracks in the cannon? Hadn't he seen how she had taken care to wrap the ropes around the cannon, layer after layer, every one as strong as her longing for revenge?

And he had, and they had held; thin little blades of papervine had bound the red thunder in.

She went back to the tree, took up her baby from his cradle made from papervine and kissed him, and wept.

'We will fire again,' Pilu yelled, in the confusion. 'We will destroy your big canoes. We have made the challenge of single combat. You must accept! Or do you want to swim home?'

Raiders clustered around Cox, who was swearing at them.

'What have we got to lose, Mr Cox?' Daphne shouted above the hubbub. 'Don't you think you'll win?' And then in the island tongue she hissed: 'We will sink every canoe! Our guns are well guarded!' Mau whispered to her and she added, 'If you raise a weapon in the Kahana circle they will kill you, Mr Cox. It's against all the rules!'

There was a heavy thudding, which turned out to be Milo thumping his chest. 'Who will fight?' he yelled. 'Who will fight?'

'All right! I'll fight!' Cox snarled. He pushed away a few hangers-on and dusted off his shirt. 'Huh, and I'm supposed to be king in this vicinity,' he complained. 'You wouldn't find the Brigade of Guards coming over all treasonable like this, my word, no!' He glared at Milo. 'I'll fight the big one,' he said. 'It's not like he'll be easy to miss.'

'You have a plan, don't you?' Daphne hissed to Mau. 'You're not going to let him shoot Milo dead, are you?'

'Yes, I have a plan. No, he's not going to shoot Milo. We'd say Milo is chief if one of the Raiders was fighting, because he'd win. But I can't let Cox shoot Milo. He's so big, so easy to sho—'

Daphne's expression went solid as understanding came. 'It's you, isn't it . . . ? You are going to fight him.'

She was jostled out of the way as Milo dropped his huge hand on the boy's shoulder, causing him to stand a bit lopsidedly.

'Listen to me!' he declared to the Raiders. 'I am not the chief! *Mau* is the chief. He has risen from the country of Locaha. He set the dead men free. The gods hid from him in a cave, but he found them and they told him the secret of the world! And he has no soul.'

Cor blimey! thought Daphne. One of the footmen had

been sacked for saying that when she was eight, and until she'd sailed on the *Sweet Judy* she'd thought it was the worst swear word in the world. It still felt as if it was.

Cor blimey! That was the most words that Milo had ever said in a *day*! They might have been said by his brother, because they were the truth, disguised as lies, and there was something about that fact which made them echo in the head. They seemed to be doing so in the heads of the warriors. They stared at Mau in astonishment.

A heavy hand landed on Daphne's shoulder, too, and Cox said, 'Missie? I'm going to have to shoot the little bugger, right?'

She spun round and shoved his arm away. But he caught her tightly by the wrist.

'I could shoot *you*, Cox, whatever you say!'

Cox laughed. 'Oh, you've got the taste for killing, missie?' he said, his face a few inches from hers. 'Mind you, poisoning don't really count, I always think. Did he gurgle? Did he go green? But well done for bashin' two of Polegrave's teeth right out, the evil little monkey . . . He didn't try to mess you up, did he? I'd shoot him if he tried anything unsavoury. Oh, but in point of fact I shot him yesterday, cos he really was a pain in the arse, excuse my French—'

Daphne managed to pull her arm free. 'Don't touch me again! Don't you even *suggest* that I'm like you! Don't you—'

'Stop.' Mau didn't shout. His spear shouted for him. It was aimed at Cox's heart.

No one moved for several seconds and then Cox said, slowly and carefully, 'Ah, is this your beau? What *will* dear Daddy say? Oh my word! An' you taught him how to talk, too.'

The cannibal twin of the Prime Minister stepped between them with his hands raised, and suddenly a lot of spears and clubs were being shaken.

'No fight yet!' he said to Cox in broken English, and turned to Daphne. 'The boy has no soul?' he said in the island tongue.

'The wave took away his soul, but he has made himself a new one,' she said.

'Wrong. No man can make a soul!' But he's worried, Daphne thought.

'This one did. He made it outside himself. You are walking on it,' she said. '*And don't try to shuffle sideways.* It covers the whole island, every leaf and pebble!'

'They call you a woman of power, ghost girl.' The man took a step backwards. 'Is this true? What is the colour of birds in the land of Locaha?'

'There are no colours. There are no birds. The fish are silver, and as fast as thought.' The words were just there, ready, in her head. Great Heavens, she thought, I *know* this!

'What is the length of time you may stay in the land of Locaha?'

'The fall of a drop of water,' said Daphne's lips before she had finished hearing the question.

'And the soul who makes his own soul . . . he was in Locaha's land?'

'Yes. He ran faster than Locaha, though.'

The dark, piercing eyes stayed fixed on her for a while, and then it seemed that she had passed some test.

'You are very clever,' said the old man shyly. 'I would like to eat your brains, one day.'

For some reason the books of etiquette that Daphne's grandmother had forced on her didn't quite deal with this. Of course, silly people would say to babies, 'You're so sweet I could gobble you all up!', but that sort of nonsense seemed less funny when it was said by a man in war paint who owned more than one skull. Daphne, cursed with good manners, settled for, 'It's very kind of you to say so.'

He nodded and headed back to his fellows, who had clustered around Cox.

Mau approached her, smiling. 'Their priest likes you,' he said.

'Only for my brains, Mau, and even if he had them for lunch I'd still have more than you! Didn't you see that gun he's got now? It's a Pepperbox. One of Father's friends had one! It has six barrels. That's six shots without reloading! *And* he's got an ordinary pistol, too!'

'I shall move fast.'

'You can't run faster than a bullet!'

'I shall stay out of their way,' said Mau, with infuriating calmness.

'Look, don't you understand? He's got two guns and you've got one spear. You'll run out of spear before he runs out of gun!'

'Yes, but his gun will run out of bang before my knife runs out of sharp,' said Mau.

'Mau, I don't want you to die!' Daphne shouted. The words echoed back off the cliffs, and she blushed crimson.

'Then who should die? Milo? Pilu? Who? No. If anyone is going to die, it should be me. I've died before. I know how it's done. No more discussion!'

CHAPTER 14

DUEL

*B*ehind them the hubbub of the meeting had stopped.

Silence fell over the war canoes, lined with faces, the cluster of Raider chiefs on the shoreline, the people who had crept out to watch from the cliff. The sun was too bright to look at, and was already boiling all the colour out of the landscape. The world was holding its breath.

There would be no count, no signal. There were no rules, either. But there was tradition. The fight would start when the first man picked up his weapon. Mau's spear and knife were on the sand in front of him. Ten feet away, Cox had laid down his guns only after a lot of argument.

Now it was just a case of watching the other man's eyes. Cox grinned at him.

Hadn't every boy dreamed of this? To stand in front of

the enemy? And they were all here together, under the white-hot sun, all the lies, all the fears, all the terrors, all the horrors that the wave had brought, all here and in mortal form. Here, he could beat them.

And all that mattered was this: *If you don't dare to think you might, you won't.*

Mau's eyes creaked with staring. He was nearly blinded by the fierce sunlight, but at least there were no more voices in his head—

Except . . .

It is a good day to die, said the voice of Locaha.

Mau's arm shot out, hurling the handful of sand into Cox's eyes. He didn't wait, he just grabbed his knife and ran, listening to the cursing behind him. But you can't cheat when there are no rules. He'd picked up his weapon when he put his spear down. He didn't have to *say* he'd chosen the sand itself. It was a good weapon, too.

Don't stop. Don't look back, just keep running.

There wasn't a plan. There had never been a plan. All there was was hope, but there was little enough of that and there was something the ghost girl had taught him on the very first day they met: guns did not like water.

The lagoon was where he belonged right now and he fled for it, dodging and weaving as much as he dared. The water was his world. Cox was a big, heavy man and water would drag at his clothes. Yes!

He heard a shot fired and a bullet sang past his head. But here was the lagoon and he dived in when the water was hardly above his knees. He would have to come up for air, but surely the man would not dare to come in after him?

Out towards the middle of the lagoon, where the damaged canoes were drifting, he stopped and made use of their cover to grab some more air. Then he peered round the canoe to find Cox – and he was right there on the shoreline, already sighting on him.

Mau dived, but Cox had expected that. Perhaps it was true. The man *could* see into people's heads.

He turned to look back. He couldn't help it. Men face the enemy, just once . . .

And what Mau saw was the bullet coming. It hit the water a few feet in front of him, trailing bubbles – and stopped inches from his face. He gently picked it out of the water as it started to fall, and then let it go and watched in wonder as it dropped to the sand.

How had that happened? Bullets really *didn't* like water . . .

He climbed up to the surface for a mouthful of air and heard another bang as he dived again. He turned to watch another trail of bubbles head towards him and the bullet bounced off his arm. Bounced! He hardly felt it!

He struck out for the gap into the deep water, which was half blocked with floating weeds today. At least it gave him some cover. But what had happened to the bullets? A bullet certainly hadn't bounced off Ataba. It had made a big hole, and there had been a lot of blood.

He would have to surface again, because Cox was probably even more dangerous when you couldn't see where he was.

He grabbed the edge of the coral, steadied himself on a root of an old tree that had wedged in the gap. Very cautiously, he pulled himself up.

And there was Cox, running, running along the spit of old coral that led from the shore around to Little Nation and the new gap. Mau heard his boots crunch on the coral as he ran, speeding up while the watching Raiders scuttled out of the way.

The man glanced up, raised his gun and, still pounding over the coral, he fired twice.

A bullet went through Mau's ear. The first thought as he dropped back through the water was about the pain. The second thought was about the pain, too, because there was so much of it. The water was turning pink. He reached up to his ear and most of it was not there. His third thought was: Sharks. And the next thought, happening in some little world of its own, said: He has fired five shots. When he has fired all the bullets he has, he will have to load the guns again. But if I was him, I would wait until I'd had one last shot with the big pistol and then reload it, keeping the little pistol ready to hand in case the darkie suddenly came out of the water.

It was a strange, chilling thought, dancing across his mind like a white thread against the – terrible red background. It went on: He can think like you. You must think like him.

But if I think like him, he wins, he thought back.

And his new thought replied: Why? To think like him is not to be him! The hunter learns the ways of the hog, but he is not bacon. He learns the way of the weather, but he is not a cloud. And when the venomous beast charges at him, he remembers who is the hunter, and who the hunted! *Dive now! Dive right now!*

He dived. The tree half wedged in the gap was tangled up in a mass of seaweed palm fronds, twisting everything together as the tides rolled it. He ducked into its shadow.

Already the tree had become a world of its own. Many of its branches had been ripped off, but the trailing weeds had colonized it and little fish darted in and out of the forests of green. But better than that, if he tucked himself up between the tree and the edge of the gap, he could just get his face out of the water and be lost in the mass of vegetation.

He dropped back under the surface; the water around him was going pink. How much blood could one ear contain? Enough to attract sharks, that's how much.

There was a thump and the whole of the tree shook.

'I've got you now, my little chappie,' said the voice of Cox. He sounded as though he was right above Mau. 'Nowhere to go now, eh?' The tree rocked again as the man walked up and down in his heavy boots. 'And I won't fall off, don't you worry about that. This piece of wood is as wide as bloody Bond Street to a sailor!'

There was another thump. Cox was jumping up and down, making the tree rock. It rolled slightly and a bullet went past Mau's face, before he pulled himself back into the shadows.

'Uh-oh. We're bloody bleeding,' said Cox. 'Well done.

All I'm going to have to do is wait for the sharks to turn up. I always like to see a shark having his dinner.'

Mau worked his way along the bottom of the log, hand over hand. The trail of pinkness followed him.

There had been six shots. He raised his head in the shelter of a clump of weed, and heard a click.

'Y'know, I'm really disappointed in those cannibal johnnies,' said Cox, right overhead. 'Too much talk, too many rules, far too much mumbo-jumbo. *Jumbo* mumbo-jumbo, ha, ha. Milk and watery bunch, the lot of 'em. Been eating too many missionaries, if you ask me.' There was another click. Cox was reloading. He had to use two hands for that, didn't he?

Click . . .

Mau reached down for his knife and his belt was empty.

. . . *Click.*

So he swam face upwards along the underside of the trunk, his face only a foot or so from the bark, which was covered with tiny crabs.

That is how it would end. The best thing to do would be to leap up and get shot. That would surely be better than a shark's teeth. And then everyone who knew about the Nation would die—

Are you totally stupid, Mau? It was the new voice, and it said: I'm you, Mau, I'm just you. You will not die. You will win, *if you pay attention*!'

Click . . .

The pale green weed in front of him moved and he saw something black. In a moment where time stood still, he brushed the weed aside and saw it, wedged firmly in the trunk: a trunk that was full of little marks to show where men had helped other men.

He had been proud of himself that day. He had hit the tree with the *alaki* axe-head so hard that it would take all the next boy's strength to pull it out. The next boy was him.

Without thinking, and watching himself, somehow, from the outside, he grabbed the handle and raised his legs until they were firm against the underside of the trunk. The axe was stuck fast.

'I can hear you wriggling about,' said a voice right above him. 'You will be wriggling a whole lot faster in a moment. I can see the fins coming. Oh my giddy aunt, I wish I'd brought sandwiches.'

Click . . .

The axe came loose. Mau felt nothing. The greyness was back in his mind. Don't think. Do the things that must be done, one after another. The axe was free. Now he had it. This was a fact. The other fact was that Cox had now loaded his pistol.

Mau dragged himself branch by branch to the little area where he could breathe without being seen. At least, the area where he *hoped* he could not be seen. As he ducked his head down, a bullet went past it. Five bullets left, and Cox was losing his temper: he fired again (four bullets left; a fact), and Cox was right above him, searching for movement in the tangle of floating greenery. The bullet had come down as straight as a spear but had tumbled and lost its way. It's hard to run through water, Mau told himself. The more you try, the harder it gets. A fact. It must be the same for bullets. A new fact.

'Did I get you that time?' said Cox. 'I hope I did for your sake 'cos they're getting closer. Actually, I was just saying that to be nice, 'cos I want to see you wriggling. I want to stay here until I sees the sharks burp and then I will go back and have a nice chat with your little lady.'

Mau's lungs were beginning to hurt. He made the tree trunk wobble, then let himself sink. He didn't hear what Cox shouted, but four bullets splashed into the water high above him, left trails of bubble for a few moments, and then just tumbled away in the current.

Six shots. Only the little pistol would be left. No, Cox would have to reload. And that needed both hands. A fact.

Now there had to be more facts, one after the other, all falling carefully into place like little grey blocks.

Mau rose fast, dragging the axe behind him. He grabbed the stub of a broken branch with his free hand, got a purchase with his feet on another and, with his lungs on fire, let all the momentum of his rise and all the strength left in his body flow into his arm.

The axe came out of the water in a great curve, moving in space but not in time, water droplets hanging in the air to mark the arc of its passage. It blocked the light of the sun, it made the stars come out, it caused thunderstorms and strange sunsets around the world (or so Pilu said, later on) – and as time came back at double speed, the axe hit Cox in the chest and he went backwards off the log. Mau saw him raising his pistol as he sank, and then his expression changed to an enormous grin, with blood at the corners, and he was dragged into the swirling waters.

The sharks had arrived for dinner.

Mau lay on top of the log until the commotion died down. And he thought, in those little white thoughts that scribbled their way along the redness of the pain in his lungs: That was a really good axe. I wonder if I'll be able to find it again.

He pushed himself onto his knees and blinked, not quite certain who he was. And then he looked down and saw the grey shadow.

I will walk in your *steps for a while*, said a voice just above his head.

Mau pulled himself onto his feet, not an unbruised thought in his head, walked to the far end of the log and stepped onto the path across the broken coral. Greyness filled the air around him as he walked, and on either side the great wings of Locaha beat gently. He felt like . . . metal, hard and sharp and cold.

They reached the first of the big war canoes, and he stepped onto it. The few warriors who hadn't already jumped into the water fell to their knees, terrified. He looked into their eyes.

They can see me. They worship me, Locaha said. *Belief is a hard thing to believe, is it not? For now, at this time, here in this moment under these stars — you have the gift. You can kill them with a touch, a word, by the passing of your shadow.*

DUEL

You have earned this. How would you like them to die?

'Take your captives to the shore and leave them there,' Mau said to the nearest men. 'Pass this command along and then go. If you stay here, I will close my wings over you.'

That is all? said Locaha.

Thoughts pieced themselves together in the chill on Mau's mind as he turned and headed across the coral.

'Yes,' he said, 'it is.'

I would have acted differently, said the voice of death.

'*And I would not, Locaha.* I'm not you. I have choices.'

Mau plodded on, in silence and grey shadow.

This day turned out well for you, said the voice of Locaha.

Mau still said nothing. Behind them the Raiders' fleet was boiling with terrified activity. There will be so many new mouths to feed, he thought. So much to do. Always, so much to do.

I am not often surprised, said Locaha, *and you are wrong. There is one choice I can make, in the circumstances . . .*

The sand under Mau's feet turned black, and there was darkness on every side. But in front was a pathway of glittering stars.

Mau stopped, and said, 'No. Not another trap.'

But this is the way to the Perfect World! said Locaha. *Only a very few have seen this path!*

Mau turned round. 'I think that if Imo wants a perfect world, he wants it down here,' he said. He could still see the beach around him, but it was indistinct, as if it was behind a wall of dark water.

This one? It's far from perfect! said Locaha.

'It's a little more perfect today. And there will be more days.'

You really want to go back? said Locaha. *There are no second chances – there are no chances at all. There is only . . . what happens.*

'And what does not happen?' said Mau.

That? That happens, too, somewhere else. Everything *that can happen must happen, and everything that can happen must have a world to happen in. That is why Imo builds so many worlds that there are not enough numbers to count them. That is why His fire glows so red. Goodbye, Mau. I look forward with interest to our next meeting. You turn worlds upside down . . . Oh, and one other thing. Those others I mentioned, who have been shown the glittering path? They all said the same thing as you did. They saw that the perfect world is a journey, not a place. I have only one choice, Mau, but I'm good at making it.*

The greyness faded, and tried to take memories with it. Mau's mind grabbed at them as they streamed away and the grey barrier faded and let the light rush back in.

He was alive, and that was a fact. The ghost girl was running along the beach with her arms reaching out, and that was another fact. His legs felt strange and weak, and that was a fact which was getting more factual with every passing minute. But when she held him as they watched the tragic cargoes unloaded, and did not move until the last war canoe was a dot on the never-ending horizon . . . that was a fact as big as the Nation.

CHAPTER 15

THE WORLD TURNED
UPSIDE DOWN

*M*au awoke. A strange woman was spooning gruel into him. When she saw his eyes open she gave a little shriek, kissed him on the forehead, and ran out of the hut.

Mau lay back and stared up at the ceiling, while it all came back. Some bits were a little blurred, but the tree and the axe and the death of Cox were as clear to him as the little gecko watching him from the ceiling with upside-down eyes. But it was as if he was watching someone else, just a little way in front of him. It was another person, and that person was him . . .

He wondered if—

'Does not happen!' The scream was like lightning through his head, because it came from a beak about six inches from his ear. 'Show us your' – here the parrot muttered to itself, then went on, rather sullenly – 'underthings.'

'Ah, good. How are you?' said the ghost girl, stepping inside.

Mau sat bolt upright. 'You've got blood all over you!'

'Yes. I know. Bang goes the last good blouse,' said Daphne. 'Still, he's much better now. I'm pretty proud of myself, actually. I had to saw a man's leg off below the knee! And I sealed the wound with a bucket of hot tar, exactly according to the Manual!'

'Doesn't that hurt?' said Mau, lying back on the mat again. Sitting up had made him dizzy

'Not if you pick it up by the handle.' She looked at his blank expression. 'Sorry, that was a joke. Thank goodness for Mrs Gurgle; she can make someone sleep through *anything*. Anyway, I think the man is going to live now, which is more than he would with that terrible wound in it. And this morning I had to cut off a foot. It'd gone all . . . well, it was awful. Those captives were treated very badly.'

'And you've been sawing the bad bits off them?'

'It's called surgery, thank you so very much! It's not hard if I can find someone to hold the instruction manual open at the right page.'

'No! No, I don't think it's wrong!' said Mau quickly. 'It's just that . . . it's you doing it. I thought you hated the sight of blood.'

'That's why I try to stop it. I can *do* something about it. Come on, let's get you up.' She put her arms around him.

'Who was that woman who was feeding me? I've seen her before.'

'Her real name is Fi-ha-el, she says . . .' said Daphne, and Mau clutched at the wall for support. 'We used to call her "the Unknown Woman". And now we call her "the Papervine Woman".'

'Her? But she looked completely different—'

'Her husband was in one of those canoes. She went right up to it and dragged him out by herself. I'm blessed if I know how she knew which one he was in. I sent her to look after you because, well, it was his leg I had to saw off.'

'Newton was greatest!' screamed the parrot, bouncing up and down.

'And I thought the parrot was dead!'

'Yes, everyone thought the parrot was dead,' said Daphne, 'except the parrot. He turned up yesterday. He is minus one toe and a lot of feathers, but I think he will be fine when his wing heals. He *runs* after the grandfather birds now. They really hate that. I've, er, started doing something about his language.'

'Yes, I thought you had,' said Mau. 'What's New-Tan?'

'Newton,' Daphne corrected absent-mindedly. 'Remember I told you about the Royal Society? He was one of the first members. He was the greatest scientist there has ever been, I think, but when he was an old man he said he felt that he had been like a little boy playing with pebbles on the beach while a great ocean of truth lay undiscovered before him.'

Mau's eyes widened, and she was shocked to realize
that it had been a long time since she'd seen him look so
young.

'He stood on this beach?'

'Well, er, not *this* beach, obviously,' said Daphne.
'Possibly not even any beach. It's what trousermen call a
metaphor. A kind of lie to help you understand what's
true.'

'Oh, I know about *those*,' said Mau.

'Yes, I think you do.' Daphne smiled. 'Now come out
into the fresh air.'

She took Mau's hand. There were a few nasty grazes
that he didn't remember getting, his whole body felt stiff,
and there was a ragged wound where the flesh of his ear
had been, but it could have been a lot worse. He remembered the bullet in the water, slowing down and dropping
into his hand. Water could be hard, you only had to belly-
flop from a height to know *that*, but even so—

'Come *on*!' said Daphne, dragging him into the light.

The Women's Place was full. There were people in the
fields. The beach was busy. There were even children playing in the lagoon.

'We've got so much to do,' said Mau, shaking his head.

'They are already doing it,' said Daphne.

They watched in silence. Soon people would spot them
and they would be back in the world again, but right now
they were part of the scenery.

After a while the girl said: 'I remember when it was . . .
just nothing, and there was a boy who didn't even see me.'

And the boy said: 'I remember a ghost girl.'

After a longer silence, the girl asked: 'Would you go back? If you could?'

'You mean, without the wave?'

'Yes. Without the wave.'

'Then I'd have gone home, and everyone would have been alive, and I would be a man.'

'Would you rather be that man? Would you change places with him?' said the ghost girl.

'And not be me? Not know about the globe? Not met you?'

'Yes!'

Mau opened his mouth to reply, and found it choked with words. He had to wait until he could see a path through them.

'How can I answer you? There is no language. There was a boy called Mau. I see him in my memory, so proud of himself because he was going to be a man. He cried for his family and turned the tears into rage. And if he could, he would say "Did not happen!" and the wave would roll backwards, and never have been. But there is another boy, and he is called Mau, too, and his head is on fire with new things. What does he say? He was *born* in the wave, and he knows that the world is round, and he met a ghost girl who is sorry she shot at him. He called himself the little blue hermit crab, scuttling across the sand in search of a new shell, but now he looks at the sky and knows that no shell will ever be big enough, *ever*. Will you ask him not to *be*? *Any* answer will be the wrong one. All I can be is who I am. But sometimes I hear the boy inside crying for his family.'

'Does he cry now?' said Daphne, looking down at the ground.

'Every day. But very softly. You won't hear him. Listen, I must tell you this. Locaha spoke to me. He spread his great wings over me on the beach, and drove the Raiders away. Didn't you see that?'

'No. The Raiders ran as soon as Cox went down,' said Daphne. 'You mean you met Death? *Again?*'

'He told me that there were more worlds than there are numbers. There is no such thing as "Does not happen". But there is always "Happened somewhere else"—' He tried to explain, while she tried to understand.

When he'd run out of words she said: 'You mean that there is a world where the wave *didn't* happen? Out . . . there somewhere?'

'I think so . . . I think I've almost seen it. Sometimes, at night, when I'm watching the shore, I almost see it. I nearly *hear* it! And there is a Mau there, a man who is me, and I pity him, because there is no ghost girl in his world . . .'

She put her arms around his neck and gently pulled him towards her. 'I wouldn't change anything,' she said. 'Here, I'm not some sort of doll. I have a purpose. People listen to me. I've done amazing things. How could I go back to my life before?'

'Is that what you'll tell your father?' His voice was suddenly sad.

'Something like that, I think, yes.'

Mau gently turned her round, so that she was looking at the sea.

'There's a ship coming,' he said.

The schooner had anchored outside the reef by the time they got down to the lagoon. Daphne waded out as far as she could, regardless of her dress floating up around her, while a boat was lowered.

On the shore, Mau watched as the man in the prow of the boat jumped off as soon as it was near her and, laughing and crying together, they helped one another up the slope of the sand. The crowd moved back to give them room as they embraced – but Mau was watching the two men climbing out of the boat. They had red jackets on, and held complicated sticks, and looked at Mau as if he were, at best, a nuisance.

'Let me look at you,' said His Excellency, standing back. 'Why, you look— What happened to you? There's blood on your shoulder! We have a doctor on board, and I'll get him to—'

Daphne glanced down. 'It's just a splash,' she said, waving a hand. 'Besides, it's not mine. I had to saw a man's leg off and I haven't had time to wash.'

Behind them, a third soldier got out of the boat carrying a thick tube, which he began to unroll. He looked nervously at Mau.

'What is happening here?' snapped Mau. 'Why do they have guns? What is this man doing?' He stepped forward and two bayonets barred his way.

Daphne turned her head and pulled away from her father. 'What's this?' she demanded. 'You can't stop him walking around in his own country! What's in that tube? It's a flag, isn't it? You brought a flag! And guns!'

'We didn't know what we were going to find, dear,' said her father, taken aback. 'After all, there are cannon up there.'

'Well, all right, yes,' muttered Daphne, stumbling over her own anger. 'They're just for show.' The rage flamed up again. 'But *those* guns aren't! Put them down!'

His Excellency nodded at the men, who put their muskets, very carefully but also very quickly, down on the sand. Milo had just walked onto the beach to see what the fuss was about, and he tended to loom.

'And the flag!' said Daphne.

'Just hold onto it, Evans, if you would be so kind,' said His Excellency. 'Look, dear, we mean no harm to these, er' – he glanced up at Milo – '*nice* people, but we must back up our claim to the Mothering Sunday Islands. We hold that they are just an extension of the Bank Holiday Monday Islands—'

'Who's we? You?'

'Well, ultimately the king—'

'He can't have this one!' Daphne screamed. 'He doesn't need it! He can't have it! He hasn't finished with Canada yet!'

'Dear, I think the privations of your time on this island may have affected you in some way—' His Excellency began.

Daphne took a step backwards. 'Privations? There is nowhere I would rather have been than here! I've helped babies to be born! I killed a man—'

'The one whose leg you sawed off?' asked her father, mystified.

'What? Him? No, he's doing very well,' said Daphne, waving a hand dismissively. 'The one I killed was a murderer. And I've made beer. Really good beer! Father, you must listen right now. It's very important that you understand *right now*. This is the other end of the world, Father, it really is. This is the beginning. This . . . is the place where you might grant God absolution.'

She hadn't meant it to come out. He stood there, stunned.

She added: 'I'm sorry, you and Grandmother were shouting so loud that night and I couldn't help over-hearing,' and, since there was no point in being deceitful at a time like this, she also added, 'Especially since I was trying hard to.'

He looked up at her, his face grey. 'What is so special about this place?' he said.

'There's a cave. It's got wonderful carvings in it. It's ancient. It may be more than a hundred thousand years old.'

'Cavemen,' said His Excellency calmly.

'I think there are star maps on the ceiling. They invented . . . well – practically everything. They sailed all over the world when we huddled around our fires. I can prove it, I think.' Daphne took her father's hand. 'There's still some oil in the lamps,' she said. 'Let me show you. *Not you!*' she added as the guards sprang to attention. '*You* will stay here. And no one is to take over anyone's country while we're gone, is that understood?'

The men looked at His Excellency, who shrugged vaguely, a man who had been thoroughly daughtered.

'Whatever she says, of course,' he said.

His daughter took his hand and said, 'Come and see.'

They started off up the path but were not out of earshot when Pilu walked up to the soldiers and said, 'Would you like some beer?'

'*Don't let them drink it until they have spat in it and sung Baa, Baa, Black Sheep sixteen times,*' was the order from on high, followed by, 'and tell them we need lamp oil.'

The first thing her father said when he saw the gods was 'My goodness!' Then, after staring at things with his mouth open, he managed to say, 'Incredible! All this belongs in a museum!'

She couldn't let him get away with that one, and said, 'Yes, I know. That's why it is, in fact, in one.'

'And who will look at it down here?'

'Anyone who wants to come and see, Papa. And that will mean every scientist in the world.'

'It's a long way from anywhere important, though,' His Excellency observed, running his fingers over the stone globe.

'No, Papa. *This* is the important place. It's everywhere else that is a long way away. Anyway, that wouldn't matter to the Royal Society. They would swim up here in lead boots!'

'*Down* here, dear, I think,' said her father.

Daphne pushed the globe. It rolled a little way and the continents danced. But now the world was turned upside down. 'It's a *planet*, Papa. Up and down are just ways of looking at it. I'm sure people here won't object to copies being made for all the big museums. But don't take this place away from them. It's *theirs*.'

'I think people will say it belongs to the world.'

'And they will be thinking like thieves. We have no right to it at all. But if we don't act like stupid bullies I'm sure they will be gracious.'

'Gracious,' said her father, turning over the word in his mouth as if it were an unfamiliar biscuit.

Daphne's eyes narrowed. 'Don't go suggesting that grace is something you only find at the other end of the world, will you, Papa?'

'No, you're quite right. I will do what I can, of course. This is a very important place, I can see that.'

She kissed him.

When he spoke again, he sounded nervous and unsure of how to put things. 'So you've been . . . all right here? Eating well? Finding things to do . . . um . . . apart from sawing legs off?'

'It was only one leg, honestly. Oh, and a foot. I helped deliver two babies – well, to be honest I really only watched and sang a song the first time, and I've been learning about medicines from Mrs Gurgle in exchange for chewing her pork for her—'

'You . . . chew . . . her . . . pork for her . . .' her father repeated, as if hypnotized.

'Well, she hasn't got any teeth, you see?'

'Ah, yes, of course.' His Excellency shifted uneasily. 'And did you have any other . . . adventures?'

'Let me think . . . I was saved from drowning by Mau, who is the chief now, and, oh yes, I met a cannibal chief who looked just like the Prime Minister!'

'Really?' said her father. 'Although, come to think of it, that's not hard to imagine. And . . . er . . . and was anyone . . . did anyone . . . try to be . . . beastly to you?'

It was said so carefully that she nearly laughed. Fathers! But she couldn't tell him about the giggling maids and the kitchen gossip, let alone Cahle's jokes. She spent a lot of time at the Women's Place. Surely he didn't imagine she walked around with her eyes shut and her fingers in her ears?

'There was a murderer. He was one of the crew of the *Judy*, I'm sorry to say,' she said. 'He shot someone and then pointed a pistol at me.'

'Great heavens!'

'So I poisoned him. Well, sort of. But the Nation called it something like . . . what do you call it when a hangman hangs somebody?'

'Er . . . judicial execution?' said His Excellency, a man trying hard to keep up.

'That's right. And I broke another man's nose with a clay bowl because he was *going* to shoot me.'

'Really? Well, I suppose poison would have taken too long,' said His Excellency, trying to make the best of it. His face was ghastly in the lamplight, and it looked to Daphne as if it was made of wax and was about to melt.

'Now that I come to talk about it, it does all seem a bit . . . um . . .' She trailed off.

'Busy?' her father suggested.

And then she told him everything else – about the way the moon shone over the lagoon, and how bright the stars were, and the mutiny, and poor Captain Roberts, and the parrot, and the red crabs, and the pantaloon birds, and the tree-climbing octopi and First Mate Cox, while the gods looked down. She towed him past the hundreds of the white slabs around the walls, talking all the time.

'Look, that's a giraffe. They knew about Africa! There's an elephant further on, but it may be Indian. This is clearly a lion. One of the stones that ended up on the beach has got a carving of a horse on it, and who would bring one here? But the carvings on these other panels don't seem to show anything I can recognize, so I'm wondering if this section is some kind of alphabet – A is for apple and so on – but a lot of panels have these lines and dots around the edges, so I could be completely wrong. And see how often there is a hand somewhere in the carving! I'm positive it's there as a guide to size. And over here . . .' And so on, until at last she finished with: 'And I'm sure they had a telescope.'

'Oh, surely not! Is there a carving of one?'

'Well, no. But a lot of slabs are missing.' And she told

him about the sons of Jupiter and the snake around Saturn.

He didn't seem too impressed, but patted her on the hand. 'Or the skies were clearer once, or there was a man with extremely good eyesight.'

'But I've come up with a good scientific explanation!'

Her father shook his head. 'Much as I love you, it's a guess. And, may I say, a hope. You must work harder than that, my girl.'

Ah, those arguments we used to have coming back from the Society, Daphne thought. I'm going to have to fight. Good!

She pointed to the gods. 'They shine because they are covered with little plates of glass,' she said. 'Those are held on with lead nails. One of the boys swam over and had a look for me. The people here knew how to make fine glass!'

Her father, sitting with his back to the cool stone, gave a nod. 'That is quite likely. Many cultures make glass. We have the beginnings of a hypothesis, but you need to find your lens maker.'

'Papa, it stands to reason that sooner or later a glass-maker would notice a bubble in the glass and see how the light—'

But her father had held up a hand. 'Science is not interested in what "stands to reason",' he said. 'It "stands to reason" that the Earth is flat. What we *know* is that the Romans took some interest in crude lenses, and that eye-glasses were not invented until the thirteenth century. The

Italian Salvino D'Armate is generally credited with—'

'Why is it always so, so . . . northern hemisphere?' said Daphne. 'Turn the world upside down!' She pulled her father over to the wall near the globe, and pointed to a panel. 'You remember I told you they were very keen on showing hands holding things, too?' she said, and held up the lamp. 'There! Doesn't that look like a pair of spectacles to you?'

He looked at the panel critically, like a man trying to decide between cake and pie.

'It could do,' he said, 'but it could be a mask, or scales or have some mysterious religious significance. It doesn't help you much, I'm sorry to say.'

Daphne sighed. 'Look, if I found some evidence that they knew about lenses, would you accept they may have known how to build a telescope?'

'Yes, that would be reasonable. I won't accept that they *did*, mind you, only that they may have done.'

'Come and see.'

This time she led him to the other side of the gods, to a niche in the wall where the white panel had fallen out.

'One of the boys found them in silt at the bottom of the god pool. The glass is broken on one side and the other is cracked, but you can see they were lenses. Be careful.' She laid them carefully in his hand.

He blinked. 'Gold-rimmed spectacles . . .' But he breathed the words, rather than said them.

'Have I proved my telescope theory, Papa?' she said gleefully. 'We know that eyeglasses lead on to telescopes.'

'Once before, at least. Or since, I'm sure you would say. Why didn't you show me these straight away?'

'I just wanted to make you admit I was doing proper science!'

'Well done,' said His Excellency. 'You have built a very strong hypothesis indeed, but I'm sorry to say that you have not proved the full theory. You'd need to find the telescope for that.'

'That's unfair!' said Daphne.

'No, it's science,' said her father. '"Could have" isn't good enough. Nor is "might have"! "Did" is the trick. But when you announce this, a lot of people will try to prove you wrong. The more they fail, the more right you will become. And they will probably try to suggest that some European traveller came here and lost his eyeglasses.'

'And his false teeth made of gold?' snapped Daphne. She told him about Mrs Gurgle's proudest possession.

'I would very much like to see them. Some people will find them easier to accept. Don't be discouraged about the telescope. What is *clear* is that this place was the home of a hitherto unknown sea-faring culture that was very adept in the technical arts. Good heavens, my girl, most people would be ecstatic to have discovered all this!'

'I didn't,' said Daphne. 'Mau did. I just had to look over his shoulder. *He* had to walk past a hundred thousand ancestors. This is *their* place, Papa. Their ancestors built it. And put on the globe there the symbol of a wave breaking in front of the setting sun, which every man of the islands has worn as a tattoo for thousands of years. I saw it! And you know what? I can prove that no European has been into this cave before me.' Daphne looked around, chest heaving with passion. 'See the gold on the gods and the globe and the big door?'

'Yes. Of course, dear. I could hardly fail to notice.'

'There you are, then,' said Daphne, picking up the lamp. 'It's *still here!*'

Mau sat with one of the *Judy's* charts on his knees. This was, officially, a meeting of the island council, or would have been if anything on the island was official. Anyone could come, and because anyone could, many didn't. There were more new people to be cared for and fed; many might go back to their own islands, if they still existed, but they had to be fit and fed. That meant more work all round. And some people didn't turn up because they had gone fishing; when it comes to voting or fishing, sea bass usually wins.

'*All* the red places belong to the English trousermen?'

'Yup,' said Pilu.

'That's a lot of places!'

'Yup.'

'They're not too bad,' said Pilu. 'Mostly they want you to wear trousers and worship their god. He's called God.'

'Just . . . God?'

'Right. He's got a son who is a carpenter, an' if you worship him you climb the shining path when you die. The songs is nice and sometimes you get a biscuit.' Pilu watched Mau carefully. 'What are you thinking, Mau?' he said.

'Other people will come. Some will have guns,' said Mau thoughtfully.

'True,' said Pilu. 'There is a lot of the yellow gold in the cave. Trousermen like it because it shines. They are like children.'

'Big children,' said Milo, 'with guns.'

'What do you think we should do, Cahle?' said Mau, still looking at the maps.

The big woman gave a shrug. 'I trust the ghost girl. A father of a girl like that would be a good man.'

'How about if I take a canoe and sail it to the trouserman island and stick my flag in the sand?' said Tom-ali. 'Will that make it our place?'

'No,' said Mau. 'They would laugh. Flags are like guns which flap. If you have a flag you need a gun.'

'Well? We have guns, too.'

Mau fell silent.

'And bad gunpowder,' Pilu pointed out.

'I think . . . I think if you are a suckfish in a sea o' sharks, you must swim with the biggest shark,' said Milo. This met with general approval; the island council was still learning about international politics, but they were experts on fish.

They all looked at Mau, who was staring at the atlas again. He stared at it for so long that they began to worry. There had been something different about him since the Raiders had left. Everyone said so. He walked like someone whose feet only touched the ground because he told them to; when you talked to him he looked at you like a man scanning a new horizon that only he could see.

'We cannot be stronger than the Empire,' he said, 'but we can be something it doesn't dare to be. We can be weak. The ghost girl told me about a man called Eyes-Ack New-Tan. He was not a warrior, he had no spear, but the sun and the moon spun inside his head and he stood on the shoulders of giants. The king of that time did him great honour, because he knew the secrets of the sky. And I have an idea. I will talk to the ghost girl.'

There should be a word like 'honeymoon', Daphne thought, but not about husband and wife, rather about parent and child. This one lasted twelve days, and she felt as though she were the parent and he the child. She'd never seen her father like this before. They explored the whole of the island, he had picked up an amazing amount of the language in a short time. He went torch fishing with Milo and got rascally drunk on beer with the other men, so that they all ended up paddling one of the big canoes in several directions at once while singing the words of his old school song.

He taught them cricket and they played a match against the soldiers and sailors from the ship, with rifles for stumps. It became very interesting when Cahle was allowed to bowl.

Daphne's father declared that not only was Cahle the fastest bowler he had ever seen, but also had an almost Australian talent for vicious and forensic accuracy with the ball. After the first three whimpering soldiers were carried down to the lagoon so they could sit in the water until the stinging died away, the fourth man took one look at her thundering towards him with her right arm swinging and ran away into the woods, clutching his helmet over his groin. For the sake of the game she was banned from bowling after Daphne's father explained that women should not really be allowed to play cricket because they fundamentally didn't understand it, but it seemed to Daphne that she understood it very well, and therefore tried to get it over with as quickly as possible so that they could get on with something more interesting, since in her opinion the world was overwhelmingly full of things that were more interesting than cricket.

It was not much better for the soldiers when the islanders went in to bat. Not only were they 'devilishly good' at swinging a bat, but they had somehow picked up the idea that the ball should be aimed at someone on the opposing side. In the end the match was declared a draw because of injuries, most of them sitting in the lagoon.

And the ship came, and stopped play in any case.

Mau saw it first; he was always the first to see anything that came from the sea. It was the largest one he had seen, with so many sails it looked like a storm heading for them. Everyone was waiting on the beach as it anchored outside the lagoon and lowered a boat. There weren't soldiers this time. The boat was rowed by four men in black.

'My word, that's the *Cutty Wren*,' said His Excellency, handing the bat back to Pilu. 'I wonder what they want here . . . Ahoy, you chaps! Do you need help or something?'

The boat touched the sand and one of the men jumped out, hurried towards him and drew him, protesting gently, along the beach and away from the match.

The conversation that took place was baffling to Mau, because the man in the black clothes spoke in a whisper while His Excellency asked questions at the top of his voice, so that what he heard was a fast buzzing, punctuated with explosions, as in 'Me?' . . . 'What, all of them?' . . . 'What about Uncle Bernie? I know for a fact he is in America!' . . . 'They have lions there?' . . . 'Look, I'm really not—' . . . ' Right here?' . . . 'Well, of course no one wants another Richard the Lionheart, but surely we don't need . . .' and so it went on. Then His Excellency held up a hand to stop the man in black in mid-buzz, and turned to Mau. He looked shaken, and in a strained voice said, 'Sir, would you be so good as to fetch my daughter? I believe she is up at the Ladies' Place, stitching somebody. Er, I'm sure this will all turn out to be a misunderstanding. I'm sure it's nothing to worry about.'

When they got back, His Excellency's soldiers, who had been lounging around in their shirtsleeves for more than a week, had struggled back into their red coats and were standing around on guard, although at the moment they were unsure who they were guarding from what and how, not to mention why, and so until there were any orders to speak of they were guarding everyone from everything.

Another boat had been lowered and was heading into the lagoon, with more people in it. One of them, sitting bolt upright, was unfortunately familiar.

Daphne ran to her father. 'What's going on?' She glared at the men in the black suits and added, 'And who are these . . . people?'

'Is this your delightful daughter, sire?' said one of the men, raising his hat to her.

'*Sire?*' said Daphne. She glared at the man in black. No one should call anyone delightful without written proof.

'It turns out that I am, not to put too fine a point on it, King,' said His Majesty. 'This has not come at a good time, I must say. This gentleman is Mister Black, from London.'

Daphne stopped glaring. 'But I thought one hundred and thirty—' she began. Then an expression of horror crossed her face, and she looked back at the approaching rowing boat. 'Has my grandmother been doing anything . . . silly? With knives and guns, perhaps?'

'Her ladyship? Not that I am aware,' said the Gentleman of Last Resort. 'Here she comes now, Your Majesty. We called first at Port Mercia, of course, and picked up the Right Reverend Topleigh. I'm afraid the Archbishop of Canterbury does not travel well, but he has sent instructions for the coronation.'

'A coronation *here?* Surely it can wait!' said His Majesty.

But Daphne was watching the figure in the distant boat. It couldn't be true, could it? She wouldn't come all this way, would she? For the chance of bossing a king around? Of course she would – she would have towed the ship with her teeth! And this time he wouldn't be able to run away to the other end of the world.

'Strictly speaking, yes,' said Mr Black. 'You became King as soon as the last king died. At that very second. That's how it works.'

'Really?' said His Majesty.

'Yes, sire,' said Mr Black patiently, 'God arranges it.'

'Oh good,' said the king weakly. 'That's very clever of Him.'

'And for full ratification, you understand, you must stand on the soil in England, but in these unusual circumstances,' Mr Black went on, 'and uncertain times, and so on and so forth, we thought it might save any argument – if we were delayed, for example – if the crown was firmly on your head. It would save any nit-picking arguments – with the French, for instance – which can take such a long time.'

'There was the Hundred Years War, for one,' said a second Gentleman.

'Well pointed out, Mr Amber. In any case, we will have another coronation once we get home – which must, now, be a matter of some urgency, of course. Bunting, cheering, souvenir mugs for the children, that sort of thing. But in this case the Crown thought it would send out the right message to get you sorted out, as I might say, as soon as possible.' As he spoke, two of his colleagues began to take apart, with great care, the small crate they had brought ashore with them.

'Am I not the Crown?' said His Majesty.

'No, sire, you are the king, sire,' said Mr Black patiently. 'You are, like us, underneath it. Subject to it.'

'But surely I can give you orders?'

'You can certainly make requests, sire, and we will do our very best to help. But, alas, you cannot give *us* orders. My word, we would be in a bad way if we took orders from kings. Isn't that so, Mr Brown?'

One of the men working on the crate looked up briefly. 'It would be Charles the First all over again, Mr Black.'

'You never said a truer word, Mr Brown,' said Mr Black. 'It would be Charles the First all over again, and I don't think any of us want to see Charles the First all over again, do we?'

'Why not?' said Daphne.

Mr Black turned to her and looked for a moment as if he were giving her a very quick examination.

'Because his arrogance and stupidity nearly lost England for the Crown. Your Royal Highness,' he said eventually.

Oh dear, thought Daphne. I *am* a princess now. Cor blimey. And I don't think it's the kind of thing you can resign from! A princess! Did you hear that, Mr Foxlip, wherever you are? Ha!

'But wasn't it Oliver Cromwell who had him executed?' she managed, trying to sound regal.

'Certainly, ma'am. But Oliver Cromwell wasn't the problem. Charles the First was the problem. Oliver Cromwell was the solution. I'll grant you he was a bit of a nuisance for a while afterwards, but at least his unpleasant rule made people happy to see a king again. The Crown knows how to wait.'

'Charles the First's head was cut off,' said Daphne, watching the new boat hit the sand.

'Clearly another reason for not wanting to see him,' said Mr Black smoothly. 'We wouldn't be able to understand what he was saying.'

A plump man in clerical clothing, except possibly for the sarong, was helped out of the boat, and he in turn offered his hand to, yes, her grandmother. She was carrying an umbrella. An umbrella! It wasn't to keep the rain off, of course. It was for prodding people, Daphne *knew*.

'Ah, and here is Her Ladyship now,' said Mr Black, quite unnecessarily in Daphne's view. He added: 'She was wonderful company on the voyage out here. The nautical miles just flew past.' The little smile on his face was a masterpiece.

Grandmother looked around at the island as if inspecting it for dust, and sighed. 'One would have thought that we could have found somewhere cleaner,' she said. 'Never mind. I trust you are well, Henry, and ready for the responsibility that has been thrust upon us by Divine Providence?'

'You mean all those people dying was *provident*?' said Daphne sharply. In her mind's eye, ancestors toppled like dominoes . . . one hundred and thirty-eight of them.

'That is no way to speak to your grandmother, Daphne,' said her father.

'Daphne? Daphne? What is this "Daphne"?' said Her Ladyship. 'Ridiculous name. Don't be silly, Ermintrude. Now, can we get on with things before we get eaten, for goodness' sake?'

Daphne blushed, in anger and embarrassment.

'How dare you! Some of these people can speak English!'

'So?'

Daphne took a deep breath, and then her father's hand was laid gently on her shoulder, just as she opened her mouth. She shut it again, letting the rage seethe inside.

'That's not the way, dear,' he said. 'And we must get on.' He left her and shook hands with the bishop. 'Ah, Charlie, good to see you. Your pointy hat not here?'

'Lost at sea, old boy. And when I picked up my crosier it was full of blasted termites! Sorry about the sarong, couldn't find m' trousers,' said the bishop, shaking the king's hand. 'Wretched shame about what's been happening, of course. Bit of a shock all round. Still, it's not given to us to know the way the ways of Prov— of the Almighty.'

'It was probably an Act of God,' said Daphne.

'Indeed, indeed,' said the bishop, fumbling in his bag.

'Or a miracle,' Daphne went on, defying her grandmother to take her by the ear on *her* beach. But Grandmother did not take defiance lightly, or at all.

'I shall talk to you later about this wayward behaviour, Ermintrude—' she began, striding forward. But two Gentlemen were suddenly in her way.

'Ah, here it is,' said the bishop very loudly, and straightened up. 'Of course we don't generally carry royal anointing oil out here but my lads make a coconut oil that keeps cricket bats nice and supple. I hope that will be sufficient.' This was to Mr Black, who worried him even more than her ladyship.

'That will be fine, Your Grace,' said Mr Black. 'Miss . . . Daphne, would you be so kind as to ask the islanders if we may use one of these ceremonial stones as a throne?'

Daphne looked at the scattered god stones. They'd got rather unnoticed in the past week.

'Mau, can they—?' she began.

'Yes, they can,' said Mau. 'But tell them they don't work.'

It was, according to the history books, the fastest coronation since Bubric the Saxon crowned himself with a very pointy crown on a hill during a thunderstorm, and reigned for one and a half seconds.

Today, a man sat down. He was handed a golden orb and a golden sceptre, which the watching islanders approved of because, when you got right down to it, a sceptre was just a shiny club. Mau was happy with his fish-spear, but in their hearts the islanders knew that a chief should have a really *big* club. Later on, some of them had had a go with it, however, and considered it a bit cumbersome for a real fight. They found it far more interesting than the crown, which sparkled in the sunlight but didn't do anything useful. But because of it, and after a certain amount of talking, a man stood up who ruled so many places on the planet that map-makers often ran out of red ink.

At this point, the men in black produced some small versions of the trouserman flag, raised them enthusiastically and shouted: 'Hurrah.'

'I'd like the crown back now, please, Your Majesty,'

said Mr Black quickly. 'I will give you a receipt, of course.'

'Oh, it will all be so much better when we are crowned properly in London,' said Grandmother. 'Really this is just for—'

'You will be silent, woman,' said the king, without raising his voice.

For a moment Daphne thought she was the only one to have heard. Grandmother hadn't, because she still went on talking. And then her ears caught up with her tongue, and couldn't believe their eyes.

'What did you say?' she managed.

'Ah, you've got it right at last, Mother,' said the king. 'I'm me, not *us*. I am I, not we. One pair of buttocks on the throne, one head in the crown. You, on the other hand, are a sharp-tongued harridan with the manners of a fox *and don't interrupt me when I'm talking*! How dare you insult our hosts! And before you utter a word, contemplate this: you treasure your elevation above what you call the lower classes, who I've always found to be pretty decent people once they've had a chance to have a bath. Well, I am King, you see – King – and the very notion of nobility that you cling to like grim death means that you will *not* answer me back. You *will*, however, act with grace and gratitude during the remainder of our stay in this place. Who knows, it may speak to you as it has spoken to me. And if you are even now putting together a scathing remark, let me point out for your lengthy consideration the wonderful and highly advisable option of silence. That is a command!'

The king, breathing a little heavily, nodded to the leader of the Gentlemen of Last Resort.

'That was all right, wasn't it?' he said to the Gentlemen of Last Resort. Grandmother was simply staring at nothing.

'Of course, sire. You are King, after all,' murmured Mr Black.

''Scuse me, miss,' said a voice behind Daphne. 'Are you Miss Ermintrude?'

She turned to see who'd spoken. One of the boats had returned and picked up more of the crew, and now she was staring at a small man in badly fitting clothes. They had clearly belonged to someone who had been happy to get rid of them.

'*Cookie?*'

He beamed. 'Told you my coffin'd keep me alive, miss!'

'Papa, this is Cookie, who was a great friend to me on the *Judy*. Cookie, this is my father. He's King.'

'That's nice,' said Cookie.

'Coffin?' said the king, looking bewildered again.

'I told you about him, Papa. Remember? The pockets? The mast and shroud? The tiny inflatable billiard table?'

'Oh, *that* coffin! My word. How long were you at sea, Mr Cookie?'

'Two weeks, sir. My little stove ran out after the first week, so I made do with biscuits, mint cake and plankton until I fetched up on the island,' said the cook.

'Plankton?' said Daphne.

'Strained it through my beard, miss. I thought, well,

whales live on it, so why not me?' He reached into his pocket and produced a grubby piece of paper. 'Funny little island I landed on, too. Had the name on a brass plate nailed to a tree. I writ it down, look.'

The king and his daughter read, in smudged pencil: *Mrs Ethel J. Bundy's Birthday Island.*

'It really exists!' Daphne yelled.

'Jolly well done,' said the king. 'Do tell us all about it over dinner. Now, if you will excuse for me a moment, I have to reign.' King Henry the Ninth rubbed his hands together. 'Now, what else . . . ah, yes. Charlie, do you want to be an archbishop?'

The Rt Rev. Topleigh, who was packing his bag again, waved his hands wildly, a look of sudden dread on his face. 'No, thank you, Henry!'

'Really? Are you sure?'

'Yes, thank you. They'd make me wear shoes. Love it down here among the islands!'

'Ah, then you choose the *big sea* rather than a big see,' said the king, in that slow, plummy voice people use when they are committing a really bad pun.

Nobody laughed. Even Daphne, who loved her father very much, could do no better than a sickly grin. Then her father did something that no one, not even a king, should do. He tried to explain. 'Perhaps you all didn't notice the pun or play on words?' he said, sounding a little hurt. 'I deliberately confused "a big sea", that's with an "a", with "a big *see*", with two "e"s, meaning the area that comes under the jurisdiction of an archbishop.'

'Technically that would be a province, sir,' said Mr Black gravely. 'Bishops have sees.'

'Although an archbishop is, strictly speaking, bishop of his home see,' said Mr Red thoughtfully. 'That's why the Archbishop of Canterbury is also the *Bishop* of Canterbury. But that would be a small see, and therefore would not work for the purposes of humour.'

'There you have it, Your Majesty,' said Mr Black, giving the king a happy little smile. 'With that small amendment your wonderful pun will be an absolute hoot in ecclesiastical circles.'

'I notice *you* didn't laugh, Mr Black!'

'No, Your Majesty. We are forbidden to laugh at the things kings say, sire, because otherwise we would be at it all day.'

'Well, at least there is one thing I can do,' said the king, walking over to Mau. 'Sir, I would be honoured if you will join my Empire. Not many people get a choice, I might add.'

'Thank you, King,' said Mau, 'but we—' He stopped, and turned to Pilu for assistance.

'We don't want to join, Your Sire. It's too big and we will be swallowed up.'

'Then you will be prey to the first man who arrives with a boat and half a dozen armed men,' said the king. 'Apart from me, I mean,' he added quickly.

'Yes, Your King,' said Mau. He saw the ghost girl watching him and thought, Well, this is the moment. 'That is why we want to join the Royal Society.'

'What?' The king turned to his daughter, who was grinning. 'Did you put them up to this, my girl?'

'Papa, this is where science began,' Daphne said quickly, 'and I just gave them the words. They did the thinking for themselves. Their ancestors were scientists. You've seen the cave! This will work!'

Pilu looked nervously from the king to his daughter, and went on: 'When the Royal Society was formed, the king gave them a club as full of bigness as his was—'

'*Bigness?*' said the king.

'That was Charles the Second, sire,' Mr Black whispered. 'In fact he did indeed say that the Society deserved a mace "alike in bigness to our own" and I suppose we can only be grateful that he didn't say "biggittity".'

'– which means he thought they were as powerful as kings, and so we humbly, no, *proudly* ask that we be admitted,' said Pilu, glancing at the ghost girl. 'We will welcome all men of science as, er, brothers.'

'Say yes, Papa, say yes!' said Daphne. 'Science is international!'

'I can't speak for the Society—' the king began, but Daphne was ready for this. There was no point in being a princess if you couldn't interrupt a king.

'Of course you can, Papa. It says Royal Society outside their building, doesn't it?'

'*Your* Society, Your Majesty,' Mr Black purred. 'And based, of course, in *London*.'

'And we will give them the golden door,' said Mau.

'What?' said Daphne. She hadn't expected this bit.

'It's not going to be shut again,' said Mau emphatically. 'It will be a gift to our brothers who sailed so far that they came back.'

'That's tons of gold!' said the king. 'About eight tons at least I'd say.'

'Very well done, sire,' said Mr Black. 'To the victor the spoils.'

'Except there hasn't been a war,' said the king. 'It's too much. We can't take it! They have been kind.'

'I was merely suggesting that the people like it when kings bring valuable things home, sire,' said the Gentleman of Last Resort.

'Like whole countries,' said Daphne, giving him a sharp look.

'But this is meant as a *gift*, Mr Black. It is not the spoils of conquest,' said the king.

'Well, that is indeed a happy, if unusual, outcome,' said Mr Black smoothly.

'And you will give a gift to us, too,' said Mau. 'When much is taken, something is returned. Pilu?'

'A big telescope,' said Pilu, 'and a boat in sizeness to the *Sweet Judy*, and ten barrels of salt-pickled beef, and tools of every sizeness. Timber, metals of all kindness, books with pictures and writing inside which is about the pictures . . .'

It went on for quite some time, and when he had finished Daphne said, 'That's still pretty cheap, Papa, even with the boat. And remember, the first thing they asked for was a telescope. How can you argue with that?'

The king smiled. 'I won't. Nor will I wonder out loud if anyone helped them with the list. Anyway I rather like "metals of all kindness". And you are right, of course. Scientists will flock here. And you can keep your door, Mau.'

'No,' said Mau firmly. 'It was closed for too long, Your King. I will not let it be shut again. But there is one more request, which is very sinple. Every man of science who comes here to see what we once knew must tell us all *he* knows.'

'Lectures!' Daphne burst out. 'Oh, yes!'

'And someone, please, to teach us doctrine,' Mau added.

The bishop, who had been feeling a bit left out by now, brightened up at this point and stepped forward smartly. 'If I can help in any way—' he began, his voice full of hope.

'Doctrine to make us better,' said Mau, giving Daphne an imploring look.

'Yes indeed,' said the bishop. 'I feel that—'

Daphne sighed. 'I'm sorry, Your Grace, but he means doctoring,' she said.

'Ah, yes,' said the bishop sadly. 'Silly me.'

'Mind you, if you're good at debating, Mau might be interested.' She looked at Mau, who looked at her, and then at the Gentlemen of Last Resort, and then at the king, and then at the *Cutty Wren*, and then back at her.

And he knows I'm going, she thought. And very soon. I'll have to. A king's only child can't live on an island that's lost at sea. He could read me like a book, if he read books. He *knows*. I can see it in his face.

*   *   *

At dawn on the seventh day after the arrival of the *Cutty Wren*, Captain Samson was ready to set sail again. The ship had already picked up most of the provisions for the return leg in Port Mercia, but eight tons of gold takes a lot of sawing up when you're determined not to leave behind a single bit of gold dust.

Now the ship waited outside the reef, just visible behind the mists. It looked like a toy, but from the Women's Place, everything was a matter of perspective.

His Excellency's schooner had left yesterday, with cheering and waving and a lot less gear, lamp oil, sailcloth and cutlery than it had when it arrived. The fastest sailing ship in the world was waiting, impatient to fly.

The clearing was more or less deserted at this time of day, but there were a few snores coming from the huts and the occasional gurgle coming from the hut of the lady of the same name. The gardens were silent, listening. And the Place *did* listen, Daphne was sure of that. It made you listen, because she did, too. It must have even made her grandmother listen, because yesterday Daphne had seen her sitting next to Mrs Gurgle, who very clearly was a woman of *great* power, because it looked very much as though her new companion was chewing a lump of salt-picked beef. Her ladyship hadn't seen her granddaughter watching, which was probably a good thing for both of them.

Now Daphne looked around at the gardens. 'I've come to say goodbye,' she said. 'And thank you.' She didn't shout it out. Either the Grandmothers were listening, or they weren't.

She stood and waited. There was no reply but the vegetables' silence and, in the distance, a pantaloon bird losing the remains of last night's dinner.

'Well, thank you anyway,' she said, and turned away.

Were they real? she thought. Memory slips away so quickly here. I think it blows out to sea. But I shall remember. And in her head, a fading voice said, 'Good!' or perhaps she imagined it. Life gets really complicated if you think too much.

The king had invited the carpenter of the *Cutty Wren* – in the few days he had been there – to help with the new building already begun by the carpenter from his schooner, and soon, because people feel uneasy watching a king work with his sleeves rolled up, both crews had rolled up theirs, too. The rest of the *Judy* had become another long hut and a big heap of useful things. And, of course, the *Sweet Judy* herself. *She* had been an unexpected find.

The prow of the ship had hit squarely between two of the giant fig trees and its figurehead had been wedged, unseen and unscathed, while the ship collapsed behind her.

A couple of the sailors had nailed the figurehead over the door, to the approval of all except the king, who wondered aloud if her undressed bosom might be considered unseemly. He hadn't understood why everyone had laughed, but he had been pleased that they had. It had made up for the Big See.

Now Daphne looked up at her for the last time. There was a faint smile on the wooden lips, and someone had put a garland of flowers around her neck.

Daphne curtsied to her, because if any non-living thing had earned respect it had been the *Judy*. She had been taught to curtsy years ago, and on the island it had been a skill less useful than ice-skating, but just this once it was exactly the right thing to do.

A boat waited on the edge of the lagoon. It had been waiting for some time. The crowd had wandered off, because there is only so long you can wave and shout at something that isn't in any hurry to move and a certain boredom sets in. In any case, Cahle had tactfully and not so tactfully got the islanders to wander back up to the fields. She knew when people, come to think of it, needed space. Besides, Daphne had said all her goodbyes last night, at the big feast, and the king had been the only trouserman there to be given the Sunset Wave Tattoo and everyone had laughed and cried. The Gentlemen of Last Resort had carried the king back to their ship only a few hours ago, because he was, they said, 'a little under the weather', which is a code meaning 'too much beer'.

Now, apart from a dog warming up in the sun, it was as though she had the place to herself, but she would have bet anything that hundreds of eyes were watching her from the fields.

She looked at the beach. There was the waiting boat, and there was Mau, standing where he always did, with his spear. He glanced up as she approached, with the faint half-smile he wore when he was uncertain of things.

'Everyone else is on board,' he said.

'I will be back,' Daphne said.

Mau drew squiggles on the sand with the end of his spear. 'Yes, I know,' he said.

'No, I really mean it.'

'Yes. I know.'

'You sound as if you don't believe me.'

'I believe you. But you sound as if *you* don't.'

Daphne looked down at the sand. 'Yes, I know,' she said meekly. 'Father's going to send Grandmother to be our Ambassador to the ReUnited States, now that she's feeling better. She's worked out that she'll be able to lord it over all the snooty Bostonians, so she's trying not to seem pleased. I suppose really she will be ladying it, which is probably worse. And, well, *he* hasn't got anyone else . . . oh, except for lots of courtiers and the government and the people of the Empire, of course, but they won't know him as himself, d'you see, but just as a face under a crown. Oh, it's all so wretched. But Father needs me.'

'Yes, he does,' said Mau.

Daphne glared at him. It was stupid to think like this, but she'd wanted him to argue . . . well, not argue, more like protest . . . well . . . not protest, exactly, more like . . . be disappointed. It's hard to talk to someone who understands, and she gave up and, only then, noticed his arm.

'What happened to you?' she said. 'That looks horrible!'

'It's just bruising. I got tattooed too after the feast last night. Look.'

She looked. On Mau's left wrist was a little blue hermit crab.

'That's very good!'

'Milo did it. And on this arm . . .' He turned to show her.

'The Sunset Wave,' said Daphne. 'Oh, I'm so glad you decided to have it done at—'

'Look again, ghost girl,' said Mau, smiling.

'What? Er . . . Oh, the wave is going the wrong way.'

'The right way. It's the Sun*rise* Wave, and we are its children, and we will not go into the dark again. I vow it. It's a new world. It needs new people. And you are right. Your father is a good man, but he needs you more than . . . this island does.'

'Well I think—'

'He needs your strength,' Mau went on. 'I've watched you together. You give his world a shape. He will give your poor nation a shape. You must be with him on that ship. You must be by his side. In your heart you know this. You will have a purpose. People will listen.' He stood up and took her hand. 'I told you Imo made many worlds. I told you that sometimes I think I can see a little way into the world where the wave did not happen. Well, now you will get onto that ship, or . . . you won't. Whatever you choose, your choice will mean there are two new worlds. And perhaps sometimes, on the edge of sleep, we will see the shadow of the other world. There will be no unhappy memories.'

'Yes, but—'

'No more words. We know them all, all the words that should not be said. But you have made my world more perfect.'

Frantically, Daphne sought for something to reply, and came up with: 'The bandage on Mrs Whi-ara's leg should come off tomorrow. Er, I still don't like the look of Caah-a's hand; the *Wren*'s surgeon said he thought it was getting better, but it's worth waking up Mrs Gurgle to have a look at it. Oh, and don't let her fool you – she can't chew meat with those gold teeth, so someone else needs to do it, and . . . I'm getting this wrong, aren't I . . . ?'

Mau laughed. 'How can that be wrong?' He kissed her on the cheek, a little clumsily, and went on: 'And now we both walk away, without regrets, and when we meet again it will be as old friends.'

Daphne nodded, and blew her nose on her last good handkerchief.

And the ship sailed away.

And Mau went fishing. He owed a fish to Nawi.

TODAY

*I*n the corner of the office, a seismograph ticked away quietly to itself.

The old man stopped talking to watch a flying boat land on the lagoon. 'Ah, that will be young Jason who's come to work on the Sub-millimetre Array.' He sighed. 'I'm sure they're doing wonderful things over there, but between ourselves I've never been happy with a telescope you can't *look* into. Sorry, where was I?' he said.

The boy and the girl stared at him. 'You said the ship sailed *away*?' said the boy.

'Oh, yes,' said the old man. 'That was it. The ship sailed away. It's what they do.'

'And?' said the boy.

'That was all of it. The ship sailed away.'

'And they didn't get married or anything?' said the girl, looking truly shocked.

'Oh no,' said the old man. 'Well, they didn't get married. I'm not so sure about "anything". A kiss or two, maybe?'

'But that's just no way to end a story,' said the boy. 'He went *fishing*!'

'But it's the kind of ending you get in real life,' said the old man, 'and isn't the story about being real? Though I've always thought he went fishing so that people wouldn't see him cry. He must have felt very lonely. "If you will sacrifice," Mau said later, "then sacrifice your time on the altar of the common good. *Eat* the fish, or give it to someone who is hungry."'

He looked at their downcast expressions, coughed gently and said, 'A ship did come back.'

'And the ghost girl was on it, wasn't she?' said the girl.

'Oh yes,' said the old man. 'About a year later.'

'Ah, I knew it!' said the girl triumphantly.

'And the telescope?' asked the boy.

'Certainly! A sixteen-inch Newtonian telescope was one of the first things they unloaded! That night everyone looked through it!' said the old man. 'And there were all the things that had been on the list and six gentlemen from the Royal Society, just as promised.' The old man smiled broadly as he recalled. 'Of course, we've had quite a few scientists since then. My father told me that Mr Einstein sat in this very chair and played the violin. An interesting little fact is that my father accompanied him on the drum and the effect was considered . . . unusual. I myself was privileged to accompany Sir Patrick Moore and Professor Richard Feynman when they were up here together. Xylophone, bongos and war drum. Wonderful! Very musical people, scientists. And I was very proud to shake the hand of Professor Carl Sagan when he came here with people from the electric television. Do you remember that the ghost girl thought the glass beads on the ceiling of the cave were a star map, but she couldn't work it out? The professor showed the world that they did indeed map the stars, but the stars as they were thirty-one thousand years ago, and that was confirmed by something called Fission Track Dating of the glass our little toy stars were made of. We're learning new things all the time. I can't recall how many astronauts came here. Interestingly, although several of them went to the moon, none of them met the lady who lives there.'

'Yes, but did the ghost girl ever come back *again*?' said the girl in a determined voice.

'Not exactly, but her son and granddaughter have,' said the old man.

'Then it's still sad,' said the girl.

'Well, I don't know about that,' said the old man. 'I understand she married a very nice gentleman from Holland. A prince, I believe. And of course you know she became Queen.'

'Yes, but it still shouldn't have happened like that,' the girl insisted.

'Well, she went back for the sake of her nation, and he stayed here for the sake of his. Wasn't that right?'

The girl considered this, and said: 'I suppose they both thought more about their people than they thought about each other.'

'And you, young man?'

The boy looked down at his feet. 'I think they both thought more about their people than they thought about themselves.'

'Good answers. And I think they were happy, in their own ways.'

'But they were still sweet on one another,' said the girl, not giving up.

'What a delightfully archaic term! Well, yes, when she died – which was not long after Mau died – the trouser-men were not very happy because they wanted to bury her in a stone box in one of their god houses, but she had the Gentlemen of Last Resort on her side. They brought her here in a steamship full of ice, and she was wrapped up in papervine and weighed down with stones and sent into the dark current, where we had gently sent Mau only two months before. And then, my great-grandfather wrote, everyone cried and cried . . . as I see the two of you are now, in fact, doing.'

'It was just dust,' said the boy.

The old man smiled, and fished a handful of folded papervine out of his pocket and handed it to the girl, saying, 'Feel free to blow your nose.'

'And then two dolphins were seen swimming in the

lagoon,' said the girl firmly. She blew her nose and gave the papervine back.

'I don't recall ever being told that,' said the old man, taking it by what seemed to be the least damp corner.

'It must have happened, though,' the girl insisted. 'It's the only right ending. They would have been swimming in the lagoon, but people were probably crying too much to notice.'

'Yes, that could have been it,' said the old man tactfully. 'Now, I think, for the official bit.'

He led the way out of his little office and along a wide wooden veranda. It had one of the best views on the island. One end of it was tangled in the canopy of the low forest, so that leaves and flowers cascaded over it, and the other had a breathtaking view across the lagoon. There was a little shed at that end.

'And since the night the first telescope was set up here we have had the Tell and the Show, for young people when they come of age,' the old man said. 'Ha! By now, of course, you kids have hung out around every dome and telescope array on the mountain, right? They spring up like mushrooms, don't they? But perhaps you think you have seen it all? People hardly *look* these days, have you noticed that? It's all photography and the electric internet. Call me old-fashioned but that's not stargazing, it's just *computers*!' He stopped by the little shed. 'So I'm going to show you something that you have never seen before. It's a little trick, really, and once you think about it you will say "huh" or some similar ejaculation, but I happen to think it is rather, as you would put it, "neat".'

He undid the shed door, which ran back on little rails, to reveal a telescope very much smaller than the ones in the big white domes on the mountain top.

'Is that it?' said the girl. 'It's very small.'

'Only in size, not in history,' said the old man reproachfully, glancing at his watch and moving the telescope with the care of someone who has done this a thousand times before. 'Ah, got it first time,' he said, looking into the lens.

'It's not dark for a long time yet,' the boy pointed out.

'The universe doesn't care about that,' said the old man, stepping back. 'Go on, one of you. Take a look.'

'But the sky is still blue!' said the girl.

'Oh, be clever, then, and don't look,' said the old man cheerfully. 'I *dare* you to look!'

She looked, and gasped. 'It's in daylight!'

She stepped away from the telescope. The boy looked through the eyepiece, and backed away quickly, staring at the clear blue sky.

'Yes, it took me like that the first time, too,' said the old man gleefully. 'The planet Jupiter, in the daylight. You saw the storm belts and three of his sons, which of course we now call moons. Callisto is behind the planet right now. And it was a shock, wasn't it? A moment of uncertainty? The world turned upside down?'

'It was a bit creepy, as well,' said the boy.

'Oh, indeed. And now you know the universe isn't just a light show. They keep it running during the day, too!'

The man clenched his wrinkled hands and said: 'Live for those moments! They keep you alive! There is no better medicine than finding out that you are wrong! What did your mother put in your hand when you were born, young man?'

'Er . . . a wooden telescope, sir. So that I will want to see further,' said the boy. He was a little shaken; tears were running down the old man's cheeks, even though he was smiling.

'Good, good. And you, young lady?'

'A blue hermit crab, sir. So that I won't accept any shell.'

'That's a big totem to live up to. You must spend your life asking questions.'

'I know, sir. Why are you crying, sir?'

The old man opened his mouth, and then hesitated for a moment. 'Ah, good one! I must answer, mustn't I.' He straightened himself up. 'Because you liked my blue Jupiter. Because we keep going. Because we've come so far and have such a long way still to go. Because there are stars and blue hermit crabs. Because you are here, and strong and clever. The joy of the moment. Those sort of things. Do excuse me if I sit down.'

He walked over to an ancient cane chair, and jerked up quickly as he went to sit in it.

'Now then, Helene,' he admonished. 'You know you shouldn't be on there. I could get into trouble for sitting on a protected species, my girl!' He put a large tree-climbing octopus on the decking, and patted his pockets. 'I think I may have a dried shrimp here for a good girl . . .

ah, yes.' He held up the shrimp and said: 'Count to
. . . five.'

A wrinkled grey arm picked up a smooth pebble by the
chair and thumped on the planks five times. A pair of very
large, soulful eyes looked up at him.

'*Good* girl! She can count up to fifteen, you know,' said
the old man proudly, sitting down quickly in the vacated
chair. 'Helene's been a bit naughty lately. She had that nice
Professor Dawkins by the leg last month – we had to lure
her away with a bucket of crabs. He was very gracious
about it, I'm pleased to say. Charles Darwin spent *hours* in
the low forest when he came here, as you might expect,
and was the first to notice that the octopi used primitive
tools. They fascinated him.'

He leaned back in the chair, while Helene curled up
hopefully under it (where there is one dried shrimp, there
may be more – possibly as many as fifteen).

'Do you believe in Imo, sir?' said the boy.

'Ah, the usual question. We come to it at last. You know
Mau said that Imo made us clever enough to work out
that He does not exist?'

'Yes, sir, everyone says that, but that doesn't help a lot.'

The old man stared out at the sea. There was never
much twilight at this latitude, and the early stars were
already showing.

He cleared his throat. 'You know . . . Pilu – I mean the
first one – was my great-great-great-great-grandfather,
son to son. He was the first to learn to read and write, but
I expect you know that. It was clever of the Society to send

a teacher on that first boat. Mau had no children, although that might depend on how you define a parent and a child. One of the things he said was: "I cursed Imo because He gave the birds and animals a way to sense great waves, and didn't give it to smart beings like us. But I realize that He did. He made us smart. It was up to us to be good at it!" I think about that every time the seismograph beeps. But I'm not really answering you, am I . . . ?'

The chair creaked.

'Everything I know makes me believe Imo is in the order which is inherent, amazingly, in all things, and in the way the universe opens to our questioning. When I see the shining path over the lagoon, on an evening like this, at the end of a good day, I believe.'

'In Imo?' said the girl.

This got a smile. 'Perhaps. I just believe. You know, in things generally. That works, too. Religion is not an exact science. Sometimes, of course, neither is science.' The old man rubbed his hands together. 'Which of you is the older?'

'Me,' said the girl.

'Huh, yes, *six minutes*,' said the boy.

'Then tonight I know you guard the Nation for the first time. You have a spear? Good. You know where Mau used to stand? Good. Occasionally there is some argument about it. I'll keep an eye on you from time to time, and if I know anything, your father will be watching somewhere. Fathers do, when daughters stand guard. It's a dad thing . . . Pretend you don't see him.'

'Er . . .' The girl began to speak, but stopped and looked embarrassed.

'Yes?' the old man prompted.

'Is it true that in the middle of the night you see the ghost of Mau standing next to you?' She said it fast, as if she were just a little ashamed of even asking and wanted to get it over with.

The old man smiled and patted her on the shoulder. 'Tell me in the morning,' he said.

He watched them go, and waited until he saw her take up position on the beach, with that hugely strained expression of constipated self-importance that, he'd noticed, young people wore on these occasions. On the top of the mountain there was a rumbling of domes as the observatories woke up for the night.

The greatest scientists in the world have taught here for generations, he thought as he made himself a cup of tea, and still our children ask us: Are there ghosts? What a piece of work is Man . . .

He stepped outside, stirring the tea. The shining path glittered across the sky. Out on the lagoon, in the last ray of sunlight, a dolphin leaped into the air for the joy of the moment, the water drops making another shining path.

The old man smiled, and believed.

MAP OF TH

Antarctic Circle

FURTHER
AUSTRALIA

NEARER
AUSTRALIA

Tropic of Capricorn

Equatoria

AFRICA

INDIA

Tropic of Cancer

CHINA

THE RUSSIAS

Arctic Circle

AUTHOR'S NOTE

The great big multiple universes get-out-of-jail-free card:

This might look like a book set in the Pacific Ocean. *Nothing could be further from the truth!!!!!* It is in fact set in a parallel universe, a phenomenon known only to advanced physicists and anyone who has ever watched any episode of any sf series, anywhere. Different things happened, some people lived at different times, some bits of history have been changed, some things are made up out of real pieces (like the beer, and the last five minutes of the *Sweet Judy*) and so on. But the Great Pelagic Ocean is its own place.

Oddly enough, though, after the book was finished I learned that the Society Islands in the Pacific were named after the Royal Society in London by the famous Captain Cook, because it had sponsored the first British scientific survey of the islands. Sometimes it's hard to make things up . . .

Drowning bullets
It's true – bullets fired into water soon lose all their speed. Some high-velocity ones even ricochet off the surface. That's because the faster you hit water, the more it behaves like concrete. However, *do not try this at home*. Don't try it at school, either. I do know someone who tried it at work, but since his job is to fire guns for the movies, no one minded. He confirmed it; a bullet hitting the water slows down very fast indeed.

NATION

Blue Jupiter

It's my favourite viewing, when the orbit is right, which means it's in the eastern sky late in the day. It is remarkable what a telescope will pick up in a clear sky. But if you look at the sun directly through a telescope it will blind you, no kidding, so daylight astronomy should only be attempted with the help of an adult who knows what they are doing. Sorry, sorry, it's the ol' 'Don't try this at home' warning, in disguise.

The green cannon

It would work, probably, since papervine is so tough. In the past cannon have been made of wood, leather or even ice (a lot of ice). Mostly they were made to be strong and light enough to last for one shot. They were used in what would now be called special operations, when one shot in the right place might make all the difference. They didn't have to last long – just long enough.

Needless to say, don't try this at home.

Thinking

This book contains some. Whether you try it at home is up to you.

Terry Pratchett